HER
HUSBAND'S
RETURN

BOOKS BY SUZANNE GOLDRING

My Name is Eva
Burning Island
The Girl Without a Name
The Shut-Away Sisters
The Girl with the Scarlet Ribbon
The Woman Outside the Walls
The Girl Who Never Came Back
The Twins on the Train

SUZANNE GOLDRING

HER HUSBAND'S RETURN

bookouture

Published by Bookouture in 2025

An imprint of Storyfire Ltd.
Carmelite House
50 Victoria Embankment
London EC4Y 0DZ

www.bookouture.com

The authorised representative in the EEA is Hachette Ireland
8 Castlecourt Centre
Dublin 15 D15 XTP3
Ireland
(email: info@hbgi.ie)

ISBN: 978-1-83618-297-9
eBook ISBN: 978-1-83618-296-2

*For Tom Shaw and Alex Bird
who saved the torn letter
under the floorboards.*

Home is the girl's prison
and the woman's workhouse.

George Bernard Shaw, *Man and Superman*

ONE

NOW

@OURFOREVERHOUSE#SWEETLAVENDER

The tall, old house on the edge of Putney Common wasn't meant to be a house for two. It was built for a family. It longed to be filled with children. Opposite a school and a church, it was the perfect forever house, asking to be filled with the laughter of little ones. That was why they had bought it; and they had nearly completed the extensive renovations. But it was not to be.

Charlotte, known as Charlie to everyone since childhood, tried to hide her disappointment as she felt the years ticking away – she was soon to be thirty-eight. She shrugged off her failure and opened the door to the cellar, where she had once expected to store toys, baby equipment, and maybe a paddling pool and a tent for hot summers.

Clutching a bunch of keys in one hand, gripping the stair rail with the other, Charlie descended the rickety steps into the dimly lit cellar. The air was freshened by the ventilation grilles set high in the outer walls. She smelt sweet herbs, not damp- ness, as she approached the door at the far end. She tried one key after another and finally found one that fitted. But it was hard to insert in the rusty lock and even harder to turn. The door seemed to be stuck fast and she wanted to kick it in frustration.

She and Dan been renovating the old house for over a year, but she'd never fully explored the cellar before. She needed dry storage for her growing interiors business and was surprised this section hadn't been opened during the renovations. She hoped it might contain a useful empty space – or it could turn out to be nothing but a cramped cupboard. Determined to find out whatever was behind the door, she finally shoved it hard with her shoulder and suddenly it flew open.

Stumbling uncertainly into the darkened chamber, she felt something catch at her hair and stifled a scream. She shook her head to chase it away. With such weak light from the single bulb dangling behind her, she could not tell what she had bumped into.

But when she switched on the bright torch on her phone, she gasped. Hanging from the low ceiling she could see bunch after bunch of dried lavender, laced with strands of cobwebs. There were so many, she couldn't move without some of the stiff stems brushing her head, scattering the long-dead flower buds.

And as she turned around in the dark space, she caught their scent. Were they cut from the lavender bushes that edged the garden at the front of the house? Even though the flowers were dried and must have been hanging there for years, the scent was still distinctive, reminding her of old aunts and their pressed blouses. But beneath the perfume of lavender she caught a hint of something else, something old and long forgotten.

She shone her torch around, trying to see what else might be lurking in this chamber. The door had been locked and she'd had to search for the key. It was so stiff, she thought it couldn't have been unlocked for years, and the room didn't appear to have been used for anything other than the drying of lavender.

And then she bumped into the shelves against the side wall. Not shelves for books or useful tools, but shelves for wine. It was a tall, purpose-built wine rack. Empty now, it must once have boasted a collection of bottles, a fine wine cellar from the days when all wine had corks and was allowed to mature.

She shone her torch across the racks, hoping to find a long-forgotten vintage burgundy perhaps. It was empty, but right at the very top on the uppermost shelf she could see a green box. A shoebox, tied with a white ribbon. She stood on tiptoe and reached for it, wondering why it had been left there and wondering what it might contain.

TWO

THEN

SEPTEMBER 1940

Frankie brushed a bead of sweat from her lip. Summer would soon be over, but up here, outside on the very top of the house on the edge of Putney Common, the sun was beating down on the flat mansard roof as she lay in her underwear, stretched out absorbing the rays. The lead was hot, almost too hot, radiating through the picnic blanket she had thrown down over the dusty surface.

Bertie lay alongside, the straps of her brassiere tucked under her arms, her knickers rolled both down and up to expose as much of her stomach and thighs as was decent. 'You're quite sure we can't be seen from up here?' Her voice was drowsy on this early September Saturday.

'Absolutely not,' Frankie said. 'I've been sneaking out through that skylight since I was ten. We're higher than all the houses around us. We could strip off completely and no one would ever know.' She hadn't in fact escaped to the roof since her marriage. Dickie wouldn't have approved, just like he didn't approve of her lively best friend, whose company she could enjoy again now he was no longer here.

She raised herself on one elbow and gazed down at the

garden next door. A line of washing hung limply in the afternoon sunshine with no breeze to smooth out its creases. At times like this, with a clear, blue sky and balmy heat, it was almost impossible to believe that the country was actually at war, that she had ever heard Chamberlain's chilling declaration of war with Germany, just over a year before.

'It's heaven,' her friend said with a yawn. 'More like the exotic South of France than dreary old south London.'

'Though we haven't got any Germans to contend with,' Frankie added. 'No chance of enjoying a laze on a beach in France since they swarmed into Paris. I bet they're swanning down the Champs-Élysées all swanky in their uniforms right this very minute.'

Dramatic news of the German invasion that summer had shocked everyone in Britain. Their enemy was now only a short hop across the Channel and the war, which so many had said would be 'over by Christmas', was beginning to look alarmingly close to home.

'Wasn't it heaven though when we had that school trip to Paris?' Bertie rolled on to her side. 'Those handsome waiters really helped us with our French, didn't they?'

'Mmm, it was heaven,' Frankie said. 'And hot, just like this.' She closed her eyes, picturing their sixteen-year-old selves, only six years previously. 'Do you remember, lying on the balcony of our *pension* in our undies, then Madame Blanc peered down from the window above us and said...'

'*Jeunes filles, habillez-vous immediatement!*' Both girls shrieked the phrase at exactly the same time, their perspiring bodies shaking with laughter.

But the hilarity of the moment couldn't last long and soon Frankie's guffaws morphed into sobs. She shouldn't be enjoying herself like this when she didn't know where Dickie was and if he was even still alive. That dreadful day only a few months before, in May, when so many troops had escaped from the beaches of France but thousands had perished, overwhelmed her once more. Many women were already widows because of that disaster, but she didn't yet know whether to mourn. And, though she hardly dared admit it to herself, if it turned out that he had perished, she didn't know how she could pretend to be a mourning widow. For a moment, as she wiped her tears, she wished she could tell her best friend why she didn't miss Dickie. But it wasn't just that she couldn't find the words to describe the true nature of her marriage – the fact was, she couldn't bring herself to; she was too ashamed to tell anyone, even her best friend.

'Oh, don't cry, sweetie,' Bertie said, reaching out to clutch her friend's arm. 'He'll pop up one day soon, I'm sure of it. Missing in action means there's always hope. Everyone says it was chaos out there and lots of girls are still getting good news, even now.'

'I know,' she said, with a snuffle. 'But it doesn't stop me feeling guilty for enjoying myself when I still don't know what has happened. Sometimes I stop worrying about him altogether and completely forget I'm an old married woman of twenty-two.'

'Not so very old. Same as me and I'm still a spinster, boohoo.' Bertie paused and squinted in the sun as she stared at her. 'Do you think you'd have got married to Dickie if the war hadn't been about to happen? You hadn't known him all that long really, had you?'

At one time, Frankie thought, she'd have told her best friend everything, as they had done before her marriage, but now all she said was, 'Of course I wanted to marry him. I knew he was the one from the moment we met.' But did she really want to marry him? Or was it more as her best friend had just said, a whirlwind of hysteria and pressure to grab a suitable man before they were all gone? Everyone she knew had maiden aunts who'd missed their chance of marriage as a result of the Great War, so all the girls were aware of what it meant to miss getting their man. And Dickie was so supportive when her parents died so suddenly, one after the other, leaving her all alone to inherit this huge house and her father's property portfolio, which meant she would never be short of funds.

Everyone thought Dickie was a dear, but he was the first serious suitor she'd ever had since leaving school and starting her secretarial job at the insurance company in Hammersmith where they'd first met. He was quite a bit older than her and destined for a directorship in the company. He'd kissed her after the firm's grand Christmas dinner and dance at the Grosvenor House Hotel. From then on they were a couple and, almost the minute a second great war loomed in the months that followed, he proposed and they were married before she'd even had time to think about the kind of life they would make together and whether she was passionately in love with him.

It was a forgone conclusion that they would live in this big house overlooking Putney Common, beneath the shadow of the tall spire of St Michael and All Angels, where they had said their vows. 'A house like that needs a family, not a single secretary,' Dickie had said, carrying her over the threshold after their brief honeymoon at the Spread Eagle Hotel in Midhurst in a lumpy four-poster bed, where they'd spent a disappointing night.

'I expect I'm not the only one who's made a hasty marriage these days,' Frankie said, sitting up and twisting her rings around on her left hand. Three small diamonds flashed in the afternoon sun, paired with a slim gold wedding band. Both rings were a little big for her and constantly slipped around to the back of her finger. She ought to get them resized, but then she thought maybe her fingers would swell if she was expecting a baby. And who kept the gold if a ring was made smaller?

'Marry in haste, repent at leisure?' Bertie stared at her. 'You enjoyed your job and you were good at it. You didn't really want to give it up, did you?'

Frankie sighed. Not this again. 'It was company policy. No married women. It's not the only place that doesn't employ wives, you know. It's the same with teachers. Well, it was at our old school. They were all spinsters or widows there.' But at the back of her mind she could hear Dickie lecturing her, *Married women shouldn't go out to work. Their place is in the home, supporting their husbands.￿* Much good giving up her job did, she thought. She was an inexperienced housekeeper and cook when they first married and, despite her best efforts, he was never satisfied.

'Don't I know it, and didn't that make them all bitter and twisted? Dried-up old bags!' Bertie sat up again, pulled off her bra and swung it around her head. 'I'm all for being single, but not being boring. I'm going to have fun if this war carries on. And you should too. With no husband here to tell you how to behave, you've got to live life to the full while you can.'

Bertie had always been able to cheer her up. She was the naughtiest girl in the school from the moment they'd met, always creating havoc, always one for a jape. She'd set up the wastebin on the door that emptied over Miss Potter's head in the needlework room. And she'd taken the blame for it too, earning detention as well as lines. It was quite a surprise that she had turned out to be an excellent primary school teacher, though even that hadn't convinced Dickie to like her.

'So, what do you think I should do, then? Dickie didn't want me working again, but I'm sure that girls will soon be having to do their bit to help with the war effort. We can't leave it all to the men. Or maybe I should just find another job. I certainly can't cope with my miserable thoughts rattling around here in this house all day.'

'I'm surprised you haven't gone nearly mad already, with nothing to do. I think the only way to stay sane in this phoney war is to keep busy at work and at play. I'm sick of carting around a gas mask that's never going to be needed.'

Gas masks had been issued in 1939 to adults and children alike, with strict instructions to carry them at all times. Even versions for babies had been produced. But since the declaration of war, with little sign of the gases and bombs that the population had been warned would be terrorising the cities of Britain, people had become lax about the clumsy devices. To date, only a few light air raids had affected London, and everyone had begun to think the war wasn't going to enter British shores. Mothers had begun reclaiming children evacuated to the country and homes were growing careless with their blackouts.

'We should find a new use for the wretched things,' Frankie said. 'I heard someone say the other day they'd used theirs as a plant pot.'

'Oh, I've heard worse than that. Sometimes they've been used as emergency potties for kiddies on long journeys!'

The girls giggled at the thought of government-issue property being adapted for improper uses. 'Oh, you're just what I needed, to cheer me up,' Frankie said. 'But what are we going to do if the war carries on? Or rather, what am *I* going to do?'

'You can drive, can't you?'

'Yes, but not properly. You know we both can. But that was on a farm with an old jalopy and your uncle's tractor.' She'd loved the summers they'd shared in Devon, helping stack hay and enjoying the admiring glances of sun-beaten muscular farmhands.

'But it was still driving, wasn't it? They had wheels and engines?'

'Yes, but what are you getting at?'

'Don't you remember that newspaper advertisement I showed you over a year ago? For ambulance drivers? They offer training and a uniform. I've decided I'm going to go for it. With so many children being evacuated and schools being requisitioned, my classes are smaller, so I reckon I could manage it on top of teaching. You should join me. We might even be able to work together. Can't you just see it? The two of us haring round London, ringing our bells, rescuing the injured, being sort of modern Florence Nightingales on wheels?'

'Ringing our bells? Really?'

'Oh, come on, it will be such a hoot. We'd have caps and badges and everything. And we'd be doing something important. Much better than typing boring old letters in some stuffy old office for men who can't sign up and fight.'

Frankie thought about the office where she had once worked. It hadn't been that stuffy. There had been a smart shiny new typewriter and crisp white paper embossed with the company's name and emblem. A lady with a trolley had brought all the staff tea and coffee in white china cups, accompanied by pink wafer biscuits, at regular intervals. She had been allowed forty-five minutes for lunch, which she usually took at a nearby tea shop that emulated a Lyons Corner House, unless it was a Friday, when she liked to wander through the market buying fresh crisp lettuce or ripe strawberries.

'Come on, what do you say?' Bertie knelt before her, holding out her hands like a golden goddess. 'I'm going to do it without you if you chicken out.'

Frankie knew that Dickie would never have allowed her to do it, but he wasn't here. She felt quite daring, contradicting that critical voice that penetrated her thoughts all the time. *What? You? Driving? Don't make me laugh. That's ridiculous.*

'What kind of uniform?' she said, her head on one side, gauging her friend's seriousness.

'Oh, nothing very glam. A blue coat with silver buttons, I think. But they do have a choice of caps. Not quite as charming as the Wrens, but pretty jaunty all the same.'

'Very well. I'll give it a go. Anything to get me out of this house. Now put your clothes back on.'

Frankie stood up and threw her dress over her head. She looked around at the still blue sky streaked with puffs of cloud here and there. It felt like the perfect end to the summer, lazing up here on the roof with her oldest friend, hot and glowing from their sunbathing. She shaded her eyes against the last of the sun – and, as she did so, she caught sight of a dark streak far over there to the south, expanding by the second.

And was she imagining it or was that the drone of engines as the black grew, like a swarm of locusts, spreading over London and heading eastwards? 'Look,' she shouted, 'there's planes, hundreds of them. They're not ours, are they?'

Bertie stood up, pulling her straps back over her shoulders. The planes were flying in giant pointed V-shaped formations, one after another. 'They're heading for the East End of London. It must be the docks,' she said, clutching Frankie's arm.

And even as she spoke, they could see a cloud forming on the horizon. Not the wispy clouds of late afternoon, but the darkly ominous clouds of destruction. This was really it. Summer was over and the war had finally started at last.

The tall house overlooking Putney Common looked sad. Perhaps it was largely because of the peeling black paint on the front door and windows, or the dark ivy that climbed the walls, clinging like bushy eyebrows above the casements, but Charlie felt it was asking for their help. She gazed upwards to the elegant mansard roof that made it look a little like a French chateau, wondering which of the rooms she'd choose to decorate as a nursery one day.

Dan had found the house after many months of searching. After sifting through piles of estate agents' particulars, he had finally begun to check auction listings. 'I think that's how we'll find a bargain,' he said. 'A place that no one else wants, because it needs so much work.'

She'd agreed, of course. Anything to give them the project they both wanted and to save money. Despite the generous legacies they'd both been fortunate to receive, from Dan's uncle and Charlie's grandparents, any property with a London postcode was expensive. They both longed to have a house they could make their own, their forever house, the home where they would live for years and raise children. They'd talked about it ever since they'd married, two years previously. With Dan's skills as an architect and her talent for interior design, they were convinced they could turn a dilapidated address into their dream home.

They'd viewed the house before the auction, of course. Charlie had often watched the long-running TV programme *Homes Under the Hammer*, and knew that a prospective bidder should always inspect the property and read the legal pack before committing themselves to raising their hand in the auction room. But it had all been so rushed, they'd had very little time to do more than run up and down the stairs, exclaim at the size of the rooms, wave their way through the cobwebs and dodge the drips from the gutters. And now, at last, it was all theirs. They had the keys and could begin to plan.

The flimsy wood and wire gate that led to the front steps scraped the paving and nearly fell off its creaking hinges. 'That'll have to go,' Dan said, pulling a disapproving face. 'It probably once had a splendid wrought-iron gate and railings, look.' He pointed to the dark stumps in the wall edging the front garden. 'That would have been much more in keeping with the house.'

'Who would do that?' Charlie looked at the severed metal. 'It doesn't look right with this tatty wire fence here, either.'

'I've been told they were taken away in the war when they needed the metal. We'll replace it all eventually when we can spare the cash.'

'That sounds like it's a long way down the list,' Charlie said, conscious of the many jobs they were going to have to undertake to make the house comfortable.

'I'm sure we can manage to camp out here while we get the work done,' Dan said optimistically, as they entered the musty hallway. 'It's all structurally sound. Just needs clearing out and updating. The surveyor was very impressed with how well it has withstood years of neglect.'

Charlie kicked aside the mound of circulars on the worn doormat. The leaflets scattered across the black and white tiled floor with its collection of dried leaves. The house had never been cleared out after its last occupant had died in a care home. No relatives had come to claim family heirlooms, no charities had collected furniture and clothes. They would have to start by fighting their way through a lifetime of possessions till they could clearly see the possibilities before them.

'We could get a house clearance company in to take all this old stuff away,' Dan said, picking up a dusty photo album from the motheaten sofa in the sitting room. 'Sometimes they don't even charge to do it, if they find there are enough items of value to sell on.' He threw the album back onto the faded velvet upholstery, creating a little puff of dust as it landed.

'Maybe, but there might be things here we could use ourselves. This side table is rather nice.' Charlie wiped the dust from the rosewood veneer, which glowed as soon as its sheen was revealed. 'Anyway, I'd like to see what's here first. This was someone's life at one time. Someone must have loved living here to fill it with such good furniture.'

'Someone's junk, more like.'

'No, it's all someone's memories, the way they once lived. I don't like the idea of chucking it out wholesale. And if we're going to make this our forever home, I want to treat this house and the people who once lived here with respect.'

'Okay, okay, I get it. Here, let's have a hug to celebrate getting the house at last.' Dan threw his arms around his wife and drew her close to his chest. 'But can we please get rid of that old bed upstairs and bring our own in as soon as?'

Charlie breathed in his warm smell of freshly bathed skin and herbal shower gel. 'Of course. I wasn't suggesting we should carry on living like they had and keep all this old furniture. I just want to get to know the place before we start ripping things apart. But I agree about the bed. That definitely has to go first.'

'Good. We can't go making babies in someone's old bed now, can we? Who knows what vibes that might give out?'

She broke away from his arms and opened the large mahogany sideboard decked with cobwebbed ornaments. 'I'm going to begin by doing an inventory of stuff we might keep and what we should sell. There are some good-quality pieces here. I think I should get an auctioneer in to look at some of this. We might as well get what we can for these things. After all, what you're planning to do here is going to cost a packet, isn't it?'

Dan had big plans for the house. As well as refitting the kitchen, he wanted to create a second bathroom and a down-stairs cloakroom, remodel the bedrooms, open up the fireplaces and replaster everywhere. Heating, rewiring and plumbing would all add considerably to the total cost. 'I'm getting final figures together,' he said, 'and, yes, it's not going to be cheap. But, hey, it's going to be our home for many years. And on top of that it'll be a showcase for our work. It'll all be worth it.'

'I know. And I'm totally prepared for a long slog to get it right. I know it will be wonderful in the end and I have a really good feeling about it.' She ran her fingers over the edges of the china saucers stacked in the sideboard, alongside matching cups. 'Who did you say the house had belonged to?'

'I didn't. It hadn't been lived in for quite some time.' Dan opened the file he was carrying and leafed through the docu-ments there. 'Mrs Frances Wilson. She died three years ago. But she'd left here a couple of years before that. So, it's been empty for about five years.'

'No wonder it's so dusty and cobwebby,' Charlie said, glancing around at the furniture, the cornices, the lamps, all laced with the work of busy spiders. She drew back the green brocade sitting room curtains and the perished fabric ripped in her hands. Light streamed in through the dirty glass panes, revealing even more fine strands of gossamer silk strung from corner to corner.

'She'd owned it a long time,' Dan said, turning the pages of the deeds. 'Looks like she was the sole owner, going back to a couple of years before the war. Doesn't mention a husband though. Maybe she inherited it from her family and he died in the war.'

'That's so sad. No wonder the house feels neglected and forlorn.' Charlie looked around her at the furniture and ornaments that had once been enjoyed by their owner and were now going to be mostly discarded. 'It feels like time then stood still. Or maybe it did even before she lost him. So, they never had children? No one to take it on?'

'Apparently not. Now, are we going to spend all day wondering about the old people who lived here and never did any housework, or are we going to get cracking?' Dan patted his wife's bottom affectionately. 'I'm going to start measuring and taking notes.'

Charlie sighed, shaking off the feeling the house was giving her. It wasn't just the cold of this chilly January day; she sensed there was something else. But she knew they couldn't dwell on its past. 'I'll take a look at the kitchen. If it's not too bad, we might be able to set up camp in there. Got to have a kettle on the go.'

'Good idea. Once the guys start, they'll need constant tea to keep them up to speed.'

'And then I'll check out the bedrooms again. We'll get one of them cleared quickly. I fancy the one nearest the bathroom. It's very old fashioned, but it'll do for now.'

'And don't forget to take photos of every stage, as we make progress.'

'Don't you worry about that. I will do. It's part of my job, remember?' Charlie's hugely successful blog and Instagram account, OUR FOREVER HOUSE@CharlotteInteriors, had been tracking the search for their ideal home for months and had an enormous following, among both aspiring homeowners and decorators. Now she had the opportunity to reveal that they had finally found their ideal house, and post details of every stage of its transformation. She was confident that her photos would win her and Dan more lucrative clients.

It was the depths of winter and she shivered in the unheated house. She couldn't help feeling sad that it was so neglected; a life had been abandoned here and she couldn't understand why. But once they began work, surely the house would begin to have a happier atmosphere, wouldn't it?

FOUR

THEN

SEPTEMBER 1940

Once Bertie had left, Frankie had time to think about the huge decision she had just made. According to the radio, the Germans had now started bombing London in earnest, so ambulance drivers would be in even greater demand. But she was shocked by her daring and knew that Dickie would never approve. She could just imagine him saying, *'What on earth makes you think you know how to drive properly? You'll be turned down and look a fool. Anyway, women shouldn't be driving. Leave that to the men.'*

But women were being encouraged to drive, weren't they, now that many men were away fighting? The news was full of young women driving cars for officers, lorries on farms and for the timber business. Girls were even learning to handle the barges transporting essential goods like coal all over the country. And she'd heard that, if the war carried on for long, all young women might be forced to serve the war effort in some way if they didn't have children to care for.

So, I should do my bit too, she told herself. Dickie isn't here to say I can't. No, he isn't here to stop me or make me feel useless, like he often did before he left.

The thought made her feel a little tearful, not because she was upset by his absence, but because she remembered what her life with him had become and how she was glad he wasn't here.

When did she fully realise why he'd married her? Was it immediately after their brief honeymoon? Or did that particular night merely confirm a thousand little uncertainties that had occurred even before their wedding?

She glanced again at her modest engagement ring. He'd presented it to her in the kitchen one afternoon only weeks after her mother's funeral, when she'd made a splendid tea of cucumber sandwiches and Victoria sponge cake. He hadn't gone down on one knee, he hadn't said he loved her, he hadn't held her hand and looked into her eyes. He'd just sat at the table, stirring his tea, then pushed a little scuffed leather box across to her and said, 'I think now that you are on your own with all of this to manage, we should get married. Everyone is saying there's another war coming. You might not get another chance.'

She had been so surprised, she hadn't had time to be disappointed at this unromantic proposal. She couldn't even remember whether she'd actually said Yes. He'd taken it for granted that she'd accept and be grateful to him. And at the time she really had thought it was for the best. It had been a shock to lose her parents so suddenly from the flu that winter, and Dickie had been so sensible, standing by her side and advising on the funeral arrangements and how she must deal with the family solicitor. He had known exactly what she had to do when she was confused and lost. So, it had seemed right for her to turn to him for help and accept his proposal without question.

But even before they were finally married, little doubts crept in here and there. When they were discussing the wedding, Dickie had said it should be a small affair. 'After all,' he said, 'neither of us has any family to speak of now, and it would be a waste of money to spend a lot on giving friends free food and drink.'

Frankie had thought she'd rather like a jolly party with her old schoolfriends as a contrast to the drab funerals she'd experienced for both her parents, but she'd nodded and agreed with him. Then, when they talked about where they'd actually marry, he'd wanted to rush to the register office. 'Oh, but I've always imagined getting married in St Michael's,' Frankie said. 'I've always wanted to walk out of the front door and cross the road to the church.'

'If you must,' he'd said. 'Save money on a wedding car at least.'

'And as my father isn't here any more, I'd ask Bertie to be my bridesmaid and walk with me. I'd really like that.'

'What, her? Do you really have to?'

'I'd like someone close to me to walk with me on my special day.'

'Well, if you must. But tell her to rein in the jokes and titters. It's a serious occasion.'

Frankie had looked at him as if he was joking. Weddings were meant to be jolly affairs. All her friends' weddings were full of gaiety. And Bertie was her best friend. But she knew Dickie didn't like her very much. In fact, she rather thought he didn't like her at all. But then she wasn't very keen on Dickie's best friend, Hugo, who was to be best man. They too had been friends ever since their schooldays at a minor public school somewhere in the Midlands, and often spent weekends away training with the Territorial Army. Dickie said it meant they would both be ready for active service if their country called for them, but Hugo never smiled at her or even spoke to her when he collected Dickie for one of their trips.

'Bertie has to be there. I couldn't possibly do it without her.'

'Very well,' he'd said. 'Just tell her to behave and keep her mouth shut for a change.'

And in the end the day had been quite memorable. The sun had shone, their friends had cheered and Bertie had carried Frankie's bouquet as well as her own posy. But Dickie's eyes hadn't lit up when he saw her walking down the aisle in her white dress, he hadn't smiled and his lips had missed hers when they were invited to kiss after saying their vows.

Was that when I should have guessed how it was going to be, Frankie thought, sipping her cooling tea. It's all so clear to me now and I regret not listening to Bertie when she questioned my choice. I was so stubborn and so stupid. But I should have listened to her.

FIVE

THEN

OCTOBER 1940

The first person Frankie and Bertie encountered at the auxiliary ambulance station looked nothing like the elegant figure depicted in the recruitment poster. That had shown a confident young woman pulling on leather gloves, wearing a dark blue coat that flattered her slim figure. Her head, topped by a smart cap, was held high and she was smiling, looking more like a stylish chauffeuse than an ambulance driver.

But the girls were met by Mrs Ogilvy, the station's recruitment officer, who was tight-lipped, grey-haired and stern. When she stood up behind her desk, her baggy, belted coat didn't flatter her stout figure, and she regarded the two girls with disdain. She could have been one of the senior teachers from their old school, judging by her manner and the way she spoke to them as she ticked their names off on her list. 'Mrs Frances Wilson and Miss Roberta Richards, I gather you've both driven vehicles before, but you'll still have to be assessed by Mr Palmer before you're allowed out on the road. You will report to me at the end of every shift and will have to account for any losses or damage each and every time. Is that quite clear?'

'Yes, Mrs Ogilvy,' they chanted in unison as if they were back in the classroom.

'Once you've passed your test, you'll be issued with a coat and a hat. Protective clothing, including gumboots and rubber gloves, is stored in your vehicle. You'll also be given extra coupons for appropriate shoes. Sensible lace-ups are more suitable for the work this job entails.' She glanced scornfully at the court shoes they were both wearing for their interview.

The girls were then ushered out of the office, and followed this stern figure into the yard behind the cream stuccoed Victorian villa that had been acquired by Wandsworth Civil Defence Planning. Previously housing a dentist, a doctor and a kindergarten, the building on the Upper Richmond Road was now home to several members of staff, plus six ambulances and six converted vehicles housed in a makeshift garage of corrugated iron. The once-elegant gravelled forecourt had been expanded by the removal of dusty hydrangea bushes and the pollarding of plane trees, to make room for all the traffic that now rolled in and out of the station.

As they followed her, Bertie whispered, 'What an old battleaxe! Ogilvy the ogre! We'll have to be careful to mind our ps and qs.'

Frankie stifled her giggles. She didn't want to get on the wrong side of Mrs Ogilvy from the start and, if Bertie kept making cheeky remarks it was going to be hard to keep a straight face.

But if Mrs Ogilvy was a dragon, Jim Palmer, who was to assess their driving skills, was a darling. He shook their hands, gave them a warm smile and said, 'You might both be able to drive, but I don't suppose you've learnt about maintenance, either of you? Every driver has to be able to look after their own vehicle. Problems often crop up when you're out on a call, particularly when there's debris and broken glass on the roads.

So, we'll go over things like flat tyres, oil checks and topping up your radiator.'

They shook their heads. Servicing hadn't ever been a part of their lessons during those carefree hours careering around the fields on the farm. They looked at each other and took a deep breath. 'Oh dear, we should have worn overalls,' Frankie said.

'Never mind that for today,' Jim said. 'I'll show you the basics and then we'll go out for a short drive. I'll take you, Miss' – he pointed to Frankie – 'and Alf Stevens here will take your friend. I'm sure you'll both be fine.'

'Will we have to take a proper driving test as well?' Frankie was worried that she couldn't remember enough to drive properly.

'In peacetime maybe, but when there's a war on the rules fly out the window. As long as you can both stop and start, you'll do.' Jim and Alf both laughed.

The girls felt safe in the company of these kind, tolerant, older men, too old to fight on the battlefields this time, but still capable of fighting on the home front. Jim led Frankie over to a converted van and Bertie went with Alf to an adapted saloon car with a raised canvas roof and sides covering the area where the back seats and boot had once been.

Frankie climbed into the driver's seat and automatically reached for the gearstick. It was all coming back to her now and, although she felt nervous as she turned the key in the ignition, she soon gained confidence when they turned out of the station's forecourt and onto the main road.

'We'll go down towards Richmond Park,' Jim said. 'Plenty of space there to show me what you can do.'

The road was almost completely empty. Now petrol was rationed very few people could manage to run private cars, so many had rescued old bikes from sheds, oiled the wheels and pumped up the tyres and were using those instead. Frankie drove at a steady pace until they reached the gated entrance to the park, which was also being used partly for army camps and exercises. She briefly wondered if the deer that lived here were becoming used to the military manoeuvres or preferred to stay out of sight, deep in the woods. It was still the rutting season, when it wasn't wise to approach the stags with their fearsome antlers and barking cries to warn off other suitors.

As she drove further and the van became warmer, she became aware of a familiar smell that reminded her of shopping with her mother; a sawdusty, fatty sort of odour. She wrinkled her nose, wondering what she was detecting, then said, 'Jim, what do you think this van was used for previously?' She asked him the question without taking her eyes off the road.

'This van?' Jim frowned for a moment. 'Oh, I think this one might have been Pete Provis's van. He's got a boy doing all his deliveries by bike now. Well, what he's got to deliver that is, there's not much to go round these days, is there?'

Of course. Provis the butcher. She could picture his shopfront hung with great sides of pork and lamb, decked with plucked turkeys and chickens at Christmas, strung with links of sausages all year round. That was why the smell was so familiar. A van that had once transported joints and carcasses would now be carrying bloody limbs to hospital and body parts to the mortuary. It seemed rather appropriate, and she smiled to herself.

'It doesn't bother you, does it? Driving a butcher's van, I mean?' Jim peered at her, trying to read her expression.

'Not at all. I know we're going to be facing some difficult situations if we're accepted. I've already told myself we'll have to be prepared.'

'You'll get some training in first aid and civil defence before you go out. But there's no doubt about you girls being taken on. We're desperate for recruits. All the stations are. I don't want to put you off, but this is a risky business and we've lost quite a few people already on the bomb sites.

Unstable buildings, fires and incendiaries, they're all routine hazards.'

Frankie took a deep breath, imagining how she was going to cope, lifting a badly injured person onto a stretcher in such unstable and dangerous conditions. The worst injury she'd ever dealt with up to now had been Dickie shutting his finger in a door and losing his fingernail. He'd made a dreadful fuss and accused her of causing permanent damage when she gently bathed and bandaged his hand. Was she really going to be able to bear the sight of blood and blasted limbs?

'Don't think about it too much,' he said. 'We all have moments when it feels hard to deal with. But we're all in the same boat and no one's going to think any the less of you if you get a bit emotional or feel queasy. I know I have a few times. But that's why everyone pulls together. There'll always be wardens and fire crew at the incidents you attend, all there to work with each other. It's bringing out the best in people, I'd say.'

'I suppose that's why we've got special kit on board as well,' she said.

'Oh, you'll need that all right. With firemen dousing the flames, you'd be soaked in no time if you didn't put on the rubber suit and boots. And you must always wear your metal helmet. You never know when another loose brick or tile is going to crash onto your head.'

As Frankie drove around the park, she felt more and more that this was so far away from the war and the bombs that had been thundering down on London since that final summer day in early September. Deer lifted their heads in mild curiosity as she passed, and nervous rabbits scampered beneath the trees.

After half an hour or more of driving, she said, 'Do you think I'm good enough?'

'You'll do fine. And don't you worry about old Ogilvy back at the station. Her bark's worse than her bite. She just likes everything done properly. We can go back now and tell her to sign you up for good.'

Frankie couldn't help smiling. This felt like the best day in months. She might yet be a widow, but she was going to do her bit to help the war effort. And a bit of her cheered to think she was defying Dickie and his tendency to dismiss any attempt she made to be modern and independent.

Charlie snapped away at every angle of the kitchen. Really, the worse it looked, the better for her social media posts. Eventually she'd be posting contrasting before and after pictures, starkly showcasing the miraculous transformation she and Dan had achieved here.

The deep white sink was crazed and stained, but Belfast sinks had a value in reclamation yards. Perhaps that should be sold, or even recycled with alpine plants, which she'd seen on a garden designer's blog. And the tall, pale lemon kitchen unit, with its folding-down door that made a useful worktop, was similar to ones she'd seen on special auction sites. They called themselves kitchenalia, didn't they? The door of the small fridge had been propped open with a stool, and the inside was grimy, but it hummed when she switched it back on. It would do for now, until Dan eventually got the large pastel-coloured American-style fridge with ice-maker he longed for.

At the back of the room were two doors. The first revealed a deep pantry, with a marble shelf where pies and jellies would have cooled in the days before fridges. No food there now, but the shelves still held a few tins. Pudding basins were tiered in order of size and an empty cake tin rattled ancient crumbs when she prised off the lid. A white enamel bin, labelled FLOUR, was lined with white dust, sprinkled with the dark husks of long-dead weevils.

On opening the second door a waft of sweet, dry air scented with sawdust and rust reached her nose. She could see steps descending into darkness. Flicking on the light switch by the door revealed nothing. The light bulb must have long gone.

'Where are you?' She heard Dan calling for her.

'Here,' she yelled back. 'Did you know we had a cellar?' She turned away from the steps and closed the door.

'I saw it on the plans. Could be useful storage if it's dry.' He stood in the middle of the kitchen and flipped open the flap on the yellow cupboard unit. 'That can go for a start.'

'It's not that awful. I think it might fetch something. I've seen them before on Pinterest.'

'If you say so.' He shook his head and made another note on his iPad. 'I can't see it making much myself.'

Charlie pictured his vision for the kitchen. Gleaming slate and marble, a tap that gushed boiling water, hushed cupboard doors closed with the touch of a fingertip and not a utensil in sight. She hoped she could persuade him that the house was more suited to an Aga and a worktop made from an old bleached and sanded butcher's block, where she could roll pastry and knead dough. She smiled to herself. He'd put his foot down if she suggested a whistling kettle as well.

Dan peered into the larder. 'We might keep this as it is though. Quite a trend to have a dedicated pantry with cool shelves.' He turned to look at her. 'Once you've chucked all these old tins out, you'll have to get going on learning how to do jams and pickles.'

'Oh, ha ha.' She tapped his arm with her clipboard. 'I'm not your servant. But come to think of it, rows of Kilner jars would look great on Instagram. Maybe I could buy them in ready filled from the Women's Institute or somewhere?'

'No cheating,' he said, wagging his finger at her. 'We're accountable and authentic, remember?'

'Of course. But it would look good, shelves lined with wholesome home produce.' Charlie took a shot of the interior of the larder, capturing the rust on the old tins. 'These cans might all still be edible but who eats canned corned beef and pilchards these days?'

'If you want to stay here tonight, we can get fish and chips or a Chinese from the local high street?'

'I'd love to stay but I didn't pack a bag. And anyway, I thought you didn't want to sleep in an old bed. Wouldn't you rather wait for our stuff to arrive tomorrow?' Charlie knew there wasn't going to be much. They'd been renting a flat for two years while they searched for their perfect home and had managed to whittle down their possessions to make life simpler.

'On second thoughts I think it would be romantic,' Dan said, sliding his arm around her shoulders. 'It wouldn't hurt to sleep in an old bed for one night, would it?'

She turned her face to kiss him. He was very persuasive and very desirable. 'All right. Let me see if I can make that bedroom presentable. As long as the bed isn't crawling with mice or bedbugs we'll do it.'

He checked his watch. 'Another hour, then we can get a drink in the local pub before we pick up food?'

'Perfect. I'll finish in here, then check out upstairs. There might even be clean bedlinen somewhere.'

Dan left the kitchen, humming some unrecognisable tune. His enthusiasm for this project was one of many things she loved about him. When they'd first been introduced he'd been heavily involved in a renovation in Knightsbridge, but he'd been determined to pursue her. Their romance grew out of short texts boosted by snatched coffees, while they were both working demanding hours, knowing that they were right for each other. Marriage and moving into their tiny flat in Clapham had followed, but from the start they had both talked about how one day they would find their forever house. And now at last they had.

Charlie shook her head at these early memories and began inspecting the tall pine kitchen dresser. The top half was glazed and she could see stacks of cups and saucers, side plates for cakes, larger ones for roast dinners and dessert bowls for trifles and crumbles. Those were the days, she thought, before take-aways, when every meal was cooked at home. And with all the work that lay ahead of her and Dan, she could see them relying a lot on Deliveroo and microwave meals.

Much of the crockery was mismatched, sets that had become incomplete over the years. But maybe, she thought, she could ask a friend who sold vintage china and also catered for afternoon tea parties to take most of it. She picked up one of the plates and wiped away the dust on the sleeve of her hooded jacket. Dan would never want to use anything like this, with its gilded scalloped edge and painted roses. It would be funny to shock him tonight though and eat off this elaborate china just once, before she had to dispose of it all. Maybe not the old cutlery though, she thought as she opened the dresser drawer. It was all perfectly useable, but the yellowing bone-handled knives and tarnished forks weren't going to touch her lips tonight, smelling as they did of long-gone silver polish and dust.

Charlie looked around her. The room would be fine once it was cleared. Late afternoon sun streamed through the grimy windows, catching dust motes in its beams. She could see the overgrown garden through the French doors at the back, with mossy steps leading down to a small terrace of granite slabs threaded with weeds. She could picture herself sitting out there with her morning tea, cupping her hands around the hot brew and enjoying the dappled sunshine filtered through the trees.

She noticed a few mildewed pears in the grass, dropped from the nearest tree, intertwined with a climbing rose that must have flowered earlier in the summer. Red rosehips were all that remained of the flowers. Strong branches spread out to a companion tree, forming an archway. She could immediately picture it holding a swing, where she would play with her children, hearing them shrieking with delight. When the hard work was completed, this sad, neglected house was going to give her and Dan everything they had ever dreamt of, and she hugged herself with happiness.

'I can't believe it,' Bertie said. 'You've passed and I haven't? I'm sure I was always better at driving than you when we were learning on the farm.'

They were walking home after their interview, along local roads scattered with crisp fallen autumn leaves, their scents redolent of nuts and maple syrup. It was so unlike the bombed streets around the East End and London's docks, littered with broken glass, where every breath filled with smoke and cordite. Since that first foray in early September, the bombing of key areas of the city had been relentless, earning it the name it would bear for all time – the Blitz, short for the German term *Blitzkrieg*, meaning rapid attack.

Frankie couldn't help laughing. Her friend was so indignant at being rejected. It had been her idea, after all, to apply for this position. 'Oh, don't look so fed up. The way I see it, this is better for us. This way we'll always be together. If you'd passed, you'd have been given your own vehicle and your own routes. We might never have seen each other. At least now, with me driving and you helping, we'll be able to stick together.'

'That's true. We'd be worrying about each other all the time if we were separated.' Bertie gave Frankie a cheeky sideways smile. 'But you'll still let me ring the bell sometimes, won't you?' Converted vehicles had to use either their existing horn or a bell. Frankie's butcher's van was supplied with a handbell.

'Of course I will. As much as possible. How could I drive and ring the bell at the same time? Though I gather from Jim that the most important part of the co-driver's job generally means walking ahead with a weak torch light and clearing the road.' Blackout regulations meant even ambulances and fire crews had to dim their lights at night and civilians were shouted at by air-raid wardens if they didn't mask their torches with a thin paper shield.

'Don't I know it! The Ogre told me as much when she said I could still be *useful,* as she put it. I think there's a shovel and a broom in the back of the van for that very purpose.'

Frankie couldn't help laughing again. 'You'll be very useful then. Oh, she's a caution, isn't she? We're going to have to be very careful we don't get carried away in her hearing.'

'Tell me about it. I only just stopped myself saying I was already being useful, thank you very much, with my teaching, and she didn't have to take that tone with me.' Bertie's school had diminished somewhat since the mass evacuation of children to the countryside in the autumn of 1939, but she still had small classes to teach and reassure.

'But I'm looking forward to it, aren't you? I know we're going to have to brace ourselves for some ghastly sights, but it's such important work. I feel better than I have done in ages.'

'Still no news then?'

Frankie shook her head. 'Nothing at all. Maybe no news is good news?' She tried to sound confident, but she knew that the chances of Dickie returning were increasingly small. Even if he had been captured, if he'd been wounded as well in that mighty onslaught earlier in the year, the chances of him surviving imprisonment were slim. Of course she was worried for him, but she couldn't help feeling that he wouldn't approve of this new opportunity and her new-found independence. And she couldn't help feeling a little bit guilty when she realised she was glad he wasn't here to stop her and that a part of her was hoping he would never come back.

'All you can do is hope and pray.' Bertie flung her arms around her friend, giving her a big hug, and they both stopped in mid-stride.

'At least we're still here, unlike those poor people in the East End and other parts of London. It hardly seems like the war is actually happening out here sometimes.'

'We've been very lucky so far.' Frankie paused. 'And I've been thinking that means I might be forced to take in lodgers. The authorities haven't pushed people into doing it yet, but I can well imagine there's going to be pressure on anyone with a large house to take in bombed-out families.'

'I suppose that's true. How would you feel about that?'

Frankie pulled a face. 'It's all right for you, still living with your parents. You won't have to take in any East End street urchins.'

Bertie shrieked with laughter. 'Oh, that would be a scream! I can't imagine Mother coping with homeless snotty-nosed children. It was bad enough when my sister brought her two round to say goodbye before they went to stay with Aunt Elsie in Sussex. They didn't wipe their feet well enough for her liking. She'd have a fit if we were forced to take in lodgers.'

'Well, I might not have a choice. And I wouldn't fancy giving house room to little uncouth tykes either.' Frankie pulled a face at the thought of her lovely spacious house, filled with her parents' fine Victorian and Edwardian furnishings, being scratched and torn by boisterous little boys. Dickie would have had a fit if he was still here, no matter how much the authorities insisted he had no choice but to help the homeless. *'Come on.*

You can't go opening your home to just any Tom, Dick or Harry,' he'd have said.

'Then hang on for a bit and wait till a more salubrious area gets bombed. Then you might get a family more to your liking.'

'What? Hold out for Chelsea?' Frankie doubled up laughing.

Bertie linked her arm in hers as they continued walking. 'Someone from a good address would be much more up your street. They'd appreciate what you've got to offer.'

'They might turn their noses up at it. If they're really posh, it might not be quite what they're used to. Anyway, that sort are far more likely to have friends in grand houses in the country who can offer them a safe bolt-hole.'

'Nevertheless, however smart they are, if they've lost simply everything they might well be very glad of a lovely house opposite a grand church with a view across the common. And at least you'd know they'd have breeding and good manners.'

'What's worse, do you think? Snooty or snotty? I don't think either is particularly appealing. What would you choose?'

Bertie pretended to think deeply about the situation. 'As I'm a teacher, I'd choose snotty every time. Then I'd always feel I could improve their situation if they lived with me, by teaching them manners and giving them an education. Yes, I'd definitely go for East Enders. Besides, they might teach me a thing or two. Cockney rhyming slang for a start. Me old china!'

'What on earth is that?' Frankie was on the verge of more guffaws of laughter again.

'China, from china plate, which rhymes with mate. You're me old china, my dear.' Bertie leant into Frankie and clutched her arm again. 'Then the rabble would arrive and want a butcher's round the house, then they'd be running up and down your apples and pears in no time.'

'I don't know what on earth you're talking about, but I might not have a choice when it comes to it.'

'Then if you really have a preference, you should keep an eye on the air raids and pick an address you prefer.'

'What, rather than have them foisted on me, you mean?'

'Exactly. If you've got to share your home and your lovely possessions, you ought to have a say in it. But I'd go for cockney every time. At least they'd think they'd landed on their feet.' Bertie began humming 'Knees Up Mother Brown' more and more loudly, until Frankie joined in, and the two of them finished their walk home singing loudly as they approached the common.

'If you get a gang of snotty urchins here, they'll think they've landed up in the countryside after the smoky East End,' Bertie said, looking out over the grassy slopes bounded by trees turning colour and brambles hiding the last of that year's black-berries that hadn't yet been stripped by birds, and local house-wives keen to take advantage of free bounty wherever they could.

'But if I'm landed with the snoots they'd expect to be enter-tained.' Frankie looked worried. 'Oh, for goodness' sake, what on earth am I fretting for? It's bound to happen sooner or later and I'll just have to take whoever gets sent here. I don't suppose they'll be that happy about it either.'

'It's a dilemma all right,' Bertie grinned, enjoying her friend's consternation. 'What a choice you've got. What's the least worst? Little tykes nicking your silver or toffs turning their noses up at it? I'm glad I'm not in your shoes.'

Frankie gave Bertie a shove, which sent them both into giggles as they pushed open the wrought-iron gate at the bottom of the steps leading to the front of the house. And Frankie felt that she was having more fun than she'd had in a long time, certainly more than when Dickie had still been at home.

@OURFOREVERHOUSE#WAKEUPSMELLTHECOFFEE

There was no coffee, nor tea either, when Charlie woke the morning after their first night in the house. All she could smell was the garlic on Dan's breath as he snored beside her, and the musty scent of the old sheets she'd used for the bed. Perhaps if she'd had time to air them, they would have been fresher.

With its drawn threadwork on both the sheets and the pillowcases, the linen she'd found was worth keeping. It was good quality and had been stored in an airing cupboard, which would have kept it fresh if the water tank had been hot in recent weeks. As it was, everything felt somewhat cold and dank, despite the tiny lavender bags tucked between the layers. The front edges of the sheets, facing the door, had yellowed with age, but she planned to eventually wash it all through, adding a dash of bleach to take it back to its original bright whiteness.

Charlie slipped out of the high bed with its soft but musty mattress. They had laughed about it when they'd climbed in last night, sinking into its pillowy depths, warmed by the stone hot-water bottles she'd found. And they'd also laughed because they'd had more than one drink in the pub, elated by their purchase of the house and the excitement of the adventure that lay ahead of them.

Just one mistake surely wouldn't matter, she thought. What were the chances of getting pregnant from just one night?

She hadn't mentioned it to Dan. He'd been too eager and she too had been caught up in the passion of the moment. But she probably wasn't going to get pregnant from this one single act, was she? And if she did, what would it matter? They were already planning to have a family, to fill the house with children, and they hadn't picked an exact date to start, had they?

But she wasn't ready yet, she told herself. She wanted to prepare for future children. She needed to make the house clean and organised, with a nursery to receive the first of many babies. She couldn't imagine going through pregnancy and then cradling a baby in the midst of the chaos of builders and brick dust.

Charlie shook her head, still thick with the alcohol and excitement of the previous night. She picked up the clothes strewn on the threadbare Indian rugs that almost completely covered the floorboards, threw her T-shirt over her head and staggered to the bathroom to splash her face with cold water and rinse her mouth. She'd found some old towels the night before in a green Lloyd Loom linen chest, and now she rubbed herself dry with the thin, rough material, trying to warm herself with the weak rays of the electric wall heater.

Coffee, she needed coffee, but they hadn't brought any supplies with them; perhaps the high street had a café serving drinks and even breakfast.

After quickly pulling on the rest of her clothes, she left Dan to sleep and slipped out of the back door, through the garden and out of the side gate. A dog walker was whistling to her black Labrador on the frosted common, a motorbike whizzed past and she could hear distant traffic on the main road. Everyone was stirring, even though it was early on a Saturday morning.

She was pleased to discover that the village high street would serve all their needs. Unlike many London suburbs, where shops were boarded up or converted to vape shops or charities, this was a thriving community. There was a butcher, a hardware shop, a hairdresser, a little general supermarket and a chemist. She could even see a florist with a green awning and buckets of fresh flowers standing outside.

And to Charlie's relief, there was a café. Despite the early hour, Nicky's Café was warm and welcoming, decked with multicoloured bunting and furnished with a variety of chairs painted in pastel tones of pink and pistachio green. Definitely not the greasy spoon builders' café she had been expecting.

Ten minutes later, walking back with cups of coffee and freshly baked croissants, Charlie felt excited to be entering her new home. Today was the first day of their new life in the old house and it felt right. She put aside her qualms about the consequences of the previous night and told herself if it had made her pregnant, it wouldn't be disastrous, it would just be sooner than they'd expected. Anyway, there was work to do, there wasn't time to go rushing off to ask for a morning-after pill just in case.

Inside the house, she heard Dan in the bathroom overhead. She hoped he'd found the handbag-sized packets of tissues she'd left out in lieu of toilet paper. Another trip to the little shops in the high street would soon be necessary.

'I've got breakfast,' she called up the stairs. 'It's down here in the kitchen.' Her breath was visible – even inside the house, the air was chilly.

Charlie sat down at the Formica-topped kitchen table with its matching red-cushioned stools, which had probably been purchased in the 1950s. She'd rinsed a couple of the old bone-handled knives so they could spread the pats of butter she'd brought from the café. Apricot jam would have made it perfect, but the crisp croissants were still delicious. She huddled in her thick jacket, hoping the fan heater would help to warm her.

When the weather improved, she'd open the French doors to the garden every morning. But for now a blackbird was trilling and a thrush pecked at fallen fruit on the lawn, while at the far end she saw the ginger muzzle of an urban fox stare at her, then slink through the hydrangeas among the shaded shrubs. That's where we'll put a Wendy house for the children to play in, she told herself.

'I could murder a full English,' Dan said as he burst into the kitchen and grabbed the food. 'Do they do that there as well?' He took a large bite of his croissant, crumbs falling to the table, some catching in the stubble on his chin.

'They do, but we'd have to eat it there. It wouldn't be take-out, unless you'd be satisfied with a bacon roll. We could go tomorrow morning. They're open on Sundays as well.'

'Mmm, we should do that.' Dan moved to the garden doors and stood there blocking the light and her view.

'What do you want to do first today?' Charlie sipped her coffee. It was cooling quickly in the chilly house, even though she'd come back as quickly as she could.

'I thought we should make a list, room by room, of what gets chucked and what can be sold. And at the same time make a note of any features we're keeping, like the cornices and those fancy ceiling roses.'

'We can do that together. I've got a few ideas about where to sell some things. And I need to finish taking pictures from every angle before we start pulling the place apart.'

'Have you posted anything yet? Are your followers responding?'

'So far, I've only shown the peeling front door both shut and slightly open. The tarnished lion-head door-knocker got the most likes. They're dying to see more, of course. But I'm being careful not to give away the exact location, so you don't have to worry about that. I know how to protect our privacy.'

'Good, we don't want to be fighting off looters all of a sudden. In fact, I'm surprised this place hasn't been broken into before now.' Dan grabbed his second croissant. He didn't bother with the butter, just tore it in half and stuffed a chunk in his mouth.

'Lucky for us it hadn't been vandalised either,' Charlie said, pushing past him to brush the crumbs from her jacket out in the garden. 'Now, if we're spending another night here, I need to pop back to the flat for a few things. The van bringing the last of our contents isn't coming till Tuesday.'

'We'd better make a list of what Brad and his guys should be taking away with them as well. Once the van's empty, they can load up furniture we definitely don't want to keep.'

'They're on board for that already. I'll give them clear instructions on what goes into storage to sell and what they can dump.'

Dan tossed back the last drop of his coffee, then hugged her from behind, pulling her close to him. 'Last night was fun, wasn't it, despite the old bed?'

Charlie could feel him hardening behind her. She was momentarily tempted, but she pulled away. She didn't want to repeat the risk she'd taken the night before. Spinning round, she quickly kissed his cheek, grazing her lips on his stubble. 'It was great, but I need a shower before we have a repeat performance.' And I need to pick up my pills, she told herself.

NINE

THEN

OCTOBER 1940

Nervously turning the key in the ignition, Frankie told herself not to worry. Jim was coming with her on her very first call-out. And Alf was going out with Bertie to show her the ropes.

'Best you have a practice run with us to start with,' Jim said after she'd been signed up. 'You'll soon get the hang of it, but this way we can make sure you're both familiar with the usual procedure.'

Frankie didn't feel the slightest bit diminished by this suggestion. He didn't talk down to her the way Dickie always had. It wasn't that Jim didn't trust her driving, more that she didn't trust herself to remember all the rules in the midst of the chaos she knew they were likely to face after an air raid.

They set off down the familiar stretch of road that led to Putney Bridge and, as they crossed over the river, Jim said, 'This end of London hasn't been getting it like the docks in the east, but there's a few landmarks the Jerries have set their sights on. Let's hope they're not having much luck tonight.' The station had received a call that residential streets west of Battersea Power Station were ablaze and a number of casualties were reported.

Because of the pattern of bombing, the roads leading towards Battersea from west London were clear of debris and Jim didn't have to keep leaping out of the van with his broom and torch. But as they neared their destination, it was clear that the tarmac was littered with shards of glass, smashed tiles and fallen bricks. 'Hold on a tick,' Jim said. As the van slowed down, he jumped out and cleared the worst of it away so she could continue driving through.

Once they were at the site, Frankie parked and opened the back of the van ready to take the casualties. Shouts and shrieks filled the night. Firemen were aiming great arcs of water at the fires and wardens were guiding walking wounded towards the two ambulances. They splashed through the puddles spreading through the debris, and Frankie was glad she'd changed into the boots she'd been told to use.

'Just remember,' Jim said, 'the worst must always go first. Fractures, cuts and bruises can wait if there's anyone in greater need.'

Frankie tried to remember the first aid lecture she had been given in preparation for this moment, but, as the distressed women and children came towards her, she found it hard to decide who was most in need of help. A very pregnant woman wrapped in a grey blanket staggered forward. 'It's coming,' she said. 'I'm sure of it. Must be the shock. My Henry only took five hours and this one feels like it'll be even quicker.'

That decided it. Frankie helped her into the rear of the van, hoping she wouldn't have to help deliver a baby as well as dealing with the other casualties. Two wardens carrying a stretcher brought her an unconscious elderly man and his wife, who had blood streaming down her cheek from her head. She clung to her husband's hand. 'We'd better take them together,' Jim said, helping them into the van. 'He looks like he might not last long.'

As the van filled up, Frankie wondered what would happen

first before she even reached the hospital. A birth or a death? Suddenly it was all too real.

She glanced around to see where Bertie had ended up. Alf had driven the converted sedan car and had parked further down the road. In the light of the fires, she was sure she could see Bertie, dressed in her galoshes and rubber suit, bending over at the side of the street. The poor girl appeared to be vomiting.

What a waste of that nice cottage pie we had at the station before leaving, was Frankie's first thought. Her second was, is it worse down there? Has Bertie just seen something so awful, she can't hang on to her tea? She quickly turned her attention back to her passengers, glad she didn't feel queasy.

'We're ready to go,' Jim said, easing himself back into the passenger seat. 'You still okay to drive?'

'Of course,' she said. 'Where am I meant to be going?'

'We're taking this lot over to Hammersmith,' Jim said. 'It's a bit further, but the nearest hospital is overrun, so that's our best bet. We'll drop them all off, then come back for the bodies.'

Frankie remembered her briefing from Mrs Ogilvy. She had made it clear that their priority would always be those who could be saved. 'You have to concentrate on the living. The dead can wait.'

Jim echoed this instruction as they drove away from the ruined street. 'Don't worry about what we're going back for. The dead aren't going anywhere. They'll still be there when we get back.'

Frankie concentrated on the road and on his directions as they travelled to the hospital. She could hear groans in the back and couldn't tell whether they were the cries of the injured or were coming from the lips of a woman soon to give birth.

At the hospital, staff were waiting to escort her passengers, and a pair of porters came through with a stretcher for the labouring woman. 'It's nearly here,' she shrieked as she was carried inside. Another pair of older men pulled out the stretcher bearing the elderly man and, as he felt the cold night air on his face, he opened his eyes and said, 'Take me home, James.'

As soon as the van was empty, Jim said, 'Come on, we've got to finish up now. We've got plenty of sacks, haven't we?'

Frankie remembered seeing a pile of hessian in the back of the van. 'I think so,' she said. 'But I've no idea if there will be enough.'

'We'll see when we get there. Put your foot down and let's get this next bit over as soon as we can. Then we can go back to the station for a nice mug of cocoa.'

By the time they returned, the street was even wetter than before as pools of water gathered from the firehoses, making a sticky mud of brick dust, scattered with shards of glass. Some local residents were already out with their brooms, sweeping the remnants of neighbouring houses into piles at the side of the road. It was so encouraging to see how these people, who earlier in the evening had fled to hide in shelters and cellars, were restoring order to their neighbourhood, in spite of their own losses and even injuries.

After parking further down the street, Frankie and Jim approached a warden who waved to them. 'We've laid them out for you,' he said, pointing to a row of bodies. 'They're the whole ones and the rest of the bits are over there.' He turned again and indicated an area along the pavement.

'We'll do the whole ones first,' Jim said, taking some of the sacks out of the van. 'We'll lift them together as even a small person is darned heavy when they're a dead weight.'

He was right, Frankie thought. She'd never seen, let alone lifted, a dead person before. It surprised her that she didn't feel upset as she moved their legs and folded their stiffening arms. A couple of them were in their nightclothes and must have already retired for the night when the raid began. A young woman with a peaceful face was covered with a blanket and, as Frankie lifted her, she realised she was naked beneath the scratchy grey woollen fabric. She must have been taking a bath, or perhaps her clothes had been ripped away in the blast.

Once they had finished moving the intact corpses, Frankie and Jim turned their attention to the body parts, none of which belonged to the bodies they had just collected. Bomb blasts shattered limbs and firemen turned their hoses from dousing fires to washing down walls plastered with flesh. 'This is always the worst bit,' Jim muttered. 'But just remember, they aren't people any more.'

Picking up arms and feet with her hands encased in rubber gloves, Frankie was tempted to try to match the parts they found. But Jim quickly realised she had slowed down and spoke to her sternly. 'Don't think about it. Chuck it all in quickly.' Once they ran out of hessian they bagged up everything in potato sacks.

She was just taking the last of her sacks to the van when she heard shouting. 'Oy, clear off, you scum!' She turned round to see Jim waving his fist at a lad who was running from the end of the terrace.

'What was he doing?' As she asked the question, she felt a kind of numbness creeping around her throat.

'Cheeky beggar was raiding the gas meter, I reckon. It happens all the time. That and nicking watches and rings off the bodies. That's the worst kind. I expect a few bits went like that tonight too.'

'How on earth can people do things like that?' Frankie felt thirsty and shaky at the same time.

Jim took his helmet off and scratched his head. 'Beats me, every time. But this war is bringing out the best in some and the worst in others.' He looked at Frankie with a frown. 'You look done in. Come on, we'll shift this lot and then get back.'

'What about Alf and Bertie?' Frankie turned round to see

where they were and caught sight of her friend pulling the canvas around the back of their vehicle.

'Looks like they're finished up too. Let's beat them to it. I'll drive for a change.'

Frankie was glad to slide into the passenger seat and let Jim drive off. Her legs seemed weak and she was exhausted. They headed back to the hospital to drop off their sacks at the mortuary.

On arrival, she suddenly thought she would enquire about their previous, living passengers. 'We dropped off a woman in labour earlier this evening. Has she had her baby, do you know?'

'I'll just check,' the nurse said. She came back a few minutes later, saying, 'She's had a girl. You got her here just in time. And she's asked for your name. Says she wants to name her baby after the lady who got her here.'

Frankie told her, and couldn't stop smiling as she hopped back into the van. So, this had been an easy call-out, Jim said. She'd just about coped with seeing the injuries and dead bodies, but they wouldn't all be this easy, she knew. But she also felt elated that she, a young woman, had tackled her first mission without crying, fainting or being sick. Maybe she'd finally found her calling. That would be something to tell Dickie – and for once he couldn't belittle her.

TEN

NOW

@OURFOREVERHOUSE#VINTAGEHOMEWARE

Charlie had finished cataloguing the salvaged contents from the old house. Dan had been all for clearing it out immediately, but she was glad she had stalled him and arranged to have the best bits put into storage. Then, after identifying pieces she thought they could eventually use themselves when the renovation of the house was completed, she had realised she could develop another business opportunity.

Excited by her new idea, she had decided to launch the project with its own identity and social media platform before she revealed everything to Dan. And now, just over a month after they had completed their purchase of the house, they were sitting in the local café waiting for their regular breakfast order. With the kitchen filled with dust and soon to be dismantled, the café was becoming a second home for them, particularly while they had little heating in the house.

'Do you remember how dismissive you were of all the furniture and stuff in the house?' Charlie stirred sugar into her cappuccino and gave her husband a mischievous smile.

'Couldn't wait to get rid of it. You've done a good job getting the place cleared out.' He'd been happy to see it all go, leaving them with the bare minimum of furniture, including their own bed from the flat.

'Well, you might be pleased to know that other people don't share your opinion.'

'What, you've sold some of it already, have you?'

'Bit by bit. And not only am I selling it, I've set up another branch of my business and it's going crazy. I might have to find more stock when all this has gone.'

'You're joking. Those fancy plates and motheaten chairs, they're actually selling?'

'Not everything, but a lot is. I don't know whether it's just because my followers want a piece of @ourforeverhome or whether there really is a long-term market for vintage, but yes, it's all selling like hot cakes. Instagram is the most fantastic marketplace.'

'Good thing, with the estimates I'm getting for the work on the house. I'm not yet into our contingency fund, but it's getting close.' Dan frowned and looked at the notes on his phone. 'This is turning out to be a very expensive project.'

'You're not beginning to regret buying it, are you? I mean, we'd been searching for ages and this was the best place we'd found by far.'

'No, no' – he shook his head – 'it'll be worth it in the end. But I'll have to keep working on other projects on the side to pay for it all. I'd hoped to ease up on my own work to some extent to concentrate on this for a bit. So, just as well you're bringing in a bit extra.'

'I'll do my best. I've got a couple of projects of my own going on too. I've been asked to style the showhouse at a new development in Morden and there's the possibility of a big house conversion in Wandsworth. That one's quite similar to what we're doing here, so it's familiar territory.'

The café's waitress slid hot plates onto the table, filled with the establishment's Full Monty breakfast, along with a plate of brown and white toast for them to share. Charlie stared at the glistening yellow of the fried egg, the grease of the rashers of bacon and the earthy smell of the mushrooms. Suddenly, she didn't feel quite so hungry. In fact, she felt nauseous. She pushed back her chair and stood up.

'What's the matter?' Dan was patting the bottom of the brown sauce bottle. It spurted over his food.

'I forgot something. You carry on, I'll be back in a second.'

Charlie rushed outside before he could stop her. She didn't know whether she needed to run back to the house or just hover nearby, but she knew she had to be out in the cold air of that early February morning, not breathing in the greasy smells of bacon and eggs. She went round the corner out of sight and leant against the old red public phone box, taking deep breaths. She couldn't understand it. She was always ready for breakfast and they'd been coming to this café a couple of times a week since moving into the house.

Charlie leant forward, hands on her knees. The nausea was subsiding. Maybe she just needed to eat. Yet again, they'd stayed too long in the friendly local pub the night before. It was probably just a bit of a hangover, wasn't it?

She pulled her phone out of her pocket to check the date. They'd moved into the house a month ago. She'd had her last period shortly before the sale had completed, hadn't she? The last few weeks had been such a whirl of activity, she struggled to remember. Maybe that was it – her period was due and, on top of the alcohol, her body was complaining. Of course, that was the answer. It couldn't be anything else, could it?

She straightened up, took another couple of deep breaths and walked slowly back to the café. Her breakfast would be getting cold. It might be even more unappetising by the time she sat down again.

Dan looked up as she returned. He'd almost finished his

food and was mopping the plate with a corner of buttered toast. 'Everything all right?'

'Sure, fine.' She cut a piece of bacon and popped it in her mouth. The egg was congealed and she covered it with her toast. If she managed to eat some of this, she'd feel better, she was sure. She wanted to push her suspicions to the back of her mind. Now was not the time to be worrying about a baby when she wanted to focus on the house and her other baby – her new vintage goods business.

'Aren't you going to eat all that?' Dan's fingers hovered near the second rasher of bacon on her plate.

'No, you finish it. I'm not as hungry as I thought.' Charlie pushed the plate towards him.

Ravenously, even though he'd already eaten all of his own large breakfast, he finished the food, including the cold egg. Through a full mouthful, he said, 'I was making friends while you were gone. Nicky here' – he jerked his head towards the waitress standing behind the counter, who gave a little wave – 'used to keep an eye on our house. And she knew the last owner.'

Charlie smiled at her. 'Did you know her well? I'd love to know more. I'm so curious about the house and its history. It's got such an atmosphere.'

Nicky came closer, tucking her tea towel into the waistband of the apron she wore over black T-shirt and leggings. 'I didn't know her ever so well, but my gran was her best friend. They'd known each other since school.'

'Maybe I could chat to your grandmother?'

'Sadly not. She passed away a few years ago. My mum looked after Mrs Wilson for a bit, then the job passed on to me. Kept it in the family, like. But by the time I took over from Mum, Mrs Wilson had moved into the nursing home, so I was only checking on the house when I went round.'

'That sounds nice and neighbourly.'

'Well, she and Gran had been close when they were young. It was only fair.' Nicky took their plates back to the counter, then turned round, her blonde ponytail bobbing over her shoulder, and said, 'By the way, I've got a load of keys from the house. I'll bring them round, shall I?'

Dan shook his head. 'We changed the locks straight away. There wouldn't be much point.'

'But that was just the front door,' Charlie said. 'Anyway, I'd love to have a chat about your memories of the house. Come round any time.'

Nicky smiled. 'I'll nip home after my shift and pop in this afternoon. I'm interested to see what you're going to make of the old place.'

ELEVEN
THEN
OCTOBER 1940

Two weeks after they'd joined the ambulance service, Frankie glanced in the mirror to adjust her cap before leaving for the station. Bertie wore hers at a rakish angle, dipping over one eye, but Frankie had caught sight of a disapproving frown from Mrs Ogilvy on seeing her friend looking so elegant.

As she tucked her hair under her cap, she caught a sickening reminder of Dickie preening in his uniform shortly before he left for training at Sandhurst. He and Hugo had signed up together and had both had their uniforms tailored at Gieves & Hawkes, Savile Row tailors to the military since the days of the Duke of Wellington and Nelson. He'd stood there in the hallway, turning this way and that, unaware that she was watching, while he smiled to himself and stroked his neatly trimmed thin moustache. He obviously thought he cut a fine figure in his captain's uniform.

Well, he wouldn't have approved of her driver's coat and cap. They were rough gaberdine, standard issue, not tailored and wouldn't flatter anyone, but she and Bertie didn't care for such finery in their work. They both laughed and said they were there to roll up their sleeves and wade through the broken glass and body parts to help those who could survive.

When she clocked in that day, she and Bertie were sent out on their first solo mission. It wasn't very far away, only across the river in Fulham, but hundreds of incendiary bombs had been dropped that night and fires were creeping towards the gasworks and petrol depot. Although many local residents had fled to shelters when the first warning sounded, some had been caught in the raid and half the nearby terrace of houses was in danger of collapsing.

When the girls arrived, their journey was slowed by the huge amount of debris scattered across the nearby streets. Frankie couldn't safely drive through the piles of bricks and glass. Bertie jumped out, pulled on her boots and grabbed her broom to begin clearing a path through the shattered fragments for Frankie to move further forward. The flames of the fires flickered on the glittering shards and there was little need for Bertie's torch. She swept the splinters aside and soon beckoned for the converted butcher's van to follow.

'Don't come any closer,' a warden suddenly shouted. 'The fire crew are trying to get the fires near the gasworks under control. It's a ticking bomb. The whole lot could blow up yet.'

Frankie leant out of her window and looked towards the giant looming gas tank, shadowed against the moonlit sky. 'We'd best be quick then. Where'd you want us first?'

The warden pointed towards the two houses in the terrace that were still relatively intact. 'We can't be sure they've all cleared out. And down the other end we can hear some cries under the rubble.'

'We'll tackle that first then.' Frankie jumped out, then pulled on her rubber overalls. She grabbed her metal helmet and torch and Bertie did the same. The two of them walked at a steady pace down to the end of the street, where another warden was kneeling next to a pile of bricks from the collapsed house.

He looked up as they approached. 'Young lady called Carol,' he said. 'Says she's got a baby down here with her. She doesn't think she's hurt, just trapped.'

'We'll see what we can do,' Bertie said, kneeling down beside him. 'If we can lift this slab together, we might be able to see more.'

With the warden's help, they were able to move the large piece of brickwork, part of the exterior wall of the house, revealing a deep, black hole. 'It must be a cellar,' Frankie said. 'They must have thought they were all safe down there.'

Bertie shone her torch into the hole, catching sight of a white face with streaks of grime. 'Carol? Can you hear me? I can see you now. Do you have a baby with you?'

Two arms lifted a bundle above the woman's head, trying to reach their outstretched hands. Frankie lay down, trying to stretch as far as she could.

'Please take her for me. She's only a month old.' Her faint, frightened voice only just reached them. She must have used all her energy in shouting earlier, to draw them across to where she was trapped.

'I can't quite get to her,' Frankie said. 'I'm going to have to lean right over the edge.'

'Don't you do that, miss,' the air warden said. 'The edges could crumble and you might fall. Here, I'll have a go.' He lay down on his stomach on the brick-strewn ground and bent forward into the hole, but his wide shoulders wouldn't fit through. A little shriek from below alerted them to the fact that his stout body was breaking off more debris around the edges of the gap.

'Why don't I try?' Bertie said. 'I'm the smallest, but you might have to hang on to my legs.' She took off her bulky coat and, wearing just her warm cable-knit sweater and trousers, shuffled forward on her stomach and edged herself over the rim. Her thick clothes meant she was still too bulky for this narrow opening, so she wriggled back up and pulled off her jersey, revealing her strappy vest and bra, then she managed to squeeze through and stretch her arms all the way down.

Frankie and the warden each grabbed one of her legs and held on tight. It felt like her friend's leg was slipping inside the rubber of the overalls they had to wear, and Frankie was afraid she might end up with just the gumboot in her hands.

They soon heard a muffled, 'Got her. Pull me up,' from Bertie and they dragged her back to the top. She held a little bundle, wrapped in a woollen shawl that had once been white, but was now reddish brown with brick dust. She handed it to Frankie. 'I'll go back down and see if I can reach for the mother,' she said, and lowered herself into the hole again, while the warden hung on to her legs.

Frankie peeled the shawl back from the baby's face. It was still sleeping. She touched its cheek and found it was cold. It's just because it's a chilly night, she told herself. It's going to be fine. She opened her coat and held the little bundle close to her chest, hoping the warmth would penetrate the shawl.

'Pull me up,' Bertie's muffled shout drifted out of the hole. A second warden rushed over to join the first in pulling her up by her legs. Frankie watched her emerging, her hands tightly gripping those of the young woman they'd heard calling. As the two of them were heaved out of the cellar, their hands firmly clasped to each other, like links of sausages, Frankie heard the wardens gasp. Then one of them said, 'Slow down a bit, let's help the young lady out careful like.'

Bertie let go of her hands and crawled to one side to help gently lift the woman out. They laid her on her back. She was silent now, after all her cries when she was buried. And she'd left her legs behind in the basement. They'd been severed above the knee.

'Oh, dearie me,' one of the men said, straightening her crumpled, soiled dress to cover the wounds. He felt her wrist, then her neck. He shook his head. 'What a pity. She's gone.'

'No, she can't be,' Bertie cried. 'Her hands were warm. She held me tight. I could feel her gripping me.' She leant forward to see better. 'Carol? Can you hear me?'

'It's no good,' the warden said. 'It's a shame, but it happens all the time. It's the shock mostly. And, in her case, loss of blood.'

Bertie began to cry, then looked up and turned round to Frankie. 'Her baby. Where's her baby?'

Frankie opened her coat to reveal the little bundle. Its body was warmer now but it was still sleeping. She held it out in her arms so Bertie and the men could see.

All three looked at the peaceful little face and one of the wardens produced a silver Vesta match case from his pocket. He wiped it on the sleeve of his coat and held it to the baby's nose and mouth. But the silver still shone as if it had just been polished. There was no breath left to mist the surface. He gave a deep sigh. 'Poor little mite. It's gone too. Maybe just as well, as the mother didn't make it.'

Frankie felt a large lump building in her throat. No, she mustn't cry. She must bury her feelings. She leant forward over the young woman's body and placed the baby on her chest, then folded her arms around her tiny child. 'They're together at least. And they'll be buried together.'

All four of them were stricken with silence for a moment, staring at the sleeping mother and child. Then Frankie covered them both with the blanket she'd fetched from the van and one of the wardens spoke. 'Right now, we've got injured down the road in need of attention. You'd better leave these ones with us for now and get to those you can help. Off you go.'

The girls stood up. They both took a deep breath. 'Have you got a hankie?' Bertie was still sniffing. She was shivering too with the cold, as she pulled her sweater over her head. 'Carol told me the baby's name, you know. Alicia Rose. Isn't that pretty?'

Frankie felt tears threatening to spring to her eyes. 'That's lovely. I'll try to remember that name. We'll never forget this, will we?'

They held hands for a minute, then walked briskly to the van to fetch more blankets. The living were waiting for them and the dead could wait.

Charlie was trying to ignore the loud sound of drilling and concentrate on loading more photos onto her vintage site when she caught sight of a slight figure in black approaching the French doors to the kitchen.

It was Nicky, who waved and, as she opened the doors, said, 'Sorry to barge round the back like this. I tried knocking on the front door, but I don't think anyone heard me.'

'It's mayhem. I can hardly hear myself think.'

'You can always come round to the café and use the wi-fi there, you know. Escape for a bit of peace and quiet, though when the workmen come in for breakfast it can get a bit hectic.'

Charlie laughed. 'That might just be the answer. I'm off out with clients some days, but today I just needed some quiet time. Some hope!'

Nicky reached into her shoulder bag and pulled out two bunches of keys. 'I don't know why there's so many, but we've got all these. My mum double-checked and none of them are ours, so they must all be from here.'

Charlie picked up the first bunch, which ranged from a giant key that looked as if it belonged to a fort and not a suburban house to a more normal-looking Yale key. The second bunch was equally varied, but none of them were new. 'Gosh, it's going to be fun, trying to work out where these all came from.'

'Mum thinks some of the smaller ones are from drawers or cupboards, like a wardrobe or dressing table,' Nicky said, pointing to a small key with an ornate fleur-de-lis design.

'I guess that's most likely. Trouble is, nearly all the furniture has been moved out now, so we can get on with the work. And some of it's already been sold.'

'Yeah, I told her they wouldn't be any good to you. But she said, you never know, they might want to unlock something. That's my mum for you, ever hopeful.'

'Well, thank her for me. That's very kind of her to be so thoughtful.' Charlie stared at the collection of keys with a puzzled expression. 'But I don't understand why they didn't just stay here in the house.'

Nicky shrugged. 'Me neither. But Mum said Mrs Wilson insisted. Of course, I didn't really know her that well, because she was in a home by the time I took over from Mum. I was more like a caretaker really, just checking that the place hadn't been broken into or had a burst pipe.'

'Oh, I see. But your mother knew her well?'

'Fairly. She always said she was very private. Not that chatty. Not like me!' Nicky laughed. 'I'll talk to anyone! Still, that makes me perfect for the café.'

'It's a very friendly place. We like it very much. And until we get this place fully sorted it's going to be a lifeline. I think you're going to be seeing an awful lot of us.'

'Rather you than me.' Nicky pulled a face. 'I don't think I could stand all the dust.'

'I'm not sure how long I'm going to stand it either. It's not so bad when the men have gone home for the day and it's quieter, but right now it's driving me mad.' Charlie snapped her laptop shut after blowing dust from the keyboard. 'Do you know what? I think I'm going to take up your suggestion and work in the café for the rest of the day. My fingers are almost numb with cold too.'

'Don't blame you. It's colder in here than outside. I'll walk round with you, if you like.'

'But you've finished for the day, haven't you?'

'Yeah, but there's always something I can be doing. Besides, I might sit down myself with a cuppa for a change.'

Charlie gathered up her belongings and threw the bunches of keys into her shoulder bag for safe keeping. The two of them left through the kitchen door and out into the garden.

'I remember that pear tree,' Nicky said, pointing to the bare branches. 'My mum used to come back with loads of fruit and make us crumbles. She bottled lots too.'

'How lovely. I'm rather afraid a lot of the fruit must have gone to waste last year. And I won't be able to use them without a proper working kitchen this year either. Do you think she'd like some pears if we get a good crop?'

'I'll ask her. She loves cooking. Oh, you'd love her pear and raspberry cake. She makes it for the café sometimes. I'll get her to do one and save some for you.'

'That sounds delicious. I could have a sneaky treat while I'm meant to be working. Better not tell Dan. He'd be jealous.'

The café was nearly empty apart from one of the workmen from the house waiting to take away cups of coffee in a cardboard tray. Charlie sat a corner table, gradually warming up after the chill of the house, and Nicky joined her with mugs of tea and two slices of Bakewell tart.

'Did your mother make this as well?' Charlie broke off a piece of the crumbly almond pastry. Her earlier nausea had vanished and she suddenly felt hungry.

'Another of her specials,' Nicky said, stirring her tea.

'I'd love to meet her,' Charlie said. 'I've got so many questions about the house.'

'She'll have loads of questions for you too, I expect. But I'm sure we can arrange something for when she's not at the Women's Institute, arranging flowers in the church or baking.'

'She sounds like a busy lady.'

'Never sits still. Always doing something. But I'm sure she'd love to meet you, and she'll want to know all about what you're doing with the house.'

'She'll be shocked, won't she, that we're changing it?'

'Probably. She doesn't like change much and she was very fond of that house. Always saying how beautiful it was, full of lovely things.'

Charlie felt a slight pang of remorse, thinking how successful she'd been in selling much of the contents. 'Oh dear. Will she be upset now we've cleared everything out?'

'I expect so. But Mrs Wilson told her to choose a couple of favourite bits of china when she knew she'd be moving into the care home.'

'Oh, I'm glad about that. So she's got some good memories of it then.' Charlie took another bite of the tart. The raspberry jam that lined the crust was thick and juicy; obviously home-made.

'You know, I'm very surprised the house wasn't cleared out when Mrs Wilson finally moved away. Quite a responsibility for you and your mother to keep looking after it.'

'We were just following her wishes. Anyway, she still paid Mum and me a bit to keep an eye on it. And she left Mum a generous legacy in her will. It was meant for my nan, but as she wasn't around any more, it passed to Mum. And then she said I should have it and that was how I could set up the café. So we've got good memories of Mrs Wilson.'

'That's lovely for you all. But isn't it sad that there was no family to leave it to?'

Nicky peered at Charlie over the edge of her mug. 'Sad no family could ever be found, you mean.'

'What are you saying?'

'That's why the house and everything had to be looked after. In case she turned up one day.'

'I don't understand. You mean there was a relative who could have inherited?'

'Well, that's the thing, you see. Nobody really knows. Mrs Wilson made a will, leaving everything to her daughter. But she never left an address for her.'

'So where is she?'

'Exactly. And that's why it took so long for the solicitors to clear things up after she died and say the house could be sold.'

'And the daughter gets the proceeds?'

'No. They never found her. So, the Crown gets the lot. As if they need it. Perhaps they'll give it all away to charity.'

Charlie was baffled. 'But why did she say there was a daughter?'

Nicky shook her head. 'Don't ask me. I don't know when the will was made. Maybe she was a bit batty by the end. Sad really.'

'And did the daughter have a name?'

'You'll have to ask my mum that. She knows more about all this than I do.'

THIRTEEN

THEN

NOVEMBER 1940

Swilling her scrubbing brush in a bucket of cold, soapy water with a dash of disinfectant, Frankie thought this was the worst part of being a member of the ambulance crew. After every call-out, when they finally returned to the station, exhausted and longing for a hot drink and the chair by the fire, they had to clean out their vehicle, ready for their next mission. Sometimes there was little more than a few smears of blood, but tonight she rinsed away blood, vomit and urine with several buckets of water, hoping the smell would have gone by the time she next took the van out. Dickie would never have approved of her doing such menial work and for a moment she wondered if he'd enjoyed being an officer, ordering others to do the messy jobs. She was sure he would never have got his hands dirty.

She'd told Bertie to get herself home on her bike so she could grab a few hours' sleep before she had to be in school. She'd cycle home herself once she'd had a mug of cocoa and a biscuit, if there were any.

'Mrs Wilson,' a sharp voice rang out across the yard. 'You're a blanket short. This isn't good enough.' After every trip, blankets had to be counted, and any badly soiled ones were handed in for cleaning. And Mrs Ogilvy took her task very seriously indeed.

'Oh, am I? Sorry.' She tried to recall her passengers that night and whether one might have left the van wrapped in a grey blanket. It had been extremely busy and she had driven out twice, collecting a van-load of distressed and injured civilians each time. 'Oh, now I remember. There was one young lady who'd lost just about all her clothes. I think she must have kept the blanket. I could hardly let her walk into the hospital wearing nothing.'

Mrs Ogilvy sniffed. 'They'd have covered her up soon enough. Don't let it happen again.'

She turned on her heel and walked back into the station with her record book under her arm. Frankie took a deep sigh, threw the dirty water from her bucket down the drain in the yard and told herself not to say a word. Rules were rules and blankets were in short supply.

But she couldn't have made the poor girl expose her body on the doorstep of the hospital, could she? Injured passengers were often in such a sorry state that she found herself willing to bend every rule and regulation to help them through their ordeal. But that wasn't how the service worked, according to Mrs Ogilvy.

After leaving the van's back doors open to air the interior, she returned to the warmth of the station. Her hands were frozen from the icy water she'd had to use to wash out the van, even though she'd worn the thick rubber gloves provided to all crew members. Jim and Alf were huddled close to the coal-fired range that heated the staffroom.

'Here, have my seat,' Jim said, leaping up. 'I've warmed up now. I expect you're frozen right through.'

'I am rather. Thanks.' She gratefully took his seat. 'Is there any cocoa tonight?'

'Not only that, but Di's made potato scones. Tatty scones my old mum used to call them.'

'Mrs Ogilvy? Scones?'

Jim winked. 'Told you she wasn't all bad. Just make sure you let her know how good they are. We might be in luck again another night, you never know.'

Frankie rubbed her hands and warmed them by the fire. 'Don't let me nod off. I'm so tired I could easily fall asleep right now.'

'Tough one tonight, was it?' Jim peered at her under lowered, bushy brows, as he packed shreds of tobacco into his pipe.

She nodded. None of them ever went into details about their shifts. They all had grim stories they'd witnessed, hidden away in their memories. Talking about them, describing the horrors, didn't help. It was better to tuck it all away beneath a cover of chumminess with each other. 'And I'm simply starving,' she said with a huge grin, hoping it had fooled them and that the gloss of imminent tears didn't show.

'You'll feel better once you've got this down you,' Alf said, handing her a steaming mug of cocoa.

And at that moment, Mrs Ogilvy bustled in from the little kitchen that served the station, bearing a plate of triangular potato scones. Thin-lipped, she placed them on the table, saying, 'Before all this rationing nonsense I'd have served them with butter, but you'll just have to put up with them plain like this.'

'They're very welcome all the same, Mrs O,' Jim said, helping himself to one. Then he remembered his manners and held out the plate so Frankie could take a scone.

It was hot and floury, seasoned well with salt and pepper. Buttered they would have been heaven, but, plain though they were, each mouthful was warm and filling. Frankie nibbled hers around the edges, while the men took great bites and demolished their share in seconds.

Mrs Ogilvy sat on a hard wooden chair at the table, her back ramrod straight. Frankie couldn't help wondering what she had done earlier in her life. She hadn't heard talk of a current husband or children. She looked as if she might have been a stern schoolmistress or a strict hospital matron, someone used to handing out orders to giddy girls.

'What do you say to a game of cards?' Alf produced a pack from his pocket and pulled another chair up to the table.

'Not for me, thank you very much,' Mrs Ogilvy said, standing up again to take empty mugs and cups through to the kitchen.

'How about you, miss?' Alf turned to Frankie. 'We often play to pass the time, waiting for a call-out.'

'I'm afraid I really don't know any card games, other than Snap and Solitaire. They're not much use, are they?' She'd played those games as a child, but Dickie had never approved of women playing card games. She could just hear him now, saying, 'The female mind can get addicted to games of chance. Best left to the men, I say.'

Jim pulled out a chair and sat down at the table too. 'How about we teach the young lady something easy first, Alf?'

Frankie felt less tired than she had a few minutes before, and quite liked the idea of staying to enjoy the camaraderie in the station. 'What do you suggest? You don't play for money, do you?'

'It's a lot more entertaining if we do,' Alf said. 'Only pennies, mind.'

'I've got a few pennies in my handbag. I could go and fetch it.'

'Oh, don't you worry about that. Alf's got the kitty. Some of the lads take it seriously, but we only do it for fun. We put it all back at the end of the game.'

Alf fetched a jar from a high cupboard tucked in the wall beside the fireplace. It was half full of coppers. He counted out a dozen for each of them and then shuffled the cards. 'We'll start with Newmarket,' he said. 'See how you get on.'

Soon, Frankie was quite absorbed in this fast game of chance, and found that she was winning. She was enjoying herself enormously and had totally forgotten her tiredness. 'Doesn't Mrs Ogilvy ever play?'

'She don't approve,' Jim said. 'She thinks gambling's a sin.'

'But it's only pennies and you're not even going to keep them.'

'That's as maybe. But it's the thin end of the wedge according to her.' Alf slammed his cards down and pushed his last couple of coins across to Frankie. 'Best not tell her we've corrupted you.'

Frankie couldn't help laughing. The food, the fire and the game had erased the dread of the nightmares that would arise from that evening's shift. And now she just felt exhausted again. 'I need to get home before I fall asleep on my bike,' she said. Though the thought of leaving this warm and cosy group, and being alone in her cold house, wasn't appealing.

'You sure you're fit to cycle home? Mrs O will sort you out for the night if you're dead on your feet. She's in charge of the girls' billet. You won't be disturbed.' Jim slipped his cards back in the pack.

'Do you know, for once I might just do that. I haven't needed to stay over before now, but tonight I think I might go straight off as soon as my head hits the pillow.'

'Best do that then. Better you hit the sack than the pavement cycling home, I'd say.' Alf patted her on the back. 'Get a good night's kip and you'll feel right as rain in the morning, all ready to face another day and whatever the Jerries bring us next.'

Dan pinched one of Charlie's chips and dipped it in the pool of ketchup. While their kitchen wasn't in working order, their dinners alternated between Chinese or fish and chips. Some-times they ate out, but they both preferred squatting together on cushions on the floor of the house, talking through the progress they'd made that day as they picnicked on food they'd brought back. Tonight they were sitting at the red Formica table in the kitchen, with a small electric fire glowing to keep them warm in the chilly house.

'I don't know why you're so keen to find out more about the previous owner,' Dan said. 'That's all in the past. This house is getting a fresh start.'

'But aren't you just the tiniest bit interested?' Charlie wasn't eating much. She'd been feeling queasy again.

'I don't see the point. This is our house now. I don't want to know about someone else's sad, miserable life.'

'I didn't say it was sad. I said it was strange, that's all. You've got to admit it's odd that the daughter couldn't be found. I can't help wondering why.'

'So what?' he said, grabbing another chip. 'But knowing you, you're not going to let it lie, are you?'

Charlie speared a piece of fish. She'd peeled off the thick, soggy batter. 'I'm just curious, that's all. I'd like to know more about the history of our house. And it might be interesting to talk to Nicky's mother. See what she knows.'

Dan rolled his eyes. 'I can see this going on and on. Just don't let it get in the way of the work we need to do here. I don't want you saying oh, we can't go ripping out Mrs Wilson's old bath cos that's where she bathed her daughter, or some other nonsense.'

Charlie laughed. 'As if. I can assure you, I'm not going to get sentimental or maudlin. I'm going to satisfy my curiosity and leave it at that.' She looked at her congealing food. 'You can finish this, I've had enough. Anyway, tell me how you got on with your job today.'

He brightened. 'Bloody brilliant. When we unblocked the fireplace in the sitting room, we only found the original marble mantelpiece had been stuffed inside the chimney all along! They'd used it to block up the space. It's all in bits but the boys reckon it can be restored and fitted back together. We'll be able to have a beautiful authentic mantelpiece around a real working fire.'

'That's fantastic. Why on earth would anyone want to do that?' Charlie sipped water. Her stomach was settling now she wasn't looking at those greasy chips and batter.

Dan pulled a face. 'I guess it was just one of those things they did in the Sixties and Seventies. People thought they had to modernise old houses. They got rid of real fireplaces and switched to electric or gas, put hardboard over panelled doors and boxed in turned spindles on staircases. Vandalism really, losing all those lovely original features.'

'And you think all of that was done here?'

'Not as much as in some of the houses I've worked on. At

least when a feature has been covered up it hasn't been destroyed. I'm glad to say that this house is relatively unscathed. It's still got a lot of character we can work with and enhance.'

'Good. I like to think it's been cared for.'

'There you go again. You're injecting a personality, not just character, into this house.'

'No I'm not.'

Or am I, she pondered. The more she heard about the house's past, the more she felt there was an air of sadness and mystery. She shook herself. Dan wouldn't like it. Then she remembered. The keys. She reached for her bag and pulled out the two bunches.

'What's all this?' Dan screwed up the greasy chip shop paper, wiped his hands on his jeans and reached for the keys.

'Nicky came round with them. Apparently, they've all come from the house or bits of furniture that were here. I'm not going to try and match them all up – anyway, some pieces have been sold already. But one or two might belong to internal doors that we're keeping.'

Dan slipped the keys around the first ring one by one, and paused at the large rusted key that was about four inches long. 'This is interesting. I bet this one could tell a story or two.'

Charlie slapped his knee. 'Now you're doing it! And you told me off for fantasising.'

He laughed. 'I have to admit something like this makes me think. Where on earth does it belong? I can't think of a lock here that would fit a beast like this.'

'It's a bit like a fairy story, isn't it? You know, the princess is locked in the tower and has just one night to find the key that will save her life.'

'Can you turn it into something for Instagram?'

Charlie jangled the two bunches on their rings. 'Maybe. The princess and the key, instead of the princess and the pea?'

'What's that?'

'Oh, I don't suppose you were into fairy stories as a kid, were you? All the girls will know that one.' She spread the keys out in a circle on the floor. 'They'll make quite interesting photos, so I'll find a way of saying something about them.'

'Anything that keeps the funds flowing in.'

She stood up and walked over to the larder door to try one of the larger keys. 'I can turn it into a game, guessing where the keys belong.'

'I expect you'll find that most of them are redundant. Locks could have been changed over the years and these weren't thrown away.'

'You're probably right, but it can make an interesting story hunting for the right lock.' She pulled the key out of the larder door and inserted it into the door to the cellar. 'This should be locked. Once we have kids, we won't want anyone tumbling down the stairs in the dark.'

'Ooh, creepy,' Dan said in a spooky voice, coming up behind her suddenly, making her jump.

She squealed, then laughed. 'It will save money if we don't have to change locks, idiot.' The key turned and the door locked. 'Look, this key fits.' She turned it back and the door was unlocked. 'One down and about twenty or so to go.' She turned the bunch of keys over and over in her hands. 'It's very odd that these weren't left in the house, don't you think? Why did Mrs Wilson insist they were taken away? It's almost as if she didn't want anyone to go round locking and unlocking things.'

Dan hugged her. 'It's a start. We'll leave that key in the door.'

Charlie fumbled to take the key off the ring, then handed it over to him to prise the metal open. 'Some of these keys are quite decorative. I might make a display with them once I know they're not going to be any use. It could be quite attractive, don't you think?'

She fanned the collection against the wall. 'I could do it in order of size perhaps.'

'Very nice. But we're a long way off that. The rewiring starts tomorrow. You'll have to put your decorating ideas on one side till we've done all the basics. Then we can start having fun.' Dan kissed the top of her head. 'Now can we go to bed? I'm shattered and the guys will want an early start.'

Charlie yawned. 'Of course. I put our new electric blanket on earlier. Just promise me you haven't put a dried pea in the bed.'

'Dried pea?' He shook his head, looking confused.

'Oh, I forgot. You're not a prince and I'm not a princess.' She laughed and pushed him away. 'And besides, I'm meeting Nicky's mum soon. She knows much more about Mrs Wilson and the house. I'm looking forward to hearing what she has to say.'

Bertie had a spark to her, a twinkle in her eye. Frankie could tell she was up to something. She'd known her long enough, since they were both ten years of age, and she knew that look.

'What are you up to? I can tell something's going on.' They were both parking their bikes at the back of the ambulance station, ready for an evening shift, waiting for calls telling them where their services were needed.

Bertie giggled. 'Haven't you noticed the weather tonight?'

'What about it?' The day had been mild for late autumn, the sky low and grey, threatening rain that hadn't come.

'You must have noticed.' Bertie stared at her, another giggle promising to burst from her lips.

'I don't know what you're talking about. Noticed what?' Bertie could become annoying when she teased her like this.

'It's cloudy.'

'So? What about it?'

'So, there won't be a moon tonight and so we're less likely to have a heavy raid.'

'Oh, I see. No bomber's moon. So, we might not get called out, you mean?'

'Exactly. And that means we could be sitting around all night twiddling our thumbs. Well, Jim and Alf won't anyway, they'll be playing cards the whole time.'

'And what do you want to do about it?'

'We should go dancing. No, not here, stupid,' she said, catching the look of confusion on Frankie's face. 'We could go to the Cinderella Dancing Club in Putney, it's only just down the road. What do you say?'

'But we'd have to go home first and get changed, wouldn't we?'

Bertie shook her head. 'No need. I've brought frocks with me.'

Frankie couldn't stop herself laughing. 'Really? One for me as well?'

'Yes, really. That blue satin one of mine you've always liked.'

'We'd have to hang around here for a bit. At least until the Ogre said we could go.'

'Of course. I wasn't going to suggest otherwise. Are you on for it?'

'Too right I am.' She could hardly believe she could be this daring. Frankie hadn't been dancing since Dickie had been called up and certainly not since she'd thought she'd lost him for good. There was still no news, so was it all right for a supposedly grieving widow to have fun? Dickie would have expected her to hide at home, fretting for him, not enjoying her new-found freedom. Would she feel guilty about going out, just as many young women were these days, enjoying themselves? Many of her friends were single or parted from husbands and fiancés, but were still making the most of their youth, dancing whenever they could.

'You looked doubtful for a moment. You sure?'

'Absolutely. I'd love to let my hair down. Everyone else is. And it would help us to put the misery behind us.' The girls had been working continuously since signing up. Some nights were so full of gruesome sights they had to hug each other to banish the tears before they drove back to the ambulance station. There had been heavy bombing almost every night since the start of the Blitz in London. The East End still bore the brunt of it, but other areas of London and cities elsewhere were also being targeted.

'Come on then. Let's go in and face the Ogre and hang around until she tells us we might as well push off. We can get ready right here in the girls' room.'

Two hours later, having been told they could stand down for the night, the girls giggled as they changed out of their uniforms and into silky dresses. 'I haven't brought evening coats or jackets as well,' Bertie apologised. 'We'll just have to wear our uniform coats on top. No one will mind.' Girls turned up to dances and dinners in their uniforms and overalls all the time, even in smart clubs in the West End. It was almost the done thing these days, proving that young women, as well as men, were putting patriotic duty first before pleasure.

'Oh, I wish I'd brought decent stockings, as well,' Bertie lamented, grimacing at her legs in their thick lisle. 'I should have thought.'

'Never mind, we'll do what lots of girls are doing now. I'll go and raid the kitchen. See if the old Ogre has any gravy browning in there.' Frankie ran downstairs to check the cupboards. Mrs Ogilvy was nowhere in sight. Hoping she was at her desk at the front of the ambulance station, busy with her rotas, Frankie scanned the shelves and the larder. She found exactly what she needed and dashed back to the bedroom.

'I haven't ever done this before, so I don't know how easy it's going to be,' she said, triumphantly holding up the packet of Bisto and a small pudding bowl. 'I'll have to mix it with some water and just guess how much to use.'

Bertie gathered her dress up around her waist and stood on

the bed, while Frankie made a pad with one of her hateful lisle stockings and dipped it in the diluted gravy browning. 'I think that looks about the right colour,' she said, wiping the damp cloth over her friend's legs.

She stood back to admire her work. 'It looks like you've been outside playing tennis all summer.'

Bertie swivelled her head to look down at her legs. 'They look great. But I need seams too. Try using my eyebrow pencil.'

Frankie delved into her friend's handbag and found the dark brown pencil. It was very blunt. 'I'll have to use mine. It's darker, but I think it will do. Now stand very still.'

She found the best way to do it was to start at the ankle and run straight up the leg in one continuous line. Bertie's skin was still slightly damp, so she didn't need to keep licking the pencil, and soon she was satisfied with her work.

'I can't see,' Bertie complained. 'Are they straight?'

There wasn't a large mirror in the room. Presumably the Ogre thought that would encourage vanity. But Frankie took a small looking-glass down from the wall and held it at an angle so the seams could be seen.

'I love them,' Bertie squealed. 'They look just like the real thing. Now I'll do you.'

Frankie hadn't yet changed into her dress, so she stood on the bed in her knickers while her legs were painted. 'Ooh, that's cold,' she laughed at the first wipe of the lisle sponge. Then she squealed at how ticklish she was when Bertie ran the pencil up her legs.

Finally, when both girls were ready, they dabbed their noses with powder and reapplied their lipstick. They pulled on their drab navy overcoats and slipped their feet into court shoes, which were far more flattering than the 'sensible' shoes Mrs Ogilvy thought they should wear on duty. The night was ahead of them, they were young women off to a dance, to partner each other if need be or young men if any were home on leave. And

Frankie put all thoughts of Dickie aside. He wasn't here to tell her how to behave and she was too young to be a mourning widow in widow's weeds. She had to live to the full while she could. She glanced at the rings on her left hand and slipped them off. It wasn't advisable to wear rings for work anyway. She should have done it sooner.

SIXTEEN

THEN

NOVEMBER 1940

Breathless from dancing, Frankie sank onto the chair next to Bertie. Her feelings of guilt and fear of Dickie's disapproval had melted away on the dancefloor and, as the music began again with a perky foxtrot, she found herself laughing.

'What's so funny?' Bertie peered at her over the top of her glass of cool lemonade.

'I can't believe that I'm having more fun in wartime than I was before.' She clinked her glass against her friend's. 'Danger by day and night, and then dancing as well. I feel so alive!'

'I think it's called living for the moment,' Bertie said. 'All the young people are doing it. They're getting engaged or married without a second thought, and lots of girls aren't even saving themselves for marriage now.'

'No, where on earth have you heard that?'

'Oh, half our old friends from school are throwing themselves at any decent men before they go off to the front.'

'Really?' Frankie looked at her friend curiously. 'But you're not like that – or are you?'

Bertie tapped the side of her nose. 'I'm not telling. It's all right for you, you're already married, but why should I end up a dried-up old maid? I might want to grab my chance while I can.'

Frankie couldn't bear to tell her that her marriage wasn't what her friend might think. That Dickie had consummated their union once and since then had turned his back on her in their double bed. Before they married, she hadn't known what to expect in terms of intimacy, but she certainly hadn't expected indifference and disdain.

'Oh, come on,' she said, leaping up and grabbing Bertie's hand again. 'Let's dance while we can.' They ran onto the dancefloor laughing. There were few men present that evening and those that were there seemed to have already chosen their partners for the night and weren't sharing their dance skills with everyone. But the girls didn't care whether they held the hand of a man or a woman. All they wanted was the joy and rhythm of dancing to chase away fears of bombs and death.

Frankie wondered whether she dared press Bertie for more information about what she had just said. Had her best friend made love with a handsome pilot before he flew off? She longed to know if lovemaking in real life could be as wonderful as films and romantic novels suggested. She had been hoping for a magical experience on her wedding night, but Dickie's pathetic poking had left her wondering what all the fuss was about.

But she didn't dare ask Bertie such an intimate question, even though they had shared many secrets in the past. And when she asked herself why she couldn't do that, she knew it was because she was ashamed of her marriage, ashamed of how she had been fooled by Dickie.

Later, they danced a quickstep followed by a calming waltz and with the lyrical music Frankie found her thoughts drifting back to Dickie's last day before his departure. That was when she had finally seen through him, had seen his true self at last.

His best friend, Hugo, had called round that day and she had absented herself, knowing they wanted to talk to each other, not her. They were both wearing their smart uniforms, and retired to the sitting room with glasses of Scotch while she sorted her wardrobe upstairs. She could hear the murmur of their voices and laughter drifting up to her room.

When the burbling quietened, she thought they must be ready to part and that she should at least wish Hugo farewell and good luck before he left. She knew he wasn't going to the front, like Dickie eventually would, as he'd been selected for important work elsewhere because of his fluent German and Italian.

She'd almost reached the top of the curved staircase when she heard their voices again in the hallway. She couldn't see them directly and they couldn't see her, but she caught their reflections in the mirror framed by the coat stand, the very one where Dickie regularly admired himself in his badged army cap.

The men reached for each other and hugged. That was to be expected, she thought. Such old friends, maybe never to see each other again. But then, to her surprise, Hugo stroked Dickie's cheek, drew him closer, and then they kissed. Not a peck on the cheek either, nor a Continental double salutation, but a long, full-blown kiss on the lips with arms around each other that seemed to last for ever. And Hugo had removed his round wire-rimmed glasses as if they'd done this many times before.

When they finally parted, Hugo replaced his spectacles while Dickie wiped his eyes on his sleeve. She caught him saying something, but could only hear a few disjointed words, '...I'll always be thinking of you, my dearest love... together again before long...'

Her heart had clenched with the shock and her legs felt wobbly and weak. She reeled back from the banister she'd been clutching, her back against the wall. At last, she knew who and what Dickie was. She felt a tinge of pity for him, mixed with anger. She could understand why he could never publicly acknowledge his real love, given the rules of society, and that was tragic. But she also resented him using her and her respectable life as a cover for his true nature.

It was startlingly clear to her now that his best man at their wedding was truly his best man – and always would be, it seemed. And when she thought how Dickie had said they should start a family when the war was over, she felt anger. How dare he try to strengthen his disguise by using her? It was plain he had taken advantage of her and had never loved her.

But she could never tell anyone. It would be the end of Dickie's military and civilian career if this was revealed. There was no room in their world for anyone who was unable to love the opposite sex. She couldn't sacrifice Dickie and Hugo to salvage her own pride. She had to live with their secret and couldn't even confide in her best friend. Taking a deep breath to calm herself and blinking back the imminent tears, she had forced herself to smile as she appeared at the top of the stairs to say her goodbyes.

And in the dance hall, as the waltz slowed to its last calming twirl, she rested her head on her friend's shoulder. 'Are you tired?' Bertie looked at her with a frown. 'It's been a busy week, we can sit the next one out if you like.'

'No, I want to dance till I drop,' Frankie said, tugging her hand. 'Besides, the next one's a Charleston. There's nothing more cheering than a Charleston. Come on, let's do it.'

They decided to meet in the café. Charlie was more than happy to leave the chilly chaos and dust of the house and work on her laptop in a calmer atmosphere that morning. And Nicky had promised that her mother would join them.

After she had been there for about half an hour, a stout woman with short grey hair marched in, bearing a cake tin. She went into the café kitchen, then came straight back out again, bearing a cake on a large plate, covered with a plastic dome.

Nicky followed her and called over to Charlie. 'Come and meet Jean. My mum.'

Charlie stood up and walked to the counter, where there was already a choice of three other cakes. 'Another lovely fresh cake,' she said. 'What have you made this time?'

'Coffee and walnut,' Jean said. 'The others are chocolate, Victoria sandwich and lemon drizzle.'

'They all look delicious, but I'd love a slice of the one you've just brought in. Coffee and walnut's my favourite. And would you like to join me? I'd really like to hear all you know about Mrs Wilson and the house.'

'Don't mind if I do,' Jean said. 'Nicky, get us some tea, will you? We'll need a whole pot and extra hot water.'

Charlie took this to mean the chat might go on for a while, and was amused by Jean's matriarchal attitude to her daughter.

When they were both seated and the tea was poured, Jean asked the first question. 'I hope you're not knocking down any walls, are you?'

'Absolutely not. The rooms are already good sizes. And we love the proportions of the house. Did you spend a lot of time there?'

Jean took a sip of her tea. 'It was just the last few years really, after my mother had passed over. Mrs Wilson was getting on and couldn't manage it all on her own. It's a big house for one person.'

'How long had she been alone? I assume there had been a husband at one time?'

Jean nodded. 'He certainly wasn't around by the time I got involved. I don't remember ever meeting him. I think he must have died in the Sixties. He wasn't that old, but I understand he'd been injured in the war and was never quite the same again. Mmm, come to think of it, I seem to remember Mum saying he left her soon after he came home and went off to live in a place she used to rent out.'

'How sad. So, she then lived there all on her own?'

'For a while, I believe, but Mum said she took it into her head to fill the house with waifs and strays after the war. It must have felt lonely rattling around in that big house. She'd had lodgers during the war and lots of people needed housing afterwards, with all the bomb damage, you know.'

'So, she became a sort of landlady, renting rooms out?'

'Well, she already was a landlady, wasn't she? She certainly wasn't short of a penny. Her father left her all his rented properties. She owned most of this street, you know, the shops and the flats and even the garages behind.'

Charlie glanced through the café window at the shops lining the street. Every single one must have had a flat above, and rents on the edge of London in this pleasant area must always have been profitable. She turned back to Jean and said, 'Nicky said she'd left the house to her daughter? Did you ever hear her say anything about her?'

Pursing her lips, Jean said, 'Well, to be quite honest, that's the funny thing. She'd never ever said a word about a daughter. Not one. And as far as I know, she'd never mentioned having a daughter to my mother either. The first I heard of it was after she'd passed on. You see, the solicitor was trying to sort out her will and make sense of it. He came to the house to look through all her papers. I was there, of course, showing him where she used to keep things, and he asked if there might be an address or photos even, so he could try and trace the daughter.'

'And did you ever find any clues, anything about her?' Charlie was far too interested in Jean's story to eat, though the cake looked tempting.

'Nothing that was any use. There were old family photos of course, but none that we could say meant there was a child related to her.' Jean pointed to Charlie's plate. 'Hope you're going to eat that. I made it fresh this morning.'

'Sorry. I was just too engrossed in your story. Please go on and I'll eat it right now.'

'Well, like I said, we couldn't find any clues anywhere. And she was quite an organised person. Important papers were all filed away in one of those old-fashioned desks. You know, with a roll-top.'

'Mmm.' Charlie tried to speak with her mouthful of cake. She'd felt nauseous earlier that morning, but sweet things suited her. 'I know the one. It was still there. It's one of the pieces I want to keep. I've put it in store for the time being. Out of the way of the dust and so on. The drawers were still full of her papers, so I'll clear those out eventually.'

'Very sensible. There were some lovely bits of furniture there. She and her parents had good taste. Of course, a lot of the stuff had been inherited by them so some of it was Victorian and old fashioned even in their day.'

'It's a wonderful house and I can assure you we want to respect it. That's partly why I wanted to know more about its past. I can sense it there all around us. It was like a time capsule when we first bought it, still full of all her possessions.'

'She never wanted to change anything. Every time I said wouldn't you like more up-to-date heating?, she'd say it had worked for her parents and would do for her.'

'But some things had been changed, surely? I mean that fireplace in the sitting room had been adapted, blocked in with a modern electric fire. I say modern, but it must have been done years and years ago?'

'Oh, that might have been her husband. I gathered he was all for changing the place, but she said to me she told him it was her house, not his. And she wouldn't listen to all his ideas.'

'Well, we're glad she didn't do as he said. Some houses get ruined when people go mad with improvements. We're trying to keep it all in character. We'll have to modernise certain things, like the kitchen and bathroom, but we want to reflect the kind of house it is.'

'I'll be interested to see it when you're all finished then. I might not want to pop round while the place is full of builders, but when you're all through it would be nice to see what you've made of it.'

'It's a shame your mother isn't around any longer to see it as well. They were good friends, I gather?'

Jean frowned. 'They were, but not so much in later years. Mum always said they were thick as thieves when they were schoolgirls and then during the war. But I think they had some kind of falling-out later on.'

'Did she ever tell you why?' Charlie finished her tea and dabbed at the crumbs on her plate with her fingertip.

'No, not really. Mum was full of tales about what they got up to when they were young, but it sounded as if, once Frankie's husband came home after the war, they weren't so close any more.'

'Who's Frankie?'

'Oh yes.' Jean laughed. 'They called each other Frankie and Bertie. Had done since they were kids. Frances and Roberta.'

'Bit like me then. I'm really Charlotte.'

'It was kind of a joke between them, but I think they also thought it sounded modern when they were dashing around in the war.' Jean put her cup down in its saucer and raised an eyebrow. 'Did you know they were both ambulance drivers in the war?'

'No, I didn't. That must have been incredibly exciting.'

'Probably. But the way my mum told it, there were times when it was bloody terrifying and just awful for them. She stopped after she had her accident on one of their call-outs. But I'm proud she did her bit and so was she.'

'That's so interesting. Do you have any photos?'

'As a matter of fact, I do. Quite a few. We're going to have to do this again, aren't we?' Jean smiled and added, 'I'll make my pear and raspberry cake for next time. Nicky collected some of the fruit from your tree when she was still looking after the house last year. Better than it going to waste, I said.'

'I'd love that. Shall we say same time, next week?'

'It's a deal. I'll bring Mum's old photo album.'

Late in the afternoon, Frankie heard the knocking, and opened the front door to a man with a thin moustache and a clipboard. 'Excuse me, miss,' he said, 'I thought this house might be unoccupied.'

'It's my house,' Frankie said. 'Mine and my husband's. Though he isn't here at present.' She still couldn't bring herself to say that Dickie was probably dead and never coming home. Officially, he was missing, presumed dead. That had to leave room for hope, didn't it? He might be injured, lying in a German hospital, unable to speak, unable to remember who he was. But days passed when she didn't give him a single thought as she raced around with Bertie through the bombed streets, collecting injured and shocked passengers. And most of the time she gave thanks that he wasn't there to stop her having such an exciting time with her best friend.

'I'm the billeting officer for Wandsworth,' the slightly shabby man said, lifting his chin in an attempt to convey his authority. 'My remit is to find suitable houses that might accommodate families who've lost their homes.'

'Aah, yes, I've rather been expecting someone would eventually call on me about this. Do you have a list of people in need? And do I have to take them all in?'

'I am officially authorised,' he said. 'I have the power to requisition properties that are vacant or have spare capacity. I take it you aren't planning to leave the house any time soon?'

'Certainly not. This is my home and it's also very convenient for my work. I'm an ambulance driver at the Putney auxiliary ambulance station.' Frankie held her head high. She wasn't going to be intimidated by this council official, whatever his title and whatever his powers might be. 'But I'm perfectly willing to help those in need, if I must.'

As she stood there with the front door wide open, chilly air blew around her ankles, along with a handful of dried leaves. 'Look, you'd better come in and tell me how this is all going to be arranged.'

He removed his hat and sidled into the hall. 'Your tenants will pay you a fixed rent, but I have to assess the available accommodation first.'

'I see. Well, perhaps we could do that quickly so I'm not late for my shift at the ambulance station. We're always extremely busy, as I'm sure you can imagine.'

'I do apologise, miss. It's standard procedure.' He looked down at his feet, then up at the flight of stairs. 'I take it there's three floors altogether?'

'Yes, three. And it's Mrs, not Miss. Mrs Wilson. I'll show you round.'

'Thank you, Miss... er, Mrs Wilson.' He thrust out his hand and she reluctantly shook it. 'Cole. Horace Cole.'

'Follow me,' she said, and began her tour, starting with the ground floor with its large kitchen overlooking the back garden. After showing him the two spacious reception rooms, both with open fires, she led the way up to the first floor.

'I'd like to continue using the front bedroom myself,' she said, showing him her room with its built-in washbasin. 'There's also a fully equipped bathroom along the corridor, so I'm sure we could manage with extra people here.'

'I noticed you have a lavatory downstairs as well, which is very convenient.'

'There's one outside too, accessed from the garden. We always called it the gardener's privy.' When we had a gardener, she thought, recalling her parents' years in the house when they'd also had a live-in maid and an occasional cook. How times had changed.

'You're very well provided for here. More than most, I must say.'

And that remark made her feel guilty. Of course she was fortunate. Her house was still standing and bombs didn't often fall this far away from central London. Apart from the restrictions of rationing and the uncertainty about her husband, she had suffered very little so far in this war. In fact, she often reminded herself she was suffering far less than she had before Dickie had left.

'Let me take you up to the top floor. There are three rooms there and one of them has a washbasin too and an open fire.'

As they stood at the top of the house, with Horace Cole estimating the size of the accommodation by pacing the rooms and making notes on his clipboard, Frankie could see that he was working out exactly how many people he could squeeze into her much-loved home. She couldn't refuse to help, but she was worried about how she would react and cope. Strangers after all this time, sitting on her armchairs, sleeping in her beds, when once it had just been her and Mother and Father, and then just her and Dickie?

She could recall the house being filled with distant relatives and house guests when she was a child, but they were all gone now and, although most of the rooms were filled with furniture, they'd been empty of life for years. Perhaps the chatter of children was what she needed to fill the melancholy hours. Gosh, if

Dickie suddenly came home, he'd create an almighty fuss if there were lodgers in the house. The thought made her feel anxious all over again. But he couldn't *suddenly* come home, could he? She was almost sure he was dead and, even if he wasn't, surely she'd be notified? And then she told herself to stop thinking about how Dickie might react. After all, there were numbers of homeless people needing somewhere to live and this was an official requirement, so she had to comply.

Finally, Mr Cole finished taking notes and went across to stand at the window of the top-floor bedroom at the front of the house. He stared out at the church and the common on the other side of the road. 'It's rather out of the way for anyone who has to get to work,' he said. 'No trains out here, just the bus. So, it might not suit everyone on our books.'

Frankie felt a slight sense of relief, mixed with a touch of regret. If she didn't help bombed-out families she'd feel guilty, but at the same time she was still nervous about opening up her house to the unknown.

'What is that building, next to the church?' He pointed to the structure over the road.

She joined him at the window. His drab grey coat smelt of mothballs with a dash of stale cigarettes. 'That's the church school. They only teach up to eleven years, but they are still open. I believe it's mixed classes, smaller than before. Some families, even around here, decided it would be best to send their children away.' And some brought them back, she thought. That year of waiting, that phoney war when homesick children pleaded to return, when tearful mothers missed their young ones.

'Then this might be suitable for a young family. We've got quite a few on the list.' He turned to look around the room and walked out to the landing at the top of the stairs. 'Yes, I could see a family occupying this floor and keeping well out of your way, most of the time. With the fire up here as well, they could be very comfortable.'

'How soon do you think they might come here?'

He looked at another page on his clipboard, running the tip of his finger down a list. 'The Browns from Mile End, Jones from Bow... Yes, I should think we could send you a family in the next few days. I'll let you know who's coming.'

They didn't shake hands downstairs in the hallway. She was keen to cut the meeting short. As she shut the door, she felt again a chilly blast of air. She glanced at the sky, heavy with grey clouds. It looked like snow.

NOW

@OURFOREVERHOUSE#GIRLSINUNIFORM

Jean was as good as her word. The following week, at the same time, Charlie arrived at the warm café in the middle of the afternoon, just as Jean was placing her special cake on the counter. She had just come back from seeing a difficult client in Clapham who wanted a child's bedroom redecorated with a gaudy hand-painted mural of a circus, and had skipped lunch.

'I'm glad I didn't have much lunch,' Charlie said, looking longingly at the golden cake studded with raspberries.

'It's always a popular one,' Jean said, taking up the broad blade of her cake knife and cutting two generous slices. 'I've had to make do with Comice pears from Sainsbury's. They're not as good as the Conference pears from your tree, so let's hope it does well this year.'

They sat down again at the same table as the previous week, while Nicky made a large pot of tea. This time she also brought a jug of boiling water straight to the table. 'So, you don't have to keep giving me orders, Mum,' she said.

Jean laughed as she poured the tea. 'She always was cheeky, that one. My eldest, she is.'

Charlie broke off a piece of the cake with a fork and popped it in her mouth. As well as the fruit, she could taste almonds and vanilla. 'This is delicious. But I haven't come here just to eat your lovely cakes. I've been thinking about all you said last week. I've got loads of questions, but the first thing I want to ask is, were you ever told the name of the daughter who couldn't be found? Nicky seemed to think you were when she first told me about all this.'

'The solicitor told me, when we were looking through Mrs Wilson's papers. I think he thought I might have heard the name mentioned at some point, but of course I hadn't. He said Mrs Wilson had left everything to her daughter, by the name of Alicia Rose. But the surname wasn't the same as hers. It wasn't Wilson. It was Wright. I don't know why it was different. Maybe she thought she'd gone and got married.'

'Oh, those are such lovely Christian names. I can just imagine a little girl with those names, can't you?'

'They are pretty. But if she doesn't exist, what's the point? I sometimes wonder if Mrs Wilson was fantasising. She was a bit vague towards the end, you know, and I don't know when she made her will. I can't help wondering if that's what she'd have liked to call her daughter, if she'd actually ever had one.'

'I see what you mean. I suppose we all do that, don't we? Think of names we'd like to use for our children. But she wasn't Wilson? So that could mean she'd moved away and got married? But they still couldn't find anyone by that name.'

Jean shook her head. 'They tried everything to find her. But no luck. You know, I already knew the names I wanted for my children when I was only about ten. That's when girls start thinking about who they'll be when they grow up.' Jean turned to look at her daughter, making a bacon sandwich for a workman waiting by the counter. 'Trouble is, awkward girls don't always like the names you've chosen so carefully for them, do they?' She added these words quite loudly.

Nicky pulled a face at her mother and pointed at her with

the sharp knife she was using to cut through the thick bacon sandwich.

'That one,' Jean said, 'wanted us to call her Tina when she was about five. Tina Turner I think it was. Children, eh? Do you think you'll bother with them?'

Charlie was slightly taken aback. She wasn't feeling quite so queasy today and the cake had helped settle her stomach, but she felt her face colouring as Jean stared at her. 'Um, we'd like to. But we ought to get the house sorted first. It's simply freezing.'

'Very wise. Wouldn't do to have builders crashing around you when you're trying to get a little one to sleep.'

'That's true.' Charlie hesitated. 'Trouble is, I think I might already be...'

Jean looked up sharply. 'You do look a bit peaky. Have you tested yet?'

'No, I've been putting it off. I keep telling myself it's nothing, just the stress of work and the house. It's been non-stop ever since we picked up the keys.'

'You go and get a test this afternoon, my girl. Do it right away. Then you'll know where you stand. It doesn't really matter, does it? A baby's not going to want everything perfect, is it? Just a warm place to sleep and a bit of peace and quiet.'

No, but I would want things to be perfect, Charlie thought. All her plans for developing the business and signing contracts with new clients might be compromised if she had a baby too soon. But maybe she'd be proved wrong if she took a test.

'Don't worry,' she said. 'I'll sort it out soon. But what I want to know right now is more about your mother and her best friend.'

Jean pulled an old black photo album out of her holdall, opened it somewhere in the middle and flipped the black pages to find the picture she wanted. 'Here we are. Frankie and Bertie, like it says.' She pointed to the silvery writing beneath the photo of two young women standing side by side, both dressed in dark belted coats, wearing dark caps. 'The uniforms were dark blue, but of course you can't tell with these old black and white photos. Mum always said the coat material was horrible, cheap gaberdine. But they had to have something to make them look official when they were on duty. That and the cap, which she said she hated too.'

'They're both very attractive.' Charlie stared at the two smiling faces, dark curled hair just touching their collars.

'Oh, they were both lookers in their day. My mum said they always carried their lipstick with them. Kept it in their coat pockets and touched it up in the ambulance mirror. Said there was a saying at that time, "beauty is your duty".'

Charlie couldn't stop herself snorting with laughter. 'Blimey, you couldn't go saying that these days.'

'I don't think they minded back then. They were different times, weren't they? And look, here's another one of them standing next to an ambulance. I think that must have been the one my mum drove some of the time. She wasn't as good a driver as Frankie, so she only drove in emergencies. I think her main job was clearing the way ahead and ringing the bell, from what I remember. I know they always went out on calls together.'

The photo showed a strange vehicle with what looked like a high canvas frame at the back. From the style of the bonnet, it looked like it had been an old van or truck.

'Bit different to a modern ambulance, isn't it?' Jean frowned. 'I seem to remember Mum saying they had to convert all sorts of vehicles as there was a shortage in those days. I'm sure she said the one they drove most of the time had belonged to a butcher.'

'I suppose they would have had to do that. There'd have been a sudden demand for ambulances with all the bombing.' She stared at the photos of the women again. 'Gosh, it makes you think, doesn't it? Here we are today, because of the brave things those young women did in those days.'

Jean gazed at the photo of her mother and her friend again, somewhat wistfully. 'They were young all right. They'd have only been in their early twenties here. Mum never talked about the awful bits. You can just imagine, can't you, going to bombed-out houses and picking up badly hurt people. They had to collect up the bodies and body parts as well.

'She liked to talk about the fun they had though. The nights at Hammersmith Palais and the Cinderella Dancing Club in Putney, though that was bombed out halfway through the war, I think she said.'

'I suppose people needed to let their hair down and forget about it all. Oh, what a shame they aren't both here to talk about it now.' Charlie continued looking at the picture of the two confident young women, feeling she had to know more about their escapades and what they could have told her about the house and its past.

TWENTY

THEN

JANUARY 1941

The day after Frankie received the letter telling her that the Jones family would shortly be arriving, she opened the door to a tiny woman with four small boys. They were all shivering, despite their coats, gloves and mufflers. The children wore knitted balaclavas that covered their ears and their knees were blue with cold despite the long socks peeping over the tops of their wellington boots, nearly meeting the hems of their grey shorts. Every member of the family carried a bundle, bag or suitcase.

'Oh, my goodness, you're all so cold. This wretched weather. What a time for you to arrive.' Frankie ushered them inside immediately, slamming the door against the freezing air. The snow had come and then stopped, but the streets were slushy and icy and the family must have walked from the nearest bus stop.

'I didn't expect you quite so soon,' she said. 'The letter only came yesterday. But never mind, I expect we can sort things out.'

'I'm sorry to be a burden, I'm sure,' Mrs Jones said. 'My two eldest went down to Somerset at first, but I said they had to come back.'

'Oh, I see. Did you miss them terribly or were they not happy?'

'We face trouble together as a family. And together we'll stay.' The woman might have been tiny, but she looked defiant. Then she glanced at the oldest boy, who was wiping his nose on the cuff of his coat. 'Tommy, stop that. Use your hankie, why don't you?'

'Put your luggage down here in the hall and come through to the kitchen as it's warmer there. I'll put the kettle on and then we can sort out your rooms. I've done my best to get them ready, but I hadn't got as far as making all the beds yet.'

'Don't you worry about that, you can leave it to us. We aren't helpless.' Mrs Jones turned to her sons again. 'Take your boots off, all of you. We don't want you messing up Mrs Wilson's lovely house, now, do we? Is it all right to leave their boots here?'

Frankie nodded and, as the boys tugged off their wellingtons, she saw thick grey socks in need of darning. Big toes and heels protruded from gaping holes. 'Have they got any slippers or other shoes they can wear indoors?'

'All gone,' Mrs Jones said. 'We lost everything. We were lucky to get given these boots.' She bent down to slip out of her own fur-lined ankle boots and pulled a pair of slippers out of her case. 'I don't like accepting charity, but what can you do when there's four of them and there's nothing left?'

Frankie saw determination in her eyes; a spirit that wouldn't be dimmed, certainly not while she had four children to protect. 'Follow me. And you must all call me Frankie, everybody does.'

In the kitchen, warmed by the range, the kettle whistled and Frankie made tea. The children sat at the scrubbed pine table, swinging their legs in their stockinged feet, hugging the hot cups of tea and taking great bites of fresh bread spread with plum jam. 'You'll be able to help me out with the jam, Mrs Jones,' she said. 'There was such a glut of plums last year we've had nothing but. I think the Women's Institute went mad trying to find enough jars for it.'

'It's most welcome. And I'm Dolly, by the way. Everyone knows me as Dolly, and my boys are Tommy,' she paused to slap his hand as he went to pick his nose, 'George, Jeffrey and Alan. They're good boys really, but it's been hard for them being cooped up in shelters and all that since we lost our house.'

'We didn't have proper beds,' Jeffrey said.

'Mum said we were lucky to have anywhere to sleep, so we had to lump it,' George said.

Alan, the smallest and presumably the youngest, didn't say anything. He sucked his thumb.

'Where's your shelter, miss?' Tommy pulled away from his mother's hand. 'For when there's bombs?'

'We've been very fortunate here. The planes seem to ignore us this far out. But we've got a cellar that we can use. I haven't had to rush down there so far. Anyway, I'm out most nights as I drive an ambulance.' She glanced at her watch. 'In fact, I ought to be going in the next hour, so I'd better show you your rooms before I head off.'

'Cor, you're a driver? Didn't know girls could drive.' George was obviously the cheeky one, Frankie decided.

'We've all got to do our bit, you know. And my friend Bertie and I are a team when we go out to help people.' She stopped short there. No need to explain what they saw and what they did. It didn't help to be reminded of how awful it was arriving to find shattered limbs and corpses, and perhaps these children had already seen enough horrors in their short lives.

Alan took his thumb out of his mouth and spoke for the first time since he'd arrived. 'Are we in the country, miss?'

Frankie was slightly mystified, but quickly realised that for a boy from the East End of London, with barely a tree in sight, this area, with its rolling grassy common and groves of mature trees surrounded by tangled brambles, was a startling contrast to rows of identical cramped terraced houses near the docks and gasworks.

'It's not far from the countryside,' she said. 'And we're very lucky to have such a large area of open space on our doorstep, just across the road from here. And a little further away, over the main road, there's Richmond Park. You can walk there from here. It's full of rabbits, squirrels and deer.'

All four boys stared at her, wide-eyed. 'Real deer? Like reindeer?' George looked incredulous.

'They aren't reindeer, I think they're roe deer. But the males still have large antlers and are quite impressive.'

'Can we go and see them? Tomorrow? Please, Mum,' Tommy pleaded, sticking out his bottom lip in a pathetic attempt to appeal to his mother.

'Now, now, that's enough questions for today. We've got to let Frankie get on. She's got an important job to do. And we've got to see about you lot going to school.' Dolly turned to Frankie. 'It's nearby, isn't it? Will they be able to walk there on their own?'

'It's just over the road. You'll be able to wave them off from the front door.'

Dolly looked relieved but the boys looked glum, so Frankie added, 'It's a lovely little school and as it's so nearby, you'll be able to play on the common at the end of the day.'

That cheered them all up and Tommy said, 'Can we, Mum? Go out to play after school?'

'We'll have to see about that.' Dolly stood up from the table. 'Now go and pick up your belongings so Frankie can show us where she wants us to stay. Quietly now,' she said as they scrambled down from their seats and rushed out into the hall to grab their bundles and bags.

Frankie led the way up the two flights of stairs, ignoring the grumbling of the youngest boy saying, 'My legs is getting tired.' When they reached the top floor, she waved her hands towards the three rooms.

'All this, just for the likes of us?' Dolly looked astonished as she peered through the doorways. 'Are you sure? We aren't sharing with anyone else?'

'I'm rather expecting the billeting officer to send me some more people, but they won't be coming up here. No, these rooms are all for you. There's a washbasin in one of the bedrooms, which also has a fireplace. And there's a bathroom with a WC down below on the first floor, as well as an indoor toilet on the ground floor.'

'I can hardly believe it. What lovely rooms.' Dolly looked quite overcome, and reached for a hankie in her coat pocket.

'And I've already covered all the windows, so you won't have to worry about any lights showing.' Unlike some round here, Frankie thought. Two nights ago, before her shift at the station, she had opened the skylight to the flat roof and hauled herself up to look at the night sky dusted with stars. Not only was there moonlight, but several roofs around her glowed with light from unprotected skylights like beacons to guide the Luftwaffe. She resolved never to tell anyone about the access to the roof so her skylight would be blacked out at all times.

'I hope you'll be comfortable up here. And, of course, you're very welcome to use the kitchen and the bathroom whenever you want. I expect we can find a way of working around each other. I'm sorry I hadn't got round to making up the beds, but there's sheets and blankets over there and I have already laid the fire for you.' She pointed to the fireplace with an armchair on either side. 'I didn't quite know how many of you there would be, nor how old the children were. If you don't think they can share a bed, there's a camp bed in the cupboard on the landing.'

'It's perfect,' Dolly said, dabbing at her eyes. 'We're ever so grateful. Aren't we, boys?' She said the last words loudly to gain the attention of her sons, who echoed her gratitude. 'Now, you've got to get on, I suppose. We'll settle ourselves in, don't you worry.'

'I don't know what time I'll get back. And I'm out nearly every night. But if I'm home, you're very welcome to join me in the sitting room downstairs. I'd appreciate the company.' *Though if my difficult husband had still been here, I expect he'd have insisted on strict rules about you keeping to your own quarters and yelled at the boys if they made the slightest noise.*

'Very well, we might just do that sometimes. But we don't want to be no trouble to you. I'll make sure this lot behave themselves.' Dolly had shrugged off her tears and was back to being the indomitable little mother hen. 'And while you're busy out there dealing with all sorts, I'll keep the house clean. I'm used to doing that. And I've missed having brass to shine and a doorstep to scrub.'

'That's very kind of you. I must say I haven't done much more than run the carpet sweeper over the rugs and flick a duster occasionally. What my mother would have said, I don't like to think.' *Or my husband, who expected the highest standards of housekeeping.*

'Well, I'll do my best to keep it all as you like it, don't you worry. Now you go off and don't even think about doing anything else for us.'

Frankie went to the top of the stairs, and had just taken the first couple of steps down when Dolly leant out of the bedroom door. 'Just one last thing? Is there a chippy down the road? I haven't got anything for the boys for tea.'

Frankie gave her directions and carried on down the stairs. She had her first family of East Enders and thought she was going to rather like them. They weren't at all snotty. Not while their strong mother was in charge. She laughed to herself. Perhaps she needn't worry about the silver after all.

Charlie quickly flushed the toilet in the bathroom, pulling on the long chain handle connected to the high cistern. She didn't want to look at the bloody mess any longer than she had to. She'd guessed something was happening when she'd felt stomach cramps that morning, and now it was all over.

Only a week ago she'd done as Jean had urged her and had stared at the thin red line on the home pregnancy test. It had reminded her of the Covid tests they'd all had to take four years before and hadn't filled her with delight. She'd always imagined that, once she and Dan were ready to conceive, she'd be thrilled with this sign that they'd been successful. But she wasn't. It had made her anxious, unsettled. She knew she wasn't ready for a baby just yet.

She hadn't told Dan about the test. She hadn't even told him what she suspected. She knew he'd have crowed about it immediately, wanting to tell everyone, wanting her to share it on Instagram. And now, she didn't have to tell him everything – or did she? It could be hard to hide her feelings, it might be best to let him know what had happened.

Charlie washed her hands, then sat down on the wooden

toilet seat lid. She took a deep breath, asking herself why she felt so conflicted. She knew she wanted to have children one day, and she knew she didn't want them yet. But something had been growing inside her and now it wasn't. Should that make her sad? Or did she feel relieved that she had escaped this time and it wasn't going to happen yet?

She shook her head. She had to concentrate. Dan wanted to talk to her about the plans for the kitchen later today. They'd decided to make this a priority so they wouldn't have to keep eating out. Besides, she was growing rather tired of all-too-frequent chicken chow mein or cod and chips. Not the café's cakes though. She'd still keep wanting to retreat to the calm of the café to escape the drilling and constant dust. In fact, that was where she wanted to be right now, sipping hot tea, eating a freshly baked cake, under the watchful eyes of Jean and Nicky. They'd sense what had just happened, she was sure. Their maternal instincts were that finely tuned. Maybe that was where she needed to be.

Charlie stood up, looked at herself in the bathroom mirror, ran her fingers through her lank hair, then blew her nose on a couple of sheets of toilet tissue. Dan could wait a little while. She'd bring back a slice of cake to mollify him.

'Is your mother coming in today?' Charlie asked as she ordered her tea and stared at the cakes on the counter.

'She'll be here shortly,' Nicky said, popping her head out of the kitchen. 'She promised me she'd make banana bread today.'

'I quite fancy that. I'll wait for her to get here then.' Charlie sat at her usual table in the corner with a good view of the door opening out onto the street. She opened her laptop and began checking through her latest photos. The responses to her most recent Instagram posts had not been as positive as she'd hoped. There was clearly a limit to how many times she could show a picture of debris and destruction. Her followers needed to see some progress in the house or they'd lose interest.

Then she remembered the keys. She'd taken photos of each of the keyrings with them all spread out in a circle. She'd also separated the keys and laid them out in rows in order of size on a large sheet of white paper. And finally there was the photo of the key in the cellar door. That was it. She'd start by showing the selection of keys, then, day by day, post more pictures of doors in the house and challenge her followers to match the keys to the locks.

Absorbed in the game she was creating, she didn't at first hear Jean push open the door with her hip, loaded as she was with a tray wrapped in a tea towel. 'Here, let me help you,' she said, jumping up, as soon as she realised Jean was struggling. She held the door as the little woman marched in, bearing her fresh-from-the-oven bakes.

'I thought I might as well do two lots, while I was at it,' Jean said, sliding the tray onto the counter. 'The bananas weren't going to get used up once they'd gone brown. Anyway, they're better for making this once they've gone off. Sweeter, I think.'

Charlie gazed at the two loaves. Their golden crusts had risen and cracked. They smelt of bananas and spice. 'Have you used nuts as well?'

'Why, is that a problem?' Jean's head whipped round. 'I had to use almonds this time, I'd run out of walnuts.'

'No, that's lovely. I like almonds.'

'I added dates as well, for extra fruitiness. Is that okay?'

'Delicious. I'll have a big slice as soon as you're ready. Are you going to join me?'

'I'll have a tea, but no cake. I can never stop myself licking the bowl with this one!' Jean chuckled. 'I know I shouldn't, but it tastes good enough to eat before it's even been in the oven.'

Charlie couldn't help smiling at this confession. 'I used to love helping to clean the bowl, as we called it, when I was a kid, too.'

Jean looked at her closely. 'You sure you're all right? Not feeling queasy any more?'

And Charlie knew she'd seen straight through her. She took a deep breath. 'No, I'm not now. Not any more.' She shook her head. 'I did the test. One minute I was pregnant and the next I wasn't.' And without knowing why, her eyes filled with tears.

'Come on, sit down, lovey,' Jean said, taking her by the arm. 'Nicky will bring our tea over. Won't you, Nicky?' She shouted the last few words in the direction of the kitchen.

They sat down together and Jean patted Charlie's hands. 'When did it happen?'

'Just before I came out. Just this morning.'

'And have you told him yet?'

Charlie shook her head. 'I hadn't told him anything. I hadn't even told him I'd done the test. And I came out straight after it happened.'

'Oh dearie,' Jean said, rubbing her hands. 'It's a shock. But you'll be fine, it being this early. You'll have plenty more chances.'

Charlie could feel the tears ebbing, but there were no sobs. Why was she crying? She didn't feel sorry, not for the lost chance of a child, not for herself. She couldn't understand it. 'I wasn't ready,' she said. 'I wasn't ready yet to have a baby.' She snuffled. 'I suppose I'm crying because I'm relieved it isn't going to happen. Isn't that awful? I mean, it was still a life, wasn't it?'

'Barely,' Jean said. 'And it happens more often than you think. And as it wasn't planned, you hadn't built your hopes up. You can stop worrying and get on with your life now, just as you were thinking you could.'

Their tea arrived, along with the usual jug of extra hot water. 'I couldn't help overhearing,' Nicky said. 'Sorry you've had to go through all that. Still, it was early days, so not as bad as some have it. Here, eat some of Mum's banana bread, it'll do you good.'

Charlie broke off a piece of the moist nutty cake. It was delicious.

'You could only have been about six or seven weeks,' Jean said. 'You might have a bit of bleeding for a few days, but you'll be fine in no time.' She took a sip of her hot tea. 'But you might want to tell your husband, in case you feel a bit down for a while. Oh and maybe see your doctor?'

Charlie took another bite of cake. Tell Dan? Tell him he'd just lost his first child? Tell him she was glad it hadn't survived? She wasn't sure yet how she'd feel about talking to him.

'I'll tell him when I'm ready,' she said. 'It was all a bit unexpected and I wasn't ready.'

'All in good time,' Jean said, patting her hand. 'But my advice to you is never have any secrets.'

TWENTY-TWO
THEN
FEBRUARY 1941

It was the second coldest winter since the war had started. Frankie didn't know whether to curse the snow or be glad that it gave the little Jones boys so much pleasure. She cycled to work along freezing roads, then tried to drive the ambulance along the slushy streets of London. At least the melting snow dampened the fires caused by the incendiary bombs, creating a blackened slush that plastered the devastated houses. But nearer home, a pillowy white quilt lay for days across the common, delighting the children, who'd never experienced such clean snow before.

In the school playground they threw snowballs and, when the day was over, they clamoured to be allowed to take turns sliding down frozen slopes on the common until the daylight faded. Frankie had never owned a sledge, but the boys improvised with a wooden crate and an old tea tray she found in the cellar.

They will be fighting over whose turn it is soon, she thought. Especially if I'm sent another family with children. Already the four boys had filled the empty house with laughter and squabbles, as they rivalled each other, running up and down the stairs at top speed and sliding down banisters. Frankie could imagine how Dickie would have been beside himself, shouting about scuffed skirting boards and worn carpet, but she just revelled in their healthy exuberance. At last the house was filled with joyful happiness.

But perhaps the deep snow had prevented the arrival of another homeless family, and she almost forgot that she was expected to accommodate more people until she received a letter at the beginning of February informing her that she could shortly expect the arrival of the Beaumont family, numbering three persons. At least I know how many to expect this time, she thought. A mother and two children, I suppose, so that will be manageable with the lively crowd we already have here.

But the Beaumonts turned out to be three middle-aged sisters. All spinsters in their late fifties and early sixties. They arrived in a black cab that had driven all the way from Chelsea, with a complaining driver who grumbled that he wanted to get 'away quick before the bloomin' snow starts up again'.

'Boys, you help the ladies with their luggage,' Dolly ordered, shooing her sons out into the street just as they'd come back from school, when they were eager to rush out onto the common for an hour of sledging before dusk fell.

Frankie ushered the ladies inside, amused to think that she was now host to both snooty and snotty refugees and that this was going to make an interesting contrast. 'Welcome,' she said. 'We leave wet boots here in the hall and I've lit the fire in the sitting room. Let me take you there first while your belongings are brought in. Then I'll make tea.'

'My dear, allow me to introduce my sisters,' said the eldest of the three. 'I'm Elspeth and this is Daphne and Cecily. We're all terribly grateful to you. Our house is in smithereens, you know. We might never live there again.'

'Our parents' house,' whispered Cecily, so quietly that she could hardly be heard.

'Whereabouts is that?' Frankie took their coats, wondering if they might wish to keep wearing them. The fire in the sitting room was alight, but she couldn't spare much coal and the wood the boys had gathered from the common was damp.

'Cheyne Walk, in Chelsea,' Elspeth said. 'Do you know it? We're quite distraught at having to leave it behind. Such a lovely house, filled with paintings. All gone now.'

'I've driven around there, I think. There's been quite a lot of bombing in the Chelsea area recently.'

'Driven, dear? Do you have a motor car?'

'Not of my own. I drive an ambulance. I work out of the Putney auxiliary ambulance station and do a shift every day – well, every night, really.'

'Oh, how very novel,' Elspeth said. 'Did you hear that, Daphne? Our hostess drives an ambulance. That's something you'd approve of, wouldn't you, you and your friends?'

Frankie was slightly confused by this remark, until Elspeth added a sotto voce comment: 'She was a suffragette, you know. Doesn't talk much though.' She glanced at her sister and said, with a knowing nod, 'Forced feeding. Hurt her throat. She doesn't hear too well either.'

Showing the women into the sitting room, which was a little less cold than the hall, Frankie wondered if they would approve of the furnishings, but they seemed to settle themselves comfortably onto the sofa and armchair, near the fire. Each of them sat primly upright with hands clasped in laps, as if they were in school during a deportment class. 'I'll fetch some tea for you now. I shan't be a minute.'

'Do you have Earl Grey?' Elspeth asked with a bright smile. 'If you've run out, we've brought some with us. I did a little bit of shopping in Fortnum's the other day in preparation.'

'I've only got ordinary tea, I'm afraid,' Frankie said.

'Well, perhaps you wouldn't mind telling one of your house-keeper's boys to fetch the hamper that's with our luggage?'

I've got to get this straight right away, Frankie thought. I can't have a hierarchy in the house. Everyone here is equal. 'Dolly isn't my housekeeper. She and her family are living here, because she was bombed out and is homeless, just like you. She likes to help, but I don't employ her.'

'Of course you don't, dear. I wouldn't dream of telling her what to do. But all the same, if one of those dear little boys can fetch the hamper, we can all share in its delights.' Elspeth had the most charming smile and had probably been used to winning over everyone around her all her life, so Frankie did as she suggested.

When the hamper was carried in with great effort by Tommy and Jeffrey, Dolly's oldest boys, the other two followed, and knelt down on the rug by the fire as it was opened by Elspeth. Their eyes were wide as they saw the contents, which were probably more extravagant than anything they had ever seen in their short lives. Cans of York ham, asparagus, beef consommé and turtle soup left them almost speechless, apart from the occasional 'Cor!'

'Here we are,' Elspeth said, taking out a decorated tin of Earl Grey tea. 'Why don't you chaps take it off to the kitchen and ask if we can have a pot of this? And when you return, I shall open this tin of shortbread.' She tapped the tartan tin with the tip of her buffed fingernail.

They took the tin out to the kitchen and Dolly poured boiling water onto two scoops of this special tea. As steam coiled from the pot, releasing its distinctive citrus-orange fragrance, she said, 'Cor, I'd sooner dab it behind my ears than drink that! I like my Rosie Lee smelling of proper tea leaves.'

Frankie was inclined to agree with her and couldn't help wondering how many more differences in taste might be uncovered in the coming weeks. They might be from totally opposite walks of life, but they were all going to have to learn to live together. And yet again she was glad Dickie wasn't here to disrupt the harmony.

When Frankie and Dolly brought in the trays with two pots of different tea, Elspeth kindly distributed the biscuits among the entire company. The boys scoffed theirs so quickly they hardly made any crumbs, but Frankie felt she had to offer the sisters porcelain plates, as they were surely used to polite company. She didn't go so far as to offer napkins as well, although she thought they might have expected that.

Elspeth delicately dabbed at her lips with a lace-edged handkerchief and said, 'We're curious to know how you manage your dining arrangements here. Do you have a cook?'

'There hasn't been one since my parents were alive,' Frankie said. 'At present, we're sharing the shopping and cooking, but as I'm often working I leave it to Dolly to organise meals for herself and the boys.'

Elspeth seemed thoughtful, as if she was preparing her next question. Then she smiled that charming smile once more and said, 'Do you think she might be able to arrange things for us as well? I'm afraid we're no use at all in the kitchen. We always had staff, you see.'

Frankie glanced at Dolly, expecting to see her with a face of thunder, but she was stifling a giggle. 'Well, I'm blowed,' she said. 'What, never even boiled an egg?'

'Not a single one,' Elspeth said. 'None of us ever had to. It simply wasn't the way we were brought up.'

'So, what have you been doing up to now?' Frankie couldn't resist asking; since the war started, so many London residents and staff had vanished to the countryside.

'We quite often have lunch and supper in a marvellous little Italian restaurant nearby and the WVS had a sweet little canteen on wheels with tea and buns. Or we'd take a delivery from Mr Fortnum. I can telephone an order for delivery here, if it helps.'

Frankie was trying to stop herself laughing. The thought of exotic produce that the Jones family had never heard of before, arriving in hampers, was simply too ridiculous. But the three genteel sisters were all staring at her with pleading eyes, begging her to believe this tale of woe and take pity on them.

'What will help a great deal,' Dolly said, with her arms folded, 'is your ration books, ladies. Hand them over to me and I'll make sure we all have enough to eat. I'm used to making do and I'm on good terms already with the butcher in the high street. If you can stomach funny foods like what you've got in that hamper, you can eat his tripe and liver. Sometimes that's all we'll be able to get.'

Frankie was impressed by this speech, and further impressed when Elspeth opened her polished crocodile-skin handbag and took out three ration books. 'What an excellent arrangement,' she said. 'And you simply must tell us what we can do to help.'

'I certainly will,' Dolly said. 'I'll have you three peeling spuds and scraping carrots before you know it. I take it you've never done that before neither.'

'Never,' Elspeth said. 'It sounds delightful. We don't want to be a burden, do we, girls?' Her sisters nodded in unison, both smiling, but both silent.

Do they even know what they have let themselves in for, Frankie thought. But if it means we can all manage to live together, I'm all for it.

Charlie didn't cry when she told Dan her news. Perhaps her tears had all drained away in the conversation with Jean and Nicky.

He hugged her tight. 'I'm sorry, baby. Do you feel okay now?'

She nodded, her face pressed against his shoulder. 'I'm fine. Really it wasn't any worse than a heavy period. And it was all over so quickly.'

'Do you need to see a doctor? Isn't that what people usually do?'

'If I'd been further along, I probably would. But this had barely started.' She gave him a playful tap as she moved away from him. 'Anyway, it's all your fault. I swear it happened that first night we were here, when I wasn't prepared.'

He frowned, as if he was struggling to remember. 'Oh... you mean...'

'Yes, I mean it would never have happened if I'd known we were going to end up spending the night here. I would have brought my stuff. I'd have taken precautions. I never meant this to happen while we were in the middle of renovating the house.'

'But I was irresistible,' he said, laughing, pulling her close again. 'And now we know everything is in working order, which is a good thing, isn't it?'

She couldn't laugh with him. She knew what he meant, after hearing too many stories of friends who'd struggled to conceive, who'd suffered several rounds of IVF, who'd failed after spending enormous amounts of money with fertility clinics. She and Dan were the lucky ones. 'That's not quite how I'd put it. But I suppose you're right in a way.'

'It's like we've just had a test run,' he said. 'And when we're properly ready to try again it will all be fine.'

But when will I be ready? Charlie thought. Do I have to say, this is the right moment? Do I have to think, I'm going to conceive on the fourth Wednesday of this month, so I can have a baby in nine months' time? Maybe it's better leaving it all to chance. She had friends who fretted over the precise moment for conception, taking their temperature, checking their fertility with ovulation tests. It sounded so unromantic, so clinical. Why couldn't it just happen, as it already had that once, in a moment of loving passion?

Echoing her thoughts, Dan said, 'I don't mind if you never take precautions again. I'd quite like to have another go at making a baby with you.'

Was there ever anything more powerfully seductive than a handsome man who said he wanted babies? Charlie melted in his arms. 'Give me a few days,' she said, then she kissed him. 'Maybe next time it will all work out perfectly for us.'

He kissed her back. 'I'll be ready to get to work as soon as you say the word, my love.'

They both laughed, then she remembered the cake. 'I brought some banana bread back for you. It's one of Jean's specials.'

He unwrapped the paper napkin and took a bite. 'Delicious! I'll make us tea to have with it. Have you got a piece as well?'

'No, I had a huge slice when I was in the café. It's such a help to escape there to work.' *And hide away from what had just happened.* 'But I'll have a tea.'

Dan boiled the kettle and popped tea bags in mugs. Charlie thought the tea brewed in a teapot in the café was superior, but couldn't object as they only had mugs for making tea in their chaotic kitchen. She rather wished she'd kept the old brown teapot she'd found in the larder, despite the cracks and the stains.

'I don't think I ever told you that Jean told me the names of the daughter?'

'Daughter?'

'Surely you've haven't forgotten? You know, Mrs Wilson's daughter? The daughter she left everything to, the one who could never be found?'

'Oh yeah, her.' Dan lifted the two bags out of the mugs and added milk. 'So, what was she called?'

'Alicia Rose. Aren't those lovely names?'

'Very pretty.' He sat down at the Formica-topped table and slid a mug across to her.

'One day, if we have a girl, I'd like to use those names. What do you think?'

He blew on the hot tea. 'If you want. Yeah, they've very nice names. But what if we have a boy? Any ideas?'

She shook her head. 'I've never thought about either sex before. Jean said she thought all girls picked names they liked from an early age. But I never have. What would you like to call a boy?'

He frowned in thought. 'Not a diminutive. You know, a shortened name. I know some of your friends have got Freddies and Jimmys, but I always think you don't know what your child is going to be when they grow up.'

Charlie laughed. 'So, you've really been giving this some thought, then? I've never imagined you devoting time to choosing baby names.'

'To be honest, nor did I, but when it comes down to it I feel it's a serious matter. Needs some proper consideration. After all, once it's registered, that's it for life.' He finished his cake, screwed the napkin up into a ball and lobbed it into a lined bin on the other side of the room.

'So, what would you like to call a boy?'

'George, after your father? Or Charles, after mine?'

'Some people are going for really old-fashioned names again now. I met someone with an Arthur the other day. He might grow into it eventually, but right now it seemed odd for a toddler in a pushchair sucking his thumb, clutching a toy rabbit.' Charlie couldn't help laughing.

Dan pulled a face. 'No, don't let's have any Victorian monstrosities like that. No Herberts or Horaces. And no modern celebrity names either, no Liams or Harrys, and no Harpers or Taylors if it's a girl. Just something sensible and solid.'

'Ooh, get you. Going all conservative and sensible.'

Dan stood up and came round the table to envelop her in his arms. 'It's not a decision to be taken lightly. If we're going to do this, we're going to do it properly. Just like everything with this house. Now, forget the baby names for the moment, let's concentrate on the kitchen.'

And suddenly Charlie felt better. She knew it was all going to be all right. Her husband loved her, he longed to have children with her and he wanted to make this house a home fit for a family. She could relax and breathe again.

It was a struggle to stop the ambulance slithering down the slope of the high street towards Putney Bridge. Although the main roads had been cleared of snow, the slush had frozen, turning the surfaces into slippery rinks. Frankie drove slowly in a low gear, hardly daring to touch the brakes.

'If we manage to get back to the station tonight, I might join you and stay over,' Bertie said. 'We'll never be able to cycle home while it's like this.'

Their dimmed headlights were mirrored in the ice, and on either side of the road banks of snow reflected what little light they had to guide them eastwards towards Fulham. 'We may end up sleeping in the ambulance at this rate,' Frankie said. 'At least we've got plenty of blankets.'

'Certainly not. I'd like a nice cosy bed back at the station. The Ogre might have some soup heated up for us by the time we finish. And at least they keep the place warm for us at the end of a shift.'

'Warmer than my house, I'd say. We're practically living in the kitchen. It's better to keep the range going than lighting fires in different rooms.'

'How are your lodgers getting on with each other? At loggerheads yet?'

It was a week since the arrival of the spinster sisters. 'It's extraordinary. The two groups are so utterly unalike but they are getting on all right together. Well, I mean, Dolly is in charge of everyone and I think she's loving having total control of the ration books and all the shopping and cooking.'

'Can she actually cook? I thought East Enders all lived on pie and mash, eked out with scraps from the fish and chip shop.'

'It turns out she was in service before she had the boys. She was a scullery maid somewhere in Mayfair, but the cook took a liking to her and taught her the basics so she could help out.'

'Well, what a turn-up for the books. I'd say you're really lucky. And the boys are causing havoc?'

Frankie couldn't help smiling at the memory of the clamour they made rushing off to have snowball fights and coming back, wet and cold, to sit by the range. 'It's a bit of a fug when they're all crammed into the kitchen. The boys are drying out from playing in the snow and of course they've all got chilblains. But it's very jolly with the radio on and Dolly bossing everyone about. I came in the other day and they were all laughing their heads off, listening to Gert and Daisy.'

'Oh, I love them,' Bertie said. 'They're just like us, but funnier.'

That made Frankie laugh again, a laugh that turned into a shriek as she slid across the ice when she tried to turn right off the bridge. 'Eeek, that nearly did for us. This drive is hopeless tonight. How on earth are we going to get back again, let alone carry people to hospital?'

'Just take it slowly. We've taken the call. They're expecting us to turn up now.'

They pushed on and, as they neared the disaster area, they could see the flames and hear shouting from the fire crews. Bertie hopped out and pulled on her boots from the back of the van. 'There's less ice here with the heat of the fires, but it's going to be a sight when it freezes up. Just look at that spray from the hoses.'

They could see droplets of icy water adding to the snow and ice that every street in London was having to contend with that winter. 'I won't drive any further then. Let's find out what they've got for us.' Frankie clambered out of the van, nearly slipping on the slick surface of the road. She grabbed her gumboots from the back and changed out of her driving shoes.

The road was so icy, the girls clung to each other as they walked towards the conflagration. A warden waved his arms above his head, directing them to a group of people huddled in the remains of a bus shelter at the end of the row of damaged houses. 'They're walking wounded,' he said. 'The rest have had it, so get this lot out of here before they catch their death of cold.'

'We've got blankets in the back of the van,' Frankie said, reaching out to take the arm of an elderly woman trembling with cold and shock. Rivulets of blood had congealed on her forehead. 'We'll soon have you in the warm.'

'Let me help you both,' Bertie said, taking the hands of two little girls, whose hair was matted with blood. 'It's very slippery out here, so we'll all hang on to each other.' The children clung to her, but a little boy followed, skating across the ice as if it was a rink, with shrieks of delight that made the girls laugh, despite their injuries. It was good to hear laughter in the midst of disaster.

When they had everyone packed into the back of the ambulance, wrapped in blankets, Bertie closed the door and said, 'Right, let's get going before the weather gets any worse. It's freezing hard. The drive here was bad enough but it's going to be even icier going back. You'll be skidding all over the place and this time you've got a load of casualties on board.'

'I know, it's a huge responsibility. I'll have to be really careful.'

Just then, the warden came running up to them. 'Hang on a minute,' he shouted.

'We haven't left anyone behind, have we?'

'No, but this little thing might belong to one of them.' He opened his coat to reveal a tiny white cat, its fur smudged with soot. 'I heard it mewing in the ruins.'

Bertie opened the back of the ambulance. 'Anyone here lost a white cat?'

The bundled figures shook their heads, until a small voice from one of the girls said, 'That's Mrs Lane's Maisie.'

'Oh, that's Elsie's cat,' the elderly lady said in a shaky voice. 'She doted on her Maisie.'

'I take it that Mrs Lane is one of the residents we won't be helping tonight,' Frankie said, stroking the cat's head.

'I'm afraid so,' the warden said. 'She didn't make it. Shame, it's a dear little thing.'

'We'll have to take it with us,' Frankie said. 'We can't leave it here. It'll starve or freeze to death. Here, Bertie, tuck it inside your coat. And keep it still while I drive.'

'You're mad,' Bertie said. 'The Ogre will never let us keep it in the station. How are you going to sneak it past her?'

'I'm not.' Frankie laughed, though her heart was in her mouth as she swerved along the frozen road. 'You're doing the sneaking.'

'Why me?'

'Because I'm always in trouble with her. Anyway, I'll distract her when we get back and you can run up to the bedroom and tuck it under the covers. It'll be like a hot-water bottle for you later. I'll take it home with me tomorrow.'

Eventually, after a hair-raising journey via the hospital to deposit the injured, they made it back to the ambulance station. They parked the van in their designated spot under the corrugated iron shelter and went inside. Mrs Ogilvy was pouring tea from the large pot that served the crew and halves of baked potato were steaming on a plate in the middle of the table.

'We'd both like to stay over tonight, if it's all right with you,' Frankie said as Bertie slipped upstairs behind her, clutching her coat close to her chest. 'It's been touch-and-go driving out there tonight.'

'I hope that doesn't mean you've damaged your vehicle, Mrs Wilson,' Mrs Ogilvy sniffed with disapproval.

'No, it's fine. I've been very careful. But it's been more exhausting than usual. The roads were treacherous.'

'Hmm, well I suppose you can both stay. You know where to go.'

'Oh, come on, Di,' Jim's voice boomed across the room and he pulled a chair closer to the fire for Frankie. He was the only crew member who dared to call her by her first name, let alone abbreviate it. 'Have a heart. The girls have been out all night, they're half frozen.'

Bertie slipped back into the room behind him, giving Frankie a wink. 'Ooh, potatoes, are they for us?'

'One half each,' the Ogre said, turning her back on them to return to the kitchen. 'And there's no butter, only margarine.'

'Who cares?' Frankie said, grabbing a chunk and sprinkling it with salt and pepper. 'After the night we've had, hot food and drinks are just the ticket.'

'We were worried about you girls out there tonight,' Jim said. 'In normal times you'd have to be off your head to go out on a night like this.'

'But these aren't normal times and, in some ways, I'm quite glad they aren't.' Heads turned to look at Bertie, who was sipping a scalding mug of tea. As she realised everyone was waiting for her to explain, she added, 'Just think about it. In normal times we wouldn't be doing anything as exciting as this. We'd be expected to keep house, darn socks and look after husbands and children. We'd never be skidding around in an old butcher's van, scaring everyone silly!'

'Bertie's right,' Frankie said, struggling with a mouthful of hot potato. 'I was bored stiff before the war, waiting for my husband to come home from work every evening. This job is terrifying sometimes, but I'm loving it. I could never have imagined doing anything like this in peacetime.' *And I could never have imagined my husband letting me do it in the first place. So don't ask me if I miss him, because I honestly don't. My life is better without his constant sniping at me.*

The post that morning had reminded her again how glad she was that Dickie wasn't in the house. She'd received a letter from Hugo, desperate for news about his friend. It wasn't the first she'd received and, from the tone, she was sure it wouldn't be the last. He'd been in touch soon after Dickie went missing, saying, *'I've not received any letters this week. If you have any news please write to me immediately at Room 47, Foreign Office.'* Hugo wasn't next of kin, he wouldn't be kept informed, so he had to plead with her for news: *'if you get even the tiniest hint that my dear friend is alive, I beg you to let me know immediately as I cannot sleep for fear that he will not return to us.'* She thought it ironic that he wrote *'us'* when he was the only one of the pair of them anxious for Dickie's safe return. And she didn't miss the few letters Dickie had written since joining up either, as they'd always been full of boring instructions about when to pay the coal merchant and so on.

'Good on you,' Alf said, raising his mug of tea to salute them. 'That's the spirit. While our boys are fighting over there, you girls are keeping things going.'

'But be careful, all the same,' Jim said. 'It's not just civilians who are casualties in this goddamn awful war. Many of our lot are falling by the wayside as well.'

'There's been another report tonight,' said Alf. 'Ambulance

crew and firemen over in Chelsea. A building collapsed and caught the whole lot of them.'

'Chelsea? That's where three of my lodgers came from. They've never worked or lifted a finger in the house in their lives. Living in my place with a bossy little East End matriarch has been quite a change for them. One of them was a suffragette, so that's probably the most exciting thing she ever did.'

'Then she should approve of the work you girls are doing now,' Alf said. 'They fought to get opportunities for women as well as the vote. You've got her to thank for what you're doing now.'

Frankie reflected on how quiet Daphne was. She'd paid a price for her campaigning, even though she'd helped women to get what they demanded. Perhaps she should get to know her better and thank her for her sacrifice.

For the second time in the space of two months, Charlie stared at the thin red line. This time she wasn't afraid of the result; she rather found she was hoping it would be positive. And perhaps this time it would last longer than before.

She left the bathroom and found Dan in the bedroom, rifling through the clothes he'd thrown on the chair the night before. 'Look at this,' she said.

'Does that mean what I think it means?'

'It sure does.'

'Bingo! How do you feel?'

'Not sick, like last time. Perhaps that's a good sign.' Charlie pulled off her nightdress and found clean underwear in the big blue IKEA bag she was using as a wardrobe till they'd got some bedroom storage sorted. But how did she really feel? Slightly nervous, wondering if this pregnancy would succeed?

'Here, big hug,' Dan said, wrapping his arms around her and kissing the top of her head. 'You're going to be a mum and I'm going to be a dad. That's great news.'

'But don't go telling everyone yet. I know you're pleased about it, but it's early days. Anything could happen.'

'Okay, I won't. You sure you don't want to tell your parents?'

'Maybe soon, when I've got used to the idea.' *When I feel sure this isn't going to be like last time.* Her mother would be thrilled. She was longing for grandchildren and had refused to downsize from their farmhouse in the Hampshire countryside, saying she wanted to have space for visitors, then qualified it by saying she wanted to fill the house with grandchildren. Charlie's sisters hadn't yet responded, so she felt something of an obligation to perform.

'And don't go telling your parents, either,' she added. 'You know how your mother's been going on about when we were going to start a family.' Dan's parents lived in London. Far too close for Charlie's liking. Her mother-in-law was very capable and would want to help at every opportunity.

'I promise. My lips are sealed.' Dan zipped his mouth with a gesture. 'But eventually we'll have to. You won't be able to hide it once you start expanding.'

Charlie felt her midriff ruefully. 'I might have to stop eating cake from the café.'

'Don't you dare,' Dan said with a smile. 'Just eat healthily. Anyway, with all the running around you're doing with the house and your own work, you're not going to pile on weight. I'm sure you can allow yourself the odd piece of cake or two.'

'I might just do that. I'm going back there today as a matter of fact. Jean has some more photos for me to look at. I love chatting to her and finding out more about the house.'

'And telling her our news?' Dan raised an eyebrow. 'That I'm not allowed to tell anyone?'

Charlie couldn't help laughing. 'Jean's got a kind of radar. Knowing her, she'll sense it the minute I walk in the café. I know she will. I tell you what, I won't tell her, I'll just wait to see if she guesses. She could certainly tell last time.'

Later that morning, Charlie walked to the café in early

spring sunshine, humming as she strolled. The bare branches of the trees on the common were beginning to grow a veil of misty green. It felt as if everything was fruitful and bursting with new life.

Jean was already behind the counter when Charlie arrived, saying, 'What have you got for me today?'

'Apple cake,' Jean said. 'That all right with you?'

'More than all right,' Charlie said. 'And it's Dan's favourite too. You'd better give me a couple of slices to take away as he's working with the electrician and they'll both want a piece.'

'Got to keep on the right side of your tradespeople,' Jean said. 'And tea and cake usually does the trick.' She cocked her head. 'You're looking bonny. And you look pleased with yourself too.'

Charlie couldn't help giggling. Jean's sixth sense was working and it hadn't taken any time at all. 'I'm hungry and ready for cake.'

'Aah, got an appetite this time, have you?'

'How do you do it, Jean, how can you tell?'

'You're glowing. I can always tell when someone's got a bun in the oven. Go and sit down and I'll bring your cake over.'

Charlie did as she was told. She could hear Jean relaying the good news to Nicky in the kitchen. Her earlier instinct to keep the news to herself was abating. Perhaps this would be something to share with her followers. They'd love to see how she'd decorate the baby's room and she began to imagine painting a frieze of animals around the walls on a background of primrose-yellow paint.

Jean joined her and Nicky brought their tea. 'I take it you've only just heard?'

'Yes, I did the test this morning. So, fingers crossed for this one.'

'Well, you're looking good. Not peaky like last time.'

'I felt sick right from the start then and this time I don't.'

Charlie broke off a piece of the moist cake, studded with sultanas and visible chunks of apple. She could smell cinnamon and nutmeg. 'In fact, I feel ravenous.'

'That's a good sign,' Jean said, stirring sugar into her tea. 'But don't push yourself too hard. I know what you young mothers are like, trying to juggle work and everything. You might need to rest more than you've been used to. And look at you with all the house repairs still going on and working on top of it.'

'I know, but I love the work and the house is exciting. I was just thinking I must decide how to decorate the nursery.'

'Which room are you going to use?'

'I was wondering which room might have been used for Mrs Wilson's daughter…'

'If she'd really had a daughter, you mean,' Jean said.

'Oh, I know you're sceptical, but I'd like to think she had her baby. And there's one right next to our bedroom I think had been used as a dressing room, judging by the furniture that was there. It isn't big, but then you don't need much room for a cot, do you? And before you ask, no, I haven't found a cot anywhere in the house.'

'You'll want space for a comfy chair and a small chest of drawers. That can double up as a changing place, you know, where you can lay the baby down on a mat.'

'Oh crumbs, I have no idea what I'm going to need. This is all new to me.'

'It's new to everyone the first time, love. You'll be an old hand with the second.'

'Hang on a minute, Jean, I've got to get through this one first!' But Charlie laughed and added, 'I can see I'll be coming here for advice every second of the day.'

'Babies, dogs, husbands, they're all welcome here,' Nicky said as she sat down for a minute at their usual table. 'But you don't need to go rushing off and getting baby stuff straight away. There's plenty of time.'

Charlie breathed a sigh of relief. 'But it's made me think. There was a small chest of drawers I put into storage. I was thinking of selling it but I might get it brought back here. It could be just what I need. I think it was a bit scratched and stained, but I might paint it.'

'You're going to have a lovely time getting the room ready,' Nicky said. 'I remember with my first one, I couldn't resist getting a picture for the wall and a mobile to hang over the cot. And then when she arrived and I knew I had a daughter, I couldn't stop buying little dresses and so on.'

'You went a bit mad,' Jean said. 'But it all looked perfect. And you had that lovely bedside light as well. A cat, wasn't it?'

'A duckling; it was so cute I couldn't resist.'

Charlie loved hearing them talk. She almost hugged herself with thoughts of how perfect the nursery was going to be.

TWENTY-SIX

THEN

MAY 1941

Daphne wasn't the only quiet one of the Beaumont sisters. Cecily was quiet too, in that she spoke in a whisper, when she did indeed speak.

'It seems you always have to be the spokesperson for both your sisters,' Frankie said as she admired Elspeth's watercolour of the church. 'But I suppose it's not unusual for the eldest in a family to take charge.'

Elspeth had set up her easel in the afternoon sun, at the top of the outside steps leading to the front door. The little white cat rescued from the bomb site sunbathed at her feet. It had taken a liking to the three sisters, especially Daphne, whose lap it usually occupied while she crocheted or knitted. All the Beaumonts were great knitters, and said they had become used to making socks and mufflers for the young men of the last war and didn't see why they shouldn't do the same for those fighting in this one. However, at present they were mostly engaged in knitting socks for the four Jones boys, whose toes and heels regularly emerged from the few socks they'd brought with them.

Frankie had come out to collect the afternoon post lying on the doormat. She glanced at the single envelope there, another pleading letter from Hugo, and slipped it into her pocket to open later. She felt sorry for him, but couldn't help him cope any better with his distress than she was coping with her guilt and shame.

'They've both had such a hard time, dear,' Elspeth said. 'I was their big sister, and I've had it easy by comparison.'

'Both of them? I know you said about Daphne being a suffragette, but Cecily too?'

'Yes, dear, the poor girl lost her sweetheart in the last war. Never really got over it. She was devastated at the time. Wouldn't eat for days. I remember Mother saying how she was always asking our cook to tempt her appetite. Such a sad time.'

'I'm so sorry to hear that. And did Daphne also lose someone in the Great War?'

'No, dear, she was never interested. Always said she wasn't going to be a slave to a man.' Elspeth dabbed a stroke with her fine squirrel-hair brush on the steeple of the church, high-lighting the weathervane at the top so it appeared to have caught a glint of sun. 'But she was in pieces when her very dear friend Julia died in prison. Holloway was very harsh on them, you know.'

'Does she ever talk about the campaigning she and her friends were involved in? I'd be very interested to hear more about her time then.'

'I doubt she'd want to talk about it, dear. Naturally she's proud of what they achieved in the end, but they did so at a great cost to many of them. And of course, losing so many young men in the war, when they'd stood up so fiercely for women's rights, was salt in the wound in many ways.'

'I don't quite know what you mean.' Frankie watched Elspeth add the final touch to her picture, then sign it with a flourish of her brush.

'The suffragettes weren't against men, not all of them. They just wanted to have more opportunities. But then, when the war was over, there weren't enough men left for all of them to marry anyway. So, the opportunity that most of them had expected to have was snatched away from them. If the same happens with this war, you'll think yourself lucky you're already married.'

Frankie felt a moment of guilt, comparing her situation to the sisters'. Elspeth thought she should be grateful to be married, but then she didn't know the truth about her marriage. She couldn't tell her the truth, she couldn't even say she no longer missed Dickie. Elspeth was so easy to talk to, she'd have liked to tell her how much she regretted her marriage, how Dickie had duped her and why, but she couldn't bring herself to do so. Instead, she tried to shake the thoughts from her head, saying, 'And what about you? Was there ever anyone special in your life too?' Elspeth had been so open with her that Frankie felt she could dare to ask the question.

'Oh, I only ever wanted to be an artist. I certainly didn't want children and marriage. But Mother and Father became ill in the same year and my sisters needed someone in charge of the household, so, instead of doing the equivalent of the Grand Tour, I stayed in this country, painting watercolours of people's houses and gardens. It was quite nice earning a little pin money.'

'You mean you've sold your paintings?'

'Lots of them, dear. And I lost several when our house was bombed, which was a shame. But never mind. It's very picturesque here, so I'm sure I can knock out quite a few paintings in no time.'

'When the weather's fine, you should walk across the common to the windmill. That would make a lovely picture.'

'What a charming thought. We could take a picnic. And those dear little boys could come with us. Do you know, one of them – Alan, I think his name is – has quite a talent for drawing. I could see him becoming a very good artist. Or an architect, I said to his mother.'

'And what did Dolly say to that?'

Elspeth laughed, 'Oh, she said he'd go out to work in the market like his father and grandfather before him. Though she didn't say it in quite those words. But I understood the sentiment. They don't have the funds for a long education, unfortunately.'

Of course they don't, thought Frankie. Those boys will be sent off to work as soon as they are old enough, unless they are sent off to war if this one keeps going. She couldn't bear the thought of those cheeky, lively boys growing old enough to fight and be killed, and could imagine how Dolly must pray for an early end to the war.

She stood back from Elspeth's easel and admired the finished painting. It caught the slant of sunlight on the church and there was a glimpse of the little school tucked away at its side, shielded by the chestnut trees. Come the autumn, the boys would be so excited when they found they could collect conkers and learn how to use them with their classmates.

Frankie sighed. She'd have to leave soon for her shift at the ambulance station. After the early intensity of the bombing, the last three weeks had been very quiet. She and other members of the crew hadn't had much to do, other than play cards and pull faces at each other behind Mrs Ogilvy's back.

She glanced up at the sky. It was a perfect afternoon, but she felt uneasy. Was it too perfect? Had the Blitz finally stopped? It had been relentless, from the start on that last perfect day of late summer in September. But for the last three weeks there had been little action from the skies above London.

Frankie shook herself, but still felt a shiver of apprehension. 'I'm going to make tea,' she said. 'Shall I bring a cup out for you?'

'No thank you, dear, I'm coming inside now.' Elspeth was folding up her easel and putting her tubes of paint back in their box. 'Here, why don't you have it?' She offered Frankie the finished painting.

'Oh, I couldn't possibly. I thought you were going to sell your pictures.'

'I will again one day when my agent reopens his gallery. But this one is for you. I enjoyed doing it.'

'That's terribly kind. If you're sure, I'd love to keep it. It will be a reminder of your time here.'

Frankie took it through to the kitchen, intending to find a space for it when she could. And a frame too, though she doubted she could find a picture framer working in the midst of war-torn London. She made two pots of tea, as had become the custom. Earl Grey for the sisters, good old English tea for her and Dolly. She laid the tray, then stopped, with a puzzled look, and checked the cutlery drawer.

'Dolly? Have you seen the sugar tongs? You know, the ones that go with the sugar bowl to this set. Have you washed them or put them away?'

'I thought they were still there. I'm sure they were there this morning after breakfast. And I don't have sugar with my mid-morning cuppa. And the ladies don't have it in their fancy tea, neither.'

'How odd. You don't think one of the boys could be playing with them?' The minute Frankie asked, she knew it was the wrong thing to say.

'Certainly not.' Dolly's face was thunderous and she looked as if she was straining not to say more. 'But I'll ask if they've seen them. We can make do with a teaspoon for now.'

Charlie could remember taking old lady clothes and sturdy shoes out of the wardrobe, but she couldn't think why she hadn't emptied the chest of drawers before it left the house. Hunting through Brad's packed storage unit, where they'd stacked furniture from the house, she found it tucked behind the sofa and armchairs, with a large marble bust on top. The unit was dry but it still smelt of old velvet and dust.

After shifting the chairs aside and heaving the bust onto a table, she was finally able to open the drawers. There were several layers of motheaten sweaters, old stockings and long nightdresses, interleaved with lavender bags. It all had to be thrown away; it wasn't even worth taking to a charity shop.

She opened the bottom drawer to find more of the same, and started pulling it out and stuffing it into a black bin bag. But the last handful was different. The pieces of clothing were smaller, wrapped in tissue paper. She stopped grabbing random piles and unfolded the fabric. Tiny vests, nightdresses embroidered with lambs and rabbits, and little knitted bootees and bonnets of the softest wool had all been stowed away in the drawer.

Could these have been made for a doll? No, they were more likely handmade baby clothes, carefully stored away from moths. She spread each perfect piece on her lap, admiring the neat stitches and satin ribbons. The garments were pristine, a perfect set of clothes for a new baby. Somewhere in the back of her mind she could recall the word layette, used by someone at some time, an older aunt or cousin with a newborn, describing the set of clothes they'd knitted for the newcomer. So, that was what she'd found here, perfectly preserved in tissue and lavender: a layette for a new baby.

Could this have once belonged to Alicia Rose? Maybe Mrs Wilson couldn't bear to give it all away once her baby had outgrown the clothes. Charlie could understand the sentiment of keeping a baby's first possessions – in fact she rather thought her own mother had kept all three of her daughters' first cut lock of hair and first milk teeth, as well as some little mittens and a christening gown.

Charlie laid the clothes out on top of the chest. They were as good as new. And that decided her: she would keep them and hope to use them one day. They were old fashioned and totally unlike the stretchy all-in-ones she'd seen her friends pulling onto their babies' limbs, but they were perfectly serviceable, and she rather liked the idea that the house was helping her prepare for her baby.

Brad helped her heave the chest into the boot of her Land Rover. It was a large car for London, she knew, but so useful for carting furniture and decorating materials to various jobs.

As she drove back to the house, she thought about how she'd make the nursery fresh and light.

When she turned into the high street and passed the café, an urge to stop first and have tea with Jean and Nicky occurred to her. She could show them the set of baby clothes and get their advice on whatever else she'd need. She pulled over into the parking bay. It only allowed an hour, but she'd never seen it being policed since they'd moved here. A light rain was falling and she shivered, wondering when the warmth of spring would arrive for good.

Inside the café, the windows were steamed up and Jean was mopping the counter. 'I've got something to show you,' Charlie called over as she sat down.

'I assume you want your usual tea and cake,' Jean said, lifting the lid on the nearest platter. 'Apricot and almond slice do you?'

Charlie nodded and took the tissue-wrapped parcel out of her bag. When Jean sat down, she removed the top layer of paper. 'I've just found these at the bottom of the old chest of drawers that I'm keeping for the nursery. I thought I might be able to use them.'

Jean inspected the clothes one by one. 'Well, will you look at that! These are all handmade. Just beautiful,' she murmured. 'You don't see baby clothes like that these days.'

'Aren't they lovely? And they're in perfect condition too.'

'And just look at that embroidery,' Jean said, running her finger beneath a little line of yellow chicks on a white flannel nightdress.

'Do you think she made these herself? Mrs Wilson?'

Jean pursed her lips. 'It's possible. I remember my mum saying Frankie was a dab hand at make do and mend. They both were, I think. They were always making their own clothes in the war, whenever they got their hands on a bit of fabric, or remodelling old dresses.'

'I suppose they had to then, with all the shortages. So, do you think it's possible she could have made these?'

'Very likely, I'd say. But, you know, it looks to me like they've never been used.'

'Oh, you don't think perhaps she was expecting and then it never happened?' Charlie put her hand to her mouth and gave a little gasp. 'Oh no, or worse, it didn't live?'

'Or it could just have been wishful thinking.' Jean refolded the little nightdress.

'You mean, hoping she would get pregnant and have a child one day. How sad.'

Jean stroked the little knitted bonnet. 'This is lambswool. The best she could get. I don't know the answer, my dear, but I do know that whoever made these little clothes put a whole lot of love into them. So, if you love them you should keep them and use them. It's such a shame they've never been worn.'

'You don't think it's bad luck if they were originally made for a baby that didn't make it, do you?'

Jean frowned and shook her head. 'Don't be so silly. You're not superstitious, are you? Goodness me, times gone by, loads of babies, and mothers too, didn't make it. Things are different now. Go on, you use them if you want to.'

But as Charlie gently rewrapped the garments in their layers of tissue, she couldn't help wondering, and she also couldn't help feeling a twinge in her stomach. She told herself it was nothing, it was just because she hadn't eaten since break-fast. She took a bite of the apricot slice. That would soon deal with the hunger pangs.

TWENTY-EIGHT
THEN
MAY 1941

Frankie soon forgot all about the sugar tongs, as that night the Luftwaffe returned to London with a vengeance. It was the most intense raid the city had suffered since the Blitz had begun back in September the previous year. The muddy brown River Thames was transformed by the full moon into a silver ribbon, guiding 500 German planes carrying 700 tons of bombs that rained down over poor and rich alike from the docks to Westminster.

'It's never been as bad as this before,' Bertie said, looking out of the window as their ambulance raced from Putney to Pimlico. 'It looks like the whole of central London is on fire.'

'Bloody moon,' Frankie grumbled. 'To think we used to gaze at it and think how beautiful a moonlit night was.'

'My uncle always called it a hunter's moon, the night of the full moon. I suppose that's when they could go out and clearly see the rabbits in the fields around the farm.'

'And now it's known as a bomber's moon. All right for them up there, with a full view of the city. It's like they've a clear map laid out before them, showing them exactly where to go.'

'At least we can see the road better than most nights. I shan't

have to get out with the lantern to light your way for a change.'
Bertie laughed, then shrieked. 'Hang on, what's that over there?
It looks like a ghost.'

Frankie screeched to a halt. A white figure in floating robes
was coming towards them, arms outstretched, screaming, 'Help
me, help me!'

Bertie jumped out, her boots crunching on the broken glass
that was scattered everywhere. 'We're here now,' she called out.
'We're here with the ambulance to help you.'

As the figure came closer, it was clear that it was a woman
of later years, her silver hair loose and streaming down her back.
Her bare feet were a mass of cuts from the broken glass and she
was wrapped in a white sheet over a long white nightdress.

'Stay where you are,' Bertie said. 'There's even more glass
over here. We'll come and get you.'

The woman screamed again, looking upwards and pointing.
'They're coming back again, look, there they are!'

Bertie looked up at the sky above. There was a bobbing
silver barrage balloon, illuminated by the bright moon. 'It's
nothing to worry about, it's meant to stop the planes.'

Frankie joined her and they pulled the stretcher out of the
back of the ambulance. It was the only way to ferry the woman
over the sea of vicious, glittering shards. They lifted her up
and carried her safely across to the back of the old butcher's
van.

'Now you just lie there while we drive a little further on to
see who else needs our help.' Frankie longed to tease the shards
of sharp glass from the woman's bleeding feet, but the light was
so poor, she couldn't be sure she could do it without causing
more harm. Bertie began sweeping the road in front of them and
Frankie started the engine again, hoping the glass wouldn't
damage the tyres and they would make it safely back to base
eventually.

'There, ahead of us,' Bertie said, pointing with her broom.

'The warden is telling us to slow down.' Frankie stopped and jumped out again, telling their injured passenger to stay put.

'It's a home for the elderly,' the warden said as he came closer. 'They really don't know what's hit them.'

'Oh, that explains it. I think we've got one of them in the back already. A woman with badly cut feet. We thought she was a ghost at first.'

'Some of them can walk, but they're all very confused and don't understand what's happening.'

'We can only take the injured ones, I'm afraid. Our brief is to get them to the nearest hospital. But it might be a case of whichever hospital is going to be easiest to get to in these conditions.' Frankie looked over her shoulder at the sound of yet another blast.

'Normally I'd advise you to try St Thomas', but with it being on the river I doubt you'd have an easy drive over the bridge. You'd be better off heading for the Royal Brompton. It's no further.'

Frankie could imagine what a target all of London's bridges were on this bright moonlit night. A little van zipping across any of the bridges would be like a fly crawling up a window-pane. Easy to spot, easy to crush. The cross painted on their canvas roof offered no guarantee of protection.

'Thanks,' she said. 'We'll scoop up whoever needs help most and head over that way. It wasn't so bad this time coming through Chelsea. We'll do what we can here and head back if we're not sent elsewhere.'

With the help of a couple of wardens, the girls slowly managed to take half a dozen of the home's residents across to the waiting ambulance. They had to walk carefully, but fortunately all of them were wearing shoes or slippers, unlike the first woman they'd met.

Frankie escorted a doddery old man shaking his head and saying, 'We should have finished them off the first time. No good bloody Huns.' He wasn't very badly hurt, but he was very old and his head was bleeding.

She could recall her father using that term. In this war they were Jerries or Krauts. Huns sounded like something from the last century, but he was right. It was happening again and she couldn't help thinking how terrible it was for a man of his age, who had probably lost dear friends and relatives the first time around, to see such destruction all over again.

'Let's get you into the ambulance,' she said, 'along with your friends from the home. We'll have you safely in the hospital in no time.'

'They're not my friends,' he said. 'My friends, my brothers and my sons, all died in the last war.' He sounded close to tears as well as being angry.

Once she had deposited him in the back of the ambulance, she and Bertie checked whether they would have to come back for anyone else. 'There's a couple of injured staff members,' the warden said, 'but they've only got slight cuts. Not worth you coming back for them. The rest of the residents were bed-bound and couldn't be got out of the home in time. So, the smoke got them. But maybe not the worst way to go if you're that old.'

Frankie wasn't sure of that sentiment, and kept thinking about it as she walked back to her vehicle. She had just turned the key in the ignition when there was an almighty crash behind them and a cloud of brick dust enveloped the street and covered the windscreen.

'Was that another bomb?' She turned to look behind them. Wardens and firemen were running out of the way.

'I'm getting out to check,' Bertie said, opening the door on her side. 'Might as well find out if there are more casualties after we've got rid of this lot.'

'The building collapsed,' shouted a warden. 'It's fallen on half the fire crew. I'd be surprised if they make it out of there.'

'We'll phone it through from the next phone box we pass,'

Bertie said. 'Or we might see a place with an "A" sign in the window. They'll let us use their phone. You go back and see if you can help. But be careful.' She jumped back into the van.

'Right, let's get out of here before anything else falls on top of us,' Frankie said. 'Honestly, I never thought how dangerous this job was going to be when you talked me into doing our bit.'

'You didn't need much persuasion, as I remember. I think you were bored stiff. You needed a bit of excitement in your life.'

It wasn't just excitement I needed, I was trapped and longed to be free, Frankie thought. I was in a prison and I couldn't break out even when Dickie was no longer there. Now, I'm freer than I ever was before and I barely think about how my marriage made me miserable. She didn't voice these thoughts to Bertie, but snorted as she laughed. 'Well, let's hope nothing else happens before we get this lot to the hospital.'

Bertie craned her neck to look over her shoulder at the old people huddled in the back of the van. 'Poor old dears, let's give them a song. Take their minds off it.'

'"Pack Up Your Troubles"?'

'Yes, that'll do,' Bertie said, kicking it off. She turned to their passengers and yelled 'Join in, everybody!'

And the girls sang loudly and the old people sang feebly all the way to the Royal Brompton Hospital, arriving in better spirits than when they left.

When did I change, from not being ready to have a baby, to really wanting one?, Charlie wondered as she splashed her face with cold water. Her red eyes betrayed her distress.

This time she had cried when the bleeding started. It had slipped away so easily, this tiny beginning of a new life. Slipped into the toilet bowl, no more solid than a large clot from a heavy period, but this time she thought she saw a fragment of white or grey tissue among the bloody mass. Was that it? Had that been her second baby? She stared at it for a moment before pulling the chain and flushing it all away.

I shouldn't have started making preparations, she told herself. It's my fault for thinking this one would work out, that I could get ready for it. If I'd done nothing, maybe this wouldn't have happened.

She blamed the baby clothes she'd found. That was when it had first felt real, as if there actually was a baby growing inside her. And because of the clothes she'd been eager to begin preparing the nursery, insisting that this particular room had to take priority over everything, so she could start decorating. Dan hadn't been pleased with the interruption to his schedule, but she'd diverted their painter from the kitchen to roller pale yellow emulsion over the walls so she could start painting a line of fluffy chicks, based on the embroidered nightdress. Standing on a sturdy footstool, she'd completed three so far, pecking at grains of corn and tufts of grass.

She'd been so pleased with her achievement, she'd ignored the first cramps, then the first spots of blood. Perhaps if she'd rested, stopped all her frantic painting on top of her trips out to see clients, she'd still be pregnant. And now she wasn't and she felt so desperately sad.

Stop feeling sorry for yourself, she repeated, biting her lip to stop herself from crying. You're young, there's plenty of time and you've got a whole house to finish. She sniffed hard and blew her nose. It was time to face Dan.

There was never anywhere private for them to talk during the day. The house was constantly filled with busy workmen drilling, plastering and painting. She beckoned to Dan, took him away from the measuring of a skirting board, took his hand and pulled him out into the damp garden. White petals from the arching pear tree and its neighbour drifted around them like wedding confetti, while the air was filled with the scent of blue-bells and primroses.

'What's the matter?' He took her in his arms.

He knew, she was sure. They were in tune. 'I'm sure I've just had another miscarriage. This one isn't going to happen either.'

He held her closer without speaking for a moment. 'I'm so sorry. Are you in pain?'

'Not any more. I'm fine. I'm just a bit sad this time. More than I was before.'

He squeezed her tighter. 'Me too. But it lasted a little bit longer than the first one, didn't it?'

'Not very much. Only a week or so. Maybe I should have

rested more. And I helped Brad lug that chest of drawers into the back of my car.'

'Don't go lugging anything around in future. You've got to look after yourself.'

'But these things happen. Everyone says it's very common in the first few weeks. And it can mean there was something wrong with the baby and it would never have lasted.'

'Don't you think you should get checked out this time? Just to be on the safe side?' He held her at arm's length, studying her face.

Charlie shook her head. 'Maybe I will, just to make sure it's all gone. But there's no point in asking why it's happened. I've heard doctors aren't interested in investigating further until you've miscarried three times.'

'Really? That seems a bit harsh.'

'That's what I've been told by friends who've been through it.'

'But if you want to see a doctor, you should. You don't have to put up with this three times before seeking help, surely?'

Charlie shrugged. 'Well, I guess we'll just have to try again and see if we are third time lucky. And if not...' She wiped away a tear that escaped.

'Oh, don't cry. I'm sad too, but really, it's okay. We'll be fine together.' He wrapped her close again.

She stifled her sobs. 'I didn't care the first time, but this time I'd begun to look forward to it, begun to imagine it being here with us. I was enjoying decorating the room too.'

'It will happen for us eventually,' he said. 'Our time will come.'

'And,' she said, pulling away from him, 'we can stop worrying about working on the nursery and concentrate on the kitchen. So that's one good thing. What do you need me to decide today?'

He laughed. 'How about coming out to choose tiles with me?'

'Where are you thinking of going?'

'First let's take a look at that expensive handmade place over in Wandsworth. Get an idea of designs. Then we'll go to the trade warehouse and get a bargain. I was thinking something practical like quarry tiles on the floor and a light colour around the cooking area and sink.'

Charlie was in agreement with this tactic. So far, they'd been to every reclamation yard around London and nearby in their search for an authentic cast-iron fireplace surround for the bedroom. Shot-blasted, it looked good as new, and fitted perfectly with the original green and blue art nouveau tiles that surrounded the fire. They'd scoured eBay and picked up kitchen cabinets that they fitted with new handles and painted a soft sage green. They had to cut costs wherever they could, but try not to compromise on quality.

Dan glanced at his watch. 'Look, it's still early, so why don't we grab a bite to eat in the café first before we go? I didn't get any breakfast and I'm sure you could do with a snack to keep you going.'

Charlie thought about the knowing faces she'd encounter there. She wasn't ready for that yet. Nicky and Jean would know what had just happened as soon as she walked in. 'I'm okay,' she said. 'Why don't you nip round there and grab your-self a bacon roll for now? You can eat in the car while I drive.'

'Good idea. That'll save time. I want to get back here before the guys knock off today.' He stopped at the garden doors. 'You sure you don't want anything?'

'Oh, go on then. Grab me a coffee and a roll, same as you. I can save it for later.' While I save my feelings for later too, she thought, forcing a smile as Dan waved to her.

She took a moment, breathing in the fresh spring air scented with sweet smells of blossom. Roses were already beginning to bud on the stems that clambered through the pear tree.

With a deep sigh, she went back inside the house and up the stairs to the little room she had become so fond of. The chest had been sanded, ready for painting pale blue. Its white porcelain knobs had been washed and were waiting to be reattached. The line of yellow chicks would not be joined by newly hatched brothers and sisters; they would remain as lonely triplets for some time to come.

Charlie looked around at the freshly painted walls and the newly cleaned window. It looked towards the nearby common, where she'd imagined walking with a buggy or pram and later on running through puddles with chubby little legs in little red wellies. She wondered if she could bear to collect the blue and white curtains she'd ordered from a local seamstress she always used for furnishings.

The frosted white lamp in the shape of a rabbit sat on the top of the chest, its flex and plug still curled around its body. It would not be glowing at night in this room for a long while yet.

She picked up the baby clothes, still wrapped in tissue, and shoved them roughly into a paper carrier bag. She couldn't bear to look at them now. She threw the bag into the bottom of the chest and kicked the drawer shut.

THIRTY

THEN

MAY 1941

That particular night of air raids seemed to be never-ending. Once Frankie and Bertie had helped their elderly passengers out of the ambulance at the hospital, they phoned back to the station and received instructions to go out again. Bombs were still raining down on the whole of London and by the time the night was over 1,500 people were dead, including several ambulance and fire crew personnel, plus a number of wardens. There were even more people looking for shelter somewhere, as another 11,000 homes had been destroyed.

When the girls finally finished their shift, they felt as if they and their ambulance were drained of every ounce of energy as they crawled along the streets back to base. 'I never want to see a night like that again,' Bertie said, shakily lighting a cigarette. She held it to dry, chapped lips no longer protected by the balm of lipstick. Her pale face was daubed with soot rather than rouge.

'Give me a quick puff of that,' Frankie said, holding out her hand. A pale pink and lemon dawn was breaking over a city strewn with debris, glittering with broken glass, wreathed with the mist of smoke from burnt-out buildings. 'It's a terrible sight, but beautiful at the same time, just like one of those Impressionist paintings,' she added. 'I'll have to describe it for Elspeth. She'd appreciate the comparison, being an artist, I'm sure. Don't you agree?'

There was no answer from her friend. Bertie was slumped against the window, fast asleep. Frankie reached for the cigarette smouldering in her hand. There was no point in wasting it and she needed something to keep her awake and alert until she reached the station.

When she finally pulled into the backyard, all the other vehicles were already under shelter, cleaned and refuelled, ready for another night of action. Frankie staggered out of the cab of her van. She had been driving on and off for nearly twelve hours without a break. All she could think of was hot tea and a warm bed. She was too tired to cycle home, so she hoped she'd be able to bed down at the station until the next call-out. And for once, she decided she would clean up her van once she'd rested, so she began to walk towards the back door.

But Mrs Ogilvy was standing there, arms folded. 'You're not leaving your vehicle in that condition, I hope, Mrs Wilson?'

Frankie's shoulders drooped and she sighed. 'But I'm dead on my feet. You know how long I've been out. I promise I'll do it before my next shift.'

'You'll do it right now. Just like everyone else does.' The Ogre was standing her ground.

'She said she'll do it later and she will.' Bertie had hauled herself out of the van and was by her side. She put a protective arm around her weary friend. 'I'll ring the school and tell them I'll be there later today, and I'll help her do it once we've had a bit of a rest.'

She and Frankie pushed past this stubborn, unsympathetic woman and walked through to the staffroom, where the fire was still burning and there was a hot pot of tea on top of the range.

Mrs Ogilvy followed them, still fuming. 'This really won't

do,' she said. 'The rules are that every driver and their partner clean their vehicle immediately on their return. And I expect you've lost your blankets as usual.'

Frankie was pouring herself and her friend the longed-for cups of tea when Jim chipped in. 'Oh, give the girls a break, Di. It's all very well for you, sitting here all night just stoking the fire and boiling the kettle. They've been out there for hours right in the thick of it.'

'I bet you girls could tell some tales about tonight, couldn't you, eh?' Alf joined in, pushing a plate of broken biscuits towards them. 'Go on, help yourselves. We've had it easy here.'

'We've been hearing about the casualties from other stations,' Jim said. 'It's been a bad night all round. So we've been keeping our fingers crossed for you two, haven't we, Alf?'

His mate nodded his head with a smile, and said, 'We said it wouldn't be the same without our best girls here. And we aren't including you in that either, Di.'

Bertie grabbed her tea and a couple of biscuits. 'I've got to get to that bed before I fall asleep standing up. You coming?'

'Right behind you.' Frankie turned to look at Mrs Ogilvy, her arms still folded and with a thunderous face. 'Don't worry. As soon as I wake up, I'll be out there getting the van ready for whatever we may face tomorrow. Goodnight.' As she climbed the stairs after her friend, a shaft of sunlight burst through the stained glass of the landing window, scattering jewels of red and green over her dark uniform.

The girls threw themselves onto the beds fully clothed. Frankie just managed to pull her shoes off before her head hit the pillow.

'I enjoyed the look on the old ogre's face,' she said as she pulled the blanket over her shoulders. But there was no response: Bertie was already fast asleep.

Frankie smiled to herself and shut her eyes, hoping to drop off as quickly as her friend, but her mind was still whirling with the dreadful scenes they'd encountered that night and her limbs felt as if she was still driving her van impregnated with the smell of body parts and the ghosts of butcher's sausages. Then, in the midst of the dreamlike images of bombed buildings and fraught victims, came Hugo's words from his latest letter, pleading for news and for hope: '*I don't know how I shall go on living if Dickie doesn't come back. Please do what you can to find out where he is.*'

She felt pity for Hugo of course; she could understand how heartbreaking it was for him, just as it was for anyone who feared the loss of their beloved. But at the same time, there was nothing she could say to ease his pain. She'd written him the briefest of letters a couple of times, just to confirm that she'd had no news either.

She didn't know exactly where Hugo was or what important war work he might be doing, but she was fairly sure he was safely tucked away, far from the thick of it, unlike her, driving through shattered glass and explosive gases night after night. Part of her longed to tell him that, while he might miss the love of his life, she was hoping that Dickie would never ever come back. But she decided she shouldn't add further to his distress. It wouldn't help either of them.

And with that final thought she was at last able to fall deeply asleep.

The sugar tongs were the first of several such mysterious disappearances. Frankie still wondered if one of the boys could be responsible but certainly didn't dare ask Dolly again. In fact, it was Dolly who one day voiced her own suspicions.

Frankie had returned to sleeping in the house again most nights. Since that terrible raid earlier in the month, the skies had quietened down and her shifts were calmer and often spent playing Pontoon with Jim and Alf, listening to their theories on why the Blitz had suddenly stopped. 'They're only leaving us alone because they've got the Russkies to deal with now,' Jim said. 'They'll be lucky,' said Alf. 'Look what the Russian winter did for Napoleon's army. It'll be the same all over again for the Jerries, mark my words.'

And there was more time to go dancing with Bertie, though she had less need of the diversion than when they had been rushing from one terrible bombing to another, night after night. She was glad of the rest after the destruction of 10 May, when so many had lost their lives and their homes. The pressure to collect all the hundreds of bodies became so extreme that council dustcarts were pressed into service, using potato sacks to gather all the dispersed body parts, while firemen hosed the walls of bombed houses to wash away the fragments of mangled flesh.

Today, Frankie was helping Dolly clear the table after breakfast. Dolly always made porridge for everyone in the mornings, using some of the milk from their plentiful ration. The boys ate first, then scooted gleefully off to school, where they now had several friends. The Beaumont sisters came down a little later after the early morning chaos, and were now occupied in dusting and running the carpet sweeper over the rugs.

'Blow me,' Dolly suddenly said. 'I could have sworn there was a little spoon that went with this here mustard pot.'

'There is,' Frankie said. 'It's silver, just like the pot. They've always been used together.' The two women stared at each other, a curious look on both their faces.

'Now then, it's not one of my boys, if that's what you're thinking. They know what's right and wrong, they do.'

'Don't worry, I believe you. They're all such good boys.' If a little boisterous and rowdy sometimes, Frankie thought. She'd nearly been knocked over by all four of them charging down the stairs that morning, racing to scoff their breakfast at top speed to give them time for a game before school.

'Something funny's going on 'ere, if you ask me,' Dolly said. 'That's two little pieces of silver not where they should be. What else has gone missing?'

Frankie tried to think. There wasn't much in the way of family silver, apart from a canteen of cutlery that fitted snugly into a felt-lined mahogany box, kept on top of the dresser. She thought that was unlikely to be targeted as it was inaccessible. She checked the dresser drawer where unmatched spoons and napkins were always kept. 'That's funny. I can't find the strawberry spoon,' she said. 'I don't think we've used it since you've been here. It's a pierced silver spoon shaped like a large strawberry, used for sifting caster sugar over berries. I really only ever use it when they're in season.'

'And that's gone too, you say?'

'It would appear so. How very strange.'

'I think you'd better have a jolly good look round the house. You've got a lot of nice bits and pieces. See if anything else has wandered off. I think someone's got light fingers, if you ask me.' Dolly pursed her lips and carried on clearing the table so she could wash the dishes and cups.

'I'll help you with the drying up, then I'll do a little check. I'm sure they've just gone astray. With so many extra people in the house and everyone helping in various ways, I'm sure they've just been put back in the wrong place.'

'If you say so.' Dolly sniffed, her hands deep in hot soapy water. She rubbed at a bowl, then stood it in the rack on the draining board.

When all the breakfast plates and cups had been returned to the dresser, Frankie tried to think what in the house might appeal to a human magpie. The house was so cluttered with her parents' possessions as nothing had ever been thrown out, apart from their very old-fashioned Edwardian clothes. It was hard for her to list all of the varied contents, so all she could do was cast around and try to think if everything looked as it should.

She started with her own bedroom, as it had often been empty during those fraught nights of the heavy air raids when she was out driving, and would have presented an opportunity. Her dressing table looked just as it always did to her casual eye, but as she studied it, she realised that a silver hatpin adorned with a large amber bead wasn't in its usual place, stuck into a tasselled green velvet cushion along with several other long hatpins. They had all belonged to her mother, who had never left the house without a grand hat. Frankie had little use for a hatpin these days, being more accustomed to wearing her ambulance uniform cap or a protective steel helmet.

Then she remembered Dickie's grandfather's silver pocket watch, which he never wore, but kept in the top drawer of the tallboy where his clothes were neatly folded. He'd never forgive her if that had disappeared too. She could just hear him remonstrating, '*See, this is what happens when you let all sorts share the house and you don't even have the sense to keep the bedroom door locked! What do you think the key is for, you stupid girl?!*' She felt sick at the thought that she might not find it. Some days she was sure he would never come back, but when things like this happened she couldn't help feeling afraid of his reaction if he turned up safely in one piece after all.

She added the watch to the mounting list of small treasures and continued checking other rooms. She didn't like to search the top floor where the Jones family lived – she could safely leave that, she thought, to Dolly's sharp eyes. And she was reluctant to look in the Beaumont sisters' room, shared by the three of them, with two sleeping in a double bed and the third in a single.

Deep in thought, Frankie finally went into the sitting room, where Elspeth was ineffectively but willingly dabbing a duster along the mantelpiece. She tried to think what might be tempting here in among the cushions, the vases and pictures. And then she remembered her mother's sewing box. She rarely opened it as she had her own in her bedroom.

Frankie sat down in the armchair next to the box on its stand. It was filled with reels of coloured thread, skeins of embroidery silks and crochet hooks. But where was the silver pincushion? Her mother had been a keen needlewoman, and she had preferred to use a cushion on a band that sat on the back of her wrist as she sewed. But where was her grandmother's pincushion, a Victorian novelty in the shape of a hedgehog?

It was a sweet little silver creature with a black velvet back that only really looked like the animal it was supposed to represent when it was studded with dressmaking pins. Frankie had been allowed to play with it as a child, but always had to return it to the sewing box. 'Oh, where on earth is it?' she sighed with exasperation after removing all the cotton reels.

'Have you lost something, dear?' Elspeth turned round with her sweet smile. 'Can I help in some way?'

'I'm not really sure you can, but it is extremely annoying all the same. I can't find my grandmother's pincushion. It should be here. It's a silver hedgehog.'

'Oh, how very novel. I've never seen one made to look like a hedgehog. My mother had a dear little silver pig, which she adored. All gone now of course, along with everything else in Cheyne Walk. But I should think a hedgehog would look much better stuck all over with pins than a pig.'

'Yes, yes, I dare say,' Frankie said, shaking her head with frustration. 'But I just can't find it. And annoyingly it's not the only thing I can't find today.'

'What else have you lost, dear? Perhaps I can help you look.'

'It's so odd. I expect they've just been put back in the wrong place, but Dolly and I think we've lost the silver sugar tongs, the mustard spoon and a silver spoon for sifting sugar over strawberries. Oh, and a hatpin as well and an old pocket watch. I think that's all, but I can't be sure because this flipping house is so full of so many things. And I don't like to think they've been taken deliberately. But I am particularly annoyed about the watch. Who would have known it was ever there in the first place?'

'Silver, did you say? Is everything that's missing silver?' Elspeth raised an eyebrow and twisted her duster in her hands.

'Yes, why do you ask?'

'I think we need to have a quiet word with Cecily. Come with me.'

They left the room to find her sister was staring in a puzzled fashion at the wooden Ewbank carpet sweeper, emblazoned with the sign of a lion and Union Jack flags. 'I think it's broken,' Cecily said in her faint, whispery voice, pointing to the trail of dust on the carpet.

'I expect it's full,' Frankie said. 'You're meant to empty them from time to time. Didn't Dolly show you?'

'Empty it? How am I supposed to do that?' Cecily continued to stare at the mess on the carpet as Dolly joined them.

'Blow me, I thought everyone in the world knew how to use one of these,' she said, taking hold of the gadget's handle and marching it back to the kitchen.

'We never swept the carpets at home,' Cecily said. 'Did someone do it for us? Was it the maids?'

'Yes, dear, those were the days when we had maids to look after us.' Elspeth took her sister by the elbow and steered her back towards the sitting room. 'Now do you think you might have seen Frankie's pincushion? It's shaped like a hedgehog.'

Cecily's eyes widened and her mouth opened and shut.

'Where is your handbag, dear?' Elspeth still held her sister's arm. 'Why don't we take a little look in your handbag? Come on now, where is it?'

'It's upstairs, Elspeth. I'll go and fetch it.' Cecily pulled away from her sister's grip and turned towards the door.

'I'm coming with you,' Elspeth said and followed her, with Frankie close behind.

They all trooped up to the Beaumonts' bedroom, where the beds were neatly made with the coverlets free of creases, and eiderdowns folded back across the bottom now the weather was warmer. Cecily sat down on the double bed, clutching her handbag close to her chest. It was a large bag, more of a carpet bag than a modern handbag, made of richly patterned tufted material and with a bamboo handle.

'Give it to me,' Elspeth said, holding out her hand. 'Don't make me force you.'

Cecily sat like a sulking child, scowling and holding her bag tight. After a moment she reluctantly released it and passed the bag to her older sister, then scowled some more.

Elspeth prised open the bag's clasp, then tipped the contents out onto the white bedspread that covered her own bed. Humbugs, loose coins and safety pins tumbled out, along with a powder compact, a purse and all the missing items of silver. 'There you are,' Elspeth said, turning to Frankie. 'Take whatever belongs to you.'

'How did you know where everything would be?' Frankie gathered the items together in her hands.

'I'm afraid it's a little habit of hers. I should have been more vigilant. Mother said it started when she lost her fiancé. A way of treating herself to another kind of treasure, I suppose. I'm so sorry. I do hope it won't happen again.'

Cecily hung her head, then hopped off her bed and began scrabbling at her scattered possessions, throwing them back into her capacious bag.

Frankie felt a deep pang of sorrow for her. What kind of compensation was a silver hedgehog or sugar tongs for the loss of her much-loved sweetheart and the future she had once expected, leading not to marriage and children, but to endless spinsterhood? Could the same be happening to me, she wondered? Am I compensating for the almost certain loss of my husband with my risky job and carelessly dancing the night away? Though I have to admit, those distractions stop me thinking about my disastrous marriage and my fear of Dickie's return.

'Don't worry,' Frankie said. 'We won't talk about this again. But I must tell Dolly straight away. She was concerned we'd think it was one of her boys.'

Elspeth sadly shook her head. 'Those children are good honest lads. They're going to come out of this dreadful time as trustworthy citizens. That last war has a lot to answer for. I just hope we don't end up saying the same about this one.' Elspeth put her arms around her sister. Her eyes were filled with tears and Cecily sobbed against her shoulder.

Charlie watched the doctor scribbling his notes. After a third miscarriage, she'd felt obliged to consult her usual doctor, who'd sent her to see a consultant. She struggled to stay free of tears when she related her history. She hadn't felt emotional the first time it had happened, but after a second and now a third, she felt she was a sad failure.

'There's nothing obviously amiss,' he said, closing her file. 'But no definite cause is found in about half of all miscarriages. And most women who've miscarried three times go on to have a successful pregnancy. Quite often everything comes right of its own accord eventually, without any intervention.'

'So, you're saying I'm completely healthy and should just keep trying?'

'When you feel ready, there's no reason why you shouldn't. There's no reason to suspect these were ectopic or molar pregnancies, so you'll probably be fine next time.'

'But isn't there anything I can do to reduce the chances of it happening? I'm not going to feel very confident about trying again.'

'If you conceive a fourth time, come and see me again and

we will do some tests to determine what we might need to do to support your pregnancy.'

Charlie left the smart private consulting room feeling there was no certainty that she could do this. Her head was full of thoughts of blood tests, hormones, aspirin and all the remedies the doctor had mentioned. Who knew it could be this complicated trying to achieve something women the whole world over did all the time, whether they actively wanted to or not?

It had never occurred to her, when she and Dan had blithely talked about finding their forever home for the family they anticipated having, that they could be left with a big empty house and no children to fill the vast space. If she kept losing babies, would they still want this huge house? And would Dan lose interest in her as well as the house? The thoughts were so depressing that she had to slip into a nearby café to indulge in a cappuccino and pain aux raisins.

We would still enjoy the house, she told herself as she stirred sugar into the coffee. We'd have plenty of room for us each to have a work space. No need to rent separate offices like they'd done when they were limited to their small but expensive central London flat.

Or we could end up adopting. We could be like celebrities with an assortment of rainbow children from different nations. They could run up and down the stairs, play hide-and-seek in the many rooms and swing high in the garden.

But they wouldn't have Dan's eyes or my nose. They wouldn't remind us of our parents, grandparents and siblings. They wouldn't be ours, the children we'd always planned to have.

It saddened her even more to contemplate a childless scenario, the two of them in old age, pursuing their own interests and having no younger generation to benefit from their hard work. It's not what I'd ever imagined for us, she told herself. I've just got to get a grip and keep trying. She took a last bite of the pastry and resolved to give Dan a big smile and a hug when she went back to the house.

As Charlie parked the car outside the house, she thought it looked much happier than the day they'd bought it. The dark, rambling ivy had been cut back, the black door and windows repainted a glossy bright white, and the shrubs in the front garden were looking trim, especially the bushy lavenders that edged the front wall. But although the house looked less sad, she still felt it was searching for something, peering out through its many windows across to the church, the school and the common. She told herself not to be so silly – the house couldn't have lost something.

In three months, the year would draw to a close and then she'd make a wreath studded with berries for the front door. She and Dan were invited to visit both sets of parents, but they'd already decided that they'd like to spend their first Christmas in their new house on their own. It was nowhere near finished and she wasn't sure she'd be cooking a dinner with all the trimmings if the kitchen wasn't completed in time, but they'd both agreed that, if they had a roaring fire and a meal heated in the microwave, they'd be blissfully happy.

But as she walked up the steps to the entrance, the idea crept into her head that maybe the house was the reason she couldn't hold on to a baby. Was this house, where a woman had planned for a baby and then maybe lost it, this house where a woman thought she'd had a daughter, who could never be found, bad luck for her? She knew from the pencilled measurements on the doorframe of one of the rooms at the very top of the house that children had once lived here and thrived, but maybe they hadn't been born here.

Charlie entered to the usual level of dust and mayhem, the decorator's ghetto blaster competing with loud drilling. The house smelt of fresh paint and sawdust. Dan was on his knees, painting the skirting board in the long hallway, and looked up when he heard her close the door.

'How did it go?' He stood up, paintbrush in hand.

'Apparently there's nothing wrong with me, so we can keep trying. He said if I start to experience problems again, then they will do further tests, but at this stage there's nothing to suggest we won't be successful next time.'

Dan rested the wet brush on the lid of the paint pot. He held out his arms to hug her. 'Good. I'm sure we'll make it happen one day. Maybe just as well we've had a delay with all this mess going on around us.'

She pulled back from his grasp and looked him in the eyes. 'I was wondering if we could escape the mess for a bit. Maybe just a long weekend. And maybe that would be a good time to try. What do you think?'

'Where would you like to go?'

'As long as it doesn't involve a long drive or a plane, I'm up for going anywhere.'

'So, this country then?' He thought for a moment. 'How about that hotel we stayed at in Rye? Not too far away, long walks, sea air, great food? You liked it, didn't you?'

'That or somewhere like that would be perfect. You decide.'

She slipped away to the almost completed kitchen. It was workable now and, although she didn't have the longed-for Aga, which Dan had pointed out would be too expensive to run, she had a range-style cooker in dark green, complementing the sage green cabinets. He'd got his way with the boiling-water tap though, which she now used to make a mug of mint tea.

Sipping the hot brew, she mulled over the idea of escaping from the house. It was mad, wasn't it, to even begin to think that this place, the house they'd searched for over many months, could be the source of her troubles? But the woman who once lived here had prepared for a baby, yet the daughter she'd named in her will could not be found. Charlie had now had three miscarriages, so that was three babies lost – or was it four? Should she count that of the previous occupant?

So, would a weekend away solve her problem? Would conceiving elsewhere bring good luck? She felt sure it was worth taking the chance.

THIRTY-THREE
THEN
MAY 1941

Elspeth was the first to notice how the pear tree was smothered in blossom, one morning after breakfast. 'My, what a beautiful sight,' she said. 'I must catch it immediately with my paint-brush.' All was calm after the horrors of that night earlier in the month. Here in this village on the edge of London, peace reigned far from the devastated streets of the city.

'All right for some,' Dolly grumbled. 'I've got a mountain of potatoes to peel if we're to eat tonight.' Daphne quickly offered to help, joined by Cecily, so Dolly was soon more like her normal cheerful self.

'You'll be glad of the pear tree in the autumn,' Frankie said. 'It usually bears tons of fruit. I haven't made much use of it in recent years, but with so many mouths to feed, I think we'll be glad of it this year.'

'Every little helps,' Dolly said. 'And now you've done such a good job with the boys, helping to dig the garden over, we're not going to be struggling for veg.'

Frankie hadn't minded sacrificing her poorly planted flower beds at the front and back of the house. Dickie would have been furious. He liked a neat, orderly garden with rows of stiff, uniform bedding plants. But Dickie wasn't here and she felt bold defying him, almost suppressing a giggle at the thought of his disapproval. And the boys didn't need a lawn for games of football when they had the grasslands of the common as well as the school playground.

The borders were now planted with rows of cabbage seedlings, lettuces and carrots. The boys had strict instructions to water them and pick off any caterpillars, slugs and snails. They had also been excited when they helped Frankie erect tall cane wigwams, which young runner bean plants were starting to climb, winding tendrils around the sturdy poles.

'Cor,' Tommy said, 'We never 'ad beans up sticks in Bow. And we didn't know cabbages grew in the earth.'

Dolly smiled at her boys working hard in the garden, with muddy knees and hands, though she said, 'I'm piling them all in the bath tonight, and goodness knows how much extra washing they're making for me.'

But Frankie could tell she was thinking this way of life, out here, nearer to the country than the city, further from the depressing ruins of the bombed streets, was good for them. And she also thought how well her two groups of lodgers were learning to live with each other. Now the weather had improved and they could all spend more time outdoors, the Beaumont sisters were teaching the Jones brothers about nature. 'We had many long holidays with our cousins in Wilt-shire when we were young,' Elspeth said. 'Our uncle was very knowledgeable about British wildlife and the countryside. We'd have happily gone to live with our cousins when we lost our home, but they're crammed into the lodge house at present as the main house has become a hospital for wounded soldiers.'

And in return for this education, the boys were teaching the genteel elderly ladies cockney rhyming slang. 'Come and have a butcher's at this,' Elspeth said to Frankie's surprise one day, drawing her attention to another watercolour she had just completed.

'Do you see that bird with a flash of blue on its wings?' Daphne could be persuaded to speak about her favourite subject, ornithology. 'That's a jay, related to the magpie and jackdaws.'

'I've just seen the most beautiful bird in the world,' Alan ran to tell his mother. 'We only 'ad sparrers and pigeons in Bow.'

And Cecily was hugely knowledgeable on plants and trees. 'Come with me and we'll see how many different trees we can find on the common,' she said, taking the hands of the two youngest boys. 'How many do you think there are?'

George frowned, thinking hard. 'There's conker trees and one that has acorns. Two, miss.'

Cecily laughed. 'I think we'll find there's many more. And I'll show you where to find the best blackberries, which we'll pick later in the year, when the summer is over.'

Frankie was glad to see her occupied with this innocent pastime and not filching more silver. These shared activities were helping everyone to cope with the daily reports of how the war was progressing. Jim and Alf had been right about Germany turning its attention to Russia, so Frankie hoped London would not be subjected to such heavy bombardment again.

'What do you do with all your pears, then?' Dolly was staring at the tree sprinkled with white blossom.

'Our cook used to bottle them or stew them, but they are just as nice eaten fresh from the tree,' Frankie said. 'They're Conference pears, very sweet.'

'Not sure I'd know how to bottle anything,' Dolly said.

'I know, you simply must join the Women's Institute. They'd be such a fund of information for you. They know all about preserving foods. And I'm sure we've got all the old jars our cook used to use down in the cellar.'

'Women's Institute? You sure they'd have me?'

'I don't see why on earth not. It's for all kinds of women. They're very friendly. I'm sure they'd welcome you with open arms.'

'But I've got nothing to give them in return.'

'Don't look so worried. You might have buckets of pears to give away this year, if the tree does a good job.' The blossom hadn't been caught by the early spring frosts that had nipped the magnolia at the front of the house, so there was a good chance that every little flower would produce fruit and the household would be inundated with pears. 'And then you might be able to exchange our harvest for whatever someone else has a surplus of.'

'I'll do it then,' Dolly said. 'I'd like some cooking apples or rhubarb. So where do I find all these women?'

Frankie couldn't help smiling. 'I'll ask around in church on Sunday. Come with me and I'll introduce you. I think they meet on a Thursday in the school hall when the children finish for the day.' Her East End lodgers weren't used to regular church attendance, and Dolly usually stayed in the house preparing lunch while Frankie went with the devout Beaumont sisters. She'd also suggested several times that the boys might like to attend Sunday school in the afternoon, but they were always bursting with energy after enjoying Dolly's Yorkshire puddings and were desperate to race off to the common.

Dolly continued looking up at the pear tree, as if she was willing it to produce its bounty at top speed. Then she turned round and said, 'Do you miss Mr Wilson?'

Frankie was taken aback by the sudden question and it struck her that these days she hardly ever gave a thought to Dickie. If he'd still been here, he'd never have tolerated strangers in the house. Nor would he have allowed her to be a reckless ambulance driver, even though all young women now had to take on roles that helped the war effort in some way. She wouldn't be out dancing several times a month with Bertie either, whether dancing with each other or meeting men on leave. Life would in fact be very dull, and she thought again, with a tiny pang of guilt, that she didn't really miss him at all. In truth, she was glad he wasn't here.

She thought of his early letters, before he went missing, full of instructions about how to run the house, such as, *'Now you've told me the window cleaner has joined up, you'll have to do the job yourself unless you can find a replacement. You can't let the house fall into disrepair and, remember, I said the painter should be booked for the spring. Don't forget, and to tell him to fix that bit of rotten window frame I pointed out before I left.'*

But all she said was, 'I worry about him. I still don't know for sure if he didn't make it or is perhaps a prisoner of war. There hasn't been any more news since he went missing. What about you? What about Mr Jones?'

Dolly's lips trembled as she said, 'I haven't heard for a while. Fred's unit's in North Africa. I bet he hates it there. Never did like the heat or funny food.' She dabbed at her eyes with the corner of her apron. 'I tell the boys he'll be home one day. I want them to know how brave he's been.'

'Of course he'll make it home. And your boys will be so proud of their father. They'll want to hear all about his adventures. And he'll be proud of them for looking after their mother so well. They're wonderful boys.'

Dolly beamed, then sniffed. 'Look at me, dawdling. This will never do. I'd better see what those useless ladies have done with my spuds. They take half the flesh off with their peeling.' She turned and went back to the kitchen, then called from the door, 'And I'll put up with the Women's Institute if it means I can feed us better.'

Frankie couldn't help thinking how different her feelings were from Dolly's. Here she was, hoping that Dickie didn't come back, while Dolly was praying for her husband's safe return. Just before he'd left, Dickie had talked about starting a family when he came home. At one time, before she knew everything about him and Hugo, she'd have been compliant, but now she knew why he'd really married her she could only think that he wanted children to complete his cover, strengthen his disguise for his true nature. She couldn't bear to think about it.

THIRTY-FOUR
THEN
JUNE 1941

Frankie was collecting that day's delivery of milk from the front doorstep when she suddenly thought something outside the house didn't look quite right. She couldn't understand what it was at first. She stood back, staring, until she realised that the iron railings that topped the low wall enclosing the front garden had disappeared. They had been a feature of the house for as long as she could remember.

She walked down the steps to street level for a closer look. The black wrought-iron railings, topped with a row of fleur-de-lis motifs, had been sawn off close to the very top of the wall. Only crude stumps remained, embedded in the coping stones that topped the bricks. And not only that, but her lovely cast-iron gate with twisted scrolls had gone as well and nothing was left, not even the metal gateposts and hinges. Who had taken them and when?

She'd returned from her shift at the ambulance station in the early hours and gone straight to bed and hadn't of course noticed anything amiss in the dark. She'd been so tired, she couldn't even remember whether there'd actually been a gate to open last night.

Before she could prevent it, she found herself thinking how on earth she was ever going to explain this to Dickie. Stop it, she thought, he might never come back. But she could hear him ranting at her, *'What do you mean, you didn't give permission? How on earth did it happen then? It's going to cost a packet to get them made specially and replaced. They're an important feature of this property. You stupid woman. It would never have happened if I'd been here.'*

It couldn't be anything to do with the rag and bone man, could it, surely? He'd been a familiar figure in the area for as long as she could remember, but she didn't think he'd been round recently with his sturdy old horse pulling his cart and his cry of 'Any old iron?' Anyway, he always paid for scrap iron and she hadn't ever known his like to steal railings right from under the noses of householders.

When she went back into the kitchen to put the milk bottles on the cool marble shelf in the dark pantry, Dolly was washing more of the boys' socks. Her arms were plunged into soapy suds, her sleeves rolled up.

'Dolly, did you know that our railings have gone missing? Did you see who took them?'

'Oh, yes – sorry, I meant to say, but you were so late back. Yesterday afternoon, it was.'

'Who was it? Not the rag and bone man, surely?'

'Don't be daft. Men from the council, I should think.'

'But why? Shouldn't they have asked permission first?'

'Government orders, they said. I heard them at it and went out to see what on earth was making such a racket. Scrap metal for the war effort, or something, they said. You must have heard about it. Everyone round here knows. Even the school has lost its railings and they've got to put up a fence to keep the little ones in the playground.' Dolly rinsed the socks out, wrung them into tight sausages, dropped them into an enamel bowl, then dried her hands on her apron.

'No, I hadn't heard anything about it. I'm completely shocked. It looks totally wrong out there. I liked my railings. And my lovely gate. I don't know how I'm ever going to explain it to Dickie.'

'Well, I told them they should have asked you first, but they said orders is orders and everyone has to give up their fancy railings. I said you weren't going to like it. And then they said that if we had any aluminium pots and pans, we had to give those up as well.'

'And did you do that?'

'No, you don't have any. Most of yours are enamel wearing into holes. There's a couple of iron ones, but we're allowed to keep those apparently.'

Frankie couldn't help but laugh. It sounded so amateur, the council and government turning into scrap iron merchants, leaving housewives with the remnants to feed the nation. 'And what are people going to do when their cooking utensils fall apart?'

Dolly looked serious for a moment, then she too began laughing. 'We'll have to manage. We'll solder the pans. It don't last long, but it's what we've always done. Can't go hungry now, can we?'

'Oh, it's ridiculous. First, we solve the great silver theft, and now this. Whatever next?'

'I say we have a cuppa. That always makes everything seem better. You put the kettle on while I hang these socks out. Honestly, I can't keep up with these boys. As soon as I darn them, they're in holes again. Daphne's doing her best to knit more, but she'll be out of wool soon and then I don't know what we'll do.'

'Do you know, I might still have some of Father's old sweaters at the back of the wardrobe. They're far too big for any of us, but they could be unravelled and used to knit new things for the boys. We certainly can't have them going without.'

'Well, that's very kind, I'm sure.' Dolly stepped out into the garden to peg the socks alongside other items of laundry on the long line strung from the pear tree and across to the fence. The Beaumont sisters seemed to exist without producing a lot of washing, although stockings, silk knickers and lace-trimmed vests were sometimes draped briefly on the pulley-operated airer that hung above the bath upstairs.

Frankie was just pouring boiling water onto a spoonful of tea leaves in the brown teapot they always used in the kitchen when Dolly came in from the garden, frowning.

'What's wrong now?'

'That garden always smells of smoke. Like bonfire smoke. How am I meant to get the washing clean when someone's always got a bonfire going?'

'I don't think that's anyone round here. Not our neighbours anyway.' Frankie was puzzled, but as she poured the tea she suddenly remembered. 'It could be the fires in Richmond Park. I heard Jim and Alf talking about it. They're calling them starfish sites.'

'And what's all that about then?'

'It's meant to lure German planes away from the built-up areas where people live.'

'But the park's only just over the road from us, isn't it?'

'I know, but if we keep our lights hidden with the blackouts, I suppose the idea is that it will look as if the park is a built-up area and planes will be tempted to drop their bombs in that direction.'

Dolly leant out of the French windows and looked up at the sky. 'So, they'll fly right over our heads. What if their bombs fall too early? What if they're butterfingers?'

'Don't think about it. We've been safe so far. Let's hope it carries on like that.'

They sipped their hot weak tea. They'd agreed to eke out the tea leaves so they'd always have enough to brew. Dolly said,

'I'd like a strong cuppa, but this'll have to do. We'll be drying tea leaves and using them again before you know it.'

'You think it will come to that? My, my, aren't times hard!' But Frankie couldn't help laughing. A weak cup of tea wasn't the worst hardship she could think of, now stories were filtering through about the Germans' relentless march through Poland and into Russia. 'Do you think we'll have to make do with anything else?'

'Well, I can't say I'm 'appy with your butcher's sausages. Got too much fat and meal in them for my liking. But I s'pose they're filling enough, though they spit like the devil when they're cooking. And as for the eggs, well, there's not nearly enough. How am I meant to bake without eggs?'

'You've been managing very well, Dolly. I know it's hard, but I really appreciate how you're keeping us all well fed.'

'I think we should get some hens, then we'd have more eggs. The ladies have got delicate appetites and sometimes an egg is all they want.'

Frankie rather thought that the Beaumont sisters had selective rather than delicate appetites, and should eat whatever Dolly managed to rustle up, but she said, 'Let's do that. The boys would love it, wouldn't they? Collecting the eggs and feeding the hens, it would be great fun for them.'

Dolly finished her tea and, with a smack of her lips, said, 'I'll get on to it right away. Your Mrs Simmonds in the Women's Institute knows someone who can help. The boys can start making a coop for them.'

'There's an old rabbit hutch in the cellar. They could use that.'

Dolly's face brightened. 'Not for hens, they won't. Why didn't you say before? We could have been eating rabbit pie once a week if I'd known.'

'Oh, I never thought, of course. It was for a pet – Gwendoline. She was never very friendly.'

'And now we can't be having them as pets. Mrs Simmonds knows a man. We'll be having rabbits for the table before you know it.'

'Gosh, Dolly. You're so resourceful. I hope the boys don't get too fond of them. I loved my rabbit until she kicked me.'

'They'll love a tasty pie more.'

Frankie laughed and picked up the empty milk bottles to put outside on the front step. She shook her head at the sad sight of the naked wall. All that was left to mark the boundary of her property was the lavender bushes. And she fretted again about how she'd tell Dickie, even though she kept telling herself he probably wasn't coming back.

Charlie woke to a rosy dawn rising over frosty marshes, where wreaths of mist swirled above the banks of reeds and water-ways. She peered through the low, diamond-paned windows at the empty landscape leading to the sea beyond.

After a late departure from London, they had arrived just in time for dinner in an oak-beamed and panelled bar, where a wood fire smouldered in an inglenook fireplace. They were both so tired from a busy day and the drive down to Rye, they fell into bed straight after dinner and were soon asleep.

She looked over to where Dan was still snoring, cushioned by the thick blankets and deep pillows. 'I'm going to make us tea in the room and then we should get breakfast before they stop serving.' A smell of bacon and coffee had already drifted into the room.

He groaned and half-opened his eyes. 'Is it morning already?'

'It is and it's a beautiful morning. There's a wonderful soft light over the marshes. I say we get out as soon as we can, then get back for lunch. And then' – she gave him a cheeky smile –

'we could have an afternoon nap with a cuddle. What do you say?'

He smiled at her. 'What about now? Double insurance?' He held out his arms.

Later, after breakfasting on poached eggs and smoked haddock, they were both in good spirits. In warm jackets, woollen hats and sturdy walking boots, they set off along the estuary towards the coast. The sky was a clear blue, the sun sparkled on the curving rivulets of water and it felt good to be breathing the fresh chilly air blowing from the sea. Wading birds picked their way through the reeds and mud and cries from birds whirling overhead pierced the silence. It felt far from the traffic of London and far from the noise of drilling and banging in their house. The air was clean, untainted by the smells of turpentine and linseed oil.

'This must be good for us after months of breathing in so much brick and plaster dust, day after day,' Charlie said. 'We haven't had a good walk out in the countryside for ages.'

'Not since before we bought the house, I suppose. The last time must have been when we went away that weekend for your friend's wedding in North Devon.'

'That was nearly a year ago. We've been working flat out ever since.' Charlie lifted her face to the sun and whipped off her woolly hat, to feel the breeze blow through her hair.

'Once the house is finished, we'll have a proper break. Somewhere hot or somewhere quiet like this?'

'I'd like that, but if I get pregnant again I think that will have to dictate where we can go. We'll have to see how I'm feeling.'

He stopped walking to put his arms around her and kiss her. 'That will come first, I promise you. We'll do everything we can to make sure you don't have any more trouble. I don't want you suffering and worrying.'

She nuzzled into his chest and enjoyed feeling his arms holding her safe. Then she looked up into his eyes and said, 'If we don't ever succeed, we will be all right, won't we?'

'What do you mean, don't succeed?' He laughed.

'I mean, if we keep on failing, if I can't ever get pregnant, will you mind very much?'

He held her at arm's length and studied her face. 'It's never going to affect us, if that's what you mean. At the moment, it's what we both want, but if it doesn't work out then it won't stop us being together, loving each other.' He kissed her. 'There, is that what you want to hear? Now put your hat back on. You know how you hate getting your hair tangled in the wind.'

She laughed and pulled the hat back over her head. 'We'd better get a move on if we're going to see the sea and get back for lunch.' She tugged at his arm and they set off again at a faster pace.

When they finally reached the beach, they walked along the sands towards a grey clapboard shack with outside seating. A short menu of local fish and seafood was chalked up on a blackboard propped against the wall. 'That was quite a walk,' Charlie said. 'I'm feeling hungry already. Let's eat here instead of going back to the pub.'

Inside the shack, over bowls of garlicky moules marinière and tubs of crisp French fries tossed in truffle oil and sea salt, they enjoyed glasses of cold white Chablis and the peaceful view of the sea, a sparkling grey-green, against the radiant blue sky. 'Those strips of colour are all you need to suggest a beach scene,' Dan said, framing the view with his fingers. 'I could happily stay here and paint seascapes all day long.'

'It's so peaceful. I feel rested after even just this short time here.' Charlie dipped her fries into the hot broth of cream and wine around the plump mussels.

'I'm glad you suggested getting away. I think it's doing both of us good. We've been working non-stop on both the house and our own projects ever since we completed the purchase. We should allow ourselves more breaks like this.' Dan mopped up the juices with the crusty baguette served in a basket on the table.

'We ought to fit in as many minibreaks as we can before we're lumbered with babies,' Charlie said. 'It won't be so easy escaping once we're tied down with car seats, buggies and carrycots.'

'Then we should make the most of this break, while we've got the chance.' Dan clinked his wine glass with hers. 'Here's to making a baby and having fun.'

She sipped her wine, then said, with a mischievous smile, 'We could hide in the sand dunes on the way back, if no one's around to see us.'

Not much later, after brushing themselves down from rolling in the sand, laughing at their brazenness, they hugged. 'Clean fresh air, couldn't be better,' Charlie said, kissing Dan back. 'Now we'd better get walking before the light goes.' She grasped his hand and pulled him out of the mounds of dunes where they'd hidden.

They walked briskly while they could still see the path through the watery marshes clearly. On either side birds called for the last time as they settled for the night, while a murmuration of starlings swirled overhead in the fading light. And Charlie felt at peace at last.

Although the work was no longer as frantic as during those months when the Blitz pounded London day after day, Frankie and Bertie were still kept busy. They might no longer have been facing the terror of nightly air raids, but their ambulance was still frequently in demand. Whether the injuries were from damaged buildings finally collapsing, fires or accidents caused by the blackouts, people often needed to be ferried to hospital. There were fewer dead bodies, but still large numbers of wounded.

One night they were called out to a row of terraced houses in Fulham, where a badly bombed property at one end had suddenly collapsed, causing some of the neighbouring homes to topple like a line of dominoes. 'There's injured in just about every one of them,' the warden said when they arrived. 'They weren't meant to ever go back home, but you know what people are like. They won't listen and carry on trying to live when it's all in pieces.'

Frankie knew only too well what he meant. Everywhere, householders were desperate to return home, to protect their properties, to try to live as they had before. People couldn't wait to leave the communal shelters filled with crying children and the fug of unwashed bodies and damp blankets. 'Come on, let's get started,' she said. 'Take us to the most urgent cases.'

The furthest houses had minor injuries requiring bandages and plasters; the nearest had the most damage and there the girls found broken bones, terrible lacerations and concussion. Those most badly injured were too stunned to cry, but the groans of the others were pitiful to hear. 'We'll ferry these ones over first,' Bertie said, 'and come back for the rest.'

They took the worst cases across to the ambulance on stretchers, then helped those who could still walk. Just as they were thinking they had a full load, there was suddenly a loud crash and yet another nearby house collapsed in a tumble of bricks and dust.

'Blast it,' the warden shouted, dashing across to the pile of rubble. 'We told them not to smoke.'

The girls closed the doors on the van and ran after him. There was a smell of gas. 'Keep back,' the warden yelled. 'It might go off again.'

'Someone was desperate for a fag,' Bertie said. 'I know how they felt.'

'Stupid though, when they'd been warned,' Frankie said. 'The gas leaks every time.'

'It looks like they've had it,' the warden called from the ruins, shaking his head. 'A woman on her own. Poor sod. You might as well leave now. We'll clear this up for when you get back.' He went to join his companions and firefighters dealing with a small fire at the far end of the terrace.

'Don't you go lighting up after that warning,' Frankie said to her friend. 'You've seen what can happen.'

'Ha ha, I'll have a sneaky one in the cab once we're on our way. Race you back.' Bertie hared off back to the ambulance.

Frankie began following, but a movement near the ruins caught her eye. Perhaps the woman wasn't dead after all. She turned back to check and saw it wasn't a woman, but a man, rifling through the debris. And then she heard the distinct chink and rattle of coins. He was raiding the gas meter, emptying out all the shillings.

'Hey!' she shouted and he looked up. But he wasn't the slightest bit alarmed by her warning – he just carried on filling his pockets with money. 'Hey! You there, you can't do that!'

He began running away, leaping over the fallen bricks, and she chased him, yelling at him to stop. He reached the end of the terrace where the worst damage had occurred and bent down to grab a brick. Frankie knew what he was about to do, but didn't react quickly enough. He threw the brick at her head, knocking her tin helmet aside. She felt a sharp pain on her forehead and stumbled forwards, losing her balance in the rubble.

As she fell to her knees on top of the broken glass and shattered bricks, she felt shards piercing her hands. Bertie rushed to her side. 'Frankie, are you all right? No, don't stand up. Let me look at you first.'

Dim torchlight shone on her face. 'Good thing you were wearing your helmet. It's not too bad. Just needs a plaster, though you'll have a shiner by the morning. Can you walk?'

'I think so,' she said in a wobbly voice, feeling shaky after the drama and the shock. 'I knew these sites attracted looters, but I never expected to nearly catch one.'

'You all right, miss?' Two wardens came running up, having heard the shouts. 'If we see him at it again, we'll give him what for.'

'Scum like him, should be locked up. You're lucky he didn't do worse,' his mate said. 'Coward, attacking a brave young lady like you.'

'I'm going to be fine,' Frankie said, looking at her bleeding hands. 'But maybe I shouldn't drive just this once.'

'You take your time,' one of the men said. 'We can find someone else to drive if you want to take it easy.'

'Don't bother,' Bertie said, with a wink at her friend. 'I'm qualified as well. I'll drive us to the hospital.'

Frankie didn't bother to challenge her. With her head beginning to throb and her legs feeling weak, she was just glad to sit in the passenger seat and get back to the station.

'I guess the meter money was all he got this time,' one of the men said. 'We've seen worse. If they can get to the bodies, they're after rings, ration books and purses. Scavengers they are, stealing when people are at their lowest.'

'That's not the half of it,' his mate said. 'We've caught them cutting off dead fingers if they can't grab the rings quick enough. Nasty pieces of work, they are.'

Frankie shuddered, thinking she'd had a lucky escape. 'I won't try to catch them next time,' she said. 'I'll leave it all to you chaps.'

'You do that, miss. And good luck to you both.'

The girls returned to the van. 'I wouldn't mind that fag now,' Frankie said as she eased herself into the passenger seat. 'I think we're far enough away from the gas leak.' She tore her hankie in half and tried to bandage her hands. What a fuss Dickie would have raised if he'd seen her coming home with bleeding hands. He'd never have allowed her to carry on with this vital work. She could just hear him now: *I told you it's not suitable work for a woman, look what a mess you've got yourself into. You stupid woman, you should stay home and leave the dangerous work to the men.*

'Hang on a sec,' Bertie said, fumbling in her coat pocket for cigarettes and a lighter before putting the key into the ignition. 'And you'll have to remind me how this thing works.'

'You're joking. Don't tell me you've forgotten how to drive?'

'Course I haven't,' Bertie said, handing over a lit cigarette. 'I'm teasing you. I'll get us back, don't you worry.'

She started the engine, then pulled away from the ruined terrace of houses with a series of noisy jerks as she pushed through the gears, both of them laughing at her dreadful driving. And Frankie tried to push the resurgent thoughts of Dickie out of her head. He's never coming home, she kept repeating to herself, as if the more she said it and thought it, the more likely it was to come true.

Frankie could hear the crashing of saucepans from the hallway, accompanied by a low, angry muttering. She entered the kitchen to find Dolly drying up the pans with a thunderous face.

'Whatever's the matter? Is one of the boys in trouble? Has Tommy got detention again?'

Dolly looked even angrier. 'It's not my lads that are turning this place upside down, it's those daft old biddies! Just take a look out there!'

She waved towards the garden, where two of her boys were bent low, creeping around with their arms outstretched. The doors to the rabbit hutches were wide open. Maisie the cat was sitting on top of one of the hutches, watching the whole scene with intense curiosity.

'Let them all out, she did. Said the sweet little bunny rabbits wanted to come out and play on the grass! After all that effort an' all.'

'I'd better go out and help them then,' Frankie said. 'They're going to be terribly hard to catch. Which one of the Beaumont sisters was it?' She was trying not to burst out laughing – the situation seemed so ridiculous, all of them hunting for the rabbits. Nothing like this could ever have happened when Dickie was around. He wouldn't even let her have a cat and when she'd said she'd like a small dog he'd refused, saying she wouldn't know how to train it properly.

'Oh, I don't know. The quiet one.'

'Daphne? And she spoke to you about letting them out?'

'No, not her. Well, I think she did it, or helped. It was the other one who spoke. The one who nicked the silver.'

'Oh dear, that's Cecily. I'll have to have a word with Elspeth. But first I'd better help the boys get all the rabbits back in their hutches as quickly as we can. Is the buck rabbit out as well?'

'He certainly is. And we don't want to lose him.'

Frankie ran outside to where little grey rabbits were hiding under bushes and nibbling the lettuces in the vegetable patch. She knelt down beside the canes of beans and quickly managed to grab one about to eat through the main stem, which would have destroyed the entire plant.

There must have been a dozen or more hopping around the garden. Since acquiring the doe and the buck, there had been two litters, with seven kits in each, which grew rapidly on the groundsel and dandelions the boys diligently picked from the common every day. Dolly said it was good for them to take responsibility and to learn about 'the birds and the bees' from the rapidly reproducing rabbits. Frankie thought they would also learn about life and death when the young rabbits were plump enough to be worth eating, as Dolly said she'd deal with dispatching them when the time came.

'I've got another one, miss,' Tommy said, as he approached the hutch with a wriggling bundle of grey fur. Then George managed to pounce on one too and popped that into the hutch along with its sibling.

'How many more have we got to find?' Frankie was

crouching down, trying to see if any others were hiding under the redcurrant bushes. 'And have we found their father yet?' The buck was just as vital to the production of rabbit meat as the mother and both were yet to be caught.

'My dears, I'm so very sorry for all the drama,' came a refined voice from behind her. Elspeth was coming down the steps into the garden. 'How can I possibly be of help?' She was all fluttering hands and trembling speech.

'Oh, you can't go crawling round on your hands and knees like us,' Frankie said. 'Leave that to me and the boys. Just tell us if you spot one.'

Elspeth bent her head to inspect the borders of the garden. 'Daphne put her up to it, I'm sure. She can't bear to see anything locked up. She's never been the same since Holloway.'

Frankie was sympathetic about the brutal treatment meted out to the suffragettes in prison but all the same, that didn't warrant the release of rabbits being fattened up for the pot. Dolly had been so proud of getting the buck and doe and seeing the first litter arrive. She hadn't yet produced the promised rabbit pies and stews, but assured everyone that there would be plenty to go round once the youngsters were plump enough, after a few more weeks.

'And if they breed like rabbits' – she laughed – 'and we can't keep up, we'll sell them off to the neighbours. They'll be glad enough of some more fresh meat, I'm sure.' With good supplies scarce at the butcher's shop, despite Dolly's attempts to flatter him, Frankie and the rest of the household were all looking forward to a change in their diet.

'Oh dear, there's another one,' Elspeth called. 'Quick, he's wiggling on top of her.'

Frankie turned round to see the buck under the giant rhubarb leaves, mating with the doe. Intent on his task, he didn't see her creep up on him and throw her cardigan over the pair of them. They hadn't planned for another pregnancy so soon, but this would mean more baby rabbits in just over a month, they reproduced so quickly. Dolly's plan to sell or barter rabbits could well become necessary sooner rather than later.

'Hold the hutch door,' she called to Tommy. 'I've got them both wrapped up.' She bundled them into the open hutch and the door was bolted fast.

'We've got nearly all of them,' George said. 'Just two more to find. Me and Tommy will keep hunting for them.'

'Good boys. You're doing really well.' Frankie stood up, her bruised knees aching from crouching down under the shrubs. Her head ached too, though the wound caused by the looter was almost completely healed.

'My dear, I'm so very sorry that my sisters have caused such a lot of trouble,' Elspeth said in a wheedling tone, twisting a lace-edged handkerchief in her hands. 'We won't have to leave this lovely house, will we? I can promise you I will do my best to ensure there are no more distressing incidents.'

She looked as if she might burst into tears at any moment. Frankie grasped her hands and said, 'Of course I'm not going to make you all leave. Anyway, where would you go? We love having you here and so do Dolly and the boys.' Over her shoulder she could see Dolly pulling a face, but she didn't shake her head.

'Oh, thank you so much. We are so, so grateful to you. I'll try to ensure my sisters make it up to you all.'

'Well, for a start, with their knowledge of plants they could gather fresh greenstuff for the rabbits every day. With their numbers increasing, the boys have been doing their best, but they have to go to school every day as well. So why don't you ask your sisters to do that?'

'Oh, I certainly will, my dear. They'll be glad to help once I've finished talking to them both about the nuisance they've caused.' Elspeth turned towards the house and disappeared to find her sisters.

. . .

'Well, I don't call that much of an apology,' Dolly said, rolling out pastry in which she'd supplemented the rationed flour with mashed potato.

'It wasn't her fault though. The trouble is, both her sisters are a little odd.'

'You're telling me! Good thing they didn't take it upon themselves to let the hens have a run around while they were at it as well. I'm relying on the extra eggs we're getting. It's all very well for her, with all her fancy *Mr Fortnum* nonsense, but some of us have got to make ends meet and they're all doing very well out of it.' Dolly's pursed lips were a clear sign of how she was thinking.

'Let's just be glad the rabbits didn't escape onto the common. We'd never have got them back if they'd gone under the fence and over the road.'

'Hmm, just as well for them, I say. I'd have taken a dim view of those so-called ladies if my boys hadn't done all they could to get the whole lot of them back in their hutches.' Dolly sniffed.

'I think we should try to understand them,' Frankie said. 'Sadly, Dolly, I think the ladies are casualties of the times they endured before. I feel sorry for all of them, even Elspeth, who has to be the guardian of her sisters.'

'Huh, maybe you're right. Just as well they gave me their ration books, otherwise they'd only have their *Mr Fortnum* to help them have enough to eat. And now I'd better get on. It's Lord Woolton Pie tonight, like it or lump it. I doubt he ever eats it himself.'

Frankie doubted it too, but the vegetable pie, with its browned potato crust, was a hot and satisfying meal that would fill all their stomachs. She thought about how much more she would enjoy a rabbit pie, once the animals were fit to slaughter, and she also wondered how many more casualties there would be from this war. If there were people like the Beaumont sisters still suffering from the hardships that had resulted from the Great War, would the latest conflict produce a whole new generation of physically and mentally wounded souls? Would they be capable of rebuilding their lives in the cities that the Germans were intent on destroying?

And what is it going to be like for me, after the war? I've loved haring around with Bertie, scaring ourselves silly and laughing to shake off the horrors we've seen. But if Dickie comes home and picks up with Hugo again, what kind of life will I be left with then? I can't see happiness ahead for me, only disappointment and emptiness.

The more Frankie thought about the future, the more the light-hearted mood of the day evaporated. She knew that a future with Dickie wasn't what she wanted, and more than ever she longed to know for certain that he'd never be coming back home.

Dan was working on the floor in front of the fireplace in their bedroom. They had decided not to have a working open fire in there, but a simulated gas fire, which would still create the feeling of natural flames. He had prised up the floorboards ready for the gas fitter to lay the pipe and was staring at some pieces of torn paper.

'What have you got there?' Charlie was making the bed, hoping the sheets could last another few days. The weather was stormy and drying large items was a challenge. Or perhaps this time she should take them to the local launderette and use the big dryer there.

'They're parts of a letter, I think. It looks as if a sheet of notepaper was torn up and these pieces fell down between the boards.' He held out the scraps, scrawled with a few inked letters. 'I can't make out what it says. You have a go.'

It was handwritten, the letters slanted and looped in a style that was rare nowadays. It didn't make sense and Charlie could only read the following letters and parts of words, all on separate lines, as if the page had been torn into strips lengthwise:

... th... Monday... erday... I... I pos... long... I sh... I h... y...

'It does look like it's from a letter, as you say. It's certainly not a shopping list.' She gazed at it again, trying to imagine what letters could have been written either side of those that had survived. And as she did so, she had the strangest sensation that a voice was reaching out to her, and she desperately wanted to hear what it had to say. She couldn't say exactly what she was feeling, but it was something that kept happening every time something from the house's past turned up.

'Are there any more scraps under there?' She bent down to see where Dan had found the fragments of paper.

'No, that's all there was. Lots of fluff and dust though, along with mouse droppings, I should think, but no more secret letters hidden away.'

'Maybe the rest went on the fire and this fell down the crack. I'll put it in the box of bits we keep finding. I like keeping these things. It feels like we're uncovering the past and learning something about the people who once lived here.'

'I don't know why you're bothering. Is that where you've put the spoons?'

'I've put one of them in there, to remind me what we found hidden away. The rest are in the cutlery drawer, where they can be more useful.' One of the workmen had been restoring the original overhead cistern for the upstairs bathroom toilet. Inside, he'd been surprised to find a handful of silver teaspoons, tarnished but not rusted by the water in the tank.

'I still don't understand how they got in there. They were silver too. Why on earth would someone do that?'

'A mad kleptomaniac, perhaps? Though why they'd choose that as a hiding place I can't think.' Charlie thought about all the little clues they'd found to the house's past as they renovated. There were the pencil marks on that bedroom doorframe, with names and dates. Tommy, George, Jeffrey and Alan must have been little boys living here, for about three years, during the Second World War.

Although the house had been cluttered when they'd first arrived, it had not been disorderly. In fact, there were many signs that Mrs Wilson had been very organised and in control of her many possessions. Charlie couldn't help noticing when she'd opened drawers that the contents were carefully arranged. For instance, in the kitchen, the dresser had what her mother would have called an 'odds and ends' drawer. But the rubber bands were wound around each other into a ball, the ends of string were twisted together into a skein and the loose drawing pins had been gathered into a small jar with a lid. She'd even found an old household accounts book dating back to the 1940s that contained two distinctly different styles of writing. Over a period of about three years, an almost childish hand recorded pounds of sausages bought and numbers of eggs laid, followed by a more cursive hand noting deliveries and bills paid.

Charlie wished she could find out more about the past and feel closer to understanding the house. It had, at least once in its life, been full of children. She could imagine the place echoing with childish laughter as little boys ran up and down the stairs.

She'd also added a wedding photograph in a silver frame to her collection of small mementoes. A pretty woman with dark curled hair and a serious young man with a thin moustache. She assumed it was the Wilsons on their wedding day, because she recognised the woman from the old photos Jean had shown her. There was an ancient photo album too, but it was too large to go in the tin where she was keeping these mementoes and she didn't dare tell Dan she hadn't thrown it out.

'And where are you keeping all this rubbish?' Dan stood up, dusting off the knees of his trousers.

'I'm using that Earl Grey tea tin I found in the pantry. It's from Fortnum's but it's a very old design. Must be wartime, I should think. I thought it was quite sweet.' The tin was the familiar turquoise colour associated with the famous grocers, but was a little rusted around the edges.

'That rusty old thing. I'd have thrown it out at the start.'

'I know you would, and that's why I'm keeping it, along with quite a lot of other things. Like those watercolours we've found of the church, the school and the house. I think they're charming. And do you know, I looked up the artist. Elspeth Beaumont. She was quite celebrated in her day and her pictures still command a price.'

He smiled. 'So, are you suggesting we should sell them? That they're worth something?'

'No, I'm certainly not. I'm keeping them. I'm fascinated to think that she came here and was painting around the area. I keep thinking she must have been staying here. And the dates on the paintings overlap with those of the little boys whose heights were measured upstairs.'

Dan hugged her. 'I don't mind finding a space for them when we've done all the decorating and are ready to add the finishing touches. I know I want to really renovate this place, but collectables add character, so that's going to make it all the more interesting.'

'I'm so glad you think so. I've kept some pieces back in the storage unit that I would like to use when we're ready. Oh, it's going to be wonderful when it's all finished.' She patted her stomach, cradling the beginnings of new life. 'And it will be perfect for our first child.'

Dan held her at length, studying her face. 'You mean...?'

'Yes,' she said and laughed. 'Our wonderful weekend away worked. I did the test this morning. I feel really well and I think this one is going to be fine. That fresh air did the trick.'

She buried her face in the warmth of his sweatshirt, breathing in the scents of dust and fresh sweat, feeling safe and happy, convinced that nothing could possibly harm her and her growing child now.

THIRTY-NINE
THEN
MARCH 1943

Another winter had passed and still the war was far from over. Frankie and her lodgers had been fed well on rabbit stew and pie, but Dolly grumbled about the shortage of tea and sugar.

And Frankie had other important concerns. 'We're going to be in trouble when they start rationing Bisto,' she said as she dabbed at the final patch of pale skin on Bertie's leg in another attempt to emulate stockings. 'We'll just have to wear our ghastly lisle and put up with it.'

'It would be warmer, for sure. We're going to freeze tonight.' Bertie twisted round to admire her light brown legs in the mirror. 'Don't bother about the eye pencil this time. It always goes wonky. My legs look better like this, like nylons.'

'I've heard that if you can meet some friendly Americans, there's a good chance of getting real nylon stockings.'

'Now there's a thought. Where can we find some of them?' Rumours about the generosity of American servicemen had been circulating ever since the United States had joined the Allies in the war in December.

'I don't think there's much chance of meeting any of them in

Putney, so that rules out Cinderella's. We should go back to the Hammersmith Palais. I've heard quite a few of them go there, and anyway, the music they have is much more up to date.' They had gone to the Palais a couple of times since it reopened after being badly bombed in the early days of the Blitz, but it meant catching a bus there and back, while the club in Putney was within walking distance.

'Come on then, let's do it tonight. What have we got to lose?'

'Just our bus fares. Let's give it a go.'

Giggling, the girls finished getting ready and tied scarves over their hair to guard against the misty night air. The bus smelt of damp coats and mothballs, with a fug of cigarette smoke. Bertie dabbed a little scent on her wrists to combat the overwhelming smells. 'Here,' she said, 'have a squirt. We can't go attracting any Americans smelling like bag ladies.' Soap was in short supply and had been added to the list of rationed items in February. Now everyone and their clothes were less clean and grubbier than ever before.

'Give it here,' Frankie said, savouring the sweet smell of orange and vanilla. 'It's lovely. What's it called?'

'Chantilly. I got it for Christmas. I'm trying to make it last, but now everything smells so awful, I can't believe it will see me out till the end of the year.'

'Oh, it won't be so bad once the winter's finally over and everyone's put away their musty, motheaten old coats,' Frankie said, dabbing a little of the scent behind her ears, thinking this was another thing Dickie disapproved of. He'd seemed to discourage anything that made her noticeable and she'd stopped using perfume after he'd said one day, *'You smell like a tart. Go and wash it off.'* She tried to shake off the memory. 'Still, at least we'll walk in smelling gorgeous now.'

The girls whipped off their scarves in the shelter of the

dancehall entrance and checked each other's hair. They bought their tickets and left their coats in the cloakroom. The hall boasted two famous bands that night – Lou Preager and Harry Leader – and one of them was already playing to a packed, jostling crowd of dancers.

The girls had become used to seeing a largely female throng at such events, with so many young men away on active service, so they were delighted to see a good mix of men and women enjoying themselves on the dancefloor, some in uniform. 'Thank goodness, some real men at last,' Bertie said with a laugh, holding her friend's hand.

'I'm not going to wait to be asked,' Frankie said. 'The music's too good to waste. Come on, let's get dancing.'

So, as they had done many times before, the two girls entwined arms and began a jaunty quickstep, which made them both breathless. As they dashed to a finish, Frankie felt a tap on her shoulder. 'May I have the next dance?' A tall man with a smooth American accent was smiling at her and his friend was speaking to Bertie.

'I'd be delighted,' she said, as she was swept away into a soothing waltz, which allowed her to catch her breath before the next number, an energetic lindy hop. 'I don't know this dance very well,' she apologised, as she missed her step.

'No problem. Just hold tight. I'll spin and catch you.' He laughed, showing even white teeth.

As they twisted around the dancefloor Frankie caught sight of Bertie, held in a frantic whirl by her equally tall partner. Both men were brilliant dancers, unlike most of the British men either of them had ever danced with. Frankie thought of the sedate waltzing partners she'd been paired with in her earlier years and how Dickie had trodden on her toes at the company Christmas dance. That was the only time they'd ever danced together, and she knew now that he'd only asked her to dance because he'd cynically planned to make her his wife. But this kind of dancing was joyous and energetic and filled her with utter happiness; she was glad Dickie wasn't here to intervene and stop her.

'So, what do you girls do when you're not out dancing?' Their partners led them to a table where they could rest and have drinks. They introduced themselves as Edwin Wright and Jayson Sands. Both wore smart brass-buttoned uniforms, made by better tailors than had equipped many British soldiers before they left for France.

'We're both ambulance drivers,' Bertie said, with a wink to her friend.

'But it's less busy than it was during the Blitz,' Frankie said. 'Though I dare say the Germans have more plans for London up their sleeves and could very well be back with rein-forcements.'

'You betcha,' Edwin said. 'It's not over yet, by a long stretch.'

'You'd better fasten your seat belts for the next round,' Jayson said.

'Have you both seen some action already?' Frankie asked the question, then regretted it. No one on active service was meant to talk openly about what they'd seen and might yet see. *Loose talk can cost lives* was still the mantra drummed into the general population, even when having a casual conversation with friendly Americans. 'Sorry,' she said, 'I know I shouldn't ask.'

'No worries,' Edwin said. 'There's nothing to tell, anyway.'

'And who wants to talk shop when there's music to dance to?' Jayson stood up again and held out his hand. 'Another twirl around the floor?'

They were right, Frankie thought as she and Bertie were led back into the melee of frantic bodies whirling around the hall. This was all that mattered now. No thoughts of bombs tomorrow or the bombs of yesterday. This was all she had to think about. Where to place her feet, how to grab that firm outstretched hand as he flung her backwards and forwards, how to move in time to the music, how to just live for the moment. Everyone at the Hammersmith Palais was grasping a few hours of pleasure before they had to face the war again.

When the girls left the Palais after hugs and promises to return the following week, Bertie said, 'I don't suppose you told Edwin you were married, did you?'

'No, I didn't think I had to. Are you saying I should have done? Did you say anything about writing to Ralph?' Bertie was corresponding with a young man who was sweet on her, but to whom she wasn't deeply attached.

'No, I didn't see the need. I'm not the one who's married, after all.'

Frankie was quiet. Her hand strayed to her ringless finger. She'd never replaced her rings after that first time out dancing and she was hoping she'd never have to wear them again.

She so often forgot that she was married, that she had said her vows with Dickie in church, that she had promised to love and obey till death did them part. She had believed them at the time, but she knew now that the vows had never meant anything to him. And it was so very long since she'd actually seen him, so long since she'd received the news that he was missing, it seemed as if he'd never been a part of her life. Even though she hadn't been told he was *missing, presumed dead*, she couldn't help feeling that, after nearly three years with no word, he couldn't still be alive. She certainly hoped so.

For a moment, she felt guilty for enjoying herself. But then she told herself she was only twenty-four years old, after all. She was far too young to be a widow and she was certainly too young to give up dancing.

'Don't look so glum,' Bertie said. 'I'll forgive you, though thousands wouldn't. It was fun, wasn't it? And they were so nice and polite, I'm definitely looking forward to seeing them again.'

So am I, Frankie thought, remembering the warm firmness of the hands that had held her for the last dance, his broad shoulders, his flashing smile. It eclipsed all her memories of Dickie, and she smiled to herself.

FORTY

THEN

JUNE 1943

Three months after that first dance, they sat on the side of the river in the heat of the day, dangling their bare feet in the cool water. Edwin had taken off his uniform jacket and rolled up his trousers. Frankie had tucked her dress high above her knees and they were now turning pink in the sun.

'If there wasn't a war,' she said, 'this river would be filled with rowing boats, practising for the Henley Regatta.'

'The what?' He leant back on the grassy bank, squinting at the sun.

'It's an annual society event in early July. Rather fun really. Everyone dresses up to watch the boats racing past. And there's loads of Pimm's, poached salmon, cucumber sandwiches and strawberries.'

'Pimm's?'

'It's a strong drink, diluted with lemonade, served with slices of apple and cucumber and garnished with sprigs of mint.'

'Sounds kinda like a mint julep. Maybe we could get some in one of your quaint old public houses round here?'

'We could try. Or we could see what the tea rooms have to offer first, before we have any alcohol. It's strawberry season after all. If they've managed to get cream, we could be in for a treat.'

He sat up and threw his arms around her. 'Let's do both. Tea then Pimm's, then dinner, then bed.'

Frankie couldn't find it in her to blush. She was loving her time with Edwin, who was not only an excellent dancer but a skilled lover too. They had only kissed and hugged previously, but when he said he longed to take her away for a couple of nights while he had leave, they had arranged this trip to Henley. It was the kind of place she thought he'd be interested to see, a typically English village, with its typically English traditions at the heart of the most famous English river.

She couldn't get used to the kissing in public that he was wont to do, so she gave him a quick peck on the cheek, then stood up and slipped her feet back into her white shoes. 'Perfect plan,' she said. 'We'll head for that tea room overlooking the river first.'

Once he had dried his feet on his handkerchief and found his socks and shoes, they walked hand in hand along the river-bank back into the village. Frankie thought it highly unlikely that anyone she knew could possibly be visiting at the same time, but she found herself hiding behind her sunglasses and sunhat all the same. Not even Bertie knew that she had arranged to come away with Edwin.

They were in luck when they ordered their tea at the Rose Tree Tea Room, with its view across the river. 'Cream went on the rations list yesterday, but we already had plenty of it in, so you can have it with your strawberries.' The waitress rolled her eyes and tapped her order pad. 'After that, I don't know what we'll do. They're going to include condensed milk as well. Whatever next?'

Frankie didn't care what would happen next. As far as she was concerned, this tea, with scones laden with more of that Women's Institute plum jam and the strawberries, was perfect.

And when the waitress turned up with a large bowl of whipped cream, saying, 'It's all got to be used up today. It'll turn in no time in this weather, so you might as well put it on your scones as well,' she thought she was in heaven.

'We might not need dinner at this rate,' she said, eating her second scone piled with cream. 'It's not quite like the clotted cream teas you'd get down in Devon or Cornwall, but it still tastes pretty good.'

'Tastes pretty damn fine to me,' Edwin said, taking a large bite, getting cream all over his chin. 'You Brits have some strange customs, but they all seem to make sense.'

Frankie laughed. It was only afternoon tea, but it felt so daring, being here with a man who wasn't her husband. She glanced at him, his bright blue eyes and short, blond hair, such a contrast to Dickie with his little toothbrush moustache, an attempt to look older and more serious.

When Edwin had first suggested spending the night together, she had been torn. She longed to sleep with him, and it would have been easy to arrange if her house had been empty. But with the boys thundering up and down the stairs, Dolly clattering pans in the kitchen and the Beaumont sisters alert to all the comings and goings in the household, there was no way she could invite a man to stay overnight in her bedroom.

So she'd agreed to coming away, to a little inn with rooms that asked no questions, though she thought she caught a wink as Edwin signed the register as Mr and Mrs. He'd asked if she'd prefer that and she'd said yes. But when he said he'd better get her a ring to maintain the pretence, she'd said, 'Oh, don't worry. My mother's old wedding ring will do.'

It wasn't her mother's, of course, it was the slender gold ring Dickie had slipped onto her finger that day in church before the war. Did using her legal wedding ring make her a fallen woman? But Edwin wasn't to know that – and, anyway, Frankie rather thought that Dickie had, as usual, skimped on the cost of the ring and that it might even have been his late mother's.

Later, after the promised Pimm's – well, two each, in fact – she felt a little giddy and no longer thought of herself as a woman having an illicit affair. She was so relaxed and happy, though not at all hungry, having eaten not only all the fruit contained in their large drinks but also the delicious home-made fried potatoes that the pub was serving in place of crisps.

'We can't get 'em in packets no more,' the barmaid said. 'And it's not like flippin' potatoes are being rationed. All gone to cheer up the troops, so they say. I reckon Smiths isn't the only firm doing well out of this war.' Frankie was disappointed that she couldn't introduce Edwin to the delight of sprinkling the little blue sachet of salt into a packet of crisps, but the pub's offering was very welcome all the same.

Later, in the low-ceilinged bedroom, where Edwin's height meant he had to duck below the beams, Frankie lay exhausted, watching the moonlight creep through the blackout blind. She slipped out of bed and drew back the curtains and blind to look at the silvery light on the river. She opened the window and heard the sharp cry of a barn owl and then the muffled quacking of ducks settled in the reeds by the bank.

'Let's hope the Jerries aren't out tonight,' Edwin said softly. 'It's a bomber's moon again.'

'Funny how your perception changes with events, isn't it? I used to only think how beautiful the moonlight was, but it's all so different now.'

'We're all different people because of this damned war,' he said, coming to stand behind her and fold his arms around her naked body.

She could feel the softness of the hairs on his chest against her bare back. She turned slightly from side to side to emphasise the sensation. How different this was compared to Dickie's pale, skinny, hairless body. And the whole experience of being loved by Edwin was utterly different too.

In the first year of her marriage, she'd wondered why people made such a song and dance about making love. It was nothing to be excited about. Dickie rolled on top of her and then rolled off when he had completed the brief act that one time, without any words of endearment or tender kisses. On their wedding night and forever after, as far as she came to expect, she wore a long nightdress and he wore striped pyjamas. Neither of them removed their clothing or ever saw each other naked. She had assumed that Dickie would suggest it eventually and was far too shy to propose it herself. At the time she had assumed he too was shy or embarrassed. It had never occurred to her then that he couldn't desire her and never would.

But Edwin had no such inhibitions. He was comfortable to undress, let her see all of him, lie on the bed and wait for her to lie down beside him. Then he undressed her himself, kissing each part as it was revealed. He was patient and kind and seemed to know exactly how her body would respond, as it had never responded before. She was almost weak with gratitude for his gentle touches.

Still standing by the window, she turned round to kiss him and ran her fingers through the thicket on his chest. 'I can't tell you how happy you've made me,' she said. 'I've never felt like that before.'

'You just hadn't met the right man,' he said, kissing her. 'I could tell it wasn't your first time, but that doesn't matter to me. I've shown you now how good it can be, made you feel like a real woman.'

'Show me again,' she said.

Charlie ran her finger down the list of names and dates scrawled on the doorframe of one of the bedrooms at the very top of the house. She had to bend down to read it and some of the pencilled writing was rather faint. Boys' names, four of them: Alan, Tommy, Jeffrey and George.

Dan had noticed it too when they first moved in, but wanted to paint over it. 'You're not touching it,' she said. 'I love these little signs that people were once happy living here.'

The dates were all from the Second World War and the boys' growth had been recorded over a period of about three years. Charlie's parents had done the same for her and her siblings, just as many families did, and her height was still visible on a section of the wall in their farmhouse kitchen in Hampshire. Her mother said she could never allow that area to be repainted.

Assuming they had been living here through those years and not just visiting, these boys had grown well in their time in the house. Their ages weren't recorded, so Charlie tried to guess how old they might have been when the growth chart was started. Alan, always the smallest, might have been four when he was first measured. Tommy, obviously the oldest, must have been around ten or eleven by the time of the last measurement, as he'd reached 4'5". And right at the very top was another figure of 4'11" and the word *Mum*. So, their mother was a little woman who would eventually be shadowed by her tall, strong children. Charlie imagined her as a mother hen with her brood of boys.

She smiled at the chart. It made her think that this little family had loved each other and had been happy here in the house. But why had they come to live here? Were they related to Mrs Wilson? If they had been, they'd surely have been traced after her death, when her estate was being settled. And then it dawned on her that there wasn't a girl's name on the wall. There was no Alicia Rose.

Charlie looked around the three empty bedrooms, cleared of the old beds, armchairs and table that had been there when she and Dan first moved in. The smallest room, with a washbasin plumbed in, was going to be turned into a bathroom.

Perhaps the boys and their mother had occupied the top floor like a flat, separate from the rest of the house. The place was certainly big enough to have accommodated different groups of people at one time. Charlie imagined the boys sliding down the curved banisters and playing in the garden.

So for a time at least, this house, where Mrs Wilson had maybe only ever had one child, had echoed with the sound of several children. Charlie could almost imagine the shrieks and laughter of boys playing and fighting.

She ran her fingers back over the pencilled marks. She couldn't let this be painted over. She longed to know more about the boys and their life here, but so far she hadn't found any more clues.

Charlie gazed out of the window at the little school across the road, next to the church. It was still thriving, still teaching children from the age of five. Perhaps that was where Alan and his brothers had learnt their times tables and been taught to write in pen and ink. They could have run straight across the road every morning and never been late for school. At the end of the school day, they might have hurtled out of the playground and onto the grass of the common to play football and hide-and-seek, building camps in the woods and dipping nets in the ponds. And maybe Mrs Wilson's daughter had gone to the school there too.

She wandered around the rooms, wondering which one they had slept in. Perhaps their much-put-upon mother had the smallest room with the sink to herself, while the boys shared a room all together and maybe a couple of beds. The bedroom with the fireplace might have been used as their sitting room, where they could read and do their homework.

Charlie felt a mix of emotions about the children. While she was glad they had thrived here, she felt sad that she couldn't learn more about them and where they had gone after leaving the house. She was about to go back downstairs, but decided to take a last look in the cupboard on the landing at the top of the stairs. She remembered clearing out some old wooden chairs there soon after arriving in the house.

The cupboard was dusty but empty, apart from one dog-eared exercise book on the floor. She picked it up and opened it. The plain white pages were filled with childish drawings of chickens, rabbits and people. Some were of boys, some of ladies knitting, sewing or reading. She turned to the cover, where a name was printed – *Alan Jones, age 7*. She was delighted. This told her more about Alan than she could have imagined – and perhaps the portraits, comical as they were, might be his brothers and other relatives.

She hugged the book to herself. She would treasure it. It made her feel hopeful that the house would be filled with children again one day.

FORTY-TWO
THEN
JUNE 1944

One morning when Frankie woke late after a particularly long and arduous shift, she heard a scream from downstairs and then the sounds of crying. She pulled her dressing gown over her nightdress, ran to the landing, bent over the stairs and called out, 'What's happened? Is someone hurt?'

Cecily ran past her to the Beaumonts' bedroom, shaking with tears, closely followed by Daphne, who said, 'They've all been murdered. It's a massacre.' Elspeth rushed after the two of them without a word, shaking her head at Frankie.

Then Dolly called up the stairs, 'It's the chickens. They're all dead.'

'Oh no, not the hens! What, all of them?' Frankie rushed downstairs in her nightclothes to see. 'Did one of the sisters let them out?'

'No, don't go out there. No one let them out. It was the fox. Tommy isn't too upset about it, but the others were in tears, so I've sent them straight to school.'

Frankie looked out of the glass doors into the garden. Tommy was collecting bodies from the remaining scrap of lawn, which was littered with feathers. Maisie the cat was pouncing on white down floating in the air. 'The fox just killed them and left them?'

'We'll know in a minute when Tommy's finished counting. I've heard that foxes kill just for the hell of it, as well as for food. I'm hoping one or two might have survived or we'll be short of eggs again. How we're all meant to manage on one egg each a week I don't know.'

'Oh, what a shame this had to happen. The hens were shut away last night as usual, weren't they?'

'Course they were. But foxes are crafty. It must've slipped the catch. Poor things.'

Tommy came towards the door, carrying a speckled hen in his arms. Her head lolled to one side, so perhaps her neck was broken. 'She's not dead yet, Mum. And there's another that's still alive an' all. What should I do with them?'

'Try tucking them up in their nest boxes, love, and we'll see if they make it. If they last the night then maybe they'll be all right.'

'What are we going to do about the rest of them?' Frankie was appalled by the scene of carnage. 'We can't just leave the bodies lying out there like that.'

'Course we can't. Good chickens are like gold dust. We'll have to dress them for the table.'

Frankie was a little confused, and then she realised what Dolly meant. 'You mean we're going to eat them? But there must be half a dozen chickens out there.'

'Well, we're certainly not going to waste them. I'd be lucky to find any chicken in that butcher's shop of yours. We haven't had any in I don't know how long. So that's what we'll have to do. Maybe exchange a couple for more eggs now we're going to run short.'

Frankie glanced again at the garden, dusted with feathers, Tommy bending to place the two shocked survivors in the henhouse. Maisie dabbed her paw at the loose feathers and tried to shake off one that had landed on her nose. 'Well, what are we waiting for?' she said. 'We'd better get on with plucking them. I've never done it before, but it can't be that hard.' She couldn't help thinking that Dickie would have been horrified if he'd been here, but Edwin would find the whole scene amusing when she told him about the drama. The two men couldn't be more different, and she hugged the thought of her new love to herself.

'Get dressed and I'll do you a bit of toast and a cuppa,' Dolly said. 'And tell those old biddies we're going to need help. It's going to take quite a while and we don't want the meat spoiling. It looks like it's going to be a warm day, so the sooner we get them ready, the better.'

Frankie turned to go back to her room to dress and Dolly called after her, 'And tell them no hysterics, mind! We've got a serious job on our hands.'

Later, having each donned an apron, they sat with a pillowcase between their knees, tugging at feathers. Dolly had insisted on scalding each bird for a few minutes in very hot water to make the job a little easier. Frankie soon found that the breast feathers were easily removed but the legs were harder. Daphne and Cecily were very slow, pulling only a few feathers at a time, while Dolly and Frankie both managed large vigorous handfuls. And Elspeth kept holding individual feathers up to the light, exclaiming, 'My dears, just look at the colours and the structure. I must save some to paint later.'

Dolly rolled her eyes and plucked even faster, muttering, 'One feather's much like another, as far as I can see, and I've got to get all these birds cooked as soon as I can.'

'What are you planning to do with all of them?' Frankie had been wondering how even this large household was going to eat so much chicken before it went off.

'Some of these girls are older, so best cooked in the pot, I reckon. But a couple of the younger ones might cope with roasting this evening. And I won't waste a scrap. I should think I can do potted meat with the trimmings.' Dolly was so resourceful, and had become quite a good cook with the advice she'd received from the Women's Institute members.

'Your little boys are in for a real treat at teatime today,' Cecily said.

Daphne mouthed some words that Frankie couldn't quite catch, but she nodded and assumed it was a similar remark.

'They'll think Christmas has come early,' Dolly said. 'We don't have chicken any other time of the year.'

'They won't mind eating these chickens then?' Elspeth was admiring another feather, turning it this way and that. 'They'd named them, hadn't they? Isn't the one I'm plucking called Tuppence?'

'Maybe it is, maybe it isn't,' Dolly snapped. 'My boys will eat what's put in front of them. So, there'll be no talk tonight of names, thank you very much.'

Chastened, Elspeth winked at Frankie, who pulled a face in return. Dolly was in her element taking charge in the kitchen. None of them would have known what to do without her firm guidance.

'Now, if you don't mind,' Dolly said, once all the birds were goose-pimpled and bare, 'I think you ladies might be better off going and doing whatever else it is needs doing. You won't like to hang around for the next part. I've got to trim these chickens and gut them, so off you trot.'

The elderly ladies meekly did as instructed, but Frankie stayed behind. After all her dealings with injured victims of bombings and collecting corpses for the mortuary, she wasn't going to be squeamish at the sight of a chicken's innards. And in fact, her help was needed.

'Some of these birds aren't 'alf tough,' Dolly complained, plunging her hand inside the inner cavity and pulling hard on the insides. Frankie held the hen's body tight while Dolly struggled to get the guts out intact.

'I'll save the livers,' Dolly said. 'Cook them up with a bit of butter, make a nice spread. And the cat can have the lights, the kidneys and lungs.' Maisie had been mewing and rubbing around their legs all the time they were working.

Later that day, the kitchen was filled with the savoury smells of roasting and simmering chicken. Dolly had exchanged two of the birds for a tray of eggs and some home-cured bacon from a neighbour who had a cousin in the countryside with pigs.

The boys were home from school and were gathering the last few feathers off the vegetable beds and small patch of remaining grass. Tommy was adding another sturdy bolt to the henhouse, and George kept wanting to check whether the two injured hens were still alive.

Frankie was due to leave shortly for a shift at the station. A new kind of bomb was terrifying the population and causing havoc in many areas, including Wandsworth, not far away from home. 'It could be a busy night,' she said to Dolly. 'I hope you all enjoy your supper tonight.'

'Don't worry, there'll be plenty left for you when you get back. I'll leave it cooling in the pantry. Here, have a bowl of soup before you go. That'll set you up for the night.' Dolly ladled a large portion of broth swimming with carrots, potato and barley, along with chunks of tender chicken, into a deep dish.

Frankie cut a slice of bread at the bread board on the kitchen table and tore pieces off to soak up the tasty liquid, flavoured with parsley. 'Who do I owe this delicious meal to?' she asked mischievously, knowing what Dolly's reaction would be.

Dolly turned, waving the ladle at her. 'Now, I told you. No names. They never had no names. Eat up and get off with you.'

Frankie smiled to herself. She loved how Dolly ruled the roost and treated all of them like children. It gave the house a homely feel and prepared her for the worst that her nights' shifts could throw at her. That, and the thought that she would see Edwin again very soon, gave her the strength to face the destruction and distress that was sure to lie ahead.

The bombs of the Blitz had been bad enough, but the new reign of terror that began that summer was in some ways more terrifying. Instead of visible planes roaring over London, in combat with British pilots and anti-aircraft guns, now the Germans were sending unmanned rockets that zoomed towards the city, ran out of fuel and then, without warning, crashed to earth, blowing all around them to smithereens.

'They're taking their revenge,' Jim said at the station. 'All because of D-Day. They know we've got them on the run and this is their comeback.'

'It's downright underhand, is what it is,' said Alf. 'Man to man is one thing, but these rockets don't give no warning. Folk haven't got a chance.'

The rockets were called V-1s based on their German name, *Vergeltungswaffen*, but began acquiring nicknames, the most common of which was 'doodlebugs'. Everyone was learning that, if you heard one and then the engine cut out, you had to run for your life. And they were dropping in London at all times of day and night.

'Where are they coming from?' Frankie asked Edwin one

night when they met outside the Bouillabaisse Club in New Compton Street. The jazz club was a new favourite of theirs and she'd hopped onto a tube train in Putney at the end of a daytime shift to meet him.

'I guess the right people are trying to find out,' he said. He never told her why he was based near London and was careful not to say what his responsibilities were. 'Sounds like they're being launched across the Channel, because some are dropping way short of London, between the coast and the city.'

'Bit rotten then for people who thought they'd escaped the worst of it by moving out to the countryside. It seems nowhere is safe any longer.'

He gripped her hands. 'Do you have anywhere you could go if it gets worse? South London has been getting a few hits recently.'

'Yes, don't I know it! Wandsworth has been very unlucky and that's part of our patch. People managed to put up with the Blitz, because it was mostly night-time and they could arrange to sleep in shelters. But this is happening at any time of day and they just don't know how to carry on with their lives.'

'But seriously, could you go elsewhere? Somewhere safer?' He stared into her eyes. They had become very close, too close almost; she dreaded him telling her he was going to have to go away. Although she still didn't know exactly what he was doing in this war, she had picked up small clues from the way he spoke and had established that he was seconded to the War Office somewhere near Hampton Court.

'I suppose I could ask Bertie if there was a chance of escaping to her uncle's farm in Devon if things get really bad up here. But honestly, I'd rather stay and take my chances. And I wouldn't see you so much if I ran away down there.'

He kissed the top of her head. 'That's true. But I want you to stay safe. We're going to come through this, you and I, and we have a great life ahead of us.'

He often spoke like that. Not definite promises, but hints that they had a future. Frankie hoped they did, because she loved him like she'd never loved anyone before in her life. And it had made her understand the reality of her marriage more clearly than ever before. She and Dickie were both guilty. She had never truly loved him. She had been vulnerable so soon after losing her parents and he had made such an effort to be helpful. But Dickie was the more to blame, for he'd duped her into thinking he cared for her and she hadn't seen how he was using her until it was too late.

'Come on,' Edwin said, 'don't let's worry about that any more now. We've got a fun evening ahead of us.'

The club was a haunt for a number of Americans, including many of the soldiers from the Deep South, whose comrades were a source of much of the thrilling music Frankie had never heard before. The beat, the rhythm, the rich voices were exciting and added to the thrill of being with Edwin and experiencing a vastly different world to the one she had grown up in.

A couple of months later, Frankie began to think that Edwin's premonition about her safety might have been well founded. A new generation of bombs began heading to London. Known as V-2s, unlike their predecessors they were totally silent, which made them even more deadly. With no warning of their approach whatsoever, they began swiftly zipping towards the capital, but many fell short and yet again the southern counties, with their towns and villages in hitherto peaceful countryside, were more vulnerable to the Germans than ever before.

After a week of these frightening raids, with several incidents not far from Putney, Elspeth approached Frankie one day, saying, 'Would you think us all terribly ungrateful if we were to leave you next week?'

Frankie was surprised as the household had been relatively

calm in recent weeks, apart from the cutlery drawer appearing to lack the normal number of teaspoons, which she put down to Cecily's light-fingered habits. 'Why, where are you thinking of going?'

'My cousin's house in the country has room for us now. It's no longer needed and they can move back in. So, he's said he would be very happy for us to join him and his wife. There'd be room for you too if you felt like escaping to somewhere safer.'

'That's a very kind offer but I must stay here and of course I wouldn't think you the least bit ungrateful. My goodness, with these terrifying silent bombs coming over so frequently, I don't blame you one bit for wanting to escape. But you really don't have to leave here and, if you ever felt you'd made the wrong decision, of course you could come back.' When she said all this, Frankie hoped it sounded sincere, as underneath she was thinking there was no way she was leaving London while there was still a chance of seeing Edwin.

'My dear, how very understanding of you. We've all been so very grateful for your hospitality. It has been a haven for all of us. And of course, we've simply loved seeing the boys growing so.'

All four Jones boys had thrived in the fresh air close to the open expanses of the common. Their East End pallor had soon vanished in this semi-rural setting. They'd made friends at the school and had plenty of exercise kicking balls across the turf and chasing each other down to the ponds, where they'd found tadpoles in the spring. Tommy had made a small pond in the garden out of an old tin bath, so they could keep a close eye on the ones they'd caught, noting with excitement day by day how their bodies changed shape until they had finally disappeared, probably hopping into the hen run and being gobbled up in no time.

'It has been a lively household with them running around,

to be sure. And I'm so glad we've all managed to live together so well. Who'd have thought it?'

Over the next few days, the Beaumont sisters were busy packing and making plans for their journey by bus into London to catch a train from Waterloo. Frankie hoped they would make it safely to their destination, with the dreaded bombs targeting central London but often falling short.

Then, the day before they left, Dolly knocked on her bedroom door just as she was about to go down for breakfast. 'Sorry to bother you,' she said. 'But can I have a word?'

'Of course, is anything the matter?'

'Not as such, but I've something important to tell you.'

She looked so worried, standing there, her hands wringing the skirt of her apron, that Frankie assumed it must be to do with one of the boys. 'Whatever it is, tell me. Are the boys all right?'

'Yes, yes, it's not them. It's... well, Elspeth has asked if me and the boys would like to go with them, to her cousin's in Wiltshire. And I've said yes. I hope you don't mind.'

'Gosh, that's a surprise. And you're quite sure? What about the boys? Have you told them?'

'Yes. They were a bit uncertain at first, because of their friends here and that, but they're so fond of the Misses Beaumont, I think they'd go anywhere with them. Daphne has helped George ever so with his reading. He's come on in leaps and bounds since she started helping him.'

Frankie thought with fondness of how Daphne, despite her generally quiet demeanour, had read *Treasure Island* to all the boys over the winter, while everyone else had listened in if they could. Huddled around the kitchen stove, hearing about those tropical adventures, Tommy had announced that, like Ben Gunn, he too longed for toasted cheese. His mother, always trying to make ends meet, had retorted, 'And wouldn't we all like cheese on toast if rations permitted? You go and tell that to Mr Hitler.'

'Then you must all go with them. It's bound to be safer. We don't how long these terrible bombs will carry on, nor what else the Germans have got in store for us. Of course you must go.' But inside Frankie was thinking, then I'd have the house all to myself. Edwin could come here as often as he wanted. No more sneaking around, pretending to be married. How wonderful that would be!

'Well then, if it's all right with you, we'll all go together tomorrow. Safety in numbers and all that.' Dolly looked relieved and smoothed her wrinkled apron.

Frankie thought there was no such thing as safety in numbers after the disasters that had befallen large groups of people sheltering in places they had thought were safe from the bombs. Café de Paris and Bethnal Green station, both considered to be havens, death traps both of them.

'I'm up to date with all the washing and there's a pie in the pantry that'll do for tomorrow,' Dolly said. 'I hope you'll manage without us here sharing all our rations.'

'You've been simply wonderful, managing so well with the restrictions and so many mouths to feed. But I'll be fine. There's often a treat or two down at the station. Our supervisor, Mrs Ogilvy, isn't so terrible. She usually makes sure we have a brew and something to eat at the end of the night.'

'Good. I wouldn't like to think we were leaving you in the lurch.'

'You aren't at all. You must do what's best for you and the boys.' And for me too, she thought. Edwin won't let me starve. The Americans had tins of fruit, meat, fish and butter galore, as well as nylons. Dolly had been delighted with the large tin of yellow cling peaches in syrup Frankie had once brought home. Frankie hadn't told her exactly how she had obtained it, just said it was a present from a grateful friend, but now she wouldn't have to make excuses, and any more peaches would be hers and hers alone.

Charlie felt sick. Not the vague nausea of her previous pregnancies, but the ominous about-to-be-very-ill queasiness of food poisoning or a bug. Surely not. She'd barely been anywhere for a few days as she'd either been working in the house or escaping to the café when the building work became too noisy.

She'd been eating in the café even more often recently, even though the house was now heated, as she was busy and didn't have time to cook from scratch. Could it be that tuna sandwich she'd had for lunch yesterday? But the café was spotless and she was sure that Nicky, with Jean's occasional help, was meticulous about food hygiene.

But minutes later she rushed into the bathroom, slamming the door against the banging and drilling from the room next door. She heaved her breakfast into the lavatory, then paused, recognising that the pains had changed and had passed down to her lower stomach. Please not again. She flushed the toilet, pulled down her jeans and sat down. She could see that she was already bleeding heavily, and the cramps were increasing. She knew she couldn't be more than four weeks gone, so maybe it would hold or maybe it would be over soon. She couldn't move – she just had to stay where she was, waiting for this awful experience to pass.

It seemed to take ages, sitting in the cold, unheated bathroom, shivering with the chill but also the sadness of it all. A fourth life, one she had been convinced was going to survive this time, one she had felt sure was going to succeed. How was she going to break it to Dan?

But she knew that she wouldn't be able to hide it from him for long, because this time she was deeply saddened.

She put her elbows on her knees and cupped her hands around her face, wet with tears and a clammy sweat from the pain. There was one final cramp and then she was sure it was over. She couldn't bear to look at what she had just lost. She wiped herself with tissue, stuffed a sanitary pad in her pants and stood up, then pulled the chain so a swirling flush took the mess away quickly.

Charlie rinsed her mouth, splashed her face with cold water, then buried her tears in the towel. As she looked up and glanced out of the bathroom window, she saw the barren pear tree, stripped now of leaves and fruit. It was bare like her; emptied of what it had grown.

She pictured the scene she had created in her mind of a swing hanging from its branches and suddenly felt furious. Every chance she'd had of creating a child to play in the garden, to swing there, to sleep in the nursery she'd decorated, was being snatched away from her.

A vision of endless medical procedures, intrusive examinations, blood tests and injections swam before her. She didn't deserve this. It really wasn't fair. Why was this happening to her and Dan? She had a successful career as an interior designer, her husband was a great architect, they should have the perfect life, but something was stopping them from having everything they wanted.

And then it dawned on her. Everything in their lives had all been perfect until they came here, to this old house. It had begun going wrong here. They'd thought they'd found the home where they'd have children, where their lives would be complete, but it was fast becoming the house where all she could do was lose children before they'd barely begun.

It was clear to her now. This house was the problem. Years before, within these walls, a woman had prepared for the birth of a child, stitching tiny nightdresses, knitting soft bootees and bonnets. But maybe it turned out that she could never have a child, or maybe she'd lost it, just as Charlie was doing. This house was toxic. Charlie suddenly felt sure that, if she wanted to have a baby, she'd have to leave.

She unlocked the bathroom door, desperate to find Dan and get away. He was in the midst of talking to their electrician, but he stopped the minute he saw her face.

'Are you okay? What's the matter?' He steered her away and into the kitchen. 'What's up?'

She couldn't control her feelings. She'd told herself to tell him calmly, but it flooded out, along with tears, although she tried not to cry. 'I've just lost another baby. It's happened again. Four times now. I can't stay here any longer. I'm never going to have a safe pregnancy if I stay here. It's all because of this house.'

He looked so puzzled. 'But the house will be finished in a few months. There's nothing unsafe about the house.'

'But there must be. Don't you see? I can't go through with a pregnancy in this house. There's something wrong with it and it's made me lose four babies. It's cursed and it's toxic!'

'Calm down, Charlie. The house is completely safe. We've checked everything. The electrics, the gas, the plumbing... There's nothing that can harm you here. Nothing that can affect you or be making this happen. I'm so sorry, darling, but it's just bad luck.'

She pushed past him and rushed upstairs to their bedroom and began packing a bag. She could hear his steps and his shouts as he ran after her. 'Where are you thinking of going?'

'I don't know. I've just got to get out of here. Maybe I'll go to my parents. Or, I know, maybe I'll go back to Rye. That's where I last felt clean and free. I've got to go there and breathe fresh air far away from this poisonous house.'

'I don't want you driving in this state. Can't you wait until I can take you?'

'No, I've got to get out now. I can't stay here a minute longer. I'm fine to drive.'

'Okay, you know I don't want you to go, but if it makes you feel better then do it. Let me know where you've gone and I'll join you as soon as I can.' He enveloped her in his arms, giving her strength, holding her tight.

She sniffed and threw more underwear in her bag. 'Maybe I'll just need a night or two away from here and then I'll feel better.' She didn't want to punish Dan. He was trying hard to understand and to help. But it wasn't his body that was expelling the fruits of their lovemaking, it was hers. 'Don't worry, I'll book a room at the pub in Rye. My mother would only make me feel worse if I went there and she'd ask too many questions.'

'Good idea. Have a quiet night and then I'll come down as soon as you feel ready. But if you want to be left alone for longer, I'd quite understand.'

'Thank you. I think I'll be fine once I'm out of here. I just need to shake this feeling about the house out of my head and I can't do it by staying here a minute longer.'

'Go then. Drive carefully and let me know when you're there.'

. . .

Charlie called the pub and luckily bagged a room, then made herself a flask of coffee and set off. As soon as she was in the car with the engine running, she felt better. It was silly, she told herself. How could a house of bricks and mortar possibly affect her body? Maybe it was just the stress of working hard and renovating at the same time. Maybe, once it was all finished and the house was peaceful, she wouldn't have such thoughts and all would be well.

But as she turned the car round to head south she caught sight of the front of the house in her overhead mirror. Tall and dark, so full of secrets, it looked forbidding, and the windows facing the church, the school and the open common seemed to be searching for something. And yet again, she couldn't help wondering about its past and what else it could be hiding.

FORTY-FIVE

THEN

SEPTEMBER 1944

Little Alan solemnly shook Frankie's hand as he stood in the open doorway. His three brothers and the Beaumont sisters were all waiting outside on the pavement. The hugs and kisses at their departure gave Frankie a lump in her throat. He and his siblings were all tagged with luggage labels like animated parcels. 'In case they wander off,' Dolly had said. 'You never know with this lot, however hard I try.'

She stood by her son's side, waiting patiently as he said his farewell. Her lips were tightly clenched to conceal her emotions and Frankie knew she was doing her best not to break down in tears in front of her boys.

'We're going to see lots of cows and sheep in the country,' Alan said. 'And I'm going to do lots of drawings and paintings. Elspeth said she'll help me and show me how to use her paints.'

'You're very talented. I'm sure you're going to have a lovely time there.' Frankie blinked away her tears. She didn't want to let this little boy see she was upset. But despite her delight that she would soon have the house free for her and Edwin, she couldn't help feeling sad that she might never see the two families again. It had been a shock at first, realising she'd have to share her large house with homeless strangers, but she'd enjoyed the company more than she could have ever expected.

'Try and write to me,' she said. 'Do a drawing for me as well. And tell your brothers to write too. I hope you will all be very happy together.'

He ran down the front steps and out through the flimsy wooden and wire gate. Dolly followed and everyone waved goodbye. Then they all picked up their bags and began trudging to the bus stop to begin their long journey to Wiltshire. Frankie knew they'd made the right decision, with the silent stealthy bombs hitting south London so frequently, but she knew she'd miss them all the same. The house would be deadly quiet without the boys tumbling down the stairs and the constant piano playing.

She watched the group disappear round the corner of the road, then began to make plans for seeing Edwin. She couldn't contact him, but decided that, as soon as he phoned the house, she'd tell him exactly where and when to find her. If he arrived when she was on duty at the station, he'd find a door key under the third plant pot to the left of the steps to the back door.

When he called, he wasn't able to confirm exactly when he'd be available or even if he could join her that night. 'It's a little crazy here,' he said. 'I wish there was some way I could reach you during the day.'

'If your plans change and you become free, you could phone the ambulance station and leave a message.'

'With that old witch who always gives you a hard time?'

She thought for a moment. 'Well, yes, it probably would be her answering the phone. Say you're calling to confirm a delivery of peaches at whatever time you think you might arrive!'

That made him laugh. She cycled off to her duties that day in a state of heightened excitement. She didn't know for sure if she'd see him that night when her shift was over, but she kept imagining how she might return home to find him settled in her kitchen or even in her bed.

When she reached the ambulance station, everyone seemed to be hurrying around. Some were starting their vehicles, others were ferrying extra blankets outside. 'What's happened now?' She tried to get details from a driver dashing to start his van.

'Putney station or near it. Took a hit. Loads of casualties.'

She ran inside to check in with Mrs Ogilvy. 'Bertie won't be here till she's finished teaching later this afternoon. I can go out on call if someone is free to come with me.'

Mrs Ogilvy pursed her lips and looked at her chart. 'You can take Jim then. He's not doing anything useful at present. He might as well go with you. At least he always follows correct procedure.'

Frankie rolled her eyes at this barely veiled comment on her behaviour. Mrs Ogilvy never missed an opportunity to let her know she didn't approve of her or Bertie. She slipped through to the staffroom, where Jim was leaning back in his chair. His eyes were closed but his lips were clenched around the stem of his pipe.

It made her smile to see him so relaxed, but she shook his shoulder and he jerked up in his chair, dropping his pipe in his lap. 'Can't a man have forty winks?' He brushed his regulation gaberdine trousers free of the hot ash.

'We're on, Jim, you and me. Come on, let's go. I'll race you to the van.'

He grumbled, but he was smiling as he pulled on his jacket and followed her outside. They were the last vehicle left in the yard. 'Where are we off to?'

'Putney station, or nearby. I'm not sure exactly where it's been hit. I'm guessing we'll find out more when we get there.' She frowned and shook her head. 'I'm trying not to think about my lodgers. They left me this morning and I'm sure they said

they were taking the bus all the way into central London. I hope
so anyway.'

'You can't go worrying till you know,' Jim said wisely,
puffing on his pipe again. 'Concentrate on your driving.'

She tried to focus on the road ahead and what they might
find when they reached the station. Elspeth had said they
would all catch a train from Waterloo, hadn't she, and that the
easiest way to go was to take the bus all the way? But what if a
Putney bus had arrived first and they'd all decided to go that
way instead?

Frankie knew it was silly, but she couldn't help herself
thinking about those little boys and elderly ladies laden down
with their luggage.

'Watch it,' Jim shouted suddenly. 'You nearly ran into that
bollard. Do you want me to take over?'

She took a deep breath. 'Sorry, Jim. My mind was
elsewhere.'

'Well, don't let it wander any more. We've got one job to do
and that's all. You can worry about your friends later. Chances
are they're sitting in a Lyons Corner House having tea and
beans on toast.'

He was right, of course, and as she drew closer to the
disaster area, her mind switched into ambulance mode and she
concentrated on what she could do to help. As usual, the road
was littered with shattered glass and debris, and other vehicles
still burning from the blast. Wardens were already assisting the
walking wounded and some bodies were laid out on the pavement. Frankie and Jim immediately went to work, lifting the
worst cases onto stretchers and into the van.

Soon they had a full load and a warden banged on the
bonnet of the van, saying, 'You can go now. Thanks for your
help.' He and the other volunteers had already started the grisly
job of clearing body parts into sacks and another ambulance had
picked up several complete bodies.

'Well, that wasn't as bad as some,' Jim said, taking his pipe out of his pocket and relighting it. 'Given the size of the bomb, it could have been a darn sight worse.'

'With a bit of luck we'll be back at the station quite early, once we've dropped these people at Hammersmith Hospital,' Frankie said. 'Do you think Mrs Ogilvy will have made some scones for us?'

'Fingers crossed she will. That seat by the fire is calling me.' Jim winked at her. 'You might want to stay tonight and play a few games of cards, rather than go back to your empty house.'

'I might be tempted,' Frankie said, but she was thinking, the house might not be as empty as you'd think. There might be someone special waiting there for me.

FORTY-SIX

THEN

SEPTEMBER 1944

Once Jim and Frankie had cleaned their van and were ready to relax in the station's staffroom, Mrs Ogilvy was waiting for them. She hadn't made scones, but there was some cold toast on the table, along with clean cups awaiting tea.

'You've had a phone call in your absence, Mrs Wilson,' she said with a stern look. 'I'm not here to act as your social secretary, you know.'

Frankie tried not to feel provoked. 'Oh really? Was there a message?'

'No peaches till Friday. I assume that means something to you. He sounded American, too.'

'Thank you. I was expecting that.' She picked up a piece of cold toast. As she did so, Bertie came down the stairs from changing out of her day clothes into her uniform. She caught Frankie's eye and winked.

'Well, don't make a habit of it.' Mrs Ogilvy turned away in a huff, leaving Frankie thinking she was going to have three lonely evenings on her own. It was only Tuesday.

'What was all that about?' Bertie cast a scornful eye over the toast.

'Oh, you know, nothing really.' She still hadn't let her friend know quite how much she was seeing of Edwin. 'But if we're free tonight, we could go dancing. Do you fancy it?'

'Absolutely. If you've got the energy. After all, you've been out once already. All I've been doing is drumming times tables and spelling into eight- and ten-year-olds. And we may yet get another call-out.'

Frankie grabbed a cup of tea and flopped into a chair. 'I could do with some fun. My lodgers left today and the house is going to seem dreadfully quiet.'

Bertie looked up from stirring her tea. 'Where were they going?'

'Somewhere in Wiltshire. They were all aiming to get on the same train at Waterloo if they could.'

'Let's hope they didn't get caught up in the chaos there this afternoon,' Alf piped up. He'd been dozing in the other comfy chair near the stove. 'A big one dropped in Waterloo Road. Not our call-out, but loads attended and picked up there.'

Frankie clutched the edge of the table. Surely not? They must all be safe. By now they might even be unpacking their bags in their new accommodation. But how could she find out? She knew she would not be able to rest until she knew more, but she didn't have a phone number for their destination. She couldn't even remember the address written on the luggage labels tied to the boys' coats.

'You're white as anything,' Bertie said. 'What's the matter?'

'My lodgers... those dear little boys... all of them. I've simply got to find out if they're all right.' She stood up and started walking towards the door.

'I'm coming with you,' Bertie shouted.

'You can't just walk out on your shift.' Mrs Ogilvy emerged from the kitchen with another large pot of tea.

'This is an emergency,' Bertie said. 'A matter of life and death.'

'There'll be an information point at the scene,' Jim said, patting Bertie's shoulder. 'Red Cross or WVS will help you. Tell you where the casualties have been taken. Good luck, girls, let's hope there's good news.'

Bertie ran out after Frankie, who was already getting onto her bike. 'Where are we going? Putney station will still be in a mess. We'd better leave the bikes here and get the first bus into town.'

'That'll take for ever,' Frankie said. 'I have to know what's happened as soon as possible.'

'I know. We'll get a bus to Hammersmith, then take the Underground. With luck that will get us there quickly.'

All the way to Waterloo, Frankie kept telling herself that her lodgers must have reached their destination in Wiltshire safely and that she was worrying unnecessarily. 'They're probably having a slap-up high tea with Elspeth's cousins right now, boiled ham with lettuce from the garden.'

'Of course they are,' Bertie said. 'If it's anything like my uncle's farm they'll be feasting on newly laid eggs, freshly churned butter and crusty home-baked bread. They'll be having a whale of a time. And in the meantime all we've had is that bit of cold toast at the station.'

'I do hope they've got there safely. Sorry I'm being such a ninny about all this.'

'Don't be daft. You won't sleep a wink till you know for sure.'

When they finally reached Waterloo, the station seemed to be heaving more than usual. Tannoy announcements blasted the air and waiting trains were vibrating and steaming in readiness. An exit was cordoned off, leading presumably to the area that had been hit. Lines of servicemen were filing on to platforms for trains soon to depart for the coast or maybe training on Salisbury Plain. Wardens with tin hats were stationed at every exit and by every platform.

Frankie rushed up to one of them and said, 'My family was meant to catch a train to Tidworth today, but I'm terribly worried that they might have been caught by the bomb. How can I find out?'

He took his tin hat off and scratched his head. 'All the trains today have been delayed by that incident and some have been cancelled altogether. The station office will know if their train left or not, but if they were casualties then you'd best check with that Red Cross first aid post over there.' He pointed to a temporary booth on the far side of the concourse, then replaced his hat. 'They'll know if anyone was taken to hospital.'

'I'll find out about the trains,' Bertie said. 'You go and ask about casualties.'

Frankie ran to the makeshift office, which turned out not to be run by the Red Cross, but by an efficient woman in her beetroot-red and green WVS uniform. 'How can I help you?'

'I'm trying to find out if members of my family were injured here today. Their names are Jones and Beaumont.' She couldn't help herself saying 'family', even though they weren't really, because they'd become like close family members to her during their time in the house.

'Hmm, Jones is a common name, so that might be hard to check. I seem to remember Beaumont though.' She ran her finger down sheets of handwritten records. 'Yes, quite a few Joneses were taken to hospital, but a Beaumont was taken to the other first aid post round the corner. It might be best to check there first.'

As Frankie turned to leave, Bertie came running across to her. 'A train left after the explosion, so they might well have been on it.'

'I hope so, but someone with the name of Beaumont was taken to first aid. That's such an uncommon name it must be one of them. Maybe the rest got away and only one of the sisters was injured. Let's go and find out.'

At the Red Cross post, a line of exhausted people were waiting on chairs, their faces smudged with soot, their clothes covered in dust. As Frankie was looking to see if she recognised anyone, a door opened and out came Elspeth, holding Alan's hand. He had his arm in a sling and she bore a plaster on her forehead.

Frankie rushed up to her. 'I'm so glad you're all in one piece. But the others... did they manage to get the train?'

'What a surprise, dear. You shouldn't have come all this way.' Elspeth frowned. 'The others?'

'Dolly and the boys, and your sisters? Are they all right? Did they catch the train?'

Elspeth bit her lip, then looked directly at Frankie. Her pale blue eyes were watery but they weren't tears. 'Oh, my dear, what can I say? We should never have left you this morning.'

'You mean they didn't get on the train?'

'We weren't even near the platform. We were all outside. I'd told them all to wait while I went to the ticket office. I was on my way back to them when it happened. It was all so very sudden. I'm so sorry. I should have stayed with them.'

'But you couldn't have known what was going to happen. Do you mean they were all killed?'

Elspeth tried to nod, but it was obviously painful for her and she closed her eyes. 'All gone. But at least they were all together. Dolly always said they all had to stay together. All gone in an instant.' She looked down at the child whose hand she still held. 'Alan was with me because he'd lost his coloured pencils and I said we'd see if we could get some in WH Smith. That was a stroke of luck, wasn't it? He says he still wants to go to the country to see the cows and sheep. Such a dear little boy.'

Frankie felt the lump in her throat growing harder and threatening to burst open, but she couldn't distress Elspeth further. 'But the others are all gone?'

'We should have stayed together.' She shook her head sadly. 'Now it's just me and Alan.'

'I'm so sorry,' Frankie said. 'Why don't you come back and stay with me, if you want to that is?'

'Thank you, dear, but I'll still go to my cousin's. I'd like to see the cows and sheep for myself and think of those dear boys. We'll get a train as soon as we can. Luckily we had our bags with us, and Alan has his pencils now.'

'If you're sure, but if you change your mind you know you'll be more than welcome.' Frankie said goodbye and left the first aid post, Bertie by her side, arm around her shoulders. She couldn't halt the tears now. Her family, the only family she might ever have, had nearly all been eradicated in an instant. She couldn't imagine having children with Dickie if he survived and she didn't yet know if she had a future with Edwin. The house might never again echo to the sounds of children.

Gazing out across the empty marshes in the cold morning light, Charlie felt light and free. She could breathe again. Streams carved through the low grassland, meandering towards the sea, reflecting the watery light of the sun.

She was still bleeding a little, but she was not in pain, and the change of scene made her feel she was no longer burdened with a huge responsibility; she no longer had to force herself to succeed with a pregnancy. Seagulls wheeled overhead, their cries drifting away with the wind, and she imagined she was now free like them, free to enjoy the fresh air and the weak winter sunshine.

Why can't I feel like this in the house, she asked herself. Why do I always feel so anxious there? Is it because we bought the house with the sole intention of making it a family home, filling it with children? It was right to get away from there, to free myself of feeling it was my fault that my body couldn't hold on to four babies.

Knowing that the day would be even shorter than when she and Dan had last come here, she didn't want to walk far. Retracing her steps from the beach would be treacherous once the light had gone, so she wandered for a while alongside the glistening waterways and then went back through the little town with its cobbled alleys. Diamond-paned windows were filled with fairy lights and decorations. There were only two weeks left till Christmas and she hadn't even thought about buying presents, sending cards or making the house ready.

Looking at the berried wreaths of holly on cottage doorways, she remembered how she had wanted to do that this year for her first Christmas with Dan in their forever house. They'd both been so excited, talking about how it would be simple but perfect. Just the two of them in the house they'd longed for and searched for over the past two years.

I'm not being fair to him, she told herself. It's not his fault that I feel so terrible and reacted badly to this miscarriage. I can't deprive him of our very first Christmas in the house we both really wanted. We had searched for so long, he'd be heartbroken.

And I'm sure he's sad too. I know he'd love us to have a baby and then maybe more after that. If I wallow in my own misery, I'm punishing him as well as myself. I know he hasn't had to deal with the physical pain or the shock of seeing the product of a miscarriage, but he's still hurting from the loss just as much as I am. I should tell him to join me and then we could go back together to help each other heal.

Charlie took a deep breath. She felt better now she'd resolved in her mind how she could go forward. She took out her phone and texted Dan: *Please come here. Love to see you.*

And he did indeed drive over that very night, as soon as he'd finished for the day. 'I've missed you so much,' he said, wrapping his arms around her tight and kissing her hair.

'I've only been away one night, silly. But I've missed you as well. And I'm sorry for running away. We have to face this together.' His smell of sawdust and sweat was so comforting.

He sighed. 'But if you honestly feel this house isn't right for you and is affecting your health, I really couldn't force you to stay there. We could rent it out or sell it once all the work is finished. I can't bear to see you being unhappy.'

She clutched his arm. 'But that's not what you want. Besides, we searched for so long for the perfect house. Forget what I said before. It was just me overreacting to what had just happened. I was upset but it's passed. I know it's the forever house we both wanted and we'll stay there and love it.'

He kissed her. 'I'd like us to stay. We can make it into a wonderful home and we'll enjoy it, whatever happens.'

'Then stay here with me tonight and I'll drive back tomorrow. Christmas is only two weeks away. I want to fill the house with Christmas spirit.'

'No tinsel, mind,' he said, laughing.

'As if I would. No tinsel, but lots of greenery from the ivy and the holly in the garden. It needs cutting back, anyway. And lots of candlelight.'

That night in the oak-beamed bedroom in the old pub, Dan held her. He didn't try to make love to her, he just showed her how much he loved her by holding her close in the deep double bed. The room was very dark as there were few street lights in the little town. The curtains were slightly parted and Charlie could see the darkest sky, pinpointed with a few bright stars. She felt safe and knew that, whatever happened, he loved her and they would face the future together.

When they parted in the morning, Dan said, 'You don't have to come home right away. Stay another day or so if you think it will help.'

'No, I'm ready to come back. I won't be far behind you.'

Home, she thought, as she packed her bag. Of course it was home. And filling it with love was the way to make it feel like it really was their forever home. She couldn't punish him any further by staying away. She had to go back and face her demons, if there were any.

When she pulled up outside the house later that afternoon, the sun was beginning to set behind the trees on the common. A fiery red winter sky burned behind the black network of branches and the church steeple was cast in a glow of light reflected on the house. And she couldn't help but smile at the sight of the twinkling fairy lights that had been strung throughout the ivy that climbed the walls, welcoming her home. All the windows were lit, glowing with a warmth that made her feel she was right to come back and that the house wanted her here.

She knew she was smiling still as she unlocked the door and entered the hall. It was quieter than usual. Dan must have let the workmen leave early. Suddenly he was there, holding a basket in his arms. 'Welcome back,' he said.

'Where is everyone?'

'I thought it would be nice for us to have time to ourselves with no interruptions.' He was still holding the basket, covered with a blanket.

Why didn't he put it down, so he could hug her? She approached him with open arms and he pushed the basket into her hands. As he did so, the blanket moved and a black nose peeped out. She peeled back the cloth to find a golden-haired puppy looking at her with melting brown eyes.

Her first thought was confusion; that Dan could think her grief at losing a baby could be appeased by a puppy. But her second was, oh my darling, I love you. She knelt down, put the basket on the floor, and stroked the silky ears and rubbed the curled fur of its tummy.

'You don't mind, do you?' Dan's voice had a pleading edge to it. 'I know we always said we'd choose a dog together, but I heard there were puppies available. I was going to wait till Christmas, but then I thought why not have something special right away? Something to cheer us both up?'

She continued stroking, then picked up the warm, furry body, receiving wet kisses in return. 'Does it have a name? And what is it?'

'He's a miniature wire-haired dachshund. Apparently, they're very easy to train, and I've got all the puppy gear here so we won't have any messy accidents. But I thought I should let you choose a name.'

'He's adorable. Such a dear little thing.' She looked into the puppy's eager eyes, knowing she could love him whatever happened next and that he would love her.

'What were the names of Santa's reindeer?' She frowned, trying to remember.

'Oh, I don't know. Donner and Blitzen... I can't think of the rest. Wasn't there a Rudolph?'

'Hmm, that's not quite right. Oh, I know, he's Rufus. That suits him. Doesn't it, Rufus?' And she hugged the puppy tight.

The house felt strangely quiet and empty without the genteel but eccentric elderly sisters and the boisterous Jones family. No more racing down the stairs and the banisters, no more disappearing silver. Frankie often thought of their time with her with fondness, but with great sadness too that their attempt to escape to safety in the countryside had ended in such dreadful disaster. Elspeth had written once on her arrival at her cousin's home, but her note had made Frankie cry for her loss all the more.

She also missed the convenience of Dolly's home cooking that had filled the kitchen with delicious smells as well as filling their stomachs. She missed the gentle storytelling too, as Daphne had moved on to reading *Little Women*, which, despite being about girls, had been enjoyed enormously by the boys.

But she didn't miss the piano playing. Not only had Cecily been teaching little Alan to play, but she had often sat for several hours at a time, repetitively picking out the notes of 'Moonlight Sonata', over and over, until Elspeth would send her up to her room.

Frankie had once asked why she chose to play this particular piece obsessively and Elspeth had said, 'Oh, it's because of

Ralph, her fiancé. He couldn't have a funeral, you know, being one of the missing. So, she insisted on playing music she would have chosen for him. Quite honestly, I think that's what drove Mother to her grave.'

Frankie had thought about how she couldn't associate Dickie with any particular piece of music, although she had been surprised when he and Hugo had been to see *Anything Goes* without her and he'd hummed the title tune continuously for weeks afterwards. Anything goes all right, she thought, reflecting on Dickie's friendship with Hugo. She and Edwin enjoyed the vibrant sounds of big bands that made them long to hit the dancefloor. But in response to Elspeth's remark about her sister, she had simply said, 'That's so sad. Does she only play it when she's thinking of him?'

'Possibly. But think yourself fortunate, my dear. Her other obsession was "The Lost Chord"; it was most tiresome hearing that non-stop. She used to play it for Ralph to sing.' She sighed, shaking her head. 'That young man had a fine voice. Such a waste.'

And now there was no piano and no rumbustious games, but as often as possible there was Edwin. When he arrived at the end of the week after the Waterloo disaster, Frankie was still in shock from the loss of her lodgers. Her first words to him were, 'You didn't really have to bring peaches,' as he handed her a large tin.

'I thought that was your main reason for wanting to see me,' he said as he stood in the hallway, gazing at the curved stair rail and the lofty lamp fitting with its four marbled glass shades. 'All this is yours? And you won't have to take in any more lodgers?'

She burst into tears as she told him what had happened. 'It's so unfair,' she sobbed. 'It was such fun having them all here and those little boys didn't deserve to die.'

'No one deserves a German bomb,' he said. 'But the Germans sure deserve what's coming to them.'

'I didn't realise I'd miss them so much.' She sniffed and tried to smile. 'I don't know yet if I'll be asked to accommodate some more unfortunates so we'd better make the most of it while we've got it all to ourselves.' Her lodgers' rooms were cleaned and emptied and she'd also hidden all traces of Dickie.

Edwin couldn't be with her every night, so she and Bertie could still go dancing sometimes. An energetic jive banished the dark thoughts of what might happen to him, just as the piano had helped Cecily in her grief. But she found it hard to tell Bertie just how close they had become and didn't tell her he often spent the night with her.

'I was planning to set up as an architect when the war started,' he said. 'I'd qualified and had some time in a practice in Boston. But maybe when this is all over, I could try my hand in Britain. I certainly find your country more inspiring and it's sure going to need a lot of help rebuilding.'

'That would be wonderful. There's so much to see here. I don't suppose you've yet had a chance to visit all our cathedrals and grand country houses?'

'I've barely started, but I'd love to tour around when I get more free time. I want to work my way right through that guy's guide to British architecture – what's his name? Pevsner? But right now, time's limited and we're all standing by for whatever comes next.'

'I hope they have nothing sneakier up their sleeves than what we're getting right now. These silent bombs are so terrifying.' Frankie remembered the awful chaos earlier in the summer when the Guards' Chapel at Wellington Barracks was hit in the midst of a service. Maybe it was considered a legitimate military target, but all the same 121 serving men and their families were killed that day.

'Well, I guess that's part of their strategy, trying to spook the public and destroy the Blitz spirit. But you Brits are so damn stubborn, you just won't give up.'

'Too right we won't. We'll fight to the end.' She saw that Edwin was frowning and added, 'Don't you think we should?'

'This is a dirty war, honey. The Nazis brook no opposition. That's how they came to power in the first place. And I won't go into details, but they've played a pretty nasty hand wherever they've been. We're gonna to hear some shocking stories at the end of all this, I can tell you.'

'Well, if they do invade, Bertie and I reckon we could find a few ways to annoy them. And we're not the only ones who will want to make their lives difficult.'

He frowned and shook his head. 'I wouldn't recommend it. Whole villages in France and Poland have been wiped out, just because they helped Allied soldiers or harboured partisans. The Nazis are capable of anything and are totally without mercy.'

He looked so serious all of a sudden that Frankie's delight in having him here in the house was shaken. But she was determined to lighten the mood. 'Well, they're not here yet and maybe they never will be, so let's light a fire in the bedroom and take our supper in there. I hope you managed to slip some goodies for tonight into your pockets?'

From his deep greatcoat pockets Edwin produced more tins, of Spam, butter, chocolate and cigarettes. 'This is all I could get. Will it help?'

'Wonderful. Dolly used to do a clever thing with the Spam. Fritters, she called them. They're delicious with a fried egg and we've still got a couple of hens, so I'm not short of eggs.'

Later, upstairs, cross-legged on the rug by the fire in her room, they ate their supper and drank the bourbon Edwin had also brought. 'I love the idea of you being an architect here in Britain,' Frankie said. 'Do you really think it would be a possibility?'

'I don't see why not. This country's going to need more reconstruction than the US for a start, so I dare say there'd be a demand for architects. I'd just need somewhere to use as an office for calls and to prepare plans. It wouldn't have to be large. Somewhere cheap to begin with.'

'You could set up here, in the house. There's loads of room here. I know it's not right in the middle of London, but it's not far to stations and there are buses as well.'

'Right here? You mean it?' He looked reflective, as if he was imagining where he would organise his work space.

'Honestly, any of the rooms could be adapted. I mean, I know they've mostly been bedrooms during the time I had everyone here, but they can be changed.'

He held both her hands, raised them to his lips and kissed them. 'It sounds wonderful. I'd be very happy here. But what if we needed more rooms in the future?'

'What do you mean? For an expanding business?'

'No, for children. We might fill the house with children one day. Would you like that?'

Frankie briefly recalled the boys racing around the house and sliding down the banisters. She'd loved the sound of their laughter and the house was certainly very quiet without them.

'You mean, our children?'

'Yes, ours. If you'd marry me, that is.' He smiled, his twinkly blue eyes amused at her confusion.

Frankie stared at him. He really meant it. And she wanted to accept. She was sure she was a widow, wasn't she? Even though she'd never told Edwin she'd briefly had a husband, she felt sure Dickie was dead. And she'd hidden all evidence of him, the wedding photos, the clothes, so he could never have suspected. 'Yes,' she said. 'Yes, I'd love to marry you. And have your children.'

'That settles it then. We'll set up shop right here.'

He opened his arms and embraced her and, as she melted against his broad shoulders, she wondered if her lack of honesty would come back to haunt her.

FORTY-NINE

THEN

SEPTEMBER 1944

It seemed particularly cruel of the Germans to send their latest wave of bombs during daylight hours. Instead of cowering in bunkers during the hours of darkness, like frightened rabbits in their burrows, ordinary civilians were bombed while trying to maintain a semblance of normal life. Children could be walking to school, housewives queuing with ration books to feed their families, businesses trying to survive. But no one was safe from these new swift and silent bombs that appeared suddenly with such devastating effect.

Frankie's shift hours changed to meet the new demand. No longer were people hiding in basements, they were going about their normal business, just with an eye on the sky at all times. Bombs fell indiscriminately and didn't even appear to have important targets in their sights. The objective was to instil fear in the population no matter how bright the day might seem.

'They don't seem to care where the bombs land,' Bertie said as they drove to Chiswick very early one morning. Another of those deadly monsters had hit a quiet residential area just as families were getting dressed and preparing for their day. Only three were reported dead, but many had been injured and, from experience, the girls knew they would mostly be helping desperately distressed children and mothers.

'It's mean and cowardly,' Frankie said, speeding along the road. Daytime driving was far easier than the many forays she'd had to make with dimmed lights in the nightly blackout, unable to see how much shattered glass littered the roads. 'They must know they're catching civilians out, not giving them any chance to take shelter. At least before, when it was planes with pilots, it was still awful, but it was a decent fight. This is just underhand and nasty.'

'Well, that's what they are. Nasty Nazis. I don't think they even care where these bombs are falling. They're doing it just to scare us into giving up. But it won't work.' Bertie emphasised her words with a thump of her fist on the dashboard.

'Course it won't. We're not scared, are we?'

'Never. Not while we're together, like the Three Musketeers!'

'And who's the third one?' Frankie couldn't help laughing at her friend, who always managed to make her see the ridiculous side of their situation, no matter how grim it might be. It was far better that they both arrived at their destination with disaster in a positive mood than fretting for the whole journey about what life-changing injuries they might find there. Edwin's face had been so serious the other night when he talked about the Nazi mentality, she was sure he knew far more than he was telling her. But Bertie's sense of fun stopped her worrying about the horrors they were facing and what might yet happen.

'It must be over here,' Bertie said, pointing down a street where they could see a fire engine spraying water. Smoke was curling between the houses and wardens were already helping to clear debris from the road. As they drove closer, they could see women comforting children, an old man slumped on a doorstep with his head in his hands and a woman rocking a baby, her head bright with blood.

'Let's stop here,' Frankie said. 'The bomb must have damaged the gas and water mains. I can smell it already.' She parked the ambulance and they both jumped out, pulling on their wellington boots because of the water and shattered glass all around them.

They picked up their first stretcher and approached one of the wardens. 'Point us to the worst ones,' Bertie said and he waved to a group on the opposite side of the road, where a couple of women with children were sitting huddled in blankets.

'The kiddies only went back to school last week,' one of the mothers said tearfully, hugging an unconscious child with a terrible head wound. 'I should've sent him away to the countryside again, I knew it.'

'Don't go blaming yourself, Doreen,' her neighbour said, comforting her daughter with a bloodied leg, all the while ignoring her own broken arm. 'You know we've all been saying we go together. It's the Jerries you've got to blame.'

The girls helped mothers and children walk to the ambulance, then returned to lift a heavily pregnant woman on to the stretcher. 'I can't feel my baby any more,' she said, hands wrapped around her protruding stomach. 'It doesn't feel right. The blast knocked me right down the stairs.'

'Let's wait and see,' Bertie said in a soothing voice. 'Baby's probably shocked like the rest of you. Wants to hide away until we're somewhere safe.'

They slid the stretcher into the vehicle, but Frankie couldn't help noticing the blood trickling down the woman's legs. It could be a wound from the blast but it could well be worse. She knew from experience that sometimes the aftershock of a bomb did enormous damage, and looking around her, she could see that this particular bomb had wreaked havoc this early morning. It had plunged to earth, forming a huge crater in the middle of a row of neat suburban houses, all waking up to a sunny

September morning, where children were being dressed and eating porridge before school. Who would have thought that this far from the centre of London, nowhere near the hub of government, it would be worth exploding a bomb that had left three people killed outright and twenty-two badly injured?

'I think we need to get going,' Bertie said, in a quiet voice so as not to alarm their passengers. 'Some of this lot need help quickly.'

Frankie glanced in the back of the van. The boy with concussion looked grey, his lips purple, and the expectant mother was white and clammy. They had to hurry. 'The West Middlesex is the nearest,' she said. 'With luck, they won't have been as overworked as Hammersmith.'

Every time the girls collected victims, they had to judge which hospital would have room and which was closest. It could make all the difference between life and death. 'The ones we've left behind will be all right for a bit,' Bertie said. 'There might even be another ambulance coming out for them soon.'

Frankie drove as fast as she could. The roads leading away from the damaged site were clear of shattered debris and broken glass. It wasn't as bad as the many times she'd driven during the Blitz when she couldn't tell whether she was driving straight into a sea of shards that would burst her tyres.

'I've been thinking,' Bertie said. 'We've been jolly lucky, in all the time we've been doing this job, not to have been badly injured ourselves. Apart from the time you got that nasty bump on the head, we've got off lightly so far.'

'Don't speak too soon. Plenty of other drivers and wardens and fire crew have come croppers attending incidents. We must never forget how dangerous these sites are. They're so unstable – and quite apart from that, who's to say there isn't a V-2 with our names on it? Just because we're not going to the East End or the Houses of Parliament doesn't mean to say we might not be targets.'

'Oh, I don't think any of Hitler's bombs have got my name on them. I think we're going to come through all of this without a scratch, mark my words.'

Frankie wasn't so sure as they headed west towards the hospital in the early autumn morning sun. Her conversations with Edwin about a shared future made her hopeful, but he had hinted that things were going to get worse before they got better and she was apprehensive.

FIFTY

THEN

NOVEMBER 1944

It had been an exhausting week for the girls. The deadly silent V-2 bombs seemed to be falling every day, creating utter chaos. At first, the government blamed the explosions on ruptured gas mains, but no one really believed that.

'They're telling porkies,' Jim said when the crew were gathered together, sipping hot, weak tea. 'Everyone knows it's the Jerries and their wretched bombs.'

Alf joined in with further evidence. 'My mate over in Chiswick, he says they found long metal shards after that explosion. It's a German bomb every time. Gas mains, my foot. Pull the other one.'

No one knew exactly where they were coming from, or where they would land, but the girls were being kept busy with the consequences. One Saturday in November they got a call to head for New Cross in south-east London, which was much further away than their usual destinations.

'Apparently there are dozens of casualties,' Mrs Ogilvy said. 'Ambulances are being called out from all over the south. Here, take this flask of tea with you and these beetroot sandwiches. You might be out quite some time.'

'She's not such an ogre after all, is she?' Bertie said as they headed out to the van. 'Mind you, I don't really like beetroot sandwiches.'

'Better than nothing,' Frankie said. 'Pity really. I could have brought some Spam. That would have perked you up, I'm sure.'

'Oh don't! My mother thinks it's wonderful. Keeps giving me Spam for tea. I'm sick of it.'

Frankie thought she might be sick of it soon too, as Edwin seemed to bring her a tin every time he visited. She now had a small stockpile in the pantry, but as she had little time to shop and now Dolly was no longer there, rustling up hearty meals from their rations every day, she was glad there was always something she could eat when she finally got home.

'It's one of the things Edwin quite often brings me. Peaches as well sometimes, but mostly Spam.'

'Well, you can jolly well keep it.' Bertie was quiet for a moment, thinking. 'You're still seeing him then?'

'When he's free, which isn't often. Have you seen your American? What was his name?'

'Jayson. Not recently I haven't.' She gave her friend a side-long glance. 'No news from France then?'

Frankie knew what she was implying and shrugged. 'It doesn't seem likely after all this time, does it? I've got quite used to the idea that Dickie bought it early on.'

'You'll get over it. Especially with the help of your American chap.'

Frankie tried not to react, changing the subject. 'I reckon they're gearing up for a big push soon. Edwin has hinted as much. But he's also warned me against being uncooperative with the Germans if we do get invaded.'

'What? You'll just do as they say? I'm not going to do that. I'm looking forward to sticking potatoes in their exhaust pipes and sugar in their fuel tanks.' Bertie laughed and clapped her hands with glee. 'Just watch me.'

'No, he said it would be highly dangerous. They're dreadfully vindictive. Anyway, do you really want to give up your sugar ration just to annoy the Germans?'

Bertie was quiet for a moment. 'Maybe not. But I reckon I could spare a potato.' She looked out of the window. 'I think we're nearly there, aren't we?' She pointed ahead to the smoke rising above the buildings that were still standing. 'Mum wants me to check on Auntie Mavis while I'm here. She lives in New Cross. I hope she's okay.'

The centre of the town was milling with crowds of rescue workers and vehicles. Frankie found a place to stop and the girls kitted themselves out with their usual boots and overalls. The streets were ankle-deep in broken glass and many bloodstained wounded were lying on the pavements. On each side of the road, cars had been overturned by the force of the explosion and were still burning like charred metal skeletons. The air smelt like Bonfire Night, all smoky and dusty, but without the sparklers and with an undercurrent of menace from fractured gas mains.

'Bloody Germans,' a harassed warden said as the girls approached, pointing to the gigantic crater further along the road. 'Woolies got a direct hit. Packed out with shoppers, it was, being a Saturday.'

'How many casualties do you think there are?' Frankie was trying to take in the scale of the disaster. The bargains at the counters of Woolworths always attracted huge numbers of shoppers and, on a Saturday morning, the store would have been crowded. And with many husbands and young men away on active service, the victims were nearly all women and children. Shops and offices nearest to the main crater had been reduced to rubble and further down the street every window had been shattered by the blast, scattering splinters of glass all across the road.

'There must be over a hundred or more injured, I'd say.' He

wiped the grime from his face with a grubby handkerchief. 'And even more dead. Killed outright, they were. Just because they were out shopping on a Saturday morning, doing nobody any harm.'

'Come on,' Bertie said. 'We'd better get started. There's so many in need of our help.'

'New Cross Hospital is overwhelmed,' the man said. 'Better get them to Lewisham or, better still, back over the river.'

The girls began helping the injured board the ambulance. 'My mummy always lets me buy sweeties on a Saturday,' said a tearful little girl clinging to her dead mother and younger sister. 'We don't usually come to Woolies, but Mummy said we'd come here for a change instead of the corner shop.'

What a change that turned out to be, Frankie thought, helping the child stand up. Her head had a gaping wound and she looked as if she'd broken her arm. 'Let me get you into my ambulance,' she said. 'And I'll see if I can find a sweetie for you in a minute.' She usually had some barley sugars in the glove compartment. Anything, she told herself, anything at all to take the poor child's mind off the dead bodies around her.

Frankie decided to take their first consignment of badly wounded and shocked casualties to Charing Cross. Although it was further away, she reasoned it would be better able to accommodate those most in need. On their return journey back to the bombed high street, Bertie said, 'I mustn't forget to check on Auntie Mavis. Mum would never forgive me if I didn't report back.'

'I hope she's not anywhere near all this chaos.'

'She's a couple of streets away. But I'll be as quick as I can.'

Reluctantly, Frankie let her go. Being separated wouldn't meet with Mrs Ogilvy's approval, but she could understand Bertie's concern. She'd feel exactly the same if she had a relative living near such a catastrophe. She allowed herself to pause for a moment and accept a mug of tea and a currant bun from the Women's Royal Voluntary Service van on the edge of the devastation. Their bottle-green and dark red uniform reminded her of the beetroot sandwiches she and Bertie hadn't yet eaten.

As she nibbled the bun, one of the volunteers leant forward over the counter, saying, 'This is one of the worst incidents I've been to. It's all mothers and children, just going about their normal business on a Saturday. If that bomb had landed early in the morning there wouldn't be anything like the number of casualties. They'd have all been at home in their beds still.'

'It's quite heartbreaking when so many children are involved,' Frankie said. 'Their fathers are away fighting and now so many of them are going to come back home to find their whole family has been killed going about their ordinary lives. They'll wonder what they've been fighting for.'

'Don't you go getting all down in the dumps, dearie. You're doing an important job. Getting these poor people to hospital as soon as you can could save their lives. Here, have another bun to keep you going.'

Frankie accepted gratefully. This was going to be a long day, even though all around her other ambulance crews were also busy ferrying stretchers to their vehicles. She had just finished her tea and begun to wonder why Bertie was taking so long when a warden rushed up to her. 'Are you Frankie, from the Putney station? Your friend has just had an accident. You'd better come with me.'

Frankie handed back her tea mug, stuffed the extra bun in her pocket and ran with him to the far end of the street, close to the crater that had hit Woolworths. Bertie was lying down on the pavement, among large pieces of masonry. She was conscious but clearly in terrible pain. Her head was bleeding and she was moaning. 'I'm sorry, Frankie. I shouldn't have got so close. It's my flipping leg.'

Frankie looked down at the overalls stuffed into rubber

boots. Bertie's leg was bent at an awkward angle, though there was no blood.

'I bloody well tripped over in the rubble. It was my own stupid fault,' Bertie groaned. 'And Auntie Mavis isn't even there. A neighbour said she'd gone to Weston-super-Mare to get away from it all. Just wait till I tell my mother, making me come here for nothing!'

'Oh, you ninny. Never mind all that. At least you didn't kill yourself. I'll run back to the van and get help and a stretcher. You can't walk like this.'

Frankie and a warden carried Bertie to the ambulance and laid her carefully inside. 'Looks like your friend's leg could be broken,' he said. 'Will you be all right driving back on your own?'

'I'll be fine, but I'd better take a few more casualties with me. Can you help me get them on board, then I'll set off.'

A short while later, Frankie's ambulance was full, and she headed for Charing Cross again. The Woolworths site was now mostly clear of the wounded and hers was the last load for the hospital. RAF-trained sniffer dogs had been brought in to help find any remaining survivors in the debris and wardens were digging through the rubble, checking for buried bodies.

There'd be no dancing for her and Bertie for quite a while, so she'd be alone in the evenings if Edwin wasn't free. But if he was able to visit, she wouldn't mind missing the dancefloor and spending all their time planning their future together.

As she drove, she remembered the bun in her pocket and the sandwiches, which were still in the glove compartment. She reached across and pulled out the pack, wrapped in greaseproof paper. The deep red juice had soaked the bread and stained the wrapping. It looked more like a bloody bandage than a snack. Bertie would have liked that, she thought; a sandwich suitable for an ambulance. She was going to miss her companion's sense of humour.

FIFTY-ONE

THEN

DECEMBER 1944

Driving the ambulance with Jim in the passenger seat wasn't nearly as much fun as attending calls with Bertie, but his driving was much better. If Frankie grew tired, she could rely on him to drive the ambulance without stalling and jerky kangaroo hops.

'And how's your cheeky friend getting on then?' He was fond of both of them, but particularly Bertie, who pulled faces at Mrs Ogilvy behind her back, making Jim and his mate Alf nearly choke on their pipes.

'I'm hoping to see her tonight. She's been discharged from hospital, so I'll pop round to her house on my way home. I'm hoping she'll be back to work before too long.'

'I'd be surprised if she's back this side of Christmas. Not with a broken leg, she won't. She can't go hopping in and out of the van while it's mending. Nor carrying stretchers. She'll need time.'

Jim was right of course. When Frankie called at the house,

Bertie's mother answered the door. 'How nice to see you, dear, do come in.'

'How is Bertie? Can I see her?' Frankie had only been able to visit the hospital once since taking her friend there the day she'd been injured. The break hadn't been complicated, but she knew that Bertie would be in plaster for a while yet.

'She's not here, dear. We've sent her off to stay with her aunt and uncle on the farm in Devon. They came and collected her yesterday. We thought it would be best to get her away from any further trouble and get a good rest.'

'Oh, I'm so sorry I've missed her. I really wanted to see how she was.'

'Roberta's getting over the accident perfectly well, but she needs some peace and quiet. Her father and I don't think it's doing her any good staying in London with reminders all the time of what she suffered.'

Mrs Richards crossed her arms and gave Frankie a firm look. 'To be honest, you two were lucky to get away with it for so long. I dread to think what might have become of you both. All those nights you were haring around out there, putting yourselves in danger. Doesn't bear thinking about.'

'But we were always very careful. Oh dear, I'm going to miss her terribly. And when she tripped, well, it was just a silly accident really.'

Bertie's mother shook her head with exasperation. 'You know, I simply can't get over Mavis not telling me she'd gone away. Honestly, if it hadn't been for worrying about her, this would never have happened. But I don't think I could go through that again. Roberta is safe where she is and I hope she stays there now for the duration, if this blessed war is ever going to end.'

Frankie could understand Mrs Richards' concern, but all the same, she really wished Bertie could have stayed at home. She wasn't convinced that she had been mentally scarred by her accident or by the many incidents they had attended, however dreadful they had seemed at the time. Even if she couldn't serve her shifts with her friend, or go dancing for some time to come, she would have enjoyed visiting her regularly and sharing news. Life was going to be bleak when Edwin wasn't able to see her.

As she walked the streets back to her own cold, empty home, she wondered when the tall, strong American would be coming to visit her again. He rang her when he could and wrote little notes often, but that was not the same as spending a night in his arms. 'I wish I could stay here every night,' he told her, 'but the pressure's on. We've all got to be prepared for what might be coming.'

She understood, of course. Without knowing exactly what he was involved in, whatever level it was, it had to be important.

But then, one night in early December, she was given a last-minute late shift with Jim. She and Edwin had planned to see each other that night and she felt guilty when he rang to confirm and she said she was on duty. But he just said, 'Not to worry. Some of the guys are going up West tonight. I'll join them and we'll catch up very soon.'

She didn't think anything of it. Her shift that night was relatively uneventful and she retreated to her cold bed in the early hours of the morning to shiver herself to sleep, with the comfort of only a tepid hot-water bottle rather than Edwin's warm body. In the morning, she turned on the radio while she made tea and toast. She was only half listening to the news when she caught a few words about a bomb in the West End.

Last night a V-2 hit Selfridges department store along with nearby buildings and a public house, resulting in eight fatalities and a large number of casualties. The store will be closed until further notice. Bystanders say all the fir trees from the shop's Christmas displays were blown out of the front windows.

The image of the trees struck her as comical at first, but then she began to wonder where Edwin had been that night.

He'd said up West. That could mean anything. The West End was a huge area. It was more than likely that he'd joined friends for a return visit to the Bouillabaisse Club, wasn't it? And that was nowhere near Selfridges, so he was bound to be fine and she was just worrying for nothing.

But suddenly she felt she had to know where he was. She couldn't rest until she knew. But how could she find out? She didn't know his department, she didn't even have an office number. He'd always phoned her, not the other way around. And she realised with a cold shiver of dread that she didn't have any way of finding him and knowing he was still alive.

She dressed and ate a small piece of cold toast, still fretting, then prepared for her shift at the station. As she cycled there, she couldn't stop thinking about whether Edwin was well, and knew she'd be unable to concentrate on her work until she knew for sure that he'd survived the night unharmed.

As soon as she entered the station, Jim noticed her face. 'What's up with you, lass? You look as if you haven't slept all night.'

She couldn't help herself. She began to shake and felt tears welling. Before she knew it, Jim had sat her down by the stove and pressed a mug of sweet tea into her hands. 'Come on,' he said. 'You're not going out with me till you tell me what's bothering you.'

'How can I find out who was harmed in the West End bombing last night? I simply have to know. A friend... a very important friend... might have been there.'

'I know just the person,' Jim said, walking to the telephone. 'Can you tell me anything about this friend? Just so we can eliminate those who aren't of interest, like?'

'He's an American officer. His name's Edwin Wright.' She sipped her tea and tried to blink away her tears. Mrs Ogilvy had come in from the kitchen and was looking concerned, wondering what all the fuss was about.

Jim was on the phone for a while. When he hung up he said, 'He's ringing me back. Shouldn't be too long.' He glanced at Mrs Ogilvy and shook his head and she backed away.

Frankie sniffed and fumbled for a hankie in her pocket. When she couldn't find one, Jim stepped forward with a large checked handkerchief, still folded and pressed. His wife must have given it to him freshly ironed that morning and she was going to be the first to use it.

The phone rang and Jim answered. 'Yes, I see,' he said. 'It's an awful business. Thanks for checking for me.'

He turned to Frankie and said, 'I take it that this person was someone special.'

Frankie nodded and her eyes began to brim with tears again.

'Then I'm very sorry to say that last night eight Americans were killed by a V-2 that hit the Selfridges basement and a nearby pub. Your friend was one of them.'

Frankie felt as if she had been hit. She was too shocked to cry.

Jim came towards her and put his arms around her. 'There'll be no driving for you today, miss,' he said. 'I'm taking you home right away.'

Late on Christmas Eve they heard the peal of bells, followed by the rich, echoing tones of the church organ, as people began arriving for midnight mass in the church across the road. Charlie pulled back the bedroom curtains and opened the windows to hear the first bars of 'Once in Royal David's City'.

Dan joined her, wrapping his arms around her almost naked body, his chin resting on the top of her head. 'We should have gone to the service,' she said.

'But we were busy,' he said. 'We'll go tomorrow morning if you like.'

They had picnicked on smoked salmon and champagne by the bedroom fire, then made love, oblivious to the time. Rufus had been put to bed in his basket in the room next door, the room that Charlie had planned as a nursery. He was a different baby to the one she'd been expecting, but still a baby she needed to keep a close eye on.

As they stood there, she heard his squeals and a scratching at the interconnecting door. 'Don't go to him,' Dan said. 'You have to start off by being firm.'

'I won't bring him in here, I'll just check he's okay.' She

knew she was giving in, but he was still getting used to his strange new home, after all. He was eager to see her, jumping up and trying to lick her hand. She held him for a moment, but didn't turn on the light as the moonlight pouring through the window was enough. She felt peaceful, her losses forgotten for the time being, and she was glad she was here with Dan, just the two of them enjoying their first Christmas in their forever house.

When the lull of Christmas was over and work on the house resumed in earnest, Charlie settled into a new routine with Rufus. He brought such joy into her life every day. Once he'd received his full quota of injections in February, she could look forward to taking him for twice-daily walks on the common. They both revelled in the damp grass, the misty air and the early signs of new growth on the trees. The walks became part of her new routine: a quick run for him in the garden, breakfast for both of them, then a circuit of the woodland trails, followed by coffee and cake at the café.

'Is this all part of a new health kick?' Nicky was as entranced by Rufus as Charlie and always made a point of stroking him as he sat quietly at the table.

'Not exactly. More a new *make me happy* kick. And I'm loving the regular walks, and so is Rufus. Until he came along, I never seemed to walk further than the short distance from the house to here. And then I'd sit down and be tempted by your mum's cakes as well.'

'She's done cinnamon swirls today. You going to have one?'

'Oh, go on then. I might as well. It'll undo the good work of my morning walk, but that sounds lovely. Nothing for Rufus, mind.' Everyone who met him wanted to offer him treats, but Charlie was determined to keep her dog healthy even if she succumbed to calories herself.

'Tell him to stop looking at me with those pathetic eyes then. Honestly, he could melt a girl's heart, he really could.'

'I know. He is simply adorable. And he's such a good boy. I'm so glad Dan just went ahead and got him for me. He's making such a difference to my life.'

'Dan or the dog?'

'The dog, silly. He's stopped me thinking about my failures and let me just enjoy the simple things in life again.'

Nicky returned with a pastry on a plate. 'Don't talk of failures, darling. It just wasn't the right time for you. But I'm glad you're more relaxed these days. You certainly seem happier.'

'I really am. I feel free to wait and see what happens. The doctor said if there's no obvious sign of problems it can often just happen naturally in time. So, I'm going to let nature take its course.'

'That's the girl. Happy girl, happy dog, happy life. You're making me think I'd like a dog now, but I couldn't manage one with the café and everything else.'

'That would be tricky. Rufus is very good, but he needs a lot of exercise. You couldn't have him in here all day.'

'Never mind. I'll just enjoy him when he comes in with you. I'll be his auntie.'

Charlie laughed to herself as she walked back to the house. She knew that before long she'd be telling Rufus they were going to see Auntie Nicky and Granny Jean, and that he would soon know exactly what she was saying and wag his tail furiously in anticipation. She imagined Dan rolling his eyes when she told him.

The house was calmer now than it had been in the frantic rush to finish jobs before Christmas, but there was still work going on in various sections. A gas fire had been fitted in the main sitting room and a second bathroom was in progress on the very top floor. Dan said there were too many stairs to go running down to the toilet at the back of the house, and there was already plumbing on the second floor, so it wasn't an expensive job to add it.

Charlie could hear drilling and a radio far above her as she went into the kitchen. Her new home office was almost finished, but she decided to stay downstairs and work at the kitchen table as she often did.

She ran the boiling-water tap to make a quick mug of mint tea and then noticed that the door to the cellar was wide open. Guessing that one of the workmen had been checking on pipes or wiring down there, she went to lock the door. But before she could get there, Rufus dashed past her and almost slid down the steep stairs on his short legs.

'No, wait! Come back!' she called to him, but he'd already slithered down the wooden steps to the bottom and then disappeared.

'Oh, you pest,' she groaned as she switched on the light. 'And there I was saying how good you are.' His cheeky face reappeared and she called again. 'Come on, Rufus, come here.' She clicked her fingers, a sign of a promised treat, and he put his front paws on the bottom step, then tried to scrabble up. But his little short legs on his long sausage body were the wrong shape for the steep stairs. She knew she'd have to go down and fetch him.

'I'm coming. Just wait there.' But he didn't. He was excited by this new adventure and dashed off again, out of sight.

Charlie knew he couldn't come to any harm. The rooms in the cellar were dusty and decorated with cobwebs, but they hadn't been worked on or littered with nails and screws. She clambered down the narrow steps, hoping the light wouldn't suddenly fail. A single bare bulb dangled in the first chamber, giving just enough light to see the two adjacent sections. Rufus barked as he heard her coming, dashed towards her, then scooted off again.

Charlie found her phone in her pocket and switched on the torch to help her see better. She hadn't really explored the cellar before, they had been so busy with all the floors above, but she thought these dry rooms might make very useful storage. They had the smell of an old shed or the back of a church, musty but certainly not damp. A small grille set high in the wall of each of the rooms allowed a little fresh air to circulate around the cellar.

The first section was empty, but had a stone shelf that ran around the walls at waist height. The second was equipped with a wooden workbench with clamps and a lathe. Some old tools were clipped to a board on the wall and a few jars held screws and nails of various sizes.

Rufus was barking at the far end of the cellar by a closed door, so she followed the sound, shining the torch on her phone. He was scrabbling at the panels, as if he urgently needed to get through. Charlie tried the handle, but it was stiff or locked. She wondered for a moment why it hadn't been opened during the renovations. Then she remembered the old keys. One of them had unlocked the door at the top of the stairs. Perhaps that would unlock this door too, or maybe it was one of the other keys she hadn't yet located.

She ran back up the rickety stairs and could hear her puppy's bark echoing through the house. She grabbed the remaining keys from the kitchen drawer and took the one from the main cellar door as well. When she had returned, Rufus was no longer barking. He was whining. He was definitely upset.

Charlie tried the cellar door key first and, when that didn't work, proceeded to try with the next oldest. It turned with some effort, and the door creaked open only when she finally shoved it with her shoulder. Rufus dashed through and began barking again.

This chamber smelt different to the other two. There was a

strong scent of herbs – or was it flowers? As she was trying to see why Rufus was so disturbed, something caught on her hair, making her jump and nearly scream. She tried to brush it away, thinking it was another spider. Then she shone her torch around the room and upwards and was surprised to see bunches and bunches of lavender hanging from the ceiling. There were so many it was practically smothered in the dried flowers, all draped with strands of spiders' webs.

Rufus was on the floor, looking up at a kind of shelving system that reached nearly as high as the low ceiling. 'What a fuss you're making,' she said, bending to pick him up. He quietened down, but as she lifted him into her arms he gave one last piercing bark, looking intently at the shelves.

Charlie lifted her head to look where his gaze had settled. That was when she realised that these weren't ordinary shelves, but a solid wine rack. Years before there must have been a serious collection of bottles here, a veritable wine cellar with maturing port and brandy as well, but the spaces were now empty. Or were they? There was something on the very top shelf, a long box, tied with a white ribbon.

'I'm going to have to put you down now. Don't go running off again,' she said, putting Rufus back on the floor, where he continued to bark, looking up at the shelves all the while.

She lifted the box down and took it through to the first chamber, where there was a little more light. She placed it on the stone shelving, blew away the dust and pulled one end of the bow. The silky satin unravelled silently and she lifted the lid with a whisper. A faint scent of lavender wafted to her nose, with an underlying hint of decay, like old damp autumn leaves. A sealed envelope lay on top of a layer of tissue paper, sprinkled with yet more dried lavender.

She put the envelope to one side and peeled back the rustling paper, then gasped as the contents revealed themselves. She told herself this couldn't be real. She had to be mistaken.

FIFTY-THREE

THEN

JANUARY 1945

Jim and Alf were like two kindly uncles who protected Frankie from Mrs Ogilvy's withering looks. Her thin-lipped stares, her refusal to notice that she was tired and needed a reviving cup of tea, her insistence that the ambulance hadn't been cleaned to her liking, all underlined her disapproval of a married woman's grief for an adulterous liaison. She'd known from the start that Frankie's husband was missing and very likely dead, but she couldn't forgive a young widow who might have found love again.

'Come on, lass,' Jim said, offering her one of the oatcakes that Mrs Ogilvy hadn't sent Frankie's way. 'You need to keep your strength up.'

But what for? Frankie felt numb, and staggered through Christmas and New Year, hoping that the routine chores that were part of her job would help her cope. Only by burying herself in other people's troubles as she helped injured casualties could she begin to forget her own loss. But she had no body to bury, no grave to mourn beside. She assumed Edwin's body would be sent back to the US or buried in a service cemetery somewhere she would never be able to find and visit. And she missed Bertie's jolly companionship, but her friend was still recuperating on the farm.

At Christmas, the house had felt so cold and empty. Bertie's mother had invited her round for dinner, along with Bertie's sisters and various aunts and cousins. 'You're looking very peaky, dear,' Mrs Richards said, pressing her to have a second portion of the measly plum pudding that had been concocted that year from the family's limited rations. 'Are you sure you're eating properly?'

She was eating, but whether it was a balanced diet she wasn't so sure. She didn't care what she ate and, even though everyone else seemed to be thriving on restricted rations, looking healthier than ever, she felt constantly queasy and out of sorts. She excused herself after they'd listened to the king's speech on the radio, saying she had to conserve her energy for the Boxing Day shift at the ambulance station. But in truth, she couldn't bear to be surrounded by jovial chatter, paper hats and crackers, when all she wanted to do was remember her precious times with Edwin. The overexcited children clamouring for Musical Chairs and Blind Man's Buff, the adults overindulging in sloe gin, cigarettes and pipe smoke gave her a headache and she was glad to leave them to walk home alone in the icy dark, while a misty moon shimmered overhead.

It must have been after New Year when she finally began to wonder if she was sickening for something. 'You're very pale, love,' the butcher said, when she reached the head of the queue. 'I've got a nice bit of liver for you. That should put some colour in your cheeks. Why don't you have that this time and forget the sausages?'

She looked at the dark, almost black, glistening liver and felt sick. It was all she could do to hold her breath, pay for a slice and stop herself heaving all over the sawdust scattered across his floor. At home, she forced herself to cook it with half of a scarce onion that she'd obtained by giving a neighbour eggs laid by the two surviving hens, thinking it would do her good, but she hadn't felt any better.

The next morning she felt sicker than ever and, as soon as she'd splashed her face with cold water in the freezing bathroom, she heaved up last night's supper in the toilet. And suddenly it dawned on her that this wasn't a bug, a stomach upset or food poisoning.

They'd been careful, hadn't they? She'd put her missed monthlies down to her grief and the long shifts, but at last she had to admit it: she was probably pregnant.

Unable to believe that it was true, she stumbled through the next few weeks, thinking it would go away. She hadn't been aware of the moment when it had happened, nor of it growing inside her, so maybe it wasn't real. Other than the nausea, she didn't feel any different. But if this was indeed true, then this growing child was a piece of Edwin, a precious piece of the man she had grown to love, who had loved her in return, who had wanted to marry her and give her children. She'd heard stories of girls getting rid of unwanted babies and tales of disastrous consequences with excruciating pain and pints of blood. She couldn't do that to his child.

So, she continued to think she could hide from the truth. Her regulation coat and overalls covered her swelling figure, though, to be honest, she was so slender there was hardly any change to most observers. But she couldn't hide from Mrs Ogilvy's prying eyes, so she was careful to wear her coat whenever she was in the station, enveloping herself in its unflattering gaberdine folds.

As the sickness diminished, she began to feel better and even less mournful. 'You're looking more like your old self,' Jim said one day when they were on their way to a call-out. 'It's good to see you looking more cheerful.'

'I can't mope for ever,' she said, concentrating on the route. 'Life must go on.' But the fact was that she felt as if she now had a reason to live. She was carrying Edwin's child. It was an unexpected but welcome gift and she had to take care of it. She'd convinced herself that Dickie was lost for good and that only she and Edwin's child would live in the house from now on.

'That's the spirit,' Jim said. 'Got to keep buggering on, as Winnie would say.' That was reportedly Winston Churchill's favourite saying and hundreds of Britons followed suit, particularly when not in genteel company.

It was daylight and they'd been sent to attend the site of an unexploded bomb in south London. The missile must have fallen earlier in the war; it had been detonated by a trained squad, but the debris had injured some local residents. Even now that the intense bombing raids appeared to have stopped, hopefully for ever, ambulance crews were still in demand for incidents like this. These occasions were not as dangerous or dramatic as the many risky calls she and Bertie had taken at the height of the Blitz, but she knew she still had to be cautious as they approached the scene.

'Thank goodness those wretched V-2s seem to have stopped,' she said, pulling up alongside a fairly clear area of pavement. 'When they were sending those over, I always dreaded being in the middle of a call-out and suddenly getting a direct hit from a second silent bomb.'

'Don't count your chickens,' Jim said. 'It's only been quiet a week. Let's hope the dastardly Germans aren't coming up with plans for a V-3 or some other deadly device.' He dampened his smouldering pipe with his thumb and pushed it into the pocket of his thick coat. 'But perhaps the Jerries have got more on their plate now our boys are getting close.'

Frankie knew that the war in Europe was still raging. If Edwin hadn't perished on a night out in London, there was every chance he'd have been in danger across the Channel. She climbed out of the cab of the van. Her back ached and she hoped the strain wasn't showing on her face. She'd convinced herself her pregnancy still wasn't obvious, but she couldn't help noticing that the belt on her coat was tighter than it had been and she had to shift it a notch to accommodate her increased girth.

She and Jim carried a stretcher each, assuming they'd both be needed. The casualties had been gathered into a school hall not far from the scene of the explosion. 'We've been here all night,' a woman was complaining. 'When can we go home?'

'Just checking the houses are safe to return to, madam,' a warden said, raising his eyebrows as Frankie approached. 'We don't want any more accidents now, do we?'

The woman carried on grumbling but returned to her children, a weary-looking boy and girl of about four and six. 'You'd think this was the end of it, but oh no, these wretched bombs are still hidden away everywhere.'

Frankie could sympathise with her. The public had had enough. The war had been going on for over five years and they'd suffered heavy bombing during four of them. Everyone wanted an end to it and longed to welcome back husbands and brothers who'd been fighting far from home.

She forced herself to put on a bright smile. 'Well, I'm here with my colleague to help anyone who needs to get to hospital. Who's our first passenger?'

An elderly woman shuffled forward. 'My husband, please. I think he's had a stroke. It was the shock, see.'

Frankie and Jim attended to those who could walk to the van, then turned to help the elderly man onto a stretcher. 'Oh no, dear,' his wife said. 'You don't want to go lifting him in your condition. One of these men should help.' She tugged at the arm of a nearby warden. 'You're a strong chap. You can help lift this stretcher. You can't expect this young lady to do it.'

Frankie felt a hot blush spread across her cheeks. Was it now obvious? Would Jim, Alf and Mrs Ogilvy soon notice as well? The clarity of daylight didn't hide the change in her figure as much as the dark of night. She lowered her head and went outside to breathe the cool air, then strode towards the waiting ambulance. If her state was now clear to everyone, how would she face the local shopkeepers and her neighbours, let alone her work colleagues?

FIFTY-FOUR

THEN

MARCH 1945

When they returned to the ambulance station, Frankie was convinced that Mrs Ogilvy was staring at her with greater disapproval than usual. She'd cleaned out the van thoroughly and she hadn't lost any blankets this time; that look could only mean one thing. Frankie turned away from her and kept her coat buckled up, even though the staffroom was warm and filled with the fug of pipe smoke from Jim and Alf, thickened by cigarettes smoked by two newly recruited women.

She sipped a mug of tea but turned down the buttered toast that Mrs Ogilvy slammed onto the table with a glance in her direction. 'You sure?' Jim offered her the plate again but she shook her head and waved it away. Alf took an extra corner instead.

'I've got such a headache,' she said. 'I think I'll go home and get an early night.'

'You do that,' Alf said. 'You'll be right as rain tomorrow.'

She slipped out of the back door and found her bike. Mrs Ogilvy followed her and stood in the doorway, with her arms folded and her head on one side, like a curious bird. 'You'd better mind how you go,' she said. 'I'm not sure you should be riding a bike, the way you are.'

Frankie didn't answer her. She pedalled away as fast as she could. She was certain Mrs Ogilvy knew. And who might she know among Frankie's neighbours? Would word get around that a young woman with a husband missing, but perhaps still doing his duty, was in the family way?

As she cycled back up the hill to the house, she thought hard about what to do. It seemed clear to her that she couldn't continue with her job. But she couldn't bear to go back to the ambulance station to hand in her notice. She'd have to phone, excusing herself at first, saying she was ill, then have an extended period of sick leave. Or, better still, say she had to attend to an elderly relative out in the country. That was it – she'd have to say she was going away and make sure she didn't go anywhere near the station again.

The more she thought about how to hide her 'condition', as that elderly woman had put it, the more she thought she really would have to go into hiding. She didn't know anyone she could stay with out in the countryside, so there was nowhere she could go. If she'd let Bertie in on her secret, maybe she could have joined her on the farm. But she felt she had kept too much information from her best friend for too long. She couldn't suddenly spring such dramatic news upon her when she was still trying to recover.

Could she stay hidden at home until the baby was born? Could she deliver the baby all on her own? She hadn't been to see a doctor. She assumed she was healthy and it would be all right, but how could she be sure?

If she were to stay in the house and never venture out, she'd have to arrange deliveries. That was easily done. Her mother had never visited the shops in person. The butcher, baker and grocer would all be happy to retain her custom and send a boy to the house with her orders if she phoned them.

By the time she reached home, she was quite resolved to become a recluse. In the Middle Ages, women of substance shut themselves away for weeks before they gave birth. That must be where the word confinement came from. She would be like them, shut away, contemplating the challenge ahead of her, calmly awaiting her child's arrival.

Frankie parked her bike in the hall and hung up her heavy coat. She'd found the ride quite tiring, and went to lie down upstairs. She stood in front of her wardrobe mirror and looked at her figure in her regulation overalls. She was certainly thicker around the waist, but not obviously so. But then she turned sideways and could see how much her stomach curved outwards. There was no mistaking that shape. No one else was putting on weight and getting a bulging midriff on a wartime diet.

She lay down on her bed and began thinking. Could she really do this on her own? She told herself women all over the world gave birth alone, particularly in wartime. She was young and healthy; of course she could do it. More to the point, how would she prepare for herself and the baby? There were spare sheets aplenty in the house; there were also clothes that her mother had kept from her own babyhood out of sentimentality. Perhaps nappies could be made from old towels and teacloths. And an empty drawer or her old dolls' pram could serve as a cradle to begin with.

She couldn't be sure exactly how much time she had left, but the more she thought about it, the more she convinced herself she could cope. Her and Edwin's child, together in this house. She couldn't think beyond the birth and the first few days after that. They would be quite alone. No one could know. Not even her best friend.

Frankie found she didn't miss the pace of her shifts and the scrutiny of the ambulance station one little bit. Every day she found something important to do, in preparation for her child's eventual arrival. She lined her childhood dolls' pram with clean linen on top of a firm mattress she'd made from clean ticking and kapok. She washed and dried the old baby clothes her mother had saved, then rinsed and ironed a pile of large cotton dinner napkins for use as nappies. After sorting through old nightdresses and blouses, she decided to turn some of the material into tiny nightgowns, embroidered with silks from her mother's needlework box.

Gradually, she felt more and more at peace in her shrunken world, waiting to greet Edwin's child. She could feel the baby growing inside her, stretching its limbs and trying to turn. She cradled her stomach and sang to it, telling it they would meet very soon.

Her local shopkeepers had not quibbled about setting up regular deliveries, nor questioned her need to establish accounts to be settled at the end of the quarter. Her family was well respected in the area and, when she explained that she had sustained an injury from her work as an ambulance driver and needed time alone to recuperate, they had nothing but sympathy for her, along with baskets of fresh produce. The only time she needed cash was for weekly payments for the milkman, and she'd made sure she had plenty of money in the house.

Bertie's mother called round one day, but Frankie spotted her from an upstairs window and decided not to answer the door. She'd have had to invite her in, and she couldn't face her inquisitive eyes in her obvious condition. These days she had to wear unfastened skirts and loose, untucked blouses to accommodate her swollen figure. Then shortly after that, Mrs Richards sent a note saying she was going to Devon to look after Bertie and would be away until the end of the summer.

Relieved that she wouldn't have more unexpected visitors, Frankie found she was enjoying her confinement to the house. She took a turn around the back garden every day, breathing in the clean air and smelling the scent of the primroses scattered through the neglected vegetable beds. She picked groundsel for the two hens and collected the occasional egg. She was glad that she no longer had to care for the rabbits, which she had given to a neighbour when the Jones family left.

One day that spring she was standing under the pear tree, looking up through the froth of white blossom, when a voice called over the back gate. It was the boy who delivered telegrams. Too young to fight, he had the important but unsettling job of delivering news about the war in his distinctive navy-blue uniform trimmed with red piping, topped with a navy pillbox hat piped in red and decorated with a red button.

'For me?' Her voice shook. There was only one reason for telegrams in this war. If he said, 'no answer' it meant someone had died. But who? With no relatives left and Edwin gone, the only person she still cared for was Bertie.

He handed it to her without a word. She fumbled to open it, feeling confused, and read the words:

I AM SAFE IN GERMAN HOSPITAL STOP HOME WHEN WAR IS OVER STOP DICKIE

The delivery boy waited patiently. She couldn't tear her eyes away from the stark message. Her mouth was dry as she struggled to understand what was written there in black and white. Finally, she managed to summon her reply. 'Thank you. No answer.'

She watched over the garden gate as he cycled away on his regulation-issue red bike. She was left with thoughts whirling through her mind. How could Dickie be alive after all this time? She'd become convinced he'd been dead for more than four years and had barely spared a thought for him at all since meeting Edwin. Their short affair had shown her so clearly what true love could mean, and she was still grieving for her lover and their future together, not her controlling, selfish husband.

Clutching the telegram, Frankie stumbled indoors. She read it once more, then dropped it on the floor. With one hand clutched to her thudding heart, the other flew to her belly, as if the baby also needed reassurance. Her mind was flooded with questions she couldn't answer. How soon might Dickie turn up and point an accusing finger at her? How soon would he arrive and make her feel ashamed?

He said he'd be home when the war was over. But when would that be? It had dragged on for over five years. Everyone was tired and longing for an end to the worry and the rationing. The whole population yearned for the return of loved ones, but once the conflict ended she'd be confronted with the return of a husband she knew for certain she didn't love and probably had never really loved.

She couldn't be glad he was alive and would eventually come home. She didn't know when he might return and nor did she know when her baby might arrive. Which would happen first? She began to breathe quickly and felt panic rising in her breast. The only fact she could be sure of was that she was simply terrified.

FIFTY-SIX

THEN

APRIL 1945

The following day, the postman called at his normal time, soon after breakfast. As well as a cheerful postcard from Bertie, one of several Frankie had received so far, there was also a formal, official-looking letter. It was from the Red Cross, confirming the contents of the message she had already received by telegram the day before:

Dear Mrs Wilson,

We are pleased to inform you that your husband, Richard Wilson, who was originally reported as missing, has recently been found in a German hospital for prisoners of war. It appears that he was taken prisoner early in the war but had lost his identity tag and was suffering from amnesia. He has only recently regained full use of his memory and was able to tell our visitor his home address as well as his rank and regiment. He is unharmed, is being treated well and should be able to return home when a ceasefire is finally declared. If you wish to communicate with him, you may send a letter via the address on this message.

Frankie still struggled to believe the evidence before her. So, Dickie really was alive after all this time. The telegram must truly be from him. She had grown so accustomed to thinking he was long gone, that she had been a widow since May 1940, nearly five years ago. When the news back then had first reached her, when she'd been shocked by those official words, *missing in action,* she hadn't been able to stop herself rewording the message to reflect what she wished. It should have said *missing for good, never to return.* She couldn't voice her thoughts to anyone, but in her heart she knew that was what she felt. Since she'd realised the truth about Dickie, since she'd known their marriage was a sham, she couldn't celebrate his survival and hope for his return. Although she could feel sorry for his loss, sorry that he might have died in pain, the fact was that she had never grieved for him the way she had for Edwin. If anything, Edwin had felt more like her real husband; his death was when she was truly widowed.

And now? Dickie was really coming back? But when? The war was not yet over, although the Allies had the upper hand. As parts of Europe were liberated one by one and the terrible crimes of the Nazis were being revealed, it seemed as if the war might finally end in the very near future.

And then what? Dickie could be sent home to confront his heavily pregnant wife? Frankie felt faint at the thought. She could have coped with bearing Edwin's child alone, but how would she cope when she faced Dickie? She knew how he'd react. That hectoring voice she'd tried so hard to banish from her thoughts began to rail at her again, with increasingly harsh words: *'What do you mean, you were lonely? You stupid bitch! Couldn't you have waited a bit longer till you knew for sure I was never coming home? Were you that desperate to throw yourself at the first man to take an interest in you? You're pathetic and disgusting. You're nothing but a whore!'*

He was so controlling, so concerned with keeping up

appearances, he'd never understand how alone she had felt, how she had finally learnt with Edwin what passionate love could mean. Dickie would never accept another man's child. And she couldn't face giving away a child that was the product of a real love match.

Trembling, Frankie boiled the kettle. She needed to sit and think quietly. One moment she had been calmly dreaming of cradling her baby in the spring sunshine, the next that idyll was shattered and all she could imagine was stern disapproval, spiteful words and rejection.

She tried hard to think logically. The war wasn't over yet by a long shot. Dickie surely couldn't come home until it was possible to travel from Germany. The letter wasn't specific, but if he was still in Germany, it seemed unlikely that he would turn up in a day or so.

She might well have given birth by the time he returned. And if that were the case, then she could say that the baby had been orphaned and that she had longed to give it a home. Surely he wouldn't be able to refuse her that?

But she had no sure way of working out when the baby was due. She guessed it was likely to be late May or early June, as she recalled the dates when she and Edwin had made love. And if Dickie arrived and found her in an advanced state of pregnancy, she was sure he would have no sympathy for her. He might leave her, he might insist on a divorce, he might even become angry and violent.

She thought back to how he had treated her before he'd left. He wasn't normally physically abusive, it was usually his words that lashed and cut her. But he had sometimes held her wrist in a vicelike grip so tight that her skin had been bruised by his fingertips. And one time he had pushed her hard against the frame of a door and she'd knocked her cheek. That had bruised too and she'd tried to mask it with face powder and told Bertie that she'd tripped on the stairs. So, he might lash out in a cold fury when he faced her in this condition or with a newborn in her arms. And she couldn't bear the thought that her child might be harmed, whether deliberately or by accident.

Sipping her unsweetened tea brought no comfort. She couldn't work out how to face the future now. Shame and humiliation were all that lay ahead.

And then, suddenly, the decision was made for her. A pain gripped her womb and fluid leaked, soaking her dress. Her baby was coming right now.

Frankie simply couldn't know how much time she would have. Labour might take hours – it could even take days. She just knew that she had to be prepared before events over-whelmed her and she was unable to move from her bed. With pains gripping her insides and her back, she stopped now and then to take deep breaths as she climbed the stairs to her bedroom. In between contractions, she ripped up sheets, padded the mattress with newspapers and carried water and towels to the room. She spread paper across the Turkish rug beside the bed and changed out of her skirt and blouse into an old nightdress, thinking it would be more practical as her labour progressed.

When she thought she had done all she could, she stopped to picture the event ahead of her. She hoped she would soon be cradling a newborn, slippery with blood and mucus, but she knew she could end up unconscious, dying even, leaking blood onto the carpet. If she died in labour, no one would know for days, maybe even weeks if Dickie's return was delayed. The milkman might become suspicious if she didn't take in the milk every day and the local shopkeepers might wonder why she hadn't placed her regular orders, but in these days of uncer-tainty it was not unknown for people to suddenly up sticks and leave their homes for somewhere safer. No one would think to break into the house and check on her well-being.

But she couldn't bear the thought that Dickie or anyone

would find her body without a final word from her. And then she knew that she would have to leave a letter. She half thought of leaving a note for Bertie, but she had no idea if her friend would ever come back to London and Dickie was supposedly sure to return in the near future. So, she wrote:

My dear Dickie,

If you are the one who finds this letter, then I am deeply sorry. I am writing this on Monday in case I do not survive another day. I am in labour all alone and hope that I and my child will survive but it is entirely possible that neither of us will. I cannot write for long as the pains are too great, but I want you to know that I never meant for this to happen and hope you will find it in your heart to forgive me.

Your wife,

Frances

Sunlight filtered through the lace curtains. It was early morning, birds were twittering outside and fresh green leaves were bursting from the trees. Frankie opened her eyes to the battle zone where she had fought to save herself and her baby. Surrounded by crumpled, bloodstained sheets, sodden newspapers and gore, she tried to make sense of what had happened in the night.

She thought she remembered screaming towards the end, as she clutched the bars of the iron bedstead, straining to push down. She was sure she remembered the tiny body slithering out of her, dropping onto the sheets. And she could remember turning to see why it wasn't crying.

Before the afterbirth was even expelled from her body, she had unwrapped the cord from around the tiny throat. She had bent to breathe air into the tiny lips. And she had rubbed the tiny torso to make it open its lungs.

But it never cried, it never drew breath. The little girl never lived. Stunned, unable to even cry, Frankie had wrapped her in a strip of sheet and fallen asleep exhausted, with the child in her arms.

In the light of morning, she examined the perfect features, the pearly nails on little fingers and toes, the curl of her ears, the curve of her lashes, the soft strands of hair, still plastered to her head with mucus and blood. She seemed to be asleep and Frankie knew she would picture her like this for ever. She cradled her in her arms, wishing the baby could have suckled just once from her aching breasts. And she wished Edwin could have seen how perfect his daughter was.

As the sun grew brighter, she heard the church clock chime seven times. And then she knew that she had to face the day. There was no time to waste. She had to remove all signs of the birth and the life that never was.

Stumbling across the bedroom floor, Frankie went first to the dressing table, where she had left her brief note the night before. She tore it into pieces and threw them in the fireplace. Then she went to the bathroom and ran a deep, hot bath, scented with lavender. Once she had soaked away the sweat and blood, she dried her tired body and wrapped herself in her thick candlewick dressing gown. After protecting herself from the flow of blood still leaking from inside her, she went downstairs slowly.

She had not eaten since the day before, when her waters had broken and the pains had begun, and she suddenly knew she was hungry and needed all her strength. She heated the milk delivered the previous day and made hot cocoa. She boiled two eggs and ate them with thick slices of toast, and used much of her butter ration in one fell swoop.

Thus fortified, she returned to her room to dress, then picked up the stillborn baby from her pillow. She could not bear to part with her like this, sticky with blood from her terrible birth, so she carried her to the bathroom, filled the sink with warm water and washed her dear little body with lavender soap.

She dried her daughter in a soft towel, sprinkled her with scented powder and dressed her in the clothes she had prepared for her arrival. Then she laid her in the dolls' pram under an embroidered sheet and a crocheted shawl. How like a porcelain doll she looks, Frankie thought, stroking her soft cheek, her skin is so pale and waxen.

She could hardly bear to tear herself away from the sight, but knew she must. The bed had to be stripped, the newspapers and sheets burned, till there was no incriminating sign left. Every now and then she had to pause in her bedmaking, she was so tired from her labours through the night.

Once all was clear and the bed was remade, she took all the soiled materials into the garden and set light to them in the brazier always used for bonfires, adding kindling and dry straw from the hens to hasten the fire. The pyre caught quickly and smoke rose into the clear spring sky. The houses on either side were empty as the owners had retreated to the countryside, as had many other neighbours. There was no one nearby to question why she was having a bonfire on a fine day. She stood close by, hugging a cup of tea, watching the white and red sheets blacken and disappear. Evidence of her mistake had almost completely disappeared, apart from one thing.

That night, Frankie slept with the baby in her arms. I can have one night, she told herself. No more, but one night surely, before I must say goodbye? She kissed the cold cheeks, warmed the tiny fists, smelt the skin sweet from her bath.

They both slept soundly and, when Frankie woke in the morning, she resolved to finish her task. She couldn't bring herself to bury the body in the garden. The thought of earth covering that delicate face, worms creeping through the tiny body, appalled her – and what if her body was uncovered in years to come? She half wondered whether to abandon her daughter in the depths of the woods on the common, like an awful tale by the Grimm brothers, but she was afraid foxes would find her and desecrate both her grave and her body.

In the end she decided she could never be parted from her

daughter. Hers and Edwin's. She had to keep her close by. So, she went to her wardrobe and selected a shoebox that still held the pair of shoes she had worn on that romantic trip to Henley. White court shoes with a bow, that had hardly been worn and were still cushioned in tissue inside the box from Russell & Bromley.

She wrapped the little body in the tissue paper and laid it in the box with lavender bags that Daphne and Cecily had made from the garden's flowers the summer before they left. She tucked the scented bags around her baby's body and looked at the sweet face one last time. She enclosed a note of farewell before gently closing the lid, then tied a length of white ribbon round the box.

The makeshift coffin was no weight at all, Frankie thought as she carried it downstairs and then down further stairs into the extensive cellar. The furthest chamber, which had once been used for her father's wine, was cool and dry, with racks for bottles that were no longer there. She placed the box on the topmost rack, where it could only be seen if someone came searching. She resolved to return later, when that year's flowers had bloomed, with bunches of lavender to decorate this crypt.

After turning out the light, she blew a kiss towards her daughter's resting place, locked the door, then left. She would never return to look at her again, but would choose to remember perfection instead.

Charlie was so shocked, she felt as if she had stopped breathing. She quickly replaced the lid of the shoebox, grabbed Rufus and ran back up the narrow steps. She locked the door behind her and stood with her back pressed against it, panting and clutching her puppy while he nuzzled her chin.

What on earth had she just seen? She couldn't rely on her own interpretation of the sight, not after all the babies she'd thought she'd been expecting and then lost. Could it be a doll? An old doll, hidden away years ago? She had to find Dan and take him to look at it with her.

But then she remembered that he'd gone out to choose fittings for the new bathroom. He might not be back for hours. She couldn't possibly wait that long. She wouldn't be able to concentrate on anything until she'd shared this startling discovery with someone.

'Come on, Rufus. We've got to go out again. And no more tricks from you.' She reattached his lead and pulled on her coat and they ran back to the café. Halfway there she had to pick him up and carry him as his short little legs were struggling to keep up with her.

'Back again already?' Nicky laughed as she saw Charlie fly through the door with her dog. Then she noticed her face. 'Oh, my goodness. Whatever's the matter? You look like you've seen a ghost. Come and sit down this minute.'

Jean heard the fuss and popped her head out of the kitchen. 'Are you all right, love? Not the usual trouble, is it?'

Charlie eased herself into a seat, looping the dog lead around the chair leg. 'I'm not sure yet what's going on. I think I might be imagining things after all that's happened. I'm sure I'll be all right in a minute. I just need to catch my breath.'

'You just sit right there and have a cup of tea,' Jean said. 'That always helps. And I'm just about to bring out a banana bread. It goes down nicely with some butter on it. I'll do you a slice of that as well. That'll soon put you right.'

Charlie sat there, Rufus at her feet, while the two women fussed around her and then, as the café was quiet after the mid-morning rush, both sat down with her.

'Now whatever's the matter?' Jean was looking at her as if she wasn't going to move until she'd heard every last detail. 'You've got a bit of colour back in your cheeks, but you were white as a sheet a minute ago.'

Charlie had no choice but to tell them both what she thought she might have found in the cellar. 'When I opened the box and peeled back the tissue paper, I couldn't believe what I was seeing. And it was wearing baby clothes. And the awful thing is, I thought maybe it wasn't a doll. Maybe it was a real baby. But how could it be? That would be mad, wouldn't it? Who on earth would do something like that?'

Jean looked at her daughter and Nicky looked at her mother, as if they knew more than they were telling. 'Do you want us to come back with you and take a look?'

'Oh, yes please. And I've just remembered: there was also a sealed envelope in the box.'

'Didn't you open it?' Jean's eyebrows shot up in surprise.

'No, I didn't think. How stupid was that? I was so shocked, I couldn't look at the thing a minute longer. I shoved the lid back on and left in a panic.'

'I can't leave the café yet,' Nicky said. 'Mum, you'll have to go back with Charlie. You're good at being calm in a crisis.'

'Come on then,' Jean said, getting out of her chair. 'Let's go and see what you think you've found. I'm sure it's nothing near as dramatic as you're imagining. And then I can get back and help Nicky clear up in here before the lunchtime rush.'

'Come straight back and tell me what you find,' Nicky called as they went out of the door. 'I wish I was going with you.'

Minutes later, back at the house, Charlie shut Rufus out in the garden so he wouldn't get in their way. Then she unlocked the cellar door and stood on the threshold, hesitating.

'Do you want me to go first?' Jean put a comforting hand on her shoulder.

'No, I'm okay. I'm just being silly.' Charlie switched on the light and led the way down the steps. When she got to the bottom, she pointed to the box where she'd left it on the shelf. She couldn't bear to open it again and stood back, waiting for Jean to join her. 'I can't... I can't do it. You go ahead.'

Jean showed no such qualms and lifted the lid immediately. She removed the envelope and parted the tissue paper with the tip of her finger. Even though she stayed calm, she visibly jolted when she caught sight of the contents. She turned to Charlie with a sad shake of her head. 'I think your first instinct might have been right. I don't think this is any doll. Not any kind I've ever seen, anyway. I'm pretty sure this is a real baby. And it's been dead a very, very long time. I think with the dry air and ventilation in here it's mummified. There wouldn't have been much to see otherwise.'

Charlie's hand flew to her mouth as she gasped. 'But how can it be? Whose is it?'

'Well, why don't we find out?' Jean replaced the lid of the shoebox, then passed her the envelope. 'Maybe this will tell us. Are you going to open it, or shall I?'

'You do it. I'm shaking too much. I can't believe what we've just found. And what on earth do we do next?'

Jean gently prised open the flap of the envelope. 'There's a letter,' she said. 'It's quite short...' She was quiet for a moment, her lips moving silently as she scanned the lines. 'You'd better read it. I think it solves the mystery of Mrs Wilson's missing daughter.' She shook her head sadly. 'What a thing to happen and then to live with it hidden away down here, all those years.'

Frankie took the page from her and read it aloud:

26 April 1945,

To whoever finds this, if by that time I am no longer alive, please believe me that no foul play was involved in my baby's death. My daughter arrived too soon and I gave birth to her all alone yesterday. I sincerely wish she could have lived, but it wasn't to be. No one knew about my pregnancy and I told no one, not even my best friend, that I'd had her. I could not bear for her to be taken from me and cremated or buried, so I decided to keep her nearby. Once I have closed the box, I'll never look at her again. I want to remember perfection, even though she never drew breath.

I have named her Alicia Rose Wright and did not want her to die so soon. She is named after her father, Edwin Wright, who I expected to marry once the war was over. Sadly, he never knew that I was going to have his child because he was killed in a terrible bombing in the West End in December 1944.

I want whoever reads this to know that I was not an adulterous woman. At the time I knew Edwin, I fully believed my husband had been killed in France in the spring of 1940. He was eventually found alive by the Red Cross towards the end of the war and returned home. I never told him what had happened and kept this secret close to my heart my whole life.

If I have passed by the time this letter is found, please reunite us in death.

Frances Wilson

Charlie gulped and wiped away a tear. '*Not even my best friend* – she means your mother, doesn't she? Do you think she really never knew?'

Jean shook her head. 'I don't think she ever did. I never understood why they weren't that close after the war. I just put it down to how things had changed by then.'

'What do you think she means by reunite?' Charlie couldn't stop herself gazing at the handwritten letter.

'Sounds to me like she wants her baby to join her in her grave.' Jean looked sad and fetched a tissue from her pocket.

'Do you think that's possible?'

'I suppose so, but I think you'll have to do this officially. I don't think you can go running off to wherever she's buried and do it yourself.'

'Oh, what an awful thought. I suppose you're right.'

'Hardly. I should think there are steps that have to be taken. Probably calling the police first and I don't know what after that. They'll know what the correct procedure is.'

'Gosh, yes. I suppose that's right. I hope we can follow her wishes. Do you know where she was buried?'

Jean shook her head. 'A few of us went to her funeral in Putney Vale. It's the nearest cemetery. I don't remember exactly where the grave is, but I'm sure we can find out.'

She opened the box again and brushed the folds of tissue

paper aside. 'And will you look at this? These scraps of fabric are embroidered. It reminds me of the things you found in that chest of drawers. She must have really cared about the poor little mite.'

Charlie steeled herself to take a quick look without focusing too hard on the remains of the little body. The embroidered flowers were indeed similar. 'She was all ready for her child's arrival, wasn't she? She'd done everything she could to prepare for a healthy, living baby. How terribly sad.'

'It's tragic, is what it is. But look, we've got to get a grip and deal with this. I suggest we leave the box exactly where it is for now and start making calls. Will your husband be back soon?'

'Possibly. I'm not sure where he went. But I don't need to wait till he returns. I think I'd like to get things moving. I assume they'll have to take the body somewhere. Now I know about it, I want it removed as soon as possible.'

'Are you sure you're going to be okay if I leave you? I've got to go back to the café to help Nicky, but I can look in again later to check on you.'

'I'll be fine now. It was just the initial shock and finding it hard to believe what I was seeing. Thank you so much for being here with me.'

Jean gave Charlie a hug. 'That's understandable. Come and find me if it's all too much for you. And now I'd better get going. Nicky's never going to believe what's happened.'

After Jean had left, Charlie thought she could barely believe it either. Rufus was barking in the garden, begging her to let him back inside. She opened the door and smelt the fresh spring air, scented with the first cut of grass from neighbouring gardens. Blue tits were twirling around each other, just like they did in old-fashioned cartoon films, choosing their mates and nesting sites. And Charlie felt relief. The shock of her discovery had passed and she was left with a lingering sadness and sympathy for the woman who had once lived here. She knew she had a challenging task ahead, but she felt perfectly capable of handling this. She was going to reunite a sad, heartbroken woman with her baby, no matter what.

The war was finally over and all across the country everyone was rejoicing. Everyone, that is, apart from the solitary occupant of the tall house opposite the church, the school and the common. Servicemen and prisoners were returning every day to families they hadn't seen in years. Frankie knew that Dickie could be home any moment and she was jumpy, fretting about how she would face him.

Would he suspect what she had endured? Would he want to make love to her? She wasn't sure if she could yet bear any assault on her body. And could she be sure she was capable of concealing her guilt from him? She tried to remind herself of the emptiness of her marriage and that he would probably want to see Hugo as soon as he could, rather than spending time with her. Yet again, she ached for the memory of Edwin and wished he hadn't gone into the West End that fateful night. She could have celebrated if he'd survived, even though she'd have been fearful of Dickie's return.

Union Jack bunting was strung from every lamp post in the street and the school organised a party for the children. Church bells that had stayed silent for most of the long war years were ringing again to proclaim the peace. From her bedroom window Frankie observed the busy preparations as local mothers laid tables in a row, covered in white sheets for tablecloths. A procession of women entered the playground bearing cakes produced miraculously from rationed ingredients. Frankie could see flags fluttering and hear the cheering and singing from her joyful neighbours. Although some must have still been mourning those lost in the war, both overseas and at home, the general air of relief and happiness reached her ears as the school piano was dragged outside and began playing 'Pack Up Your Troubles'.

As she stood watching, there was a knock at the door. Frankie peered cautiously through the lace curtains. Bertie was standing on the front step, looking up and shading her eyes, perhaps sensing that she was there.

Despite her fear that her face would show her feelings, Frankie couldn't ignore her best friend. She hadn't seen her since soon after her accident the previous year, and hadn't known she was back home. She longed to tell her everything, but so much had happened and so much had been hidden, that she couldn't take her into her confidence now, not when Dickie might appear at any moment. She slipped down the stairs and opened the door a little.

'You are coming along to the party, aren't you?' Bertie was all smiles. 'I fully expected you'd be over there helping already.'

'No, I'm not going.' Frankie shook her head and kept the door close to her as protection.

'Why ever not? Everybody's going. Look at them all.' Bertie turned to wave at more women entering the playground with bowls of jelly and trifle, jugs of lemonade and huge tea urns. 'I'm going up West later. It'll be one big party and the pubs will be open all hours. But I wanted to see the children enjoy the party first. You'll have to come with me.' She held out her hands, pleading with her friend. 'Come on, don't be such a spoilsport. Besides, we haven't seen each other in ages. You must have lots to tell me.'

'I'm sorry, but I really can't join you. Dickie is coming home. I can't possibly let him turn up to an empty house.' Frankie wanted to pull the door shut and end the conversation before Bertie suspected she had more to say. She regretted the loss of their close friendship but couldn't risk Bertie guessing her secret .

'What? Dickie made it after all? But that's wonderful.'

It was, wasn't it? Wonderful for everyone else that her husband hadn't perished as she'd thought and was coming back to reclaim his rightful place in the house? She knew she was lucky when so many women had lost their husbands and truly mourned them. But she had lost the only man she had ever really loved and also his child, and that was the tragedy she could never speak of.

'It's all been a bit of a shock. I really did think he was dead. All that time... and now...' She could feel herself beginning to lose control, and didn't want Bertie to see her break down. She took a deep breath.

'Of course, darling, it must be such a shock for you. But you must be so pleased for him. And you can both start all over again. It will be like a second honeymoon.' Bertie was so happy for her. But then she didn't know the truth.

'I suppose so.' Frankie shook her head. 'I don't know what he's going to be like. The Red Cross found him in a German hospital.'

'Poor old Dickie.' Bertie put out a hand to pat her friend's hand, tightly clutching the edge of the door. 'He'll be so happy to be home.'

'Yes. I hope so. But it's been so long. It's going to feel strange.'

Bertie stared at her, a curious look in her eyes. 'Are you sure you're all right? You're terribly pale.'

'I'm tired. That's all. I haven't slept properly since I heard the news. As I said, it's been quite a shock. I didn't think I'd ever see him again. All that time, I thought I was a widow. I'd got quite used to the idea he was gone for good and never coming back.'

Bertie cooed sympathetically. 'I'm sure things will all settle down once he's home. You'll both be fine when you have time to get to know each other again.'

If she had ever really known him, Frankie thought. They'd never had deep conversations about their plans for the future like she'd had with Edwin. They'd never shared hopes and dreams. Never had a physical passion like a hunger for each other. Dickie had used her to hide his one true passion and had never really cared for her at all. She had been a convenient scapegoat for him and his real love in a world that would have punished him for having such a relationship. 'I must go, I'm giving the place a really good clean. I want it to be absolutely perfect for him when he returns.'

'Of course. I quite understand. Well, if you're sure you won't come to the party, I'll get going. I don't want to miss out on all that jelly and cake!' Bertie stepped down the path to the makeshift wooden gate. 'I'll call round once he's home to say hello!' She waved goodbye, then crossed the road, calling out to neighbours she knew.

Frankie watched her friend go. Bertie's injured leg was concealed by well-cut baggy slacks that flattered her figure. But she had a slight limp and moved more awkwardly than she once had done. We're all injured in some way, Frankie thought. We all bear the scars of one kind or another from this long and dreadful war.

SIXTY
NOW
@OURFOREVERHOUSE#APOLICEMATTER

As soon as Jean had left, Charlie phoned for the police. She used the emergency number, 999, even though she knew this situation might not be classified as an emergency. But the minute she said, 'I think I've found a dead body in my cellar,' she was asked a few questions and then told that an officer would attend as soon as possible.

When they arrived about an hour later, it wasn't one officer, but two uniformed figures. A very tall young male constable and a kindly older woman who reminded Charlie of Jean, with her sympathetic smile and calm manner. 'I'm PC Sharon Pierce,' she said, 'and this is my colleague, PC Dennis Murray. Would you like to take us to where you came across the body?'

Having explained briefly what she had found, Charlie led them down the cellar steps, apologising for the poor level of light from the single light bulb. Then she pointed to where she had left the shoebox. 'I brought it in here to look at because the light was better than in the back of the cellar, where it was hidden.'

'Not to worry,' PC Pierce said. 'Our flashlights will help us assess the situation.' She switched on her torch and glanced at the closed box. 'Is this exactly how it was when you discovered it?'

'No, it was tied with that white ribbon and I found it in the furthest part of the cellar. The door was locked.' Charlie pointed to the third chamber. 'And the box was on top of the wine rack.'

'We'll take a look in there in a minute, but first let's see what you think you've found.' PC Pierce pulled on thin plastic gloves, lifted the cardboard lid, then parted the tissue.

Even though she must have been a witness to numbers of unpleasant scenes during her career and seen many bodies in various states at different times, she visibly started. 'We'll have to get the on-call coroner to take a look at this to confirm, but you could well be right. It does look very like a baby.'

'And there's a letter there.' Charlie pointed to the envelope.

'Did you open it?'

'No, a friend was with me and she did. She opened it and read it, then gave it to me. If it's true, it explains what happened and identifies the body.'

The officer picked up the envelope in her fingertips and extracted the sheet of paper inside. She scanned it quickly. 'Well, this seems to confirm what we suspect, but it would be as well to get it checked officially.'

'Of course. I want this all done properly. If it's all true, it's just so terribly sad. I really feel for Mrs Wilson. She appears to have been the writer of that letter.'

'Was she a previous owner of this house?'

'Yes, she was the last owner and she carried on living here until she was very old. It seems to me that she couldn't ever bear to leave because of this... her daughter.'

'Where did you say you found the box?'

'In the back of the cellar. On top of the shelves.'

The female police officer led the way, shining her torch. Her tall colleague followed, ducking through the doorway and then bending even lower when his head encountered the bunches of dried lavender.

'She must have picked these flowers every summer until she couldn't do it any more,' Charlie said, feeling her voice breaking. 'The lavender bushes edge the front garden, just above the wall. She must have done it every year for something like sixty or more years. It's simply unbelievable.'

'People are extraordinary,' PC Pierce said in a soft voice. 'Now, I need to make a couple of phone calls and I won't get a signal down here, so I suggest we all go back upstairs.'

Back in the kitchen, Charlie offered tea and coffee, wishing she'd brought cake back from the café. Phone calls were made and she realised she wasn't going to be able to leave the house until the proper checks had been made. She sent a brief text to Dan telling him not to be alarmed when he returned.

PC Pierce explained that they had to wait for a visit from the duty sergeant to confirm whether the death was suspicious or not. 'In this case,' she said, 'with the evidence of the letter and the time that has passed, I think he will turn up with the on-call coroner, who will then liaise with the on-call funeral director.'

It seemed to Charlie that a smoothly operating machine had taken over and, although she had to be present, she was no longer responsible. Once they were all drinking tea and were waiting for the other participants to arrive, PC Murray took a statement from her and, in the middle of doing that, Dan burst into the house, clearly alarmed by the sight of the police car outside.

'What on earth is going on here?'

'I'm so sorry,' Charlie said, 'I did try texting you. It's all happened so fast. We think we've found Alicia Rose, Mrs Wilson's daughter. She's been in the cellar all this time.'

'What do you mean, in the cellar?' Dan flopped into a chair, stunned by the news. Charlie began to explain and then there was a knock at the door.

'I'll answer that,' said PC Pierce, going into the hall. 'It's probably one of our team.'

But she returned with Jean, bearing a bundle wrapped in a tea towel. 'I was on my way home, but then I saw the police car outside. And I thought, she's going to need plenty of refreshments with all these visitors.'

'There's going to be even more very soon,' Charlie said, and explained the procession of officials they were awaiting. 'She can't be moved until they've taken photos and got all the details.'

'And where will the poor little thing go then?' Jean was still standing there, clutching her bundle to her chest.

'A hospital mortuary so they can do a post-mortem.'

Jean shook her head. 'What a sorry business. Sounds like I'd better stay for a bit and keep the kettle on.' She whipped off the tea towel. 'I've brought more banana bread and fresh shortbread. I'll get the cake sliced up and pass it round. You'll all need something to keep you going.'

Charlie couldn't help smiling, and caught Dan's eye and saw he was amused too. 'Jean was the one who opened the envelope,' she said to PC Pierce. 'I was so shocked when I first found the box, I had to find someone to come back here with me and check what I'd discovered. I thought I was seeing things.'

'We'll take a statement from you as well then,' the policewoman said to Jean. 'And thanks for bringing the cake and shortbread. Tea and cake are always very welcome when we've got to hang around for a while.'

'You've all got to keep your strength up,' Jean said, bustling through the group. She found a knife near the bread bin, quickly sliced the banana bread and passed the plate to Charlie. Then she handed a second plate with the triangular shortbread to tall PC Murray, saying, 'And you can pass round the petticoat tails.' He looked a little surprised to be ordered to share the dainty biscuits, but held the plate out for his colleague. Then

Jean ran a bowl of hot water and began rinsing the used tea mugs.

'Am I allowed to see what you found in the cellar?' Dan was looking at Charlie and then at the two police officers.

'Can he?' Charlie appealed to PC Pierce. 'We won't touch anything. Just a quick look.'

'I'll come down there with you,' the policewoman said. 'We mustn't disturb the scene any further until the coroner has been and we've got all the photos we need.' She moved towards the cellar door and went first down the steps.

When the box was opened again and the rustling tissue was parted, Dan flinched with a sharp intake of breath. He turned his head away and held Charlie tight.

The officer held out the letter so he could read it, shining her torch for more light. 'It seems conclusive,' he said, shaking his head. 'What a thing to find down here,' and he hugged Charlie some more.

Back upstairs, they all drank more tea and helped themselves to Jean's offerings. 'I'd better pop back with more later as the rest of your visitors aren't here yet,' she said.

'Only if you really want to,' Charlie said. But she could tell Jean was thoroughly enjoying being a part of the drama and couldn't bear to miss a minute of it. 'And thank you for all your help.'

'I wouldn't have missed it for the world,' Jean said. 'At last, we now know the end to the mystery of the missing daughter. You couldn't make it up. Really you couldn't. Nicky is going to be beside herself when I tell her everything.'

'Then tell her there's going to be a happy ending. When this lot have done all the official business and we have permission, Dan and I will make sure Alicia Rose is laid to rest with her mother.'

Frankie couldn't know exactly when he would return. So, every knock at the door made her jump, made her stop to pat her hair in the hall mirror and check her lipstick. Sometimes it was only the milkman or the postman, but finally, a couple of weeks after the war was over, it was her disgruntled husband, standing on the doorstep in an ill-fitting uniform.

She opened the door and tried to smile. 'Welcome home, Dickie,' she said, hoping it sounded as if she meant it.

He looked behind him at the wire fence and gate bordering the front garden. 'Whatever have you done with the railings? The house looks dreadful.'

'Oh, it was a government thing. They wanted the iron.'

'Huh,' was his only answer. 'Aren't you going to let me in?' He didn't smile. 'Or does a man have to ask permission to enter his own home?'

'No, sorry, of course not. I just wasn't sure when you'd get back.'

'I thought a telegram had been sent to give you some idea.'

'No, no, I don't think so.'

He pushed past her to cross the threshold, hung his cap on

the hall coat rack and noticed her looking at his uniform. It was much too large for him. 'I know it's not a good fit. It's not mine,' he said. 'The Red Cross sorted me out. I lost mine a long time ago, I think.'

'Your old clothes are all ready and waiting for you upstairs. You've lost weight though.'

'So would you, if you'd been treated the way I've been these last few years.' He was noticeably thin and his hair was sparse, though slicked down to create the impression that he had a full head. He still wore his thin moustache, but his cheeks were scratched and grazed, as if he'd had to share a blunt razor.

'I'm so sorry. It must have been awful.'

'It was perfectly bloody. But what would you know, safely tucked away here all through the war?'

Frankie didn't want to argue the minute he arrived, but she was feeling increasingly tense. 'Why don't we go into the garden and I'll make tea? The pear tree is full of blossom and it's so pretty out there.'

He wrenched off his tie and started walking upstairs. 'I'm going to wash and change. Then I might lie down.'

She watched him walk away from her, wafting carbolic soap and stale cigarettes. He hadn't hugged her or kissed her. He didn't seem very pleased to be home.

The next day, after he'd rested and they'd shared a miserable supper mostly in silence, Dickie seemed to be in a better frame of mind when he came down for breakfast. 'I'm going back to the old firm to start with. They've lost a lot of people and are going to need someone who knows the ropes. I'll have things straightened out there in no time.' He put a spoonful of sugar into his tea and stirred.

'That's a good idea to go back where you're known. You'd soon get back into your old routine, then it won't be too much of a strain for you.' She couldn't interpret the look on his face. 'And I was thinking I'd like to go back to work too. I always enjoyed it. And it would feel strange to suddenly be doing nothing. You don't know how busy I was during the war. I signed up to drive an ambulance. Bertie and I did it together. We had such fun.'

He frowned, his eyes hardening. Now she could tell what he was thinking. And he clarified it by saying, 'You did what? Well, if I'd been here, I would never have let you do that. Far too dangerous and inappropriate. And you're not going out to work any more either, driving or office work.'

'But I enjoy working. It's very lonely being at home all day.'

'I'm sure you can find enough to keep yourself busy. My mother and yours never had any complaints. They knew their place.'

Frankie was stunned. She'd loved the driving and the danger. She'd loved the camaraderie at the ambulance station and her time with Bertie. She'd loved working in an office too, even though it was staid and uneventful compared to the drama of driving an ambulance.

'Besides, once we have children, you'll soon have your hands full. You won't be hankering after an office job then.'

She couldn't respond to that. She wasn't ready to be with child again. She knew she'd never want a child with him. And maybe she should make sure she never did. Besides, he hadn't yet touched her, not once since he'd walked through the front door. Not a single caress, a kiss or even held her hand. And although they'd shared a bed last night, he'd turned his back on her as soon as his head was on the pillow. She imagined many husbands, home after such a long absence, hungrily grasping their wives as soon as they could be alone together in the marital bed. But she assumed Dickie's inclinations hadn't changed during his long absence and he still hankered for Hugo. In truth, she was glad he hadn't touched her; it would have felt like a violation after the tenderness she'd been shown by Edwin.

'So, there'll be no more talk of you working. And once I'm back at my old job I'll want to come home to a hot meal every night and a clean shirt for the morning, so there'll be more than enough to keep you busy then.'

Now Frankie was able to summon up the nerve to speak. 'But lots of women who had jobs in the war have decided to carry on working. We all had to do our bit at the time and lots of us loved being away from the house. Girls and women have been doing extraordinary things these last few years. They've been working on farms, in forests and in factories, even flying planes, all the time their men have been away. And they don't want it to stop. Some of them say it has been the best time of their life.'

'Don't I just know it. While we were away fighting for our country, they were gallivanting around, taking men's jobs, more like.' His lips acquired a thin, cruel line and she was sure he was sneering at her.

'But they had to. They kept the country going while you were away.' *Doing what, I wonder? Were you really a prisoner? Or did you run away and hide, then pretend you'd lost your memory?* He hadn't given her an account of any kind of his lost years. He could have been on the run all that time for all she knew, hiding from the action while other men were risking their lives, facing the enemy.

'Well, they don't need to do that sort of thing any more. And beside all that, I've been thinking about this house. What do you say to us selling this old-fashioned heap and moving to one of the modern houses they're starting to build in Richmond? Then we could have proper heating and no draughts. And with the money left from selling this place I could invest in a busi-ness. One of my pals is going to start up his own insurance practice and could do with a partner. We could be set up for life if we cashed in on this house and used the capital properly.'

This was the last thing Frankie had expected. She knew he'd never really liked the house, but had been willing to accept it for its convenience when they first married. 'I can't believe you just said that. Whatever makes you think I'd agree to leave here? Besides, it's my house. My parents left it to me, not you.'

'I'm sure you can see the sense in it. A better future for us.' He looked around the kitchen. 'Are you making breakfast or aren't you?'

'But you've never said you didn't like this house before. And I don't want to ever leave it.' *Not that I can ever leave it until I am carried out of here, eventually. But I can never tell you exactly why I can't go.*

He raised an eyebrow. 'I'm very disappointed in you. I thought you'd have more sense. I'm your husband and I have a better understanding of important financial matters. You should listen to what I have to say. I only have your best interests at heart.' He stood up from the table and grabbed her arm, holding it tight, pinching the soft flesh. 'You're my wife and I know what's good for us.'

Frankie flinched but managed to stare back at him. She could see his true nature so clearly. War had not changed him. This was how he had been before he'd joined up and gone off to war. This was really the man she had married just before it all started, when she had been too blind to see for herself. Of course she felt sorry for the hardships he'd suffered, but he didn't seem to be glad to be home again.

'This house was left to me by my parents. It's mine and I'm never going to sell it.' Her mind kept flitting to that dark chamber in the cellar. If he'd been a handyman, he might have taken up woodwork down there. And if he was a connoisseur of wine, he might have found a use for the rack in the far chamber; but he was a pint of bitter and occasional Scotch man, so she was fairly confident that her secret was safe. But she could never be totally sure, so she had to stay to protect it.

'We'll see about that,' he said. 'I'm going to consult a solicitor. I think you'll find that I have every right to exercise control over important assets, even those that have been left to my wife.'

'I can't believe what you're saying. What century do you think we're living in now? You can do what you like, but I'm never leaving here. You can go if you want, but I'll never leave. I'm sorry you feel you can order me around, but I don't have to stand for it. You can continue living here, I shan't deny you that, but I shan't share a married life with you if you're going to be like this.'

She pulled away from his grasp and left him standing speechless. She went out into the garden, rubbing her bruised arm. The hens had to be let out of their coop to scratch in the run. Their soft clucking soothed her nerves and she collected two eggs from the nest box. She would have offered to boil them for Dickie's breakfast but she was too angry. He didn't deserve to be cared for after the way he'd just behaved. And when she went back indoors, she found he'd already gone without saying another word. She assumed he'd gone to find Hugo and tell him how unreasonable she was being.

SIXTY-TWO

THEN

JUNE 1945

Maurice Campbell, senior partner of Harland and Campbell, had been her family's solicitor as long as Frankie could remember. She had first met him when he and her father had provided references for her to have her own bank account to manage her father's properties after his death.

He was a grandfatherly figure, dressed in an old-fashioned black suit and a white shirt with a winged collar, who looked at her over pince-nez spectacles perched on the end of his nose. 'You're quite sure you don't want to divorce your husband? I'm sure it could be arranged with the minimum of embarrassment to yourself.'

'I would prefer a quiet, discreet settlement if that is possible. I want to ensure that Dickie leaves me alone for the rest of my life. And I think I may have arrived at an effective solution.' Frankie withdrew a wad of handwritten letters, bound with a large elastic band, from her handbag. 'These letters are from a close friend of my husband's, a male friend. They arrived at regular intervals while he was missing during the war. Dickie and his friend are now planning to set up in business together and my husband has been pressing me to sell the house to provide them with capital. The content of the letters is somewhat compromising and I am sure if it were made known, say in court during a divorce hearing, his prospects would be severely damaged.' She caught a flicker of surprise in Campbell's raised eyebrow.

'I see, and what would you like me to do with this evidence?' He held his hands in a thoughtful prayer-like attitude under his chin.

'I want you to keep them safely locked away. They are not to be revealed unless I say so. I am planning to tell my husband that he must leave the house for good and, if he objects, then I will threaten to expose him and his friend. As you can well imagine, they would not be treated kindly and would probably receive prison sentences. I don't wish for that to happen. I actually feel pity for them both and have no desire to ruin their lives.'

'Can you be sure he will agree to leave the house?'

'I think he will under these circumstances. And I also propose to buy him off. I thought I could assign one of my properties to him in its entirety. There is one on Putney Hill, a shop with a large flat above it. I believe both are occupied at present, but if the tenants are given the appropriate notice then he will have premises for both a business and a place to live. That should convince him to leave.'

'That can be arranged of course. Would you like me to draft a letter informing him of the arrangement?'

While Frankie thought in silence and Campbell waited for an answer, the only sound between them was the soft rhythmic ticking of the office clock. She wanted to see Dickie's face when she told him in person. She wanted to show him that she could stand up to him and was no longer afraid of him. 'Prepare the letter, but I'll hand it to him myself.'

He nodded then made some notes on the pad set out on the leather-edged blotter on his large partners desk. 'And one further matter, Mrs Wilson. A very important matter that we should address immediately. As it stands at present, your husband would stand to inherit your estate in the event of your demise. I assume, under the circumstances, that you would not wish that to happen.'

Frankie had not thought that far ahead, but he was right. If Dickie reacted badly, if he attacked her or she had an accident, he would get everything, and she couldn't let that happen. He didn't deserve to benefit from her death and she had to protect her secret in the cellar at all costs. 'Thank you. I hadn't remembered that. You're right of course, so I must prepare a new will today. And I know exactly what I want it to say.'

'Very good. We can make a note of your wishes right now if you know how you would like me to proceed. I think it would be well to have that prepared and signed before you say any more to your husband. In view of the circumstances and the need for a speedy solution, I suggest we amend your existing will, which I and my clerk will witness in your presence this afternoon. That document will be watertight and he would not be able to contest it.'

'I'm so glad I came to see you. I knew you'd understand how I needed to do this properly. He's a difficult man.' Frankie swallowed and took a breath as she thought of the confrontation that lay ahead of her.

'In the meantime, do you feel safe returning to the house? I take it that you are alone there?'

Frankie paused for a moment. She wasn't alone, she'd never be alone with her daughter hidden in the basement and her memories of Edwin, but she answered, 'He's gone fishing with his special friend. He said he'd be away for a week. So, I had the locks changed before coming to see you.' She felt herself blush at her boldness. 'I thought that was the best thing to do. And until the Putney property is empty, he can stay with his friend.

Hugo has a mansion flat in Marylebone, so Dickie can manage. I haven't made him homeless.'

And then an idea occurred to her. Now was the time to outline her plan. 'It may seem strange, having thrown my husband out, but I don't want the house to stay empty. I'd like to share it with others. After the initial shock of being told I'd have to take in lodgers during the war, I actually enjoyed having the company, and I know there are still so many people in need of a home at present. I'd like to think about making a formal arrangement to help families, and then the house would be filled with children again.'

'A noble gesture, Mrs Wilson. I'll draw up a draft agreement at once.' Campbell made some more notes on his pad while the clock chimed three, and Frankie felt at ease. She could now see a future, not the one she had once imagined, but a future with purpose and hopefully a degree of happiness.

SIXTY-THREE

THEN

JUNE 1945

Frankie heard him hammering at the door and yelling. She had been dreading this moment, and took a deep breath. She knew this was going to be difficult and she'd need all her courage to confront him. When she let him in, Dickie slammed the front door behind him. 'Damn key wouldn't unlock the door. What on earth's going on?'

Frankie straightened her shoulders and clenched her hands. 'I've changed the locks. You can collect your things and if there's anything else you need, I can send it on to you. I assume you'll be staying with Hugo for the time being.'

He advanced towards her but she backed away. 'What the hell do you mean? I come back after years of fighting for my country and you won't let me into my own house?'

'It's my house, Dickie, not yours. And I'm asking you to leave for good. You can't live here any more.'

'I'm damned if I will. You're my wife and this is my home.' He moved towards her again.

She stepped back further. 'Don't come any nearer. I'm telling you to leave. This house is mine and always will be.'

'We'll see about that. I'll consult my solicitor. We'll soon have this nonsense sorted out.'

Frankie held out a fat cream envelope. 'This will explain everything. I've made arrangements with my solicitor. If you leave as requested, you will receive a property in Putney for you to use as you wish. You can live there or rent it out or sell it if you want. It will be all yours. If you don't do as I ask, then I will start divorce proceedings citing your relationship with Hugo as grounds.'

His face reddened and he spluttered as he said, 'What grounds? What on earth are you talking about, woman?'

'Hugo's letters, Dickie. He wrote to me while you were missing. Poor chap, he was quite distraught. I don't think he ever considered how those letters might sound to anyone else, certainly not anyone who disapproved of such a relationship.'

'I don't believe you. You're bluffing.'

'Am I? Do you want to test me? Really, Dickie, I feel sorry for you and Hugo, truly I do. It's not your fault you couldn't love me as another man might, but that doesn't mean I have to put up with a loveless marriage. I've had enough of your mean, selfish cruelty. I want you to leave. Our marriage is over.'

'Where are these letters then? I demand to see them.'

'They are all safely deposited with my solicitor. And if anything should happen to me, he will make their content known. They are undeniable evidence, Dickie.'

He turned away and ran both his hands over his sparse hair. When he turned back to face her, he was visibly trying to calm himself and said, 'Look here, I'm sure we can sort this out. Why don't we sit down and talk properly? We haven't had a proper chat since I came back, have we?' He held out his hand, but she backed away again.

'No, I'm not giving in.'

His jaw tightened again and his brows lowered. 'You've got hold of the wrong end of the stick, you stupid girl. Hugo and I are best mates, have been since schooldays. That's all there is to it. You've completely misunderstood our friendship. Let's sort this out properly.'

'But I saw you, Dickie. I saw the two of you kissing the day you said goodbye to each other, all those years ago when the war started. That and the letters couldn't have made it clearer. Admit it, Dickie, you can only love Hugo, not me or any other woman. I was just a convenient opportunity for you, complete with property and an income. We should never have married.'

She could tell from the way his face coloured that her words had hit home. 'You should be with Hugo, not me. You tried to fool me into thinking we could have a normal, respectable marriage, when I was young and vulnerable. You even suggested we should have children to cement your mask of decency. But I can't live a lie. This is the end.'

He batted the bulging envelope against his left hand, then opened it. As he read the contents, his teeth clenched. 'Very well,' he said. 'If that's the way you want it. You're welcome to this dreary old house and all its drab, old-fashioned furniture.'

He stormed upstairs and came down about ten minutes later with a suitcase. 'I'll stay with Hugo until the Putney place is free. Send my things on.' He pushed past her and out through the front door.

'Good luck...' Frankie's voice faltered as he ran down the steps to the pavement.

He turned to look at her one last time, his face twisted in fury. 'Good riddance,' he shouted. 'I'm never coming back.'

Frankie breathed a sigh of relief as she closed the door. She stood with her back against it, trembling. How had she found the courage to face him and send him packing? Then she broke into nervous giggles. She'd done it, hadn't she? She'd sent him off and the house was now all hers and her daughter's. They would never have to suffer his slights again.

SIXTY-FOUR

NOW

@OURFOREVERHOME#PEACEATLAST

More than a year after making that shocking discovery in the cellar, on a balmy day in late June, Charlie and Dan stood beside the graves in Putney Vale Cemetery. They gazed at the simple stone bearing the name Frances Wilson and the dates of her time on this earth. To that had recently been added *Alicia Rose Wright, 25 April 1945, An angel, sadly not for this world.*

'That day we found her, I never thought it would take so long to make this happen,' Charlie said, cradling her new baby daughter against her breast. She also held a bunch of roses picked that morning in the garden of their house; the creamy pink, blowsy flowers were framed by the frothy lime-green foliage of the lady's mantle edging the borders and sprigs of that summer's lavender.

'It had to be done properly,' Dan said, turning to her to take their baby in his arms. 'You're glad we've done this, aren't you?'

'Of course. We had to respect her wishes. And it makes me feel that they are both at peace now, so we can be too. I know you think it's crazy, but I think if we'd never found her, we'd never have had this little one.' She stroked her baby's downy head. 'But I never imagined it would take so long to finally bring them together.'

She thought back to the day the police had arrived at the house. The kind, mature female officer and her young male colleague, who'd had to duck his head when he inspected the furthest chamber of the cellar and the wine rack. Neither of them had ever dealt with a case quite like this before, and they had seemed just as shocked as Charlie and Dan.

The police had arranged for an on-call coroner to come to the house and then an undertaker took the body and its box to a hospital mortuary. That was followed eventually by a post-mortem, then a coroner's report, which confirmed that what they had found was indeed a baby that hadn't reached full term and had probably been stillborn. Later, arrangements were made with another undertaker, who checked records at the cemetery to identify the correct grave and organise the interment of a second coffin.

The undertaker had said there would be no charge for the funeral. Charlie had looked at Dan and said, 'But it still has to be done properly.'

'We don't charge for anyone under eighteen years of age. It's our normal practice.'

'Thank you so much. But we would never have objected to paying. After all, Mrs Wilson's daughter died in our house. And even though it was a very long time ago, it's the very least we can do.'

And now, after a short ceremony in the cemetery chapel, they had walked to the graveside, which had been prepared for its new occupant, accompanied by Jean and Nicky, and David Paige, the vicar from the church opposite the house. The procession was completed by the presence of Alan Jones, the celebrated artist, in a wheelchair pushed by his husband Rick. They looked very alike, both with neat grey beards and parted hair.

Only the vicar wore black that day. Everyone else dressed in the light colours of summer, reflecting that although this was a solemn occasion it shouldn't be sombre. The men wore light grey suits with pink roses in their buttonholes. Alan even wore a pale pink shirt.

The undertaker walked slowly, carrying the tiny coffin in his arms. Alicia Rose no longer rested in an old shoebox, but was laid in a pure white coffin bearing her name.

They passed ornate tombs, dating back well over a hundred years, until they reached the more recent burial ground where Frances Wilson had been buried a few years previously. 'I'm so glad we've been able to do this for them both,' Charlie said as they watched Alicia Rose being lowered into the prepared grave to meet her mother.

Reverend Paige stood by the grave, his hands clasped together, and said, 'We are gathered here to witness Alicia Rose Wright being reunited with her mother, Frances, who only knew her for such a short time in life. We give thanks that she can now be embraced again by her mother and that she will now rest in peace.'

Charlie felt sad but composed. Behind her, she could hear Jean sniffling and Nicky whispering that she'd better take a tissue. Little Matilda Alicia Rose snuffled and began to complain, so Dan rocked her in his arms and she was soon soothed.

The undertaker brushed earth over the buried coffin, creating a small mound in the plot. Charlie laid her flowers on the grave, followed by posies of white flowers from Nicky and her mother.

'That was so beautiful,' Jean said, blowing her nose. 'So

simple. I wish my mum had still been here to see this. She'd have been so touched to know how Frankie had suffered.'

'Of course she would,' Charlie said. 'The letter said she'd never even told her best friend and that was your mother, wasn't it? It must have been so hard for her, bearing her troubles all alone like that.'

'Doesn't bear thinking about, does it?' Jean looked as if she might need more than the one soggy tissue at any moment. 'And then never leaving that house again, knowing what she'd got hidden down there, who'd have thought it?'

'Come on, Mum, snap out of it,' Nicky said. 'Let's all go back to the café for tea.' They had decided that the café was more accessible for Alan in his wheelchair than the house with its steps. Nicky turned to the others. 'She's made a lovely cake for today. You're in for a treat.'

That quickly dried Jean's tears. She smiled and said, 'It's my speciality. I only make it for very important occasions. Blow-away Sponge Cake with strawberries and cream, decorated with fresh and dried rose petals. In honour of little Alicia Rose.'

'Ooh, I could wolf that down right now,' Charlie said, smiling. 'With lots of tea.' She opened her arms to take her baby, now awake and gurgling. 'We all like the sound of that.'

She turned to Alan, who had also laid flowers on the grave. 'I'm so glad you were able to come today. What you've been able to tell us fills in so many gaps in the story.'

'I could never have guessed that Frankie was hiding such a sad life,' he said, removing his glasses and wiping his eyes with a large, clean handkerchief. 'When I returned to London in the Fifties after doing my national service, she welcomed me back to the house and said I had to stay with her while I attended the art school in Putney.'

'And that was the start of your hugely successful career.'

He nodded. 'I owe it all to her and Elspeth. They both showed me what a poor boy from the East End could hope to achieve. I could never have done it without their support.' Alan's work was widely acclaimed and often likened to that of Stanley Spencer.

'And it's all thanks to Elspeth's memoir that I found out about you and your family. I'd always wondered about the height chart in the top room. But it's so sad that they didn't all live to see how well you've done.'

He gave a wry smile. 'It was dreadful at the time, but in a way losing them meant my life changed for the better. Being adopted by Elspeth meant I took a completely different direction. I'd have been destined for the docks or the market if she hadn't taught and encouraged me. She made me feel I'd been saved for a reason and shouldn't waste my ability.'

Charlie sighed. She had longed to learn more about the house and its past, but she could never have imagined that it held so many stories. 'I'm so glad you've been able to tell me more about Frankie's house of waifs and strays after the war. Though I'm not saying you were one of them.'

'It was always a happy house,' he said. 'Both when I was a child and later. I don't know what it would have been like if her husband had stayed, but I gathered from her that it wasn't a happy marriage. She had great empathy, you know, and was particularly supportive when I told her how I felt about men and later when I told her that I loved Rick. She said I should be true to myself. And she also said, *"You're lucky times have changed"*, which I never really understood, but I think she meant the attitude of society towards homosexuality.'

'We'll never know her full story,' Charlie said. 'But I'm so glad you only have happy memories of living there.'

As they walked, Dan put his arm protectively around Charlie's shoulders and she smiled up at him as they all strolled together back to the café, past their house, bathed in sunlight. It seemed to be glowing with happiness that day and Charlie thought it was indeed their forever house now all the ghosts had finally been laid to rest.

Here they would rear a family of boisterous children to slide down the banisters, chase each other in the garden, swing high beneath the pear tree and hide in the Wendy house behind the hydrangeas. It would never again be a house of sadness and regrets, but forever a house of laughter and love.

AUTHOR'S NOTE

How do stories begin to germinate in an author's mind? When I speak at festivals, I am sometimes asked where my ideas come from. I often say stories are the result of being nosy; it's a flippant answer but there is some truth in that in the sense that a writer's curiosity and imagination can develop a good story from a tiny crumb.

I often think that my novels develop from a seed, which is then encouraged to grow by asking questions and examining scenarios. The original seed for this book was two newspaper clippings, saved from papers in recent years. One was headlined THE SUITCASE SECRET and the other DEATH MYSTERY OF SHOEBOX BABIES.

In both cases, these shocking news stories reported the discovery of the remains of babies found hidden in houses being cleared after the long-term occupant's recent death. Newspapers found in the hiding places indicated that the deaths had occurred many years before, in the 1930s and '40s. I can't help wondering if the bodies were deliberately wrapped in newspapers to give a clue to the date of death. But there was never anything to explain who had hidden the bodies and why.

I couldn't help asking myself what could bring someone to act in this way. What were the circumstances of the births and deaths? Why did the children die? And how did the mother feel about continuing to live with the corpse in the house? Of course, in those days having a child out of wedlock was a scandalous occurrence and to have a baby when a husband had been away fighting for years would have been totally unacceptable. Is that what drove a woman to hide her mistake or was it more complicated than that?

And then I began to think about how such a discovery might affect a young woman now living in that house who hoped to have her own children there. Would she sense that the house had a sinister secret? Could a house that had contained many lives and held many different stories create an aura that could be communicated to future occupants? It is from such thoughts that stories begin to develop, and this one led me to the tale of Frankie and her fear of discovery.

I thought at first that Frankie's hope that Dickie wouldn't return was simply a reflection of her disappointment in her marriage. But with encouragement from my editor I decided that, not only had Dickie taken advantage of her and her inherited property, he was using her to protect his reputation and his love for his best man, Hugo. In those days, homosexuality was illegal and it would have been difficult for couples in same-sex relationships to declare their love for each other. Although in artistic communities such relationships might have existed a degree more openly, in middle-class, suburban England it would have been impossible for Dickie to acknowledge his feelings for Hugo.

Not only did Dickie's deceitful marriage mean an unhappy life for Frankie, it couldn't have been that fulfilling for him either, even though it helped to maintain a respectable facade. Such marriages were known as 'lavender marriages', and were sometimes beneficial for both parties. But in this case the relationship was disappointing for both of them, and, with Dickie's controlling behaviour, it was particularly cruel and unsatisfying for his young wife. Yet despite the unhappiness he caused her, Frankie shows compassion for him and Hugo in deciding not to reveal their love in a divorce court.

Frankie's discovery of a more exciting life while Dickie was missing illustrates the new opportunities that were suddenly available to women. I can remember my Great-Aunt Nora talking with her best friend Billie about their ambulance driving in the war, and it sounded as if they'd had the time of their lives. They also recalled how they painted each other's bare legs to emulate stockings and applied eyebrow pencil seams very badly, while standing on a chair in their knickers. In my presence they never talked about the horrors they must have seen, just the thrill of working together in a way they could never have expected without a war. But of course they would have encountered terrible distress and injuries in their work at that time. Contemporary accounts of the devastation caused by bombings make it clear that the emergency services were faced with dreadful sights every time they attended, and many of the scenes I have described are taken from such reports. Collecting the body parts must have been particularly hard, requiring detachment and a strong stomach.

For many women, the ambulance service, recruitment in the army, the Land Girls service and the Forestry Commission offered them their first opportunity to learn to drive. Although formal driving tests had been introduced in the UK in 1937, they were suspended for the duration of the war when drivers were needed urgently. That is why it was possible for Frankie and Bertie to be assessed by two kindly older men at the ambulance station and not take an actual test.

To find out more about the ambulance service in the war years, I turned to the London Ambulance Service, who told me about the station in Putney and the areas it served. Craig Henty there was very patient, answering my many seemingly trivial questions about the vehicles in use. He provided essential details, such as whether the vehicles had a bell or a horn and how the vehicles were adapted for emergency use.

The dedication for this book is to my lovely nephew Tom and his equally lovely husband Alex, as they were responsible for the letter fragments found under the floorboards. When they were renovating their own house, they found scraps of paper and sent me a picture, wondering if it might inspire me. It certainly did, and I took a guess at reconstructing the letter from the handwritten fragments they found. I have no idea what the original might have said, but it certainly gave me the idea that Frankie's letter, written in desperation in the midst of her labour pains, might be found in pieces by the new owners.

I hope that in writing this novel I have tried to understand whoever was behind those shocking news cuttings and have shown sympathy for their plight. Whatever the circumstances, they must have experienced pain, distress, shame and fear. And I hope that like Frankie, they subsequently found a way to live a good life in some way.

BLOW-AWAY SPONGE CAKE

This is Jean's recipe, copied from my old school domestic science exercise book. It hasn't been converted to metric measurements, so this is exactly how it is written.

2oz plain flour

2oz cornflour

1 level teaspoon baking powder

Pinch of salt

A dash of Angostura bitters or vanilla essence

4 eggs

4oz caster sugar

1. Separate the whites and yolks of the eggs

2. Sift together the flour, cornflour, baking powder and salt

3. Beat egg whites till stiff and peaky

4. Gradually add sugar, then whisk till thick and smooth

5. Whisk in egg yolks and flavouring

6. Quickly and lightly fold in dry ingredients

7. Put mixture into two well-greased 8-inch sandwich tins

8. Bake at 400F or Gas Mark 6 for 15 minutes

9. Put on a cooling tray, then sandwich and top with fillings, such as strawberries and whipped cream.

A LETTER FROM SUZANNE

Thank you so much for choosing to read *Her Husband's Return*. If you enjoyed it and want to keep up to date with all my latest releases, just sign up at the following link. Your email address will never be shared and you can unsubscribe at any time.

www.bookouture.com/suzanne-goldring

I hope you enjoyed *Her Husband's Return* and, if you did, I would be very grateful if you could write a review. I'd love to hear what you think and it makes such a difference helping new readers to discover one of my books for the first time.

I really appreciate hearing from my readers and you can get in touch through my Facebook page, X, Instagram or my website.

Thanks,

Suzanne

www.suzannegoldring.wordpress.com

facebook.com/suzannegoldringauthor

x.com/suzannegoldring

instagram.com/suzannegoldringauthor

REFERENCES

The Blitz – Juliet Gardiner

Wartime Britain 1939–1945 – Juliet Gardiner

Nella Last's War: The Second World War Diaries of Housewife, 49 – edited by Richard Broad and Suzie Fleming

Wartime Women: A Mass Observation Anthology 1937–45 – edited by Dorothy Sheridan

Under Fire: The Blitz Diaries of a Volunteer Ambulance Driver – Naomi Clifford

Forgotten Service: Auxiliary Ambulance Station 39 – Angela Raby

ACKNOWLEDGEMENTS

I began this book thinking I would not have to do as much research as I normally do, but soon found that even the present-day timeline required careful checking. Some references I found useful are listed at the end, but for information on how the wartime ambulance service operated, I am particularly grateful to Craig Henty of the London Ambulance Service. He has said he is looking forward to reading the book, but I think the end result will be far different to what he might have imagined. I hope I have done the sterling work of the wartime ambulance drivers justice.

I also thankful to Tom Shaw and Alex Bird, to whom this book is dedicated, for finding the scraps of a letter under their floorboards. Anyone else might have thrown them away, but they thought to photograph them and send them on to me. It was great material.

Thanks are also due to Chris Jolly, a long serving police officer for his expert advice on police procedure.

While writing this novel, I was constantly encouraged by my loyal writer friends. I'm particularly thankful to Denise Barnes, Carol McGrath and Gail Aldwin for their unwavering support. The Elstead Writers Group have also been a great source of encouragement. And I am extremely grateful to my agent, Elly James of the HHB Agency, whose comments on an early draft prompted me to plot a dreadful end for most of Frankie's lodgers.

At the start of writing this novel, my husband suddenly

became very seriously ill and was in hospital for four months, followed by a long period of recovery. I am grateful to all who cared for him during that time, allowing me to continue writing as well as making daily hospital visits. Writing was a great escape for me during those weeks. I am also grateful to my husband for recognising that my work helped me remain strong for him.

And last but not least, I am immensely grateful to the whole Bookouture team who so efficiently make my books a reality. I am particularly thankful to my editor, Lydia Vassar-Smith, whose insightful comments help me to see the potential of my original ideas.

Many thanks for this, my ninth book with all of you.

PUBLISHING TEAM

Turning a manuscript into a book requires the efforts of many people. The publishing team at Bookouture would like to acknowledge everyone who contributed to this publication.

Audio
Alba Proko
Sinead O'Connor
Melissa Tran

Commercial
Lauren Morrissette
Hannah Richmond
Imogen Allport

Cover design
Eileen Carey

Data and analysis
Mark Alder
Mohamed Bussuri

Editorial
Lydia Vassar-Smith
Imogen Allport

Copyeditor
Jacqui Lewis

Proofreader
Jane Donovan

Marketing
Alex Crow
Melanie Price
Occy Carr
Ciara Rosney
Martyna Młynarska

Operations and distribution
Marina Valles
Stephanie Straub
Joe Morris

Production
Hannah Snetsinger
Mandy Kullar
Nadia Michael
Charlotte Hegley

Publicity
Kim Nash
Noelle Holten
Jess Readett
Sarah Hardy

Rights and contracts
Peta Nightingale
Richard King
Saidah Graham